Children of the Middle Sea

Michael A. Ponzio

This is a work of historical fiction; however, most places and historically documented incidents are real. Except for actual historical figures, the names and the characters are products of the author's imagination or are used fictitiously.

Any resemblance to actual living persons, businesses, companies, events, or locales is entirely coincidental.

No part of this book may be reproduced or stored in a retrieval system or transmitted in any form or by any means—electronic, mechanical, photocopying, recording, or otherwise—without the express written permission of the publisher.

Copyright © 2024 Michael A. Ponzio
Trinacria Publishing Company
BISAC: Fiction/Historical/General
All rights reserved.
ISBN 13: 978-1-7349723-6-8
Library of Congress control number: TBD
Printed in the United States of America.

DEDICATION

Children of the Middle Sea, the second volume of the Lover of the Sea series, is dedicated to my wife, Anne Davis Ponzio. She is a lover of seas and oceans, always making sure she swims, kayaks, or skis during our worldwide travels to the seven seas.

ACKNOWLEDGMENTS

Grazie mille to:
Proofreader and editor: Nancy Soesbee
Developmental editor: Edward Ferrari-Willis

This novel was enhanced by my wife, Anne Davis Ponzio.

ATTRIBUTIONS

Cover design by modification of digital rendering of the satellite view of the Mediterranean Sea. This globe rendering is a screenshot from the Globe Master geography game, shared by the game authors. For the global texture, Whole World-Land and Oceans composite image was used, created by NASA Goddard Space Flight Center (public domain). https://globalquiz.org/en/quiz-image/mediterranean-sea-from-space/ The file is licensed under the Creative Commons Attribution 3.0 unported.

The sailboat image used to indicate a scene or time change in this novel is a representation of Esmeray's fishing boat. From Wikimedia Commons, the free media repository. Attribution: Jadvinia at Polish Wikipedia. Changes made from the original: one of two images used. Jadvinia at Polish Wikipedia, the copyright holder of this work, hereby publishes it under the following licenses:

https://creativecommons.org/licenses/by-sa/2.5/deed.en.

Permission is granted to copy, distribute, and/or modify this document under the terms of the GNU Free Documentation License.

Chapter XX Illustration of Harbor of Genoa, View of Genoa by Christoforo de Grassi (after a drawing of 1481); Galata Museo del Mare, Genoa - Artist: Christoforo de Grassi. File: Genova 1481 (copy 1597).jpg - Wikimedia Commons.

This work is in the public domain in its country of origin and other countries and areas where the copyright term is the author's life plus 100 years or fewer.

All the maps were drawn by the author.

Children of the Middle Sea **is the second volume of the Lover of the Sea series.**

Ancestry Novels by Michael A. Ponzio
Michael A. Ponzio | Ancestry Novels (michael-a-ponzio-author.com)

The Ancient Rome Series:
Pontius Aquila: Eagle of the Republic
Pontius Pilatus: Dark Passage to Heaven
Saint Pontianus: Bishop of Rome

The Warriors and Monks Series:
Ramon Pons: Count of Toulouse
1066 Sons of Pons: In the Wake of the Conqueror
Warriors and Monks: Pons, Abbot of Cluny

The Lover of the Sea Series:
Lantern Across the Sea: The Genoese Arbalester
Children of the Middle Sea
The Fortunate Islands (In progress)

Nonfiction Historical:
Brig. General Daniel Davis & the War of 1812: The Destiny of the Two Swords
Memories of the Neracker Brothers: Sweet Cider & the Cider Mill

"We cannot direct the wind,
but we can adjust our sails."

Lucius Annaeus Seneca, Roman philosopher

HISTORICAL BASIS

A will dated 1279, written by the notary Ugolino Scarpa, is among the records in the city archives of Genoa, Italy. He compiled a list of the effects of Ponzio Bastone, a Genoese soldier, an arbalester (crossbowman).

The notary recorded: "On 4 February, 1279, in the inventory of Ponzio Bastone, soldier, I find two knives with handles of carved ivory, one fine steel bladed knife of Damascus steel, a silk pillow of satin weave, a bolt of the finest lightweight silk, and one barrel of dried macaroni."[1]

When I wrote *Lantern Across the Sea: The Genoese Arbalester,* the first novel of the "Lover of the Sea" series, I envisioned the life of Ponzio Bastone, an arbalester, a marine, a sailor, and a spy, during the exciting period of the maritime Republic of Genoa in the thirteenth century. Bastone meets Esmeray, a Greek fisherman's daughter, and together they join the revolt of the Sicilian Vespers. After the revolt, their adventures continue in this sequel, *Children of the Middle Sea.*

Michael A. Ponzio

---

[1] Arturo Ferretto, *Atti della Società Ligure di Storia Patria, Proceedings of the Ligurian Society of Homeland History Volume 31, Part 2,* Artisans of San Giuseppe, Roma, 1903.

AUTHOR's NOTE

As a tribute to the language, I have added a few Sicilian words (a few words my Nanna taught me), but mostly from multiple sources: the on-line translator (author Eryk Wdowiak) on the website of Arba Sicula, a nonprofit international organization that promotes the language and culture of Sicily (author and president Professor Gaetano Cippola)[2], Art Dieli's online dictionary, and the *Sicilian Dictionary and Phrasebook* by Joseph F. Privitera. This explains why many words in the novel that are Sicilian appear to the reader as misspelled Italian words. Examples: signore (Italian) which is signuri in Sicilian, mangia is mancia, grazie is grazzi, etc. Please forgive any confusion this may cause. I also include Italian vocabulary at times, usually when the speaker is not Sicilian.

To provide a richer experience, the reader may want to "pronounce" as they read the Italian words using these phonetics.
Ciciri: Che-cher-ree. Chickpeas.
Esmeray: Ez-mer-ay. Bastone's wife, one of the two main characters.
Esme: Ez-may. Esmeray's nickname.
Francesco, Bastone's brother: Fran-chess-co.
Giovanna: Jo-van'na. A Lady of Queen Constanza's court.
Grazzi: grah-tzee.
Nglisi: In-glay-say.
Mino: Mee-no. Sicilian merchant from Messina.
Bastone: Pone-zee-o Bah-sto'-nay. One of the two main characters.
Procida: Pro-chee-da. Mastermind of the revolt of the Sicilian Vespers.
Speculatore: spe-coo-la-toh-ray. Spy.

---

[2] Author Gaetano Cipolla, and the president of Arba Sicula since 1987, has edited and translated many volumes of Sicilian poetry and is one of the leading experts in the field.

PROLOGUE	1
CHAPTER I	3
CHAPTER II	11
CHAPTER III	17
CHAPTER IV	23
CHAPTER V	33
CHAPTER VI	47
CHAPTER VII	55
CHAPTER VIII	69
CHAPTER IX	79
CHAPTER X	89
CHAPTER XI	97
CHAPTER XII	103
CHAPTER XIII	111
CHAPTER XIV	121
CHAPTER XV	133
CHAPTER XVI	139
CHAPTER XVII	149
CHAPTER XVIII	157
CHAPTER XIX	167
CHAPTER XX	171
CHAPTER XXI	177
CHAPTER XXII	185
CHAPTER XXIII	193
CHAPTER XXIV	199
CHAPTER XXV	205
CHAPTER XXVI	215
CHAPTER XXVII	219
CHAPTER XXVIII	227
CHAPTER XXIX	231
CHAPTER XXX	237
CHAPTER XXXI	245
CHAPTER XXXII	253
CHAPTER XXXIII	261
CHAPTER XXXIV	271
CHAPTER XXXV	283

CHAPTER XXXVI	293
CHAPTER XXXVII	301
CHAPTER XXXVIII	311
CHAPTER XXXIX	319

PROLOGUE

On Easter Monday 1282, the Sicilian people united against the harsh government of Charles, the Angevin King of Sicily. The uprising, known as the Sicilian Vespers, raged across the island for six weeks, expelling Charles's forces. Doctor Giovanni Procida had been the mastermind behind the revolt, directing agents, *speculatori,* to secretly meet with state leaders to support the rebellion.

Within a few months, Charles regained a foothold on the island, besieging Messina. When the citizens' attempts to break the siege failed, they sent representatives to the Pope asking for the Church's protection. The Pope, who had been appointed by Charles, refused, forcing the patriots to turn to Peter, King of Aragon, for help.

Procida wanted his trusted *speculatore,* Ponzio Bastone, to lead the mission, but the spy's whereabouts were unknown. After slipping out of Messina, Procida traveled on foot for three days to the port of Riposto, gaining passage on a cargo ship to North Africa, where Peter was campaigning. As Procida sailed out of the harbor, the fatigued septuagenarian cursed the spy for having to undertake a long sea voyage to Africa. "Where the hell is Ponzio Bastone?"

Children of the Middle Sea

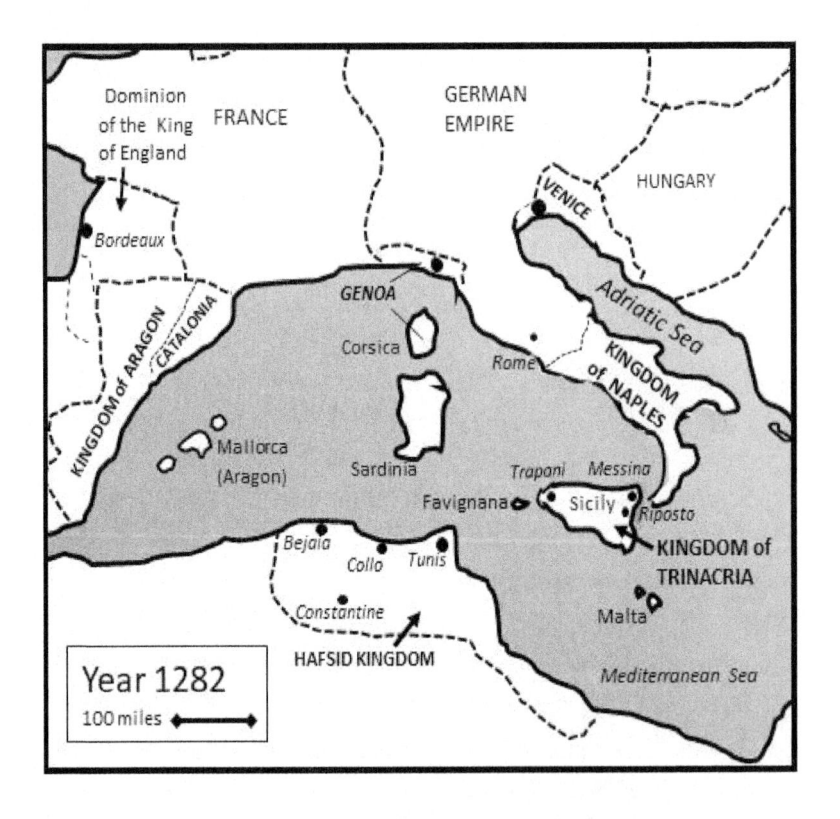

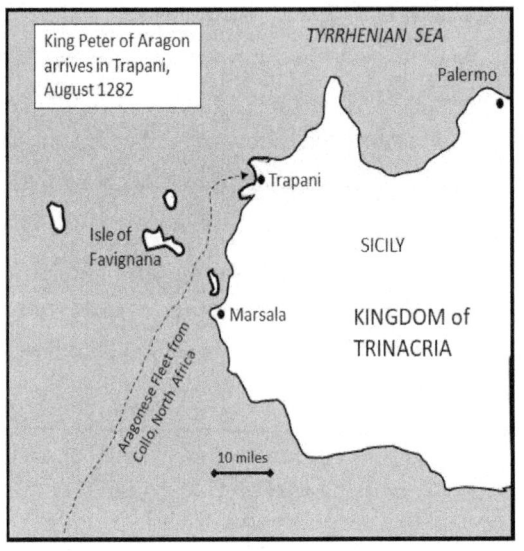

CHAPTER I

"That one's as good as dead. Leave him! Only those who can walk may board my ship."

Doctor Giovanni Procida supported the feverish man, holding the man's arm across his own shoulders, half dragging him along the gangway, ignoring the captain.

Legs planted wide, the captain blocked their way. "I said leave him!" The captain stepped forward, drawing a dagger. Procida backed away, returning to the wharf with his patient. He would not abandon him to die. A palm tree nearby provided shade, where Procida let the man sink to the ground, tipping a water skin to the man's mouth. Was this skeletal wretch really *him,* the man he sought?

The captain sheathed his knife. "If you want to return to Sicily on my ship," he yelled, "you better board now! And without that stinkin' corpse. We cast off as soon as the hold is full." He glanced at the containers of wax being hoisted onto the deck and left for his cabin.

Procida examined the sick man. He looked like Ponzio Bastone, although he was gaunt and his beard was matted. The doctor helped him drink. Peter, King of Aragon, had freed hundreds of galley slaves from the Hafsids, this man among them. Procida was astonished at the coincidence of finding Bastone. He wanted confirmation and asked, "What is your name?"

"Uh." A groggy response.

Procida gave him more water.

"Who are you?"

"I don't . . ." A blank look.

The doctor placed his palm on the man's head. He was still feverish and delirious. Procida asked again. "What is your name, sir?"

"P-Ponz . . . Ponzi, Ponzio . . ."

"Are you from Genoa?" asked Procida.

"Um . . . y-yes."

"Where is your wife? What happened?" Procida recalled Bastone's wife. She would have died fighting to prevent this from happening to him.

"Wife? Um . . . row . . . row, gotta row, now . . ."

"But . . ." said Procida. He wrung his hands, unnerved and shaken that Ponzio Bastone, formerly a robust man, had been reduced to an emaciated, weakened victim of abuse. Bastone coughed and hacked, then vomited. Procida poured water into his cupped hand and cleaned the man's face.

Procida had arrived in Collo several weeks after Peter's forces had freed the Christians taken as slaves, but many were seriously ill. Having studied at the medical school of Salerno, Procida recognized the ill men were suffering from *mal aria*, thought to be caused by foul air emanating from marshes. In Collo, he had come upon the man he now cradled in his lap. Procida watched as the last of Peter's fleet sailed for Trapani, Sicily. Peter had only allowed the freed slaves who were healthy to sail with the fleet, which denied Bastone passage.

The creaking gangway drew Procida's glance. Guglielmino Nglisi, the merchant who Procida had befriended on the voyage from Sicily, disembarked with an assistant. Nglisi had contracted the ship's owner to transport salt from Trapani, trading it for beeswax in Collo. At the wharf, the crew, using the mast boom, hoisted the last container of wax onto the ship, and the merchant's scribe finished tallying the cargo. Guglielmino noticed Procida under the tree. He waved his men onto the ship and called out, "Doctor, come! We're leaving!"

"The captain won't let me bring this man and without treatment he will die." At 72, Procida was fit, but he was having difficulty lifting the man. The merchant rushed over to help. "Thank you, Mino."

The crew was close to removing the gangway. Mino and Procida draped the gaunt man's arms over their shoulders, keeping him upright, his feet dragging. As they approached the gangway, Mino nodded to his scribe, "Go on ahead. Tell me when the captain is not looking."

The scribe returned in a moment and gestured for them to board. The gangway bounced under them and they reached the deck. They froze at a shout from the captain. "I told you, no!"

The scribe stood with his back to them, shielding them, whispering, "Go!"

They hesitated. "He doesn't see you. Go, go! The lug is just yelling at his crew."

Procida said, "We'll take him to my cabin."

The Genoese trading vessel cast off, sailing out of the harbor past a verdant promontory, the Collo Massif, the northern end of the Atlas Mountains as they ran into the sea. Once Bastone slept, Procida bent over and passed through the low cabin door, returning to the deck to inspect the welfare of the other men. The ship rolled, and he swayed as he moved among the scores of former galley slaves dispersed about the deck, controlling the urge to treat them, which risked drawing the captain's attention. Procida had learned many were from Genoa, Bastone's home, which supported his belief that the man he hid in his cabin was the speculatore, the spy he had worked with during the revolt of the Sicilian Vespers.

Procida returned to the cabin, searched his kit, and found a fleam, a sharp instrument used to puncture veins. The doctor hesitated before pricking Bastone, recalling that he had not bled a patient in years, because usually barber-surgeons did the task. When the doctor inserted the fleam's point, Bastone woke with a groan. As the blood dripped into the bowl, Procida felt a pang of guilt. Was he focused on saving this man to use him for his own political goals . . . or was it because of his compassion as a doctor?

Evening came, and the doctor squeezed himself into the small space on the floor next to the bunk. Both men slept. That night, fatigue overcame him and he never awoke to the quarreling on deck, followed by moans and scuffling, and loud splashes.

Early in the morning, Procida noted there were fewer afflicted men on deck. He carried his chamber pot containing Bastone's vomit and blood to the bow. As he poured the contents overboard through the lattice of timbers at the head, someone arrived and began urinating to his left. He recognized the captain's voice. "Ha! I hope you are enjoying the privacy of a cabin, Doctor. You don't have to squat here like a sailor, just bring your chamber pot and—" Procida was almost sprayed when the captain jerked and said, "But that bowl smells—I noticed that odor passing your cabin. You brought that sick wretch on board!"

The captain pulled up his pants, tying the drawstring as he rushed to the stern castle, heading for the passenger cabins. Procida chased him, avoiding the slicks of body fluids. They passed a sailor splashing a bucket of seawater to rinse the deck. The captain stopped, Procida almost running into him. He addressed the sailor, "Throw the sick ones overboard—the ones making this mess." Then he resumed his march to the stern.

He reached Procida's cabin and threw open the hatch. Procida's heart sank, knowing the captain would throw Bastone overboard. Ducking, the captain stepped into the cabin. "God's bones! It smells in here." He exited. "Where is he?"

Nearby, a man vomited, distracting him.

"Captain!" Mino leaned out from the door, blocking the entrance to his cabin. Procida guessed he was hiding Bastone, hoping the captain didn't enter. "My cabin smells, too. The scent permeates everything and the ship reeks of vomit from bow to stern."

The captain stomped off, directing his crew to heave more of the sick overboard. Procida followed, intervening and rescuing several men, but saving less than half from the captain's fury.

The captain went to his cabin. After giving him time to calm down, Procida knocked on the captain's door and held out a skin of wine. "Captain, can we talk?"

The captain didn't answer but stepped aside, letting Procida enter. They stared at each other. The captain's head nearly touched the low ceiling, but Procida had to stoop. Following an awkward silence, the captain sat down and gestured for Procida to take a stool. The doctor passed the skin to the captain.

Procida organized his thoughts. He had negotiated with kings and nobles, but now he needed to convince the captain to halt throwing sick men overboard. Especially Bastone, who would likely soon be discovered.

They took turns drinking from the skin. "Sir, you run a disciplined ship."

The captain passed back the skin.

Procida drained a swallow. "Which is necessary to survive the dangers at sea."

A slight nod and slow blink from the captain.

Procida sensed the captain was becoming receptive. "Are there laws on the sea?"

The captain interrupted his swallow, paused, then finished. "Laws?" He laughed. "If you mean the lessons that were beat into me as cabin boy and as a sailor. And now, yes—as a captain, I know what to do." He swigged more wine. "Like fight pirates, salvage prizes, and never abandon overboard sailors at sea."

The captain was more talkative. But the doctor had to be careful—the man was intelligent and Procida could not appear to be scheming. The captain looked as old as Procida. "How long have you been a captain?"

"It seems like forever!" He drank again. He scrutinized Procida. "You look like you have been around for a while, too."

"We have that in common, Captain." Procida added, "You had wise captains as mentors?"

The captain gazed up, as if thinking, "Yes, many over the years, and the sea itself, she . . . she taught me."

Procida remained silent, waiting. Then the captain said, "How did you learn to be a doctor?"

"From the lessons of many, many doctors—alive and dead."

The captain's eyes widened.

"I initially studied ancient books, then trained under doctors for years, and now, decades later, I am here."

The captain leaned forward, encouraging Procida to continue. "I have learned from the world about suffering, as you have learned from the sea. The men onboard can't pass on their sickness, the *mal aria*. Contracting the disease requires exposure to swamp air. Just as you said you don't abandon sailors at sea, I also follow rules—rules of a doctor—and I can't desert my patients."

"I believe you, Dottore." He raised the skin toward the cabin door. "Go take care of them."

The captain kept his word during the remaining four-day voyage across the Mediterranean Sea. As they neared Sicily, Procida remembered how hot and dry the island was in August. The doctor moved on deck to the ship rail, hoping for a breeze. But the sirocco wind did not offer any cool relief. It made him warmer instead, and the sand it brought from the Sahara Desert stung his face.

The ship skirted the west coast of Sicily, passing the port of Marsala, the coastline topped by a cloudless, deep blue sky. Lining the shore between Marsala and Trapani were lagoons, where the Sicilians collected seawater, exploiting the dry winds to evaporate the water and make salt. Mino joined him on the ship's rail, scanning the shore. "I had planned to use my own ship to trade the Marsala salt for the wax, but it's trapped in the harbor at Messina because of Charles's siege of the city. Hiring this ship cuts into profits."

"Where will you sell the wax?"

"In Palermo. There are plenty of churches that use the beeswax for candles. The Church wants the best wax, not the tallow candles that fill the church with smoke."

"And the ivory you purchased in Collo?" said Procida.

"Yes, for the nobles. I make false teeth. Beautiful, white teeth, the best!"

Mino glanced north. Sailing ahead of them, the tail end of Peter's fleet was in sight. "It's a relief that you secured Peter's help. Now, with his army here, I'd round up patriots and even join in the fight again. When Messina is free, I won't have to lease ships and steal in and out of my city. Perhaps the Aragonese fleet will make the difference and finally rid us of Charles. I remember the huge blaze in the harbor last spring. Charles's fleet going up in flames was a grand celebration!

"I understand your passion to save these men, being a doctor. Why is that one man so important?"

"His name is Bastone. Along with his wife and cousin Lucianu, they risked their lives and started the great fire you admired so much," said Procida. "An expert arbalester, his fire arrows destroyed the fleet that was to invade Constantinople."

"*Bravu!* He is an arbalester? I have a collection of crossbows myself and can't wait to hunt boars again in the Nebrodi Mountains after we get rid of the Angevins for good."

Mino sobered. "Of course, I hope Bastone survives."

The ship continued north, the seas becoming choppy in the strait between Sicily and Favignana. As the ship pitched, Procida and Mino crossed from steerboard to port, their balance hardly affected by the rising and falling of the deck since they had acclimated to rougher seas. They gazed at the small island of Favignana, a few miles distant.

"Right now, seeing Bastone in his poor condition," said Procida, "it's hard to believe just last spring he carried out missions across Sicily during the revolt."

Mino put his hand on Procida's shoulder. "And Doctor, you finished the work, convincing Peter to fight Charles. I believe he will get rid of that bastard for good."

"I agree, but a threat is looming in Malta. Charles has a garrison there and could use it as a base to attack Sicily. Most of the population is Muslim, and Charles has abused them as he did the Sicilians. Without a healthy Bastone," Procida sighed, "I may have to make a trip to rally the Maltese against Charles."

CHAPTER II

After docking in Trapani, Mino and his scribe helped Procida bring the sick men ashore. Procida embraced Mino. "Thank you for helping hide Bastone on the ship."

"*Pregu*, my friend!" Mino slapped Procida on the shoulder. "I'll unload a share of the wax cargo today, but I must leave at the sixth hour overmorrow to deliver the rest in Palermo. You will sail with us again?"

Procida nodded.

He followed the Hospitallers as they took the sick to the nearby Church of Saint John the Baptist. Many of the freed men who had sailed with King Peter's fleet had become ill during the voyage; the church's hospice only had space for twenty of the rescued galley slaves. Procida oversaw the transfer of the extra patients to the Greek Church of Saint Nicholas.

The Hospitallers confirmed Procida's diagnosis. The hospice's barber-surgeon treated the sick men by bleeding them and inducing vomiting. As knights, the Hospitallers spent many hours training for combat, and their diet consisted mostly of protein, heavy in meat and fish, which they also provided for their patients.

At the Greek church, however, the priest had recruited local women to cook for the sick. The aroma of food, pungent with garlic, soon filled the chapel sanctuary. Procida administered the bloodletting for the patients. To further treat the sick, the doctor obtained liverwort and milk thistle from the Hospitallers' extensive herb garden.

Procida worked through the night helping the men. On the second morning after their arrival, he moved from pallet to pallet, assessing the patients, noting Bastone had improved, and hoping he might communicate. When Procida spoke to him, Bastone was overcome by a lengthy coughing fit and vomited, again unable to speak. A woman rushed to aid the sick man. She turned to the doctor. "Dottore, I will finish cleaning him. Please let him rest."

Procida returned and gave Bastone potions of liverwort, which helped rid the fluid from his lungs. The doctor also provided him with tea made from milk thistle seeds, staying with him afterwards to make sure he kept it down. Bastone still didn't have the energy to answer Procida's questions.

Procida treated the others with the same potions and returned to Bastone's pallet. The same townswoman was feeding him pasta from a bowl. The aroma of garlic was strong. Smiling, she said, "Nanna's pasta will heal you, young man!"

She turned to Procida. "You are always asking him questions. Let him gain his strength! Please, sir, let the poor boy eat."

The doctor stayed to make sure he kept down the herbs he had given him, and *la nanna* stayed to make sure the doctor let Bastone rest. When she finished feeding him, Procida again tried to question him, but the grandmother flicked her hands at Procida, shooing him away, saying, "I will tell you when he is strong enough."

Exhausted, Procida went outside for fresh air to clear his head. His last meeting with Bastone had been in Mallorca the previous spring. Later, he had learned of Bastone's exploits burning King Charles's fleet in Messina harbor, using flaming arrows from his crossbow. That was three months ago. Procida supposed the Muslims captured him soon after that, took him to Collo, and forced him to hard labor as a galley slave.

It was a difficult decision, but Procida could not remain to help Bastone. He had to go to Palermo to make sure there was a balanced distribution of power between King Peter and the Sicilian nobles. His loyalty was shifting to Peter, knowing the king's military was necessary, but he didn't want to create another tyrant like Charles, who was obsessed with dominating the Mediterranean. He also had to do something about Charles's garrison in Malta. Bastone was in no condition to undertake the mission. Procida knew he must find an alternate agent, the closest being Petru in Favignana. Now, however, he knew he must focus on his plan for Peter's entry into Palermo.

It was the fifth hour, an hour before noon, the time Mino had said his ship would cast off. Procida went to the rectory, informing the priest that he would return in several days. He retrieved his duffle and exited the back door, taking a few steps along the alley. He paused, stared vacantly, hesitant to leave—there were men suffering in the church. Yet Procida continued down the narrow street, weaving through pedestrians. He walked with head down, holding the guilt of leaving sick men. He recalled part of the Hippocratic oath he had learned in Salerno: *I swear by the Lord, making him my witness, that I will come for the benefit of the sick, remaining free of all intentional injustice.* Not a deeply religious man, he snorted to himself. The original oath had been, *I swear by the gods Apollo, Asclepius, and all the gods and goddesses.* But a Christian writer had changed the phrase to *I swear by the Lord.*

A commotion at the nearby harbor front drew his attention. Procida found throngs of citizens lining Trapani's main street for a procession. King Peter, wearing armor, rode a warhorse at the front of a cavalcade of mounted knights. They had draped *caparisons,* decorative cloth coverings, on their horses. The knights wore plated shirt armor and armor leggings. They couched their lances in their right stirrups, the weapons pointing to the sky, adorned with red and yellow ribbons waving in the breeze. Each had a kite-shaped shield on his left arm. Both the caparisons and shields displayed an alternate pattern of vertical yellow and red stripes, the colors of Aragon and Catalonia. Men and beasts alike were perspiring, even in the dry air.

Standing behind a cluster of onlookers, Procida overheard their commentary. "King Peter's putting on a show with all the shiny armor and bright colors!"

"I hope Peter doesn't tax us like that bastard Charles."

"Nobody's cheering. Who asked them here? We got rid of one foreign king for another!"

After the last of the knights passed, thousands of Aragonese infantry marched by, wearing chain mail shirts and swords. Auxiliary troops followed, equipped with short swords and spears, rambling along in a less disciplined manner.

As this last contingent of soldiers appeared, grumbling came from the spectators. "Who are they? Ah, God's bones, we are in trouble if these make up the bulk of Peter's army! They wear nothing but peasant clothes."

The spectators continued to watch and groan. The warriors passed without shields or armor, each with a bundle of javelins. At each man's belt hung what appeared to be a short sword, its cruel purpose hidden by the leather sheath. The weapon, a *coutel,* part dagger and part cleaver, was unique to the fighters.

More complaints came from the crowd. "They are a sad-looking lot. There are a couple of dark ones, maybe Arabs? Mercenaries."

"That's all Peter could afford?"

Procida couldn't resist engaging the group of men who were denigrating the fighters.

"Excuse me, *amici*—friends," said Procida, "we are fortunate they are with us."

Several men turned at the interruption. Procida said, "Those warriors are *Almogavars*. They live only for battle and come from the mountains of Spain. Their kind have been raiding the Muslim lands for centuries, serving the Christian King of Aragon in the reconquest of Iberia."

"Who are you?" a man asked. "How do you know so much?"

"I saw them in Aragon," said Procida.

"Your accent," said one man, "You aren't Sicilian."

The men continued to assess him with suspicion.

Procida said, "No, but you are Sicilians—patriots—who last Easter defeated the Angevins and freed your land, armed no better than these Almogavars."

A few of the men gave friendly nods to Procida, then turned back to their comrades.

Most of the army had passed, and Procida glanced toward the nearby waterfront. He hurried down the wharf, saw Mino hail him from the trading ship. "You just made it on time." Mino took Procida's duffle and led him toward the stern cabins. "We'll arrive tomorrow at mid-morning."

Procida felt a stab of guilt for abandoning Bastone, but it promptly faded as his mind churned, planning ways to limit Peter's authority.

CHAPTER III

Procida disembarked as soon as his ship docked at Palermo and entered the city through the seagate, arriving at the Palermo Cathedral in a quarter hour. There, he mingled with nobles from across Sicily who had assembled to receive King Peter. Procida soon discovered a problem as he circulated among the lesser nobles and merchants, learning that two of the three powerful Sicilian nobles, Alaimo and Caltagirone, who had collaborated to expel Charles were absent. Only Baron Abate of Trapani was present. Alaimo was defending Messina under siege, and Caltagirone was recruiting reinforcements for the besieged city. How could Procida prevent this council from awarding too much power to Peter without Alaimo and Caltagirone present?

The Sicilian assembly debated for the next two days as Peter's army marched from Trapani to Palermo. Procida stood with a hundred others, listening as the head of the wine merchant's guild spoke from atop the raised sanctuary. "It's time to come down from our blissfulness of the people's victory. We only succeeded because it was a surprise attack on the Angevin garrisons."

The nobles let out groans. Procida knew they were proud of their success. When the jeers died down, the merchant continued, "Look now to Messina. Charles brought a proper army, but Messina will soon fall to us with Peter as our ally. We should crown Peter as the new king of Sicily."

Procida had positioned himself near Abate, the most influential noble at the assembly. He crafted his comment, aware of the baron's wish to make his city of Trapani self-governing. "Baron, without Alaimo and Caltagirone here . . ."

"Yes, Dottore, I know. We must avoid giving Peter total power." His voice softened. "You're the master negotiator. What would you do?"

"The mayors from Catania, Enna, and Syracuse are here. They agreed to speak for Alaimo and Caltagirone. Considering Alaimo and Caltagirone are risking their lives fighting as patriots, the mayors' words will tap the spectators' emotions."

Abate scanned the crowd for the mayors. "You are the better orator."

"But you are Sicilian. Caltagirone's representative should speak first, and you last," said Procida, "so your words will moderate their radical ideas. Speak from your heart."

The leader of the merchants continued, "Peter should be awarded the crown because his wife, Constanza, is Sicilian and the daughter of the last legal king of Sicily."

Cheers erupted from the crowd.

Abate climbed the steps to the sanctuary accompanied by several of the mayors from eastern Sicily. The mayor from Catania spoke first. He was playing the part well, announcing he was reading a letter from Caltagirone—fictitious lines from a parchment he held. "Sicilians should govern themselves." There were pockets of applause. A second mayor unfurled the flag of the Sicilian revolt, a trinacria symbol on a yellow and red field. "The red symbolizes the sacrifices our people have made to free Sicily!"

Next spoke Abate. "*Mbari!* As you say in Catania and Messina. Here in Palermo, you are *cumpi*! No matter where in Sicily, we are all countrymen, all patriots, no?" Abate held his arms wide, raising one hand as he said, "I am hearing: Give Peter all the power!" He raised the other hand, "I am also hearing: No foreign rulers—Sicilians should govern themselves!" He brought his palms together in the center. "Do not be sweet lest you be eaten, do not. . ."

Several in the assembly finished the proverb, shouting, "Do not be too sour lest you be shunned."

Abate smiled. "Yes! Moderation! Compromise!"

During the remaining time before Peter arrived, the nobles formed a parliament of representatives from across Sicily. They agreed to crown Peter if he gave them the rights they had enjoyed under William II of Sicily. The people had given the former king the name "William the Good" because of his fair rule and the era of peace in Sicily during his reign. Members of the parliament adopted a bill of rights written by the leaders of Messina to present the king when he arrived. Copies were read to the public at the *piazzas* throughout the city.

Peter entered the city the following day with much the same fanfare as at Trapani, and marched to the Palermo Cathedral. Procida and the Bishop of Cefalu descended the stairs to greet the king as he dismounted. Procida expected the Aragonese king to be awarded the Kingdom of Sicily. The nobles' courage had faded, including Abate, and they remained undistinguished among the other aristocrats lining the stairs to the cathedral. Procida reasoned it was proper for him to greet the king—just a week earlier the doctor had represented Sicily in their appeal to Peter for help.

Peter embraced the bishop, then Procida, the latter handing him a single-page document titled *Rights of the Sicilian Parliament and People*. "What's this?" Peter glanced at it and seemed about to toss it.

Procida held up a palm toward the king. "Please wait, Your Highness. The accord contains the same entreaties granted to Aragonese nobles in your homeland."

The king appeared irritated. The bishop added, "And our two lands have a commonality. The Pope has excommunicated both Sicily and Aragon. Your Highness, Sicily's clergy will authenticate God's approval of your coronation." Peter's face turned red, but he maintained self-control in front of the thousands of onlookers, scanning the brief document, which referenced the Aragonese parliament's rights.

He cleared his throat. "I am, um, fortunate to have your good counsel."

Peter held up the document listing their rights. "As your sovereign, I will honor all." The king, nobles, and most of the crowd entered the Palermo Cathedral where the Bishop of Cefalu crowned Peter I, King of Sicily.

Mino was increasingly frustrated after the coronation. A week had passed and the new king had made no moves to recapture Messina. Apparently, he was examining several strategies for removing Charles from the city. But Mino's business depended on his ship being on the sea, which was blockaded in Messina harbor. Desperate to save his business, he planned a way to nudge Peter into freeing Messina. Mino sought out Procida, who was staying at the governor's palace as a guest of the king. He persuaded Procida to arrange a meeting with the king.

Within a day, the king and several of his commanding officers received them. Mino wanted Procida to speak for him to advocate his plan, but the doctor advised it would be more effective if he presented it himself.

Mino and Procida stood before the seated king, both bowing. The king gestured for Mino to speak. "Your Highness, I've spent my life hunting in the wilderness and mountains near Messina. I know the best trails to reach the city unnoticed. I've heard your Almogavar warriors can live on low rations and move through rugged terrain faster than any troops. I offer my service to guide them through the Nebrodi Mountains. We will harass Charles's siege lines around the city."

"A good idea," said the king. "Yes, the Almogavars will divert enemy troops from the siege lines, giving the Messinese a chance to sortie from the city, while I bring up the main army. He downed the rest of his cup of wine. His steward poured wine for the group. "You said you hunted in the mountains?"

Mino nodded. "For many years, sire."

"What kind of game?"

"Boar, among others."

"A dangerous quarry, but . . ."

"I fought against the Angevins at Messina."

"Good," Peter said. "But you must convince the Almogavar warriors to follow you, especially the arbalesters." He tilted his head toward one of his officers, who escorted Mino to meet with the crossbowers.

Procida was content with the king's agreement with the Sicilian nobles to balance power, and now the actions had been set into motion to free Messina. He turned to his next goal, addressing Peter. "Sire, Charles still has a garrison in Malta, only sixty miles south."

The king raised his eyebrows. "Yes?"

"Your Highness, I would like leave for a few days to gather intelligence on the island."

"Granted. Keep me informed."

Excused by the king, and with his task done in Palermo, Procida headed for the harbor to find a ship and return to Trapani.

CHAPTER IV

Procida carried his cloth duffle, continuing along the wharf at *La Cala*, Palermo's inner harbor. None of the captains he had asked were sailing to Trapani. The ship he had taken from Collo was docked ahead. Procida was surprised to see Mino disembark. The merchant carried a crossbow strapped over one shoulder and a linen shoulder sack over the other.

They slapped each other on the shoulder.

"Mino, are you staying on the ship?"

"No, leaving. I sold all the wax to the two cathedrals in Palermo. But I had to sell the ivory at a cheap price. I couldn't keep it on the ship, and I don't know when the port at Messina will be open."

"How did it go with the Almogavars?"

"I got the job. I'm going to lead 2,000 fighters through the mountains to Messina."

"How did you convince them?"

"I told the officers a few jokes," said Mino.

"What?" Procida's brow furrowed. "That persuaded them you're tough enough?"

Mino laughed. "No, I told them about the first time I hunted in the Nebrodi Mountains, when I was twelve. My father took me into the wilderness, left me alone, with a dagger and crossbow. I lived off the land for a few weeks, bringing down game with my crossbow, and eventually found my way home. The Almogavars are mountaineers—we think alike. Then I described the battle of Messina when we kicked out the Angevins. When I mentioned fighting with my crossbow, the officers had me compete with their arbalesters. I equaled their skills. Now, they think I have balls. I won the officers' respect as well as their men's."

"*Bellissimo!* When I return to Messina," said Procida, "and *you* have freed the city, can I find you in the merchants' quarter?"

"When I'm home, yes," Mino admitted, "though I'm at sea most of the time. My house is near the south gate close to the church of San Filippo Neri. Anyone in the neighborhood will show you where I live."

"Your surname, *Nglisi,* means English in Sicilian. But your manners, your mastery of the language—you *are* Sicilian."

"Years and years ago—maybe a hundred years ago—my ancestor William Maccorbmack, from Ireland, arrived in Messina with the army of the English king—King Richard. The king stopped at Messina en route to the Crusades. William liked the city so much, he returned to become a merchant, and he married a woman from the village of Santa Catalina. I am named after him, Guglielmino, Little William. People called my ancestors *those Nglisi*, and my parents adopted it as a surname. But now, once more, ciao, Dottore Procida!" He hurried into the city.

Procida located a ship and sailed to Trapani. Soon after he arrived, he arranged passage to Favignana with a local fisherman. Climbing aboard the man's sailboat, about fifteen feet long, he stepped over the net, infused with the smell of sardines. He offered a silver coin, the size of a thumbnail, to pay for his trip. The fisherman held it between his thumb and forefinger and closed one eye, studying the profile of King Charles stamped on the coin. "A silver *salutu*—but it's the tyrant's money." He handed it back. "No, no, keep it, Dottore."

Procida's eyes widened.

"It's my honor to help you, Dottore. People say you took dangerous risks for Sicily."

"There are no victories without sacrifices," said Procida.

"Ah, you have even learned a Sicilian proverb."

Procida placed the coin in the man's palm, closing his fingers shut, "I insist. Do not worry that it has Charles's image. They minted this *salutu* in Messina. So it's Sicilian, not Angevin, just as this land belongs to the Sicilians."

As their eyes met, Procida sensed their hearts were in agreement. At this instant, he felt a deep love for Sicily, but he knew his political goals must take precedence.

"Can you bring me back to Trapani?" asked Procida.

The fisherman pocketed the coin. "Dottore, my boat will be your personal ferry." He untied from the mooring post. Using the fisherman's stroke, facing forward, he stood push-rowing with the oars. "Next, Peter's mug will be on our money. Another foreigner."

"But the Sicilian nobles will protect the people from Peter becoming a tyrant," said Procida.

The fisherman tugged on a line, raising the mast, the lateen sail catching the gentle breeze. "Hmm, yes. Abate did protect the Trapanesi from the filthy Angevins, but . . . he didn't stop them from raping Palermo."

The fisherman moved to the stern, manning the tiller. "I heard Peter sent his Almogavars to Messina to give Charles hell!"

He threw a wine skin, which Procida caught. "*Vino Favignanesi.* We'll be there soon."

Within a half hour, the shore of Favignana came into sharp view. Procida gave the skin of wine to the fisherman. Procida licked his lips. The fisher noticed. "You like it?"

The sweet wine was a surprise, but not to his liking. But who would dare insult a man's wine? Procida smiled and nodded.

The fisherman sipped. "This is the best wine for a fisherman on the hot days at sea."

"Yes, now that you mention it," said Procida, "I am not as thirsty as when I drink red wines."

The fisher handed him the skin. "Take another drink and close your eyes."

Procida held the wine on his tongue. "I taste . . ."

"The sea?" asked the man.

He intended to say it had a salty-sweet taste, but uttered, "Yes, yes, the sea."

They reached the village on the north shore. Inland, a hill topped by a small castle overlooked the dry, treeless, rocky landscape. The fisherman furled his sail as the boat continued gliding above the transparent water toward a sandy beach. The strand was less than a hundred feet long, bounded on both sides by the otherwise rocky shore. A lengthy net had been drawn out along the beach, a score of fishermen mending meshwork. After running the boat aground, the fisherman threw a stone anchor on the beach and hopped ashore. Procida jumped from the bow to the dry sand. Offered more wine, he declined. "Can I help you find your way?" asked the fisherman.

"I'm looking for Ponziu Petru."

The man gestured to follow. They came to a husky man with long dark hair, sitting cross-legged, tying hemp cords to repair holes in the netting. He continued his work, looking up, smiling, "*Comu jemu?*"

"I am fine," said Procida, "*E tu?*"

He turned to the boatman who had given him passage, "Thank you, signuri. Where can I find you when I need to return to Trapani?"

The fisherman placed his hand on the doctor's shoulder, looked at Petru and said, "Just ask him."

Procida turned toward Petru and crouched, his knees protesting. With his hands on his knees, he addressed Petru at a more respectful level.

"I am Giovanni Procida."

Petru glanced at him, not stopping his work. "You're late."

"Signore?" Procida, was surprised, reverting to Genoese.

"You were supposed to be here last year. Ponzio Bastone took care of everything . . . the Angevins are gone."

"Yes, yes, but they are back . . . in Messina," said Procida. "I need your help . . ."

Petru sprang to his feet, legs planted wide, looming over the doctor who stood, stumbling back. The fisherman wrapped his arms around Procida, squeezing the breath out of the doctor. He released his embrace, Procida wide-eyed, barely keeping his balance. Petru's face reddened. "Oh, I'm sorry. A jest! You are the best! The greatest patriot and not even Sicilian! Grazzi, grazzi!"

Nearby, men patching the net laughed as they continued working. Petru placed his arm around the doctor's shoulders, leading him. "Please come to my house and have some wine and something to eat." He waved at the other men. "I'll be back soon!"

The fishermen laughed, responding with a broken chorus. "Huh-uh, sure, sure, are you certain?"

At Petru's, they sat at a table outside the front of the house. Shaded by a pergola of woody vines, the fisherman's wife brought bread and cheese. Petru poured water and added wine into their cups. "So now we can talk. I'm aware of the Messina siege, but Peter is now king. He is the best choice to end Charles's reign of terror for good, no?" He tapped his cup on the doctor's. "*Cent'anni*—health for a hundred years!"

They drank. "What can I do for you, Dottore Procida?"

"You are right. I believe Peter will drive Charles from Messina, but there is another threat," said Procida.

Petru raised his thick eyebrows.

"Charles still controls Malta," said Procida, "where he has a strong garrison."

"But do they have ships? Is it a threat to Sicily?"

"My *speculatore* in Provence has reported Charles is building a fleet in Marseilles, which he will send to Malta to strengthen his position there. So, you see," he sighed, "my job is not done."

Petru's eyes grew wide. "Yes, of course—you will instigate a revolt in Malta, like the Sicilian Vespers. I can give you the name of a trusted friend in Malta . . ."

"No, no . . ." said Procida.

Petru tilted his head, puzzled.

"You. I need *you* to go to Malta, Petru."

Petru's forehead wrinkled, flicking his head back. "You sent Bastone last spring. Send him again. I'm sure Bastone is still filled with vengeance against Charles, whose men killed his brother."

Procida grimaced, his jaws clenching, recalling when he had learned Charles had unleashed his henchmen on his own family, killing his son and violating his wife. It had driven him to destroy Charles's plans to attack Constantinople.

Petru asked, "Dottore, are you feeling ill?"

"No, no. Bastone told you that? How? When?"

"He lives nearby," Petru said. "I thought you came to see him."

"I left him in Trapani a few days ago to recover from his illness," said Procida.

"You must be mistaken, Dottore. He and his wife Esmeray have fished with me many times, even in the Mattanza. I know him well. Perhaps you confused him with someone else?"

Procida scratched his head in confusion.

Petru finished his drink and stood. "Come, let's go to their cottage. I'll show you."

Had Procida been influenced by the blue eyes of the rescued galley slave? The color was uncommon. The man's physical condition could also have misled him. He recalled the man had told him his name was Ponzio and he was from Genoa, but Procida now questioned his own memory. Had he coaxed the man by *asking* him if his name was Ponzio? Plus, the man had been feverish and delirious.

They passed through the hamlet and in the bright sun walked along a path a few yards above the sea, overlooking turquoise waves. Along the way were mastic bushes, wild olive trees, cacti, rosemary, and sea marigolds. The mastic and rosemary blooms had withered months ago, but a few yellow sea marigolds still brightened the landscape. Ahead was a lone cottage made of blocks of *tufo,* soft volcanic stone, quarried on the island.

Upon entering, they found it empty. Petru hurried outside, scanning the beach next to the hamlet. "Their boat . . . they are gone!" shouted Petru.

They traded glances, both raising an eyebrow, then looking back to the shore to make sure the boat was really gone. Procida stroked his short beard, peering across the sea. Words repeating in his mind. Where in God's teeth is Ponzio Bastone?

An hour later, they sailed into the harbor at Trapani on Petru's boat, passing a ship that had just cast off. Petru beached his boat near the docks. Procida jumped off, heading toward the Greek Church of Saint Nicholas. By the time Petru reached the church, the doctor was already inside talking with the priest.

"What do you mean, he left?" said Procida.

The priest's head snapped back. "Dottore, please. No need to raise your voice. The pace of the man's recovery was incredible, but I advised him to stay a few more days. And then he decided he was well enough to return to Genoa. I couldn't force him to stay."

Procida's eyebrows knitted. "He healed that fast?"

"It seems your care must have been very beneficial, and . . ."

"And what?"

"The kind ladies bringing food claim it was their food that brought him, and several others, back to health."

"Father?"

"Perhaps the Lord blessed the ladies' food? The Hospitallers delivering herbs told me many of the men they were caring for were dying and brought some of their ill to our church. Those men fared better here when they ate the nannas' food."

"Grazie, Padre."

As Procida left, the priest said, "I hope you find him."

Procida stopped outside the church, Petru on his heels. The aroma of garlic followed them. Procida remembered the Sicilian woman's words: "Nanna's pasta will heal you, young man."

Pausing, he tilted his head forward, rubbing his temples. "I was gone only a few days. I should not have left!" said Procida.

Petru placed his hand on Procida's shoulder. "But the sick man was not Bastone. He was in Favignana."

Michael A. Ponzio

The Three Provinces, *Valli*, of Sicily

Leading Sicilian nobles in alliance with Giovanni Procida:

Palmerio Abate in the Val di Mazara.
Alaimo of Lentini for the Val di Demone.
Gualtiero Caltagirone for the Val di Noto.

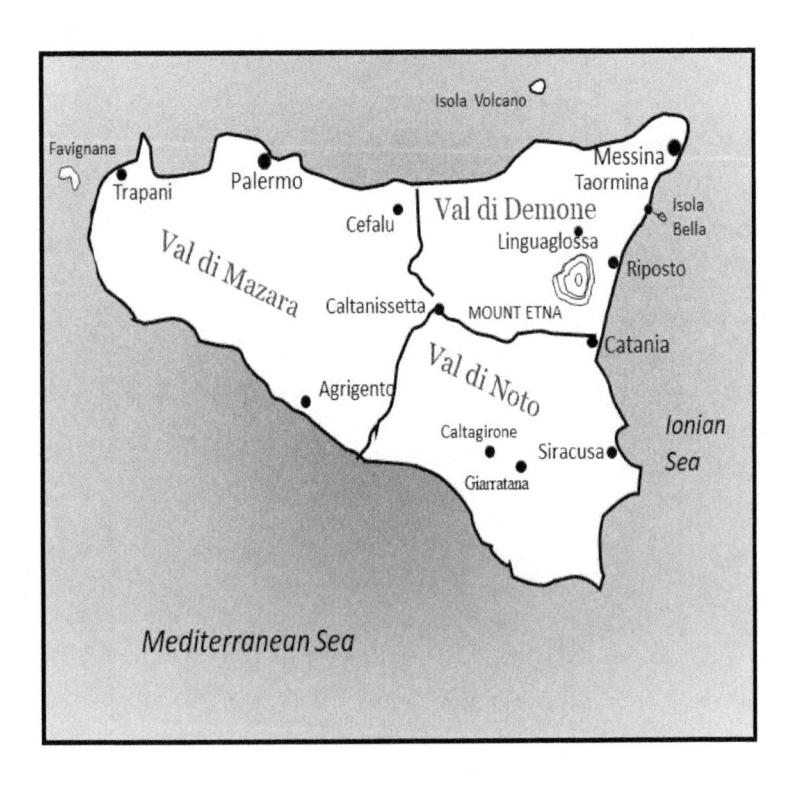

CHAPTER V

With the nor'westerly mistral winds abaft, the *Aspasia* sailed briskly along the southern coast of Sicily. On their way to Catania, they would soon pass Agrigento, two days out of Favignana.

Esmeray had been content on the small island with their daily routine sailing to the fish traps, returning to their snug cottage, leading a calm life after the stresses of the Sicilian revolt. She was also relieved that she did not have to attend Mass; to her fortune there was no priest on the island. But she did not socialize or fit in with the fishermen's wives, because she was a fisher herself.

When not fishing with Esmeray, Bastone was working in the vineyards. He helped Vincenzu, the aged owner, to maintain the vines, shielded by stone walls from the desiccating *favonio*, the dry, westerly winds.

Esmeray had everything she needed: the sea, her boat, the *Aspasia*, and Bastone. In Favignana, she had thought they had finally found a permanent home, but now as she manned the tiller, Esmeray remembered how much she loved the *open* sea, undertaking a long journey, the unexpected ahead.

She was comfortable in her cutoff sailor's pants and loose tunic, her chestnut hair free in the breeze, not having to cover it as in public spaces. Her sailboat, an archetypical Greek fishing vessel, a *trohantiras*, eighteen feet long and single-masted, was equipped with a mainsail and jib. She had added a third sail, a *genoa*, which overlapped the jib, boosting the vessel's top speed.

Bastone, with dark hair, a trimmed beard and moustache, crawled out of the tiny cabin, having slept after his turn at the helm. "There he is, *tesoro mio*, my sweetheart!" said Esmeray. His blue eyes always thrilled her. And like the sea, they changed hue with the light.

Bastone moved aft, replacing Esmeray at the helm. "You don't look tired." He tied a hitch around the tiller handle. "Esme, perhaps I will just let the *Aspasia* steer herself and we can share the cabin?"

Esmeray laughed, squeezed him, then drew back. "I thought I taught you better. That half hitch wouldn't hold the tiller." She added another half hitch to make a clove hitch. She gave him a short, sweet kiss, and made her way to the cabin, holding out her palm as if *not now*.

His proposal of intimacy reminded her they had agreed to start a family, although it had yielded no results as yet. Esmeray wondered if they would ever have children or if their life would be filled instead with secret missions. As she drifted off to her nap, she remembered one reason she had been attracted to Bastone—because of his zeal for adventure, however dangerous.

A week earlier, Peter's fleet had passed between Sicily and Favignana. Esmeray noted Bastone had been unusually quiet about it. Then when they learned of Peter's coronation as the king of Sicily, Bastone had angry words, considering it was a new invasion of his adopted country.

Esmeray woke from her nap, crawled out of the tiny cabin, and for a time was absorbed by the sea. "Are you ready for me to take the tiller, tesoro mio?"

"Va bene, I'll go a little longer."

"Bastonino, I understand why you want to consult with Caltagirone. We risked so much fighting Charles. But is it within our power—even Caltagirone's power, to oppose Peter?"

"Procida was there and gave up Sicily! And I learned why Sicilians, who had the first chance in centuries to govern themselves, had invited a foreign king. Alaimo and Caltagirone were absent. We fought alongside them during the revolt. I respect Caltagirone for his refusal to allow another foreign power to rule Sicily."

Esmeray made her way to the stern, gave Bastone a quick kiss. "I'm with you. I'll take the helm. Get some rest, sweet."

After several more days following the coast of Sicily, Esmeray and Bastone sailed into the harbor of Catania at mid-morning. Approaching the breakwater, Bastone furled the mainsail, slowing the boat, propelled solely by the jib. The city lay at the foot of Mount Etna, which the Sicilians called *Muncibbeddu,* the beautiful mountain. The volcano dominated the landscape. Black swaths of old lava flows that had reached the sea bounded the city. Overlooking the cityscape of red-tiled buildings was the Cathedral of Saint Agatha, built by the Normans two centuries before, and repaired after an earthquake a century later. But their goal now was the Castle Ursino, a walled enclave within the city, where they had heard they might find Baron Caltagirone, who had led the assault on Messina and freed the city months earlier.

After tying up at a mooring post, they stowed the tiller in the tiny cabin, disembarked, passing through the city gate. Absent since Bastone's last visit were the groups of French Angevin soldiers openly abusing the citizens on the street. The people of Catania had killed most of the soldiers in the revolt. A few who had treated the Sicilians fairly had been deported. Still present, however, were the poor, some homeless. It would take years for the economy of Sicily to recover from Charles's mistreatment.

Bastone had brought his crossbow, its case strapped to his back. Esmeray recalled how he valued the weapon, having been crafted by his father, although the men's last time together in Genoa had been antagonistic. Before they disembarked, Esmeray had donned a headband to gather her hair and slipped on an ankle length tunica. Both garments were the blue she cherished, the color of her husband's eyes. They had had years of experience working together on his covert missions as a speculatore. This one could be the most dangerous.

They reached Castle Ursino. Inside the walls was a green oasis of mulberry trees, the home of the silkworms whose threads were used to spin fine cloth. After the patriots had expelled the former Angevin baron, the castle was now used by Baron Caltagirone. Vadala, the baron's scribe, welcomed them at the gate. He embraced Bastone and slapped his back. "Too bad we don't have time for a stick match, my friend, like your last visit! The baron will be pleased to see you."

"Signuri Vadala, my wife Esmeray."

Esmeray, seeing that Vadala was a close friend of Bastone, offered her right cheek. The scribe placed his hands on her shoulders, touching his right cheek, then left. Both kissed the air. He released her, "Welcome, Signura Ponzio! Please come. The baron is discussing plans to relieve Messina." They entered the grove of mulberry trees, coming to a private glade where several men sat on stools around a small table. The baron stood as they arrived, embracing Bastone first and then Esmeray. They had shared a history; all three had been comrades in arms, fighting in the battle evicting the Angevins from Messina. His confederates remained seated, Esmeray sensing they were irritated that a woman was interrupting their meeting.

Esmeray had been in situations like this before and had discovered that being too bold or fearful would not help gain their respect. She briefly but firmly held eye contact with each man but broke off soon enough to avoid the appearance of confrontation.

Caltagirone turned to his men. "You have heard of the women, Dina and Clarenza who rang the church bells to alert the men defending Messina?"

Confused faces, but with nods.

"And you respect them for that?"

More nods and shrugs gesturing "of course."

"Have you also heard of the heroes who burned Charles's fleet in Messina harbor?" Caltagirone held his arm out toward the couple. "Esmeray slipped her boat into the harbor. Bastone set the ships on fire with flaming arrows. And now, they have just sailed nonstop from Favignana to fight with us."

The men's eyes grew wide. They sprang to their feet, slapping the couple on the back with, "*Scusi, signura, signuri, bravu, bravu!*"

Vadala appeared with a jug of wine and cups. The men insisted Bastone and Esmeray take their stools as they remained standing. Caltagirone raised his cup, all toasted and said, "*Cent'anni!*"

He raised his cup a second time and said, "*Antudu*—courage is your Lord!" The others repeated the motto of the Sicilian Vespers revolt.

Caltagirone swallowed, then said, "*Paesani* and patriots. I voted against bringing King Peter to Sicily. Now that the *Palermitani* have crowned him king, I am afraid he will never leave. The people of Palermo may want him king, but we don't have to accept him. We will slip into Messina, rally Alaimo and his men to break out of the city and drive Charles and his Angevin pigs into the sea! The Sicilian people will have control of two of the *valli* if we win Messina.

"My fearless mountain men from Val di Noto are on the march to the beaches south of Messina, where Charles beached his ships." The baron nodded to his men. "We'll ride tonight and join them this evening. Tomorrow night I'll lead the sortie against Charles's encampment." He looked at Bastone. "You had good ideas when we assaulted Messina last year."

"How far is Charles's camp from the south gate?" asked Bastone.

"Just beyond crossbow range from the city walls . . ." Caltagirone glanced toward his men, receiving nods.

"I will need a small rowboat, two small casks of pine pitch, and at least three arbalesters to go with us. I am very familiar with Messina harbor," said Bastone, "and Esmeray is an expert sailor. We can moor at the outer breakwater at night. We'll take over the lighthouse and create a distraction. We will feint a sortie from the city as you attack Charles's camp."

"This will be a race against Peter," said Caltagirone. "I heard he is sending a brigade of his Almogavar raiders with the same intent—to break the siege. Alaimo has not agreed to send sorties from the city to coordinate an attack; he is waiting for King Peter to arrive. But we must show that Sicilians can win the fight without Peter's mercenaries."

"How will the Almogavars get through the mountains?" asked Bastone.

"A Messinese who knows the trails will guide them. A merchant named Mino Nglisi. With him leading them, they could arrive any day."

With time of the essence, Caltagirone and his compatriots planned the details with Bastone and Esmeray.

That following day an hour after sunset, Esmeray piloted the *Aspasia* north along the coast, passing Charles's camp. Rising above the sea-horizon was an enormous full moon. They reached the hooked-shaped peninsula which formed Messina's harbor. From the seaside, they neared the dark, rocky shore. Bastone furled the sails, and with Esmeray at the tiller, he rowed the boat to the shallows, near the lighthouse, the fire atop kept going by monks from the adjacent monastery. Three arbalesters waded ashore with him and remained concealed in the darkness near the base of the tower. Esmeray cast off, headed south toward the Angevin camp, a rowboat in tow.

Bastone silently entered the tower, easing up the spiral stairway in the dark, but he was certain there must be an Angevin lookout atop the tower. He had only taken a few steps when he heard someone descending. He halted, steadying his dagger, light glowing around the curve of the stairs. A monk appeared carrying a torch. He saw Bastone's knife, gasped, then said, "Mother Mary! Who are you!"

Bastone held a finger to his lips. "Shhh!"

Under this breath, Bastone commanded, "Brother, do not call out. Are there Angevins at the top?"

The monk nodded and whispered, "Just one."

"Turn around and go back up. I will follow."

"There has been so much bloodshed," said the monk. "The man has not mistreated us!"

"I will do my best not to kill him. Lead the way and block me from his view."

At the top, the trap door creaked as the monk pushed it open, swinging with a thud on the floor.

A voice with a French accent said, "Brother, you must have run up the stairs. That is the fastest you have ever carried wood to the top!"

The monk stood as Bastone climbed up behind him.

"What!" said the soldier. "No firewood?"

In two quick steps Bastone crossed the small space, grabbed the Angevin's wrist, locking it against his back, pushed him against the wall pinning his other arm, and held his blade at the man's neck.

"I will not kill you—just be quiet!" said Bastone. "*Oui?*"

The soldier carefully nodded. Bastone disarmed the Angevin. He sheathed his dagger, reaching toward the monk. "Brother, give me your belt."

Bastone used the rope to tie the man's hands behind his back, pulled the soldier's liner from his helmet, stuffed it in his mouth and said, "You'll live if you are quiet."

The Sicilian arbalesters joined Bastone at the top of the lighthouse. The moon was a few fists above the horizon now. Scattered campfires marked the main encampment, beyond the faint outline of Charles's siege lines a couple of hundred yards south. With the higher elevation of the lighthouse, Bastone could land bolts inside the enemy camp. He waited.

The monk passed a skin of diluted wine to Bastone's men. "When the moon is halfway risen, a troop of Angevins will arrive to change the guard."

An arbalester sniggered. "Grazzi, Brother. They'll be easy targets."

The soldier thrashed against his bindings, his attempts at speaking muffled by his gag.

As Bastone glanced at the moon above the sea, a downdraft from the sea breeze washed heat from the lighthouse fire on him, displacing the cool night air. The warmth sent prickles across Bastone's scalp.

He recalled Caltagirone should be in position by now, his focus returning to Charles's camp. Where was Esmeray's signal?

The monk stood, turning toward the pile of wood. "I need to stoke up the fire."

Bastone nodded.

After he collected an armful of firewood, the monk was halfway up the steps to the next level. Bastone noticed a ram's horn within the bundle tucked under the man's arm. Before Bastone could stop him, the monk blew the shepherd's horn, his cheeks expanding with his effort. "BAAROOOOOM!" He sent out a second blast. Bastone reached him, knocking the horn away, which clattered onto the steps. "Are you a traitor?"

Bastone ordered his men. "Shoot into the camp."

The monk stepped close to face Bastone. He maintained eye contact and his voice did not contain deceit. "I was trying to help. The horn was to signal the Angevins if the patriots attacked from the city."

Bastone didn't have time to respond, but sensed the monk was telling the truth. His men lofted salvos of bolts into Charles's camp, hoping to cause havoc. As Bastone drew his crossbow, inserted bolts, shot, and repeated, he reflected how the monk's action was a stroke of luck. Charles's troops were heading north toward the siege lines in front of the city walls, their attention pulled away from the south where Caltagirone's men waited.

Esmeray lit the cask of pitch on the rowboat she towed, sending it drifting toward the Angevin ships along the beach. It was the signal for Caltagirone to attack. The blazing rowboat approached the beached galleys. The Angevin soldiers swarmed toward their ships to protect them from the fireship. Other Angevins hurried toward the siege lines near the city wall.

Caltagirone's patriots assaulted the south side of Charles's camp, creating further distraction. Bastone released another bolt, the silent flight of the missile disappearing into the mass of Angevin soldiers. Bastone continued to loose bolts. He glanced at the monk, who had retrieved the horn. "Keep on blowing, Brother. It's helping!"

Now, the Angevin forces were split among three sides of the camp, leaving the west side under-manned. Bastone was thrilled with the success. The Sicilians had won the race against the Almogavars. Messinese defenders had lined the walls but did not join the battle.

Caltagirone's men were penetrating the south side of the camp, when battle cries abruptly roared from the hills west of the camp. "*Desperta ferro*—awake iron!" The brigade of Almogavar warriors charged. They had been waiting in the hills and exploited the diversion of Caltagirone's assault.

Groups of Messinese now sortied from the city to join in the fight. Thousands of Angevins were killed. Charles's forces had been severely mauled, but they greatly outnumbered the Sicilians, regrouped and counterattacked. The Almogavars retreated after looting large quantities of supplies and baggage from the camp. Caltagirone's men withdrew. The patriots from the city retreated back to Messina.

Esmeray safely returned to the lighthouse, joining Bastone. In the morning, they watched Charles break camp. His army weakened and demoralized, he learned that Peter's army was approaching, and he broke off the siege, withdrawing his forces across the Strait of Messina to Calabria, his domains on the Italian mainland.

The following day, Bastone and Esmeray entered Messina. Peter had arrived and Sicily was free of the Angevins once again. The people celebrated and cheered the Almogavars parading through the city.

"A sour victory," said Bastone. "Caltagirone and his men aren't joining the celebration. I'll wager he was livid when he heard the Almogavars received the recognition for freeing the city."

That afternoon, the Messinese leaders recognized Peter as the new king of Sicily. As Bastone continued to grumble, Esmeray said, "We need to accept the inevitable. Likely the rest of Sicily will soon give their allegiance to Peter."

"Caltagirone will fight it," said Bastone. "But we are done. Let's go home."

They departed Messina and sailed to Riposto, then trekked up the road along the lower slopes of Mount Etna to the village of Linguaglossa. There they visited their friends the Ponzii, receiving a warm welcome, and a much-needed respite.

Several days later, back in Riposto, they purchased supplies, preparing their return to Favignana. Although their undertaking in Messina had nourished Esmeray with the thrills she relished, she was eager to return home. She confided with Bastone she wanted this to be their last mission. Bastone, always the merchant, planned to stop in Catania to purchase silk and trade it in Trapani, filling their small cabin with as much as it could hold. Even small quantities would bring them a good profit.

After a day's sailing, they docked at Catania, making their way through the narrow, cobbled streets to purchase silk from Bastone's friend Vadala at Castle Ursino. There, not only did silkworms create fabulous threads, but weavers also spun and wove the satiny cloth. Vadala warmly greeted them, notifying Bastone that Baron Caltagirone wanted to see him. He led them to the glade in the mulberry grove, where the baron and his lieutenants were waiting. The mood of the meeting was somber, compared to the enthusiasm when they had met before the raid at Messina. The couple remained standing as the baron spoke.

"I didn't think the Almogavars could get through the mountains that fast," said Caltagirone. "Our diversions worked, but the foreigners got all the glory. I will not give up. I have asked you here, Bastone, because of your proven stealth. And you are a true patriot. Who else would have sailed so far to further the cause?"

Bastone glanced at Esmeray. He sensed she feared Caltagirone was going to ask more of them. Her presence was a comfort, yet a terror all the same, as she could be subject to another dangerous situation.

"Sail to Reggio di Calabria," said Baron Caltagirone, "and transport two of my men to deliver a message to Charles."

Charles! Years earlier, when word had reached Bastone that his brother had been executed by King Charles's soldiers, it had driven him to join the powers involved in destroying Charles's plans to dominate the Mediterranean. Was Caltagirone going to ally with Charles? Bastone used all his control to avoid showing his anger and contempt. He steadied his breathing. Now that they knew of Caltagirone's treasonous plan, a slight reddening of the face, a twitch, unusual blinking, *anything*, could lead to the death of his wife and himself. He steadied his voice. "What is your proposition for Charles, Baron?"

Caltagirone clenched his jaw, irritated, glancing at his cronies. "Your task is to transport my men, not to deliver the message."

Bastone made sure he didn't shake his head involuntarily as he said, "Yes, Baron."

But Caltagirone calmed. "We have fought together. We trust each other, no? *Scusi*, you should know the details, being of the cause." He looked at his men, "These men are not sailors, like you. They could fall overboard. Perhaps you *will* have to convey the message?"

The men laughed, and Bastone joined, remaining focused on the baron. Since his initial glance at Esmeray, not knowing how she was handling the tension, he patted Esmeray on the shoulder, masking the gesture as if he were surrendering to hilarity, but to encourage her to join in the laughter. When she barely laughed, sounding hollow, keeping a stoic face, Bastone realized his touch may have been a mistake.

There was an awkward pause.

"As long as your men behave themselves," said Esmeray with a straight face, "I will not throw them overboard."

They all roared.

"She is a wit, Bastone," said the baron, tears coming to his eyes.

Bastone relaxed, now more confident they would survive this tense situation.

Vadala, as if on cue, arrived with wine and retreated. Caltagirone returned to the issue. "We will allow Charles to land troops at Catania, using it as a base of operations to retake Messina and Val di Demone. In exchange, he will leave Catania and Val di Noto for Sicilians to govern themselves."

Esmeray's jest diverted suspicion and relieved Bastone. He could have exploded upon hearing about the baron inviting Charles back to Sicily. He would have to cooperate. Bastone held up his cup and said, "We are honored to do the mission."

Caltagirone raised his cup with the others, toasting with the code word used during the revolt of the Sicilian Vespers: "*Antudu,* courage is your Lord!"

Bastone and Esmeray planned to spend the night in relative privacy on board *Aspasia* at the wharf. The next morning, two of the baron's men would join them for the crossing to Calabria. Caltagirone promised Bastone bolts of silk at no cost when they returned.

It was dark when they reached the boat. The cooler air of the October night was refreshing. Inside the cramped cabin, barely high enough to crawl into, Esmeray struggled to remove her tunica. Bastone pulled off his tunic and helped her get undressed. As they lay beside each other, embracing, Bastone whispered, "A good reason I admire you so much, Esme. Your clever banter helped me maintain control when Caltagirone showed he was a traitor." She answered with a warm kiss. They made time for each other, not knowing what the next few days would bring.

Children of the Middle Sea

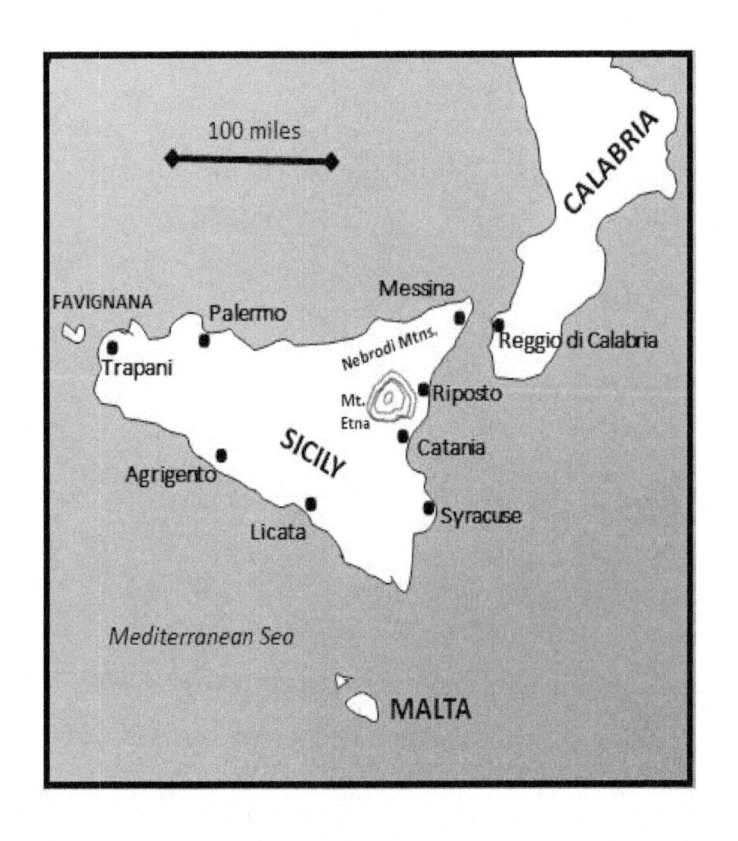

CHAPTER VI

Messina now free from Charles, Mino was relieved to be back in the merchants' quarter. Returning to the comforts of his home, he slept late into the day, exhausted after leading the Almogavars through the Nebrodi Mountains. He had turned them loose on the Angevins, marveling at their speed, outmaneuvering the armored Angevin knights and soldiers. During the raid on Charles's camp, their marksmanship with the crossbow and speed of reloading and firing had been exceptional. But the Almogavars' foremost skill had been in close combat with spear and *coutel,* a thick-bladed short sword, which they had used to cleave between the joints of the French armor. The more agile Almogavars, shouting their battle cry "Awake iron!" had overwhelmed the Angevins, driving them back to their ships, and killing thousands. Although exhilarated by the events of the last few days, Mino was ready to get back to his business affairs.

He was eating breakfast when his domestic brought him a message from Peter, who was now in Messina with his army and had established himself at Castle Mategriffon. After a long walk through the city and uphill to the castle, Mino joined the king and Procida for antipasti and wine.

"Signori Mino, you should be rewarded for your service. With your grand patriotism, you could be Messina's next captain of the people." The king raised his glass, "Saluti!" Procida and Mino joined.

"Grazzi, Your Highness, but my passion is traveling the high seas to trade."

"Hmmm. A merchant who thrives on risks and . . . dangers of the Middle Sea?"

"Perhaps, if the profits justify the hazards."

The king's glance at Procida cued him to speak. "Charles is determined to retake Sicily. Although he failed at Messina, he still has a garrison on Malta only sixty miles away. The shipments of wheat to the island halted during Sicily's revolt. The Maltese people are nearing starvation, and we could win their loyalty by providing grain."

"I will procure wheat for the crown and deliver it to Malta," Mino said.

Peter raised his eyebrows. "I hope at reduced prices. You are a patriot and Signori, we are at war."

After stroking his chin, Mino said, "For the cause . . . I can offer every ten bushels for the price of nine."

"You will still profit, I'm sure." Peter sipped, not taking his eyes off Mino over the rim of his glass.

Mino knew he wouldn't profit if he purchased the wheat in Syracuse, but he had learned grain was in surplus on the south coast of Sicily because of the interruption in exports to Malta. He would risk buying the grain there. And he proposed a scheme to ensure profits. "As long as you will lift export taxes."

The king paused as if in thought, then nodded.

Mino left the meeting pleased. Now he had a profitable reason to sail to Malta for his new venture. Malta was renowned for its beehives and honey. He hoped to bring several hives to Sicily, expand them into multiple hives to produce his own honey and wax, and sell candles to the Church.

Over the next few days, Mino readied his ship, the *Lucia*, to transport wheat to Malta. The vessel was a sixty-foot trading ship with a fifty-ton cargo capacity and was fitted with two masts and lateen sails. Under the stern castle were the captain's suite, a cabin shared by his scribe and first mate, and a third cabin for paying guests.

The *Lucia*'s crew of thirty included Messinese sailors and several cousins and nephews from the Nglisi and Danca clans. Cardo, Mino's nephew and first mate, was also an expert arbalester, as were his other nephews, having often hunted together in the Nebrodi Mountains. Pirates were common at sea and a crew that could defend the ship was essential. It was October, and the weather was unpredictable, but Mino was determined to undertake the profitable voyage.

At Catania, the sun rose over the horizon across the Ionian Sea, melting away the chill along the waterfront. Esmeray and Bastone, along with Baron Caltagirone's two envoys to Charles, boarded the *Aspasia*. After the envoys rowed the boat out of the harbor, Esmeray pointed the bow into the wind and shouted, "Stow oars!" She nodded to Bastone to hoist the mainsail. He took hold of the halyard to run up the sail but lost his grip. As the line dangled beyond his reach, he said to one man at the rowing bench, "Paisanu, hand me the line."

The envoy stood to retrieve the rope. Suddenly, Esmeray turned hard on the rudder. The boom swung, knocking the man off balance. As he was regaining his feet, Esmeray pulled the boom back and shoved it against him a second time. Losing his balance, he fell overboard. His partner glanced at Esmeray, appearing uncertain if it was an accident or intentional. Then, in a burst, he unsheathed his dagger, thrusting it at her abdomen. She slid back, pulling in her stomach as well, avoiding the point by a mere fingerbreadth. He slashed behind, but Bastone kept his distance, chopping the dagger with the sharp edge of an oar. As the dagger clattered on the deck, Bastone smashed the flat of the oar against his adversary's face, sending him to join his comrade in the sea.

Bastone ran up the mainsail. The men's shouts died away as the *Aspasia* sailed on. Bastone had an ecstatic grin. "Esme, it worked!"

From the helm, she looked over her shoulder. "Yes, *tesoro mio*, we are a good team. They can swim ashore. I'm glad we didn't kill them, though. I wouldn't want to be hunted down by their families. Now it's just revenge, not a *vendetta di sangue*."

Bastone laughed. "Just revenge, *just* revenge? Ha! Who have you become? You have always been brave, and loving fresh adventures. Now you see the threat of revenge as just a trifle danger?" Holding the line to the jib, he hesitated, looking up to the sky, "Thank you, Lord, for sending me a most thrilling wife!"

"We must hurry to Messina," said Bastone, "and report that Caltagirone has gone too far. The nobles will brand him a traitor. *He will be the hunted one*."

The sun was rising, the winds were increasing. Bastone raised the jib, then hoisted the genoa, a second, larger overlapping jib, and gained speed. Because of the nor'westerly winds, they would have to tack the sixty miles to Messina, first to starboard, then to port, zigzagging along the coast. Eager to report Caltagirone's treason to Peter, they sailed the ten-hour voyage nonstop.

Procida, appointed by the king as chancellor of the new kingdom, waited for Peter to arrive to review local affairs. It was an hour before sunset, as he gazed across the harbor from Castle Mategriffon overlooking Messina. The castle was mostly intact, although sections had been burned by the patriots during the revolt. A cool breeze, however, pushed away the odor of charred wood.

Now that Messina was free again, the doctor envisioned the new threats to Sicily. His greatest concern was the Angevin occupation of Malta, which Charles could use as a base to reconquer Sicily. Procida had to find an agent for Malta. He resisted the urge to go himself because of his age, and because the new government needed his skills to mediate between the nobles and Peter. He believed another, but less significant threat was Caltagirone, who was still unwilling to pledge his allegiance to the new king, creating a fresh crisis.

From his vantage point, Procida noticed a sailboat skirting the outside of the breakwater. It was a trohantiras, rare this far west of the Greek islands. He knew of only one boat trimmed like that: Esmeray and Bastone's boat. It passed out of view, sailing behind the lighthouse, but came into sight again near the harbor entrance. Seeing the boat reminded Procida of Ponzio Bastone, the man perfect for this mission to Malta, but he was missing from the hospice in Trapani. There were two sailors on this trohantiras. One with a slighter build was at the tiller. They furled the mainsail and continued into the harbor with the jib. Could it be *them*?

It was at least a mile through narrow streets to the waterfront. Procida, seventy-two years old, knew he could not rush down the hill. He shouted, "Steward!"

A court assistant entered the room.

Procida placed his arm around the man's shoulders and pointed. "See that sailboat? The one with two people?"

He nodded.

"Send a courier to bring them to the castle at once!"

"Yes, Chancellor."

The steward ran out of the room.

Bastone knew that Procida was in Messina and was sure he and Peter must be governing from the castle. Esmeray placed the tiller in the cabin, changed into a woad tunica draping down to her ankles, and emerged with a matching blue headband to cover her hair. She slipped on her blue shoes. She always went barefoot on her boat and usually wore just sandals ashore, but her one luxury was these shoes. They were crafted with an ankle strap and open instep, and pointed at the toes. Bastone paid the harbor master a mooring fee, which also provided security for their boat.

A young man arrived at a run as they set foot on the wharf, trying to catch his breath. "You . . . are . . . Pohn-Ponzio Ba-Bastone?"

The man appeared non-threatening, and Bastone nodded.

"Dottore Procida requests your presence. I will escort you."

Bastone glanced at Esmeray. "*Bonu*, I want to talk to him as well."

After the hike uphill, they entered the castle with their escort, freely passing through several layers of Aragonese guards. Along their route through the castle was the hubbub of new construction. The steward waved his hand. "The carpenters and masons are working day and night to repair the castle before the arrival of Queen Constanza from Aragon."

The steward led them through the castle to the great hall, where the scorched walls and ceiling still gave evidence of the fire during the revolt. Workers were sawing, hammering, and banging, repairing the damage. The activity stirred up the pungent smell of burnt wood, the odor drifting in and out of the hall with the changing sea breeze. Seemingly oblivious to the noise and whiffs of smoky residue, Doctor Procida, chancellor to King Peter, was seated at a table, his back to them, sipping wine, gazing over the harbor and city.

"Dottore Procida," said the steward, "Signuri Ponzio is here."

The doctor twisted in his chair, looking behind. "*Bellissimo!*" Setting his cup on the table, he sprang up from the chair, crossing the room and embraced Bastone.

"And, of course, Esmeray. Welcome!" He clasped her hand. "Signora, I remember our brief meeting last year. Since then, I have heard about your courageous actions in Messina harbor."

Releasing Esmeray's hand, Procida noticed she was wearing a tunica and shoes. "And you are no longer a sailor?"

"*Dottore*, the sea is . . . my blood," said Esmeray as she smiled, glancing at her husband. "We are now fishermen living on the isle of Favignana."

"But she is still quite the *lupo di mare*, sea wolf," said Bastone proudly. "An expert helmsman."

"An astounding woman!" said Procida. His attention suddenly changing, he craned his neck forward, peering at Bastone and mumbling, "The man from Collo, who I treated . . . wasn't you. The garlic . . ."

"Signore? Garlic?" asked Bastone, looking puzzled.

"You remind me of a patient with *mal aria*. I believe garlic cured him," said Procida. "I . . ."

"*Scusi Dottore,*" interrupted Bastone. "Charles is planning another invasion of Sicily. We must tell King Peter at once."

That got Procida's attention, the doctor's eyes growing wide. "What do you know?"

Bastone explained his role in helping Caltagirone lift the siege of Messina, believing the baron's goals were noble and for the good of the people. "But then he forced us to transport his messengers with the intent to get a message to Charles in Calabria. He planned to let Charles land his army at Catania. But we tricked Caltagirone's men, shoving them overboard, then sailed here."

Procida gasped. "I thought the baron was a patriot, but he is just a filthy traitor. He's angry because he wasn't awarded more land after the revolt." Moving back to the table, he retrieved his cup, swigging the wine, then gestured to them. "Sit down with me." Procida tilted his head back, shouting, "Steward!" The man hurried in. "Tell the royal secretary I want an audience with King Peter straightaway. It's urgent." The steward took a step, pausing when Procida added, "And have wine brought for my guests."

"Bastone, I want you to come with me and tell the king directly. I've told him about your skills as a spy. He knows I trust you."

A second steward arrived, carrying a tray of stoneware cups and a terra cotta jug of wine. He poured wine for Bastone and Esmeray. The three drank together, clinking their cups with a toast. "*Cent'anni!*"

Procida put down his cup. The doctor stared long at Bastone, speaking in a hushed tone to himself, "He had the same blue eyes . . ."

"Who?" asked Bastone, eyebrows furrowing, then glancing at Esmeray, who shrugged.

"Last spring, you went to live in Favignana after you burned the fleet at Messina?" asked Procida. "And you've been there ever since?"

"Um . . . yes," said Bastone, still looking baffled.

Procida pursed his lips, raising his eyes to the ceiling in contemplation, recalling he had thought the slave he'd treated for malaria was Bastone. Yet, the man had left the infirmary without a trace. Then his attention returned. "I'm sorry. It's nothing," said Procida. "Sicily needs your help once more. I have a mission for you in Malta."

Bastone exchanged skeptical glances with Esmeray. "Now? In our trohantiras? It's October. The winter storms make sailing too treacherous and it would be insane to cross on a mere fishing boat."

CHAPTER VII

Giovanna was cleaning a pair of blue shoes, sitting on the edge of the bed where Esmeray dozed after her fainting spell. Esmeray raised herself up on an elbow. "What happened?" She touched her forehead. "Oh, I have such a headache!"

"I'm sure you just need some rest, dear. You have beautiful shoes, *signura*," said Giovanna. "Where did you find these?"

Disoriented, Esmeray found it odd she had asked about her shoes, but as her head cleared a little, she realized the woman was being kind and trying to distract her from her discomfort. "Was I sick?" said Esmeray.

Giovanna handed her a cup of water. "It has honey to take away the foul taste."

Esmeray grasped she meant well. "*Grazzi*, I'm sorry, I am being rude," said Esmeray.

"*Tutti beni,* all's fine, signura. I'm Giovanna." She finished the shoes, placed them on the floor, and rinsed her hands in a bowl of water. "Maid!" A young woman appeared and took away the rags soaked with vomit. "Were these shoes imported from Constantinople?"

Despite her headache, Esmeray pushed through and tried to carry on the pleasantries. "My . . . um, sister-in-law gave them to me in Genoa."

"That was kind," said Giovanna.

"Thank you for helping me," said Esmeray. She glanced at Giovanna's clothes, then at the departing maid. "I'm sorry. You are?"

"I am the daughter of Duke Gualtieri of Messina. I am one of Queen Constanza's court ladies. The queen will arrive in Messina soon."

Esmeray's eyebrows furrowed.

"An attendant, confidante, lady-in-waiting. They chose me because I am the daughter of a Sicilian noble . . . and I am Messinese."

Esmeray said, "But you cleaned my . . ."

"Women help one another, no?" said Giovanni. "And besides, you have my respect—I know of your heroic acts in the revolt."

Esmeray's head was clearing. "Doesn't Constanza already have a confidante?" asked Esmeray.

"Yes, of course, several, but I am the most qualified *Sicilian* court lady. I will reintroduce her to the culture of Sicily after her long absence. Bella d'Amico, the queen's lady of honor, will supervise me. She fled to Aragon with Constanza when the Angevins invaded. She has been with the queen her entire life," Giovanni said.

"You are Sicilian, yet you are blond with blue eyes," said Esmeray.

"Yes, my father's ancestors were Normans." She placed her hand on Esmeray's. "When was your last monthly?"

Esmeray sat up on the side of the bed, more alert, now facing Giovanna and sensing the woman genuinely cared. "Towards the end of summer, the weather grew comfortable for about ten days or so. Then we sailed for several days to get here. Yes, I forgot, I missed my last monthly and I am almost due for my next monthly. Why?" Esmeray felt like her heart almost skipped. "Do you think I'm with child?"

Peter, Giovanni, Procida, and Ponzio Bastone sat in conference overlooking the harbor, drinking wine from the vineyards of Mount Etna. Peter's height and bulk, in addition to his royal status, rightfully intimidated many people who met him for the first time. He had fought in the wars of the Reconquista, gaining a reputation for ferocity, and he had many scars as souvenirs of combat.

But Bastone was not intimidated. He had negotiated, cajoled, argued, and had come close to insulting state leaders across the Mediterranean. He had survived many hand-to-hand fights with men as large as the king.

Bastone did respect the king for his cautious strategy in taking Messina. Instead of sailing with his entire fleet to challenge Charles, he had probed the enemy defenses using the Almogavars, then entered Messina without a major battle. Charles had fled when Peter approached the city with his main army. Peter had also used the same careful pattern earlier in the war. Initially, he had refused to ally with the Sicilian patriots unless the Pope approved. Peter had been with his fleet in Collo in Africa to reinforce his suzerainty over the Hafsids, and while there, the Pope had agreed, albeit in secret, to support the cause. Peter had then sailed to Sicily, marching into Palermo without a fight to claim the crown.

"Signore Ponzio, please tell His Majesty what you told me about Baron Caltagirone's scheme," said Procida.

"Your Grace," said Bastone, "I worked undercover for Caltagirone to raise the siege of Messina. After the battle, he requested my services again."

"I am aware of your efforts, Bastone. It ensured the success of the Almogavars," said the king.

"Thank you, Your Grace. Two days ago, Baron Caltagirone coerced me into transporting two of his men across the strait from Catania to Calabria for a meeting with Charles. His messengers were to confirm Caltagirone's alliance with Charles, inviting him to land his Angevin forces at Catania."

The king sipped from his cup and set it on the table. "And Dottore Procida told me you abandoned Caltagirone's men at sea, coming here instead. Excellent!" said Peter. "We must look at all angles, comrades. Could Caltagirone's plot inviting Charles to Catania be a ruse to distract us?"

Bastone, following Procida's lead, did not comment, sensing the king was not asking for immediate answers.

The king continued to voice his thoughts. "We discovered when Charles retreated to Calabria, the twenty galleys he had leased abandoned him and returned to Genoa. But his fleet had over a hundred vessels. He still has transports to ferry troops to Catania, but now may be short of galleys for escort."

The fact that Genoese galleys had been a part of Charles's fleet did not surprise Bastone. Genoese shipowners leased to both sides of a conflict that didn't involve their home city.

"Dottore Procida's speculatore in Provence has reported that Charles is building a fleet in Marseilles," said Peter.

"They have completed at least a score of galleys," said Procida. He glanced at Peter, explaining to Bastone, "His Grace sent a troop of Aragonese to Malta, commanded by Manfredo Lancia. Manfredo incited the Maltese people to revolt, besieging the Angevin garrison at Castle Maris. However, the Count of Malta did not join in the revolt. He remains inside the walls of the principal town, Mdina, with his soldiers, a potential threat to Manfredo's forces."

"Will Charles's new fleet in Marseilles reinforce Castle Maris, then use Malta as a base of operations against Sicily?" asked Peter. "Or will he send the galleys here to land at Catania and join Caltagirone?"

"I will keep our fleet here in the event Charles dispatches the Angevin ships from Marseilles to Sicily. And as for Malta, I have a ship ready to deliver wheat to the island. That might gain the Maltese people's favor, and perhaps influence the count to support us against the Angevins.

"Wherever Charles sends his ships, my fleet will be ready to fight. We have the most skilled leaders and sailors. My admirals have always been Catalan, but I have faith in my new admiral, Roger di Lauria, a Calabrian."

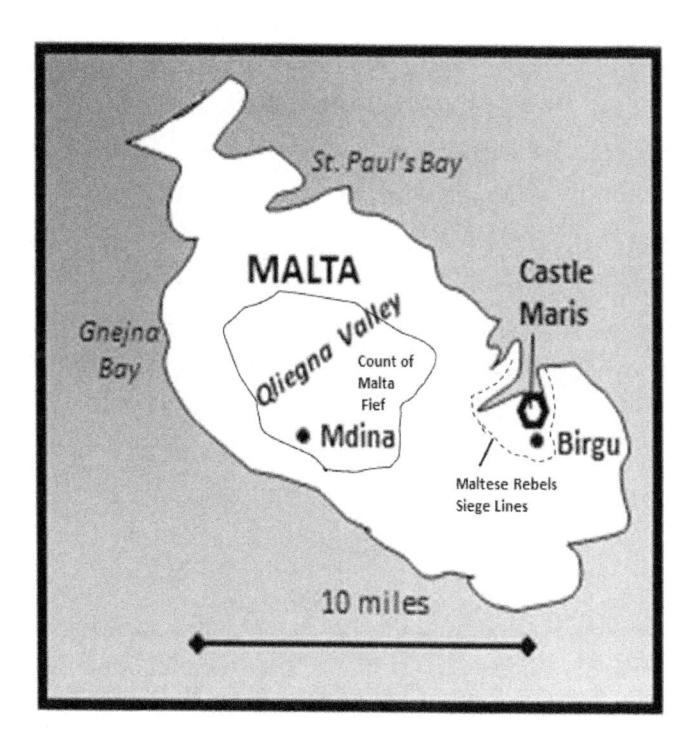

Map of Malta showing St. Paul's Bay, Gnejna Bay, Oliegna Valley, Count of Malta Fief, Mdina, Castle Maris, Birgu, Maltese Rebels Siege Lines, 10 miles scale

Peter looked at the men, pausing. "And like both of you, Di Lauria has personal reasons to fight the Angevins. His father died in the Battle of Benevento, fighting Charles's forces."

Bastone felt the heat of anger rising as the memory of his brother's death resurfaced. Procida must have told the king that his brother had been executed after being captured in battle against Charles. And he imagined the doctor having dark thoughts, recalling when Charles's men had killed his son and raped his wife and daughter.

"The doctor says you are prepared to go to Malta to advance the uprising."

The rush of heat from the anger flooded Bastone. Reflexively, he tightened his abdomen, shifting tension from his shoulders, face, and hands. At the same time, he lengthened his inhalation, slowed his breathing. He bit the inside of his lip to avoid grinding his teeth.

The doctor had lied to Peter—Bastone had not agreed to go. He peered at Procida, but the doctor refused to look his way.

Peter added, "You are charged with revitalizing the insurgency in Malta, keeping the garrison pinned down. Use your skills as a speculatore, infiltrate the baron's fief, gain the citizens' loyalty. And you may have to inspire them to rise against the count."

A renewed fury recalling his brother's death seized Bastone, overwhelmed the shock from Procida's lie. Bastone had not been cowed into cooperating. Instead, he was determined to finish the defeat of Charles. Bastone bowed his head in acceptance, sealing the pact.

Upon leaving the meeting, the king's steward guided Bastone to their room, where Esmeray was resting. On the way, unaware Esmeray was feeling ill, the thrill of the new mission surged through Bastone.

When he entered the room and saw Esmeray lying on the bed, he knew there was something not right. He reddened, feeling guilty from his focus on his mission and did not try to hide it.

He sat on the bed next to her and took her hand. *"Dolcetta mia,* are you feeling ill?"

She sat up, with a weak smile. "I'm better now, just tired and a little faint. A lady of the court helped me." She touched his forehead. "You are warm. Tell me—what is wrong?"

Bastone broke eye contact, glancing around the room as if looking for something.

"Tell me, Bastonino."

"Procida, *and* the king, are sending me to Malta on a new mission."

She squeezed his hand, her eyes watering, but there were no tears. "I am not surprised. When we sailed from Favignana, I had a lot of time thinking about—and preparing for something like this."

They laid together in silence for several minutes.

Bastone whispered in case his wife was dozing. "You haven't mentioned going with me?"

But she was awake. "I also have a surprise. The royal maid thinks I'm pregnant. She said I could stay at the castle as long as needed."

Bastone raised up on an elbow, "Esmeray!" He kissed her. "I am terrified, and yet happy, Esme!" After a long pause, he simply stated, "I can't . . ."

"You must go!" said Esmeray. "You don't think I'm strong enough? I escaped after being taken hostage, almost got killed, endured your family in Genoa, and survived your moth . . ."

"Go ahead, finish. I survived my mother, too," Bastone said after a half-hearted laugh.

"We will have a child! And you will receive the best care here at the castle. Perhaps there *is* a God caring for us."

"Whatever the reason for this gift, you *will* return. Or I'll come find you!"

Usually, in a place with such privacy and a situation as intimate, their passion would have ruled. But for now, they simply held each other, sharing a wordless, timeless comfort. Sometime later, Bastone opened his eyes, sighing, "I'm relieved you haven't insisted that you go with me."

Esmeray's thoughts retraced her life's journey. Born in Anatolia, she had lived amid a close farming community, but after a disastrous raid by Seljuk Turks, she had fled with her father to the island of Chios. They became fishermen, as Esmeray developed expert sailing skills. She was content with her life. But when her father was murdered, she fled again, with Bastone's help. After years of sailing the Middle Sea and facing dangers together, they had found an idyllic home on Favignana, but again she was uprooted, now trapped in Messina. Would she ever have a place to call home? Esmeray broke from her nostalgia, then asked, "Who is this Mino Nglisi whose ship you are sailing on?"

"A Messinese merchant. Procida knows him well. The doctor is a master schemer, occasionally infuriating me, but he is adept at selecting the ideal person for the job."

In the morning Bastone and Esmeray woke, held each other, and for several minutes shared a long, quiet embrace. Bastone gave his wife a quick kiss, bounced out of bed, and washed at the dresser commode. He pulled on his pants and tunic and added a surcoat as Esmeray watched. "Esme, I have changed my mind. Get your things together. I am not going to Malta. I'll be back soon, *dolcezza mia*— my sweetness—and we'll make our own plans."

Esmeray, stunned, had no time to respond before he hurried out. He found Procida, insisting the doctor arrange an audience with Peter. Soon, Procida and Bastone were before the king. Bastone had no leverage to negotiate or persuade Peter, so he simply stated he could not leave his pregnant wife. The king laughed. "A good jest, Bastone, but what is your real reason for an audience?"

When Bastone didn't answer, Peter blinked rapidly several times but remained calm. He said guilelessly, "Signore Ponzio, knights go to the Crusades, soldiers go to wars, sailors go on long sea voyages, and they leave behind pregnant wives. That's what men do."

Bastone stood fast. He didn't question himself and was confident of his manhood. He didn't have to be a *speculatore* to detect the king's irritation. Neither Peter's position as a king nor his status as a warrior had intimidated Bastone, but now the king's words, although without a tone of insinuation, made him feel less of a man, outside the norm for *true* men. Bastone reminded himself he didn't approve of a foreigner like Peter ruling the Sicilians. He wished he was through with this never-ending war, but he remained silent. The king frowned, but his voice remained steady. "The royal family will take good care of your wife while you complete the mission in Malta."

The doctor was looking at the floor. Bastone bowed his head, abdicating, "Yes, Your Highness."

After Procida worked with Bastone on the details of his mission, the king forbade him from seeing Esmeray again before leaving. Guards escorted Bastone to the waterfront, ensuring he boarded the ship the *Lucia*. The gangway flexed and creaked under Bastone as he crossed to the ship, the captain waiting to greet him. "Procida told me you would come. You must be Ponzio. *Ciau* Bastone!" The captain embraced him, stepping back with a knowing glance at the crossbow case slung on Bastone's back. "Bonu! An arbalester. You will fit in here."

Bastone halfheartedly returned the embrace.

"You are still recovering your strength?" said Mino. "Procida works miracles, no?"

Bastone appeared dazed. "What?"

"In Trapani . . . you were sick." Mino shook his head. "Or perhaps he was someone else—never mind. Please come to my cabin, we'll have wine," said Mino. "Your cabin is the next one over, the guest cabin. As you are a special guest—no charge."

They ducked into the captain's quarters as the crew was casting off. Mino called out in Sicilian, "Cardo! *Veni ca*—come here!"

In the cabin, Mino, Bastone, and Cardo, who was the first mate and Mino's nephew, shared wine. Bastone, rather uncharacteristically, gulped his drink.

Mino, eyebrows up, poured more. "The wine is superb, no?"

Bastone drank silently.

"Bastone, cheer up! Procida told me you left a wife, and pregnant, but you'll be back before you know it." He glanced at the case slung on Bastone's back. "I am also an arbalester. May I look at your bow?"

Bastone removed his crossbow, handing it to Mino. "What! What are these lines? A new design? Layers of wood, perhaps glued together? I have never seen this, Bastone. Where did you get it?"

Bastone finished his second cup, the wine helping him to relax. "It was made in Genoa, at the *Factoria de Balistrai.*"

"I have heard of this factory," said Mino, "an unusual organization—a trade guild, owned in common by citizens."

"Yes," said Bastone, "Similar to Genoese commercial ventures, where ships are owned by wealthy families, but common citizens' shares finance much of the trading expeditions. They share the profits."

Mino drank, then said, "Do the Genoese sell these crossbows to foreigners?"

The crossbow that Mino held and was admiring had been crafted by Bastone's father. The memory caused him to shift in his seat in discomfort, recalling the hostile parting he had suffered with his father when he'd left Genoa.

"This crossbow was made for me by my father. It is a new design and has lived up to, um, expectations. This bow can take a stronger pull than a solid wood stock. I would wager they are for sale to anyone."

"Hmm?" Mino stroked his short chin beard, then laughed. "As they say, '*A Genoese, therefore, a merchant.*' Bastone, I hope you will give me permission to shoot your fine weapon."

"Of course." Bastone raised his cup, draining it like the first two. His expression softened.

Cardo asked, "Why are we going to Licata, Uncle? The warehouses in Siracusa are likely full of grain. Licata is further west."

"I am certain the grain is cheaper." Mino took a side long glance at Bastone knowing he needed to contact a patriot in Licata for information on Malta.

Cardo said, "We'll have to pay our sailors for four or five extra days if we go to Licata. Fewer profits, Uncle."

"The lower prices in Licata and the waiver of export taxes will more than make up for the extra sailing. And this favor for the king is an investment, ensuring future shipments."

They sailed past Riposto near sunset and continued for several days, rounding Cape Passaro, turning west to arrive at the port of Licata. There Mino unloaded the wax, then contacted the local merchants, who began filling the hold of the *Lucia* with 300 Sicilian *salme* of wheat, almost 2,000 bushels of grain. Bastone went ashore. to meet an agent working for Procida to aid him in the Malta mission.

A clear blue sky and the gentle sunshine of autumn made it a pleasant walk. He could see the dome of the Church of Saint Angelo from the waterfront, surrounded by scaffolding rising above the red tile roofs of the surrounding buildings. After a few minutes' walk from the docks, Bastone arrived at a large plaza where quarried stone blocks, lumber, and tools had been stockpiled. The bustle of workers and the noise of construction echoed across the cobbled square. Bastone stood in the plaza, squinting at the men on scaffolds, shielding his eyes from the sun. Nearby, a man wearing an apron called out from a wine tavern, "*Veni! Paesani*, come and eat!"

He joined the man under a trellis in front of the tavern, the shade provided by vines growing overhead. They each took a stool at one of the outdoor tables. There were no other customers. The man called into the tavern, "Bring some refreshments for our guest." A young man placed a jug of wine, cups, a round loaf of bread, and a crock of olive oil on their table, then left.

The man said, "Animus tuus dominus."

Bastone answered, "Antudu."

"Good! And you are Genoese," said the tavern owner; "I can tell by your accent."

He held up his cup, as did Bastone, "Cent'anni!"

"Do many Genoese stop in Licata?" said Bastone.

"No, no, but I see many in Birgu, at their trading colony."

"Birgu?" asked Bastone.

"Yes, yes, the port in Malta. He slid the plate of bread to Bastone. "Please enjoy this *pani* while it's still warm."

Bastone pulled a chunk off the round loaf, the tavern keeper pouring olive oil on the bread. Bastone took a bite, his eyes partially closing, savoring the warmth, the oil, and a hint of spice he couldn't quite name.

The tavern owner laughed. "I knew you would like it! I make the best *muffulettu* in Licata! Do you like the anise I added?"

Bastone nodded with his mouth full, enjoying a hint of spice in the warm bread. He sensed the man was proud of his food and deserved a compliment, "This is *delizioso*. It needs nothing else."

The owner drank, then leaned forward, wrapping his hands around his cup on the table.

"I will tell you about Malta. The island has only two towns: Birgu, where the Genoese trade, on the harbor near Castle Maris, and the other is Mdina, a walled town on a hill a few miles inland. The Count of Malta, Andreolo da Genova, governs from Mdina, where most of the citizens are Christians. He disrespects the farmers, fishermen, and people of the countryside, mostly Muslims. The count's fiefs—cotton farms and vineyards—are around Mdina. King Charles awarded him the fief, yet the count himself is unpredictable, and likely will join whatever side is winning."

"You said the count is Andreolo *da Genova*. He is Genoese?" said Bastone. "And Manfredo is leading the revolt?"

"Yes," said the tavern keeper, "so far, Manfredo's siege is holding, but he has only a few hundred soldiers and untrained peasants."

"What is the count's relationship with the Genoese merchants in Birgu?" asked Bastone.

"The Genoese in Birgu will also try to stay out of the fight. Your contact in Malta will be a cotton farmer named Bertinu, the chief tenant for the Count of Malta. He is married to a Muslim woman, and he speaks Arabic.

"And just a few months ago, I had a conversation like this one, advising Manfredo Lancia, sent by King Peter to lead a revolt in Malta. He recruited peasants in the countryside and they have the Angevins under siege in Castle Maris, but the count has not taken sides. Manfredo is Sicilian, but you are Genoese. Perhaps you can convince the count to join the revolt."

MALTA in the Year 1283.

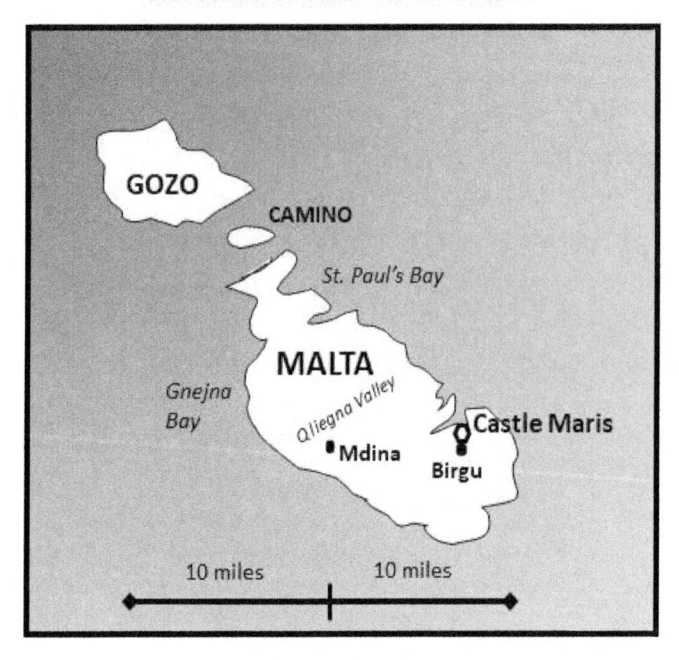

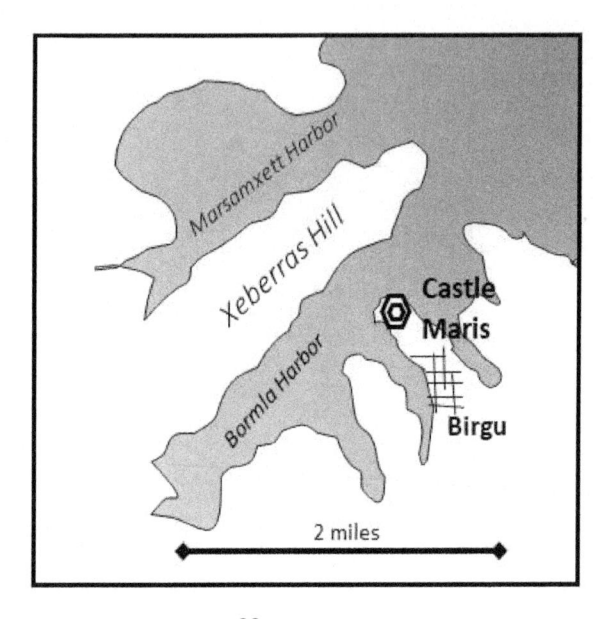

Map of Malta showing Gozo, Camino, St. Paul's Bay, Gnejna Bay, Qliegna Valley, Mdina, Birgu, and Castle Maris. Scale: 10 miles | 10 miles.

Detail map showing Marsamxett Harbor, Xeberras Hill, Bormla Harbor, Castle Maris, and Birgu. Scale: 2 miles.

CHAPTER VIII

Departing Licata the next morning, they sailed east along the coast to the fishing village of Puzzaddu, the closest point of Sicily to Malta. Mino anchored at sunset, assured by the fiery magenta sky, which predicted good weather the following day.

Casting off an hour before sunrise, Mino gazed at the horizon from the stern castle, closing his eyes as he took in a deep breath of cool air, reawakening his delight of the sea. He nodded to the helmsmen, one on each steering oar, as he ordered Cardo to adjust the sails to run on a close reach to the scirocco. The warm African wind remained steady throughout the day, pushing the ship at five knots. Mino had reckoned they would reach Malta just before sunset. They would avoid sailing at night, a wise decision in October when storms could strike with little warning.

An hour before sunset, the scirocco died, replaced by cold gusts blowing from the northeast. A sailor in the crow's nest shouted, "Thunderheads!"

Bastone came out of his cabin. "It's the *grecale*," said Mino. "We should expect heavy squalls. Bastone, stay inside." Mino ordered a helmsman to secure the deck, taking his place at a steering oar, the second helmsman remaining at the other oar. He looked up at the crow's nest, "Sailor, get down here now!"

As Bastone returned to his cabin, Mino yelled above the wind, "And close the portholes!"

The seas were increasing as curtains of rain approached. The lookout shouted, "Land to the south!"

The watch had just sighted the storm on the horizon, telling Mino it was six miles away and they had a chance to reach the safety of shore. "We're making a run to the coast. All hands on deck! Cardo, help us with the steering oar!"

Running straight leeward was dangerous, but the *grecale* wind was from the northeast and Mino could steer the ship on a beam reach, at a right angle to the heavy gusts. The ship leaned hard to starboard but clipped along briskly to Mino's thrill. "We'll make it before sunset!" he shouted. A tremendous thunderclap answered him. "I'll take the challenge you Kraken! Saint Elmo protect us!"

Approaching Malta, they sped along the shore of Gozo, the northernmost of the three main islands of the Malta archipelago. The rain crashed down in torrents and the winds intensified into gales, rolling the ship violently, waves hurtling over the sides.

"Furl the sails!" bellowed Mino. The crew quickly lowered the sails, securing the sheets to the booms with rope, righting the ship. Cardo, Mino, and the helmsman tied themselves to the steering oars. They struggled at the helm, trying to point the bow into the wind. The *Lucia* continued to flounder, now nearing the rocky shoreline of Gozo.

Intense vibrations penetrated the deck from below, giving Mino a sickening feeling, realizing the rocky sea bottom was grinding on the ship' hull. His stomach dropped quickly as a huge swell carried them above the submerged boulders and then down into the wave's trough, giving him a feeling of weightlessness. With renewed hope, the three men strained at the oars, barely clearing the island's rocky shoreline. Now at the head of the channel between the Gozo and the islet of Camino, Mino hollered, "Turn the bow at a close reach to the wind!"

They turned the ship, the nor'easterly gales pushing the ship backwards between the islands, toward the islet of Camino. Mino's voice grew hoarse as he shouted above the roar of the storm, "Cardo, it's too rough to take soundings, so get crewmen and the drop anchor when I signal. Tell the rest of the crew to go below and bail." Cardo staggered down the stairs to the deck.

The chaos of the storm was pierced by a bolt of lightning that struck the tallest mast, emitting a deafening thunderclap. With his ears ringing, Mino could see a blue glow at the mast. "Aha! Saint Elmo's fire! The saint heard my prayer!"

Mino strained with the helmsman to keep the bow pointed just off the headwind as he squinted to see through the downpour. Cardo and a handful of sailors hunkered down near the bow, clinging to the anchor, waiting for Mino's signal. As the ship pitched and rolled, the winds continued to force the ship backwards. Mino hollered to maneuver the ship to the lee side of the islet.

The storm became more brutal as waves rushed across the deck, crashing on the sailors at the anchor. Catching glimpses between the waves, Mino was relieved to see Cardo and the men still holding onto the anchor. Severe gales continued to howl with deafening ferocity, pulling on the helmsman and Mino, both barely keeping their feet. Piercing it all were high-pitched winds whistling through the rigging.

Mino glanced over his shoulder. The ship was getting close to the rocky islet behind them. He screamed, "Cardo, drop the anchor! Throw out the anchor, now!"

Cardo didn't move. Mino waved frantically, hoping Cardo would see him. Glancing behind, Mino saw the rocky shore approaching. The anchor rope might be too long to stop them, even if it was thrown overboard now. He kept on screaming and waving his arms. Finally, the crewmen dropped the anchor, the line uncoiled quickly, the ship racing towards the rock-strewn shore. Abruptly, the line snapped violently against the deck. The anchor had dug into the seabed. Mino lost hope as they continued to slip toward the dark shore. The line stretched, and Mino could feel the ship was still moving. He could do nothing but wait for the crash. The waiting seemed like eternity, but instead of the sickening sound of wood splintering on rock, the groaning of the planks signaled the line was taut, halting the ship.

The storm finally ended just before sunrise. They weighed anchor and sailed into a nearby bay on the north coast of Malta. Bastone woke and opened the porthole, sunlight streaming in. The water in the bay was like glass and the warm scirocco wind from the southwest had returned.

Bastone detected the aroma of food cooking. He ducked through the hatch to see a landscape, green from the fall rains. A few cottages made of limestone lined the bay. Boats floated on the crystal-clear water. He suspected the fishermen had wisely stored them on shore during the storm.

Mino joined the sailors gathered at the galley near midship, where a slab of slate insulated a cookfire from the wood deck. The sailors had cooked hard pasta, boiling it in a mixture of half seawater and half fresh water. They were in good spirits, comforted by the warm food, sharing their experiences of the tempest.

Mino handed Bastone a wooden bowl of penne and chickpeas sprinkled with olive oil. "Finally awake, huh?"

Bastone dug into the warm pasta. After he swallowed a few mouthfuls, he said, "Mino, have you accounted for all hands? And how did your cargo fare?"

"The crew is well. No one went overboard. We took on a lot of water, but it could have been worse."

"My compliments getting us through the storm," said Bastone.

"I've got the best crew. I only hire the most experienced. It's not cheap, but it's worth it overall." A sailor handed Mino a cup, then poured him water from a jug and added a dash of wine.

The captain drank as Bastone asked, between bites of pasta, "Have you faced such a storm before?"

"Once, no, twice before. Only when I was stupid enough to sail in the winter. And you?"

Bastone told him of his experiences with storms during the years on the *Paradisio*. He mentioned he had been an officer of the arbalesters, which he knew would interest Mino. The captain appeared intrigued by Bastone's description of the storm he and Esmeray had survived on their fishing boat, the *Aspasia*.

As he told the story, Bastone's concern for Esmeray surfaced. He hoped her pregnancy was going well. His concern was replaced by anger, remembering the king had not allowed him to see her before he'd left.

Mino snapped him out of his thoughts, laughing, "Ha! It's good I sent you to your cabin last night. From your story, it sounds like your wife is the sailor in the family!" He slapped Bastone on the back. The ship's dinghy had returned from shore, where there were a few fishing huts. Sailors were climbing to the deck.

One approached Mino. "The fishermen knew a little Sicilian and said we are at Saint Paul's Bay."

Mino peered upward, pursing his lips, as if recollecting. "Yes, yes, good. It's on my map. Did you find any beehives?"

"I got directions to the beekeeper's house."

"Row me to shore. Bastone, come along."

Mino caught Cardo's attention nearby, tipped his head back, which brought his nephew closer. "I'm going ashore for a few hours. You're in charge."

"Do you want us to dry the wet grain?" asked Cardo.

"No, no, we'll unload it this afternoon at the harbor. I learned we are at Saint Paul's Bay, less than twenty miles from Marsamxett Harbor. We'll stay out of Bormla Harbor. We must find a place to unload the wheat out of sight of the Angevin garrison, or they will confiscate it."

The sailor had remained. "Captain, the fisherman warned that pirates often anchor here."

"Harrumph! Yes, sailor, Malta has plenty of pirates." His wry smile got Bastone's attention. "Yes, Genoese pirates! But they have become, er, merchants now, no?" Mino sobered. "After I return from shore, we will cast off for Marsamxett. Bastone, from there you can begin your reconnaissance of the Angevins."

Mino headed toward his cabin, preparing to go ashore on the dinghy, but halted when he heard a shout from the crow's nest. "*Navi*—ships!"

Multiple sails were visible outside the mouth of the bay, over a mile away. A fleet was moving south parallel to the coast. Mino cupped his hands and yelled to the lookout, "What banners do they fly?"

"They are blue." The lookout shielded his eyes from the sun. "Blue, covered with yellow symbols."

"They aren't Sicilian or Aragonese or they would be bright red and yellow," said Bastone.

"But Charles's flag has a blue field covered with gold *fleur-de-lis.*"

Mino scratched his scalp. "It is an Angevin fleet. On this voyage, I didn't fly the trinacria, but even with our sails furled, I am sure they can see us." The ships continued to sail past the bay. Mino said, "They're galleys, warships. They must have crossed before the storm. Perhaps they sheltered on the west side of Gozo?"

The last one passed without turning into the bay. "That's twenty-two major galleys, eight minor galleys, and a supply ship,*"* said Bastone. "They didn't pay attention to us. Certainly, they are going to reinforce the Angevin garrison at Castle Maris."

"They'll send back a scout," said Mino. "We don't want to be here when they arrive. I'll have to cancel my plan to find any beehives. And now we can't go to Marsamxett Harbor to unload the wheat. It's the same direction the Angevin fleet just sailed."

They got underway, leaving Saint Paul's Bay, Mino piloting the *Lucia* the opposite direction the Angevin fleet had sailed. Rounding the island, he searched for a suitable cove with access to the inland city of Mdina, where he planned to trade the wheat, hoping to gain the favor of the local people. In Mdina, he and Bastone would try to secure the Count of Malta's allegiance to Peter. After sailing along the rocky western coast, Mino spotted a cove with a sandy beach, calling out to the first mate, "Furl the jib."

Scanning the shore from the stern castle, Mino unrolled a parchment showing a map of Malta. He handed it to Bastone, who steadied the map in the breeze. "Here." Mino pointed to Gnejna Bay. "According to his chart, Mdina is less than four miles inland. And we have a perfect beach to unload."

Mino anchored the *Lucia* a hundred feet from the beach and used the dinghy to bring several bushels of wheat ashore. Fishermen and their families, who had come out of their cottages along the shore in order to watch, soon joined in with their own boats to help ferry the grain. Mino rewarded them with an extra bushel for every load they brought ashore and encouraged them to spread the news of free grain to their neighbors. People from nearby farms arrived with carts and Mino persuaded them to transport wheat to Mdina, receiving extra bushels for their help.

Within a few hours, Mino and Bastone, along with a handful of sailors and several farmers leading donkey carts full of wheat, began the trek to Mdina. The city was built on a plateau hundreds of feet above the surrounding land. Nearing the city, the tallest structure, the bell tower of Saint Paul Cathedral, was prominent.

As Mino kept pace with Bastone at the front of the caravan, he said, "Charles appointed Andreolo da Genova as the Count of Malta, and gave him the fief of Mdina. My purpose is to deliver the wheat to the count. With the food shortage in Malta, do you think it will convince him to switch his allegiance to Peter?"

Bastone said, "But I have heard that the count's loyalty is fickle. And I fear he may not distribute the grain as Peter intended."

Mino looked at Bastone. "We are of the same mind. We'll withhold a large part of the grain from the count to use as negotiation for his cooperation."

Once inside the city walls progress was slow due to the narrow and crowded alleys. They finally arrived at the count's residence, *Castellu di la Chitati*—the Castle of the City, an ancient fortress within the walls of Mdina originally built by the Romans. The count heartily welcomed them, seeing the food they had brought. Mino presented him with a letter from Peter. He explained the carts full of wheat were only the first of a thousand bushels of wheat sent by the king, withholding the fact from count that they had twice that amount to distribute. While they moved through the city, Bastone estimated there were about 100 soldiers garrisoned in Mdina. The count expressed his satisfaction and arranged for helpers and armed escorts for the next series of cartloads.

Mino and Bastone returned to Gnejna Bay. Scores of farmers had gathered at the shore, bales of cotton strapped on their donkeys. Others were loading wheat into *panniers*—pairs of baskets slung over the backs of the animals.

"It looks like everyone in Malta owns a donkey," said Bastone.

Mino saw Cardo directing the boats, moving the cotton to his ship. "What is this?" Mino asked. "The grain is free for all. Didn't you tell them?"

"Yes, but they didn't want charity," said Cardo. "A few traded their cotton and others followed. One man told me they couldn't eat the cotton anyway. They are grateful and say it's a better deal than taking their products to Birgu, paying export taxes, and getting less value from the Genoese."

"This is good," said Bastone, "The people are getting what they need while keeping their pride. We'll gain their trust. But the count will need some prodding. He has offered no concessions. After delivering a few hundred bushels of wheat to Mdina, we better hope it will convince him to pledge the city as a base to attack the Angevins."

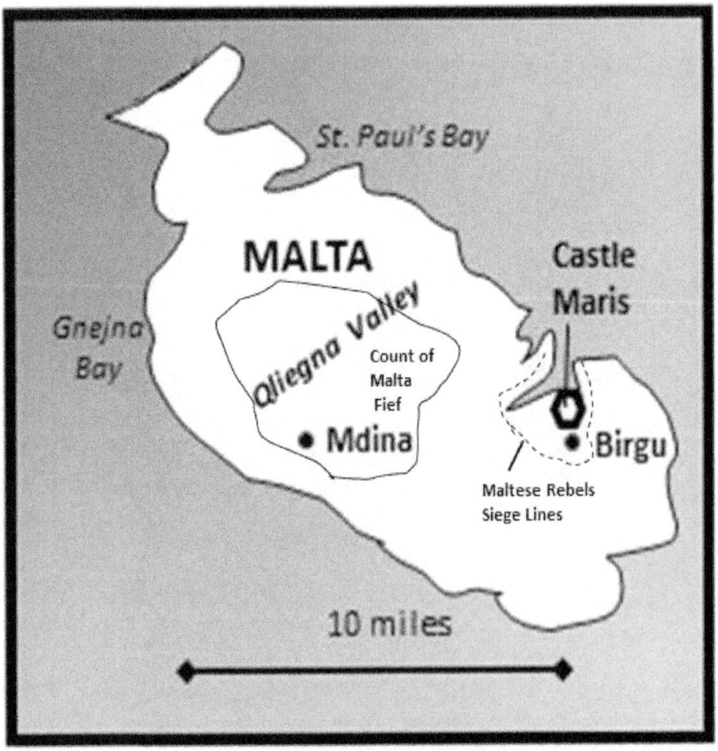
St. Paul's Bay
MALTA
Gnejna Bay
Qliegna Valley
Count of Malta Fief
Mdina
Castle Maris
Birgu
Maltese Rebels Siege Lines
10 miles

CHAPTER IX

As they promised the count, Mino and Bastone returned within several days leading a caravan of donkey carts loaded with wheat. The count embraced Mino and Bastone and offered them wine. "This Maltese vintage," said the count, "is made from the white *girgentina* grapes, from the valleys just north of Mdina."

Mino sniffed. "Fresh. With hints of citrus." He sipped. "Ah, yes, the nose doesn't lie! Very good!"

Bastone let Mino continue with negotiation and pleasant conversation. His role was to take an antagonistic approach to keep the count off balance. Bastone was blunt. "Have you been distributing the wheat to the citizens?"

"Um, yes," said the count. "I am giving the people the wheat at no cost, uh, save for a very, um, small tax."

Bastone could barely hide his disapproval. A tax on the citizenry, many of whom were starving. "King Peter waived the export taxes in Sicily. He will be pleased to hear of your generosity."

Bastone's intended sarcasm made the count squirm in his seat.

Mino sipped, paused, then said, "Count, have you tasted the mascalese vintage from Etna?"

He shook his head.

"It is a red wine, which reminds me of cherries."

The count leaned forward, showing interest. "Would you consider trading my Maltese for your Sicilian wines?"

"I am interested in trade with Malta, but first we . . . with your help . . . must expel the Angevins."

Bastone turned to the count. "The people of Sicily, with Peter's support, repulsed Charles's counterattack at Messina. Charles has retreated to Calabria. He will no longer support you."

A steward arrived, poured more wine, then promptly departed. The count said, "And taste this red wine made from the *gellewza* grapes. Does it compare to the Etna red, Mino? Did you know when the Arabs controlled Malta, they only allowed farmers to grow grapes to eat, not to make wine?"

Bastone continued, "We know Manfredo has inspired the Maltese rebels to take the countryside, ambushing Angevin patrols, and they are preventing delivery of food to Castle Maris. It will be in your best interest to join the revolt against the Angevins."

"I forbade my tenant farmers to join the uprising," said the count. "The tenant-in-chief has made sure. And a siege won't work. The Maltese may block the food by land, but Genoese merchants have ships in Birgu and will supply Castle Maris if necessary, assuming the price is right."

At the mention of the count's tenant-in-chief, Bastone recalled the man's name—Bertinu. "Count Andreolo, we have only delivered half of the wheat to Mdina," said Bastone. "It's a short sail to Birgu . . . you said the prices are favorable there . . .?"

The count's eyes grew wide. He drained his cup. "Teeth of Jesus! You just wanted me to . . ." But quickly he smiled, calming, pouring wine for himself without offering more to the others. Gulping, he paused and stated, "In exchange for the wheat, I will not side with the Angevins, but my troops will stay here In Mdina to protect the city."

"Will you promise that Manfredo's fighters can retreat behind Mdina's walls if needed?" said Bastone.

The count was silent.

"Peter knows of the recent arrival of the Angevin ships and has dispatched his Sicilian fleet, soon to arrive," added Bastone.

The count leaned back and drank without comment.

Bastone added, "Peter has given me the authority to assure you that you'll keep your fief at Mdina, if you cooperate."

"I stand on my decision not to join the revolt," said the count, "but I will give sanctuary to the Maltese rebels."

Bastone peered at the count. "And?"

"Yes, of course—that would mean—I would be committed to the revolt, but I would expect the rebels to help defend the city."

Bastone held up his cup. "Salute! We will continue the grain deliveries."

The count smiled, appearing pleased with himself. The three men toasted, stood, shook hands, sealing the agreement.

As Bastone and Mino left Mdina, they passed through three successive gates, off center from one another, creating a tortuous route designed to slow an assault on the city.

Mino said, "Peter's fleet is coming? You duped the count. Twice! And you made him believe he would keep his domain after the Aragonese take over." Mino slapped Bastone on the back and laughed.

"And your chat about Etna wine helped keep him distracted. Let's hope the count opens the gates for Manfredo's fighters when the time comes," said Bastone. "We only achieved a minor concession, but the count has every reason to be confident." He glanced back at the walls. "And look how well Mdina is fortified. Plus, I noticed most of his soldiers are Genoese arbalesters."

Esmeray stood at the walls of the Castle Mategriffon and shielded her eyes, squinting toward the docks in Messina harbor. Peter's wife, Constance, was disembarking, escorted by her entourage of ladies and royal maids. The castle was ready for Constance and her chief of the ladies-in-waiting, Bella D'Amici. The fresh scent of new beams of pine had replaced the odor of charred wood. Workers had scrubbed the stone walls blackened during the fire and covered them with tapestries of brilliant colors.

Esmeray was more nervous about Bella than the queen. What an unusual feeling. Esmeray had faced life-threatening dangers from assassins, survived fierce storms at sea, eluded slavers, and weathered constant misogynistic attacks, but now she was terrified.

"I know you are worried," said Giovanna. In their brief relationship, her Sicilian friend had always given her excellent advice, and Esmeray listened attentively.

"Yes, Bella is very demanding, but your dress we picked out for you will please her. Just remember, only talk when she asks questions. But if the queen speaks to you, talk freely, even discuss your adventures. I've heard that Constanza is always interested in learning about the experiences of capable ladies. In fact, she has invited Dina and Clarenza, two very brave ladies of Messina, to visit with her."

Giovanna's words again reassured Esmeray, as they had during these weeks of pregnancy. She placed her hand on her belly, her condition still undetectable. Giovanna noticed. "Esmeray, it will please the queen that you are *in dulci aspittari*. She has six children, and she governed Aragon and Catalonia while Peter was in Africa and Sicily."

"I'm sure the king will be pleased to see her," said Esmeray. She wished it was Bastone returning, and her unease resurfaced about his mission.

Giovanna raised her eyebrows. "The king will only have time for a brief visit with his wife. You haven't heard? Charles has challenged Peter to a duel. He will return to Aragon, then go to Bordeaux for the duel. The King of England will act as an intermediary during the contest. Constanza will rule Sicily while he is gone." She sighed, "Men!"

Over the next several days, Giovanna was busy helping the queen settle into her new residence. Esmeray walked around the castle's battlements hoping the fresh air would relieve her headaches. Although she was fatigued because of her pregnancy, she still preferred moving to sitting around the castle. During one of her circuits along the fortifications, she noted a few small galleys entering the harbor. Stopping at a crenellation in the wall, she watched them dock as armed Sicilians led scores of Angevin prisoners off the ships. She was certain these captured vessels were Angevin, when an Aragonese officer disembarked the vessel, carrying a blue flag with the yellow *fleur de lis,* the coat of arms of Charles. He would likely present it as a war prize to Peter.

The duel with Charles had not occurred and Peter had returned to Messina from Bordeaux. He met with Admiral Roger di Lauria in Castle Mategriffon. Speaking in Catalan, the king's native tongue and the language of the admiral's adopted homeland, Di Lauria reported the status of the recent hostilities. "Charles sent a few galleys to the Straits of Messina, scouting ahead of their fleet. We captured the ships and interrogated the captains. The rest of the Angevin fleet sailed west, avoiding the straits. I will have the Sicilian fleet ready to chase them down and engage in a few days. Meanwhile, I have sent a squadron to raid Charles's coastal territories in Calabria."

Peter smiled. "With your success, soon you can reclaim your Calabrian birthplace." He raised his cup. "Yes, I made the right decision appointing you as admiral."

"*Gr'acies*, Sire, but I must give credit to the marines and sailors."

Peter knew that Di Lauria had altered the fleet's structure. The king trusted Di Lauria because of his recent string of victories over Charles's fleet. Peter credited the admiral's success to excellent tactical skills in combination with his charisma, which gained his men's loyalty. Peter said, "Yes, Catalans are renowned as sailors. And my Almogavars. They are the fiercest marines."

"And Sire, the Sicilian oarsmen played a decisive role in the battles. They are free Sicilian citizens, who are especially motivated to protect their homeland."

"Yes, yes, very good idea, Admiral—extra incentive beyond their pay," Peter chuckled. "I pay the Almogavars well, but they are driven more by their warrior spirit, wages, and plunder." Peter furrowed his brow. "You only speak of the Sicilian oarsmen. What about the Catalans who were oarsmen?"

"I reassigned the Catalans to join the sailors manning the sails and rigging."

Peter tilted his head. "Hmm? Go on."

"I have both Catalans and Sicilian helmsmen on each ship. Each galley has a hundred oarsmen, who are all Sicilians. The arbalesters are Catalans. And of course, your marines, the Almogavars, make up the boarding parties."

The king raised his cup. "Excellent. Your genius has paid off. Each time Charles builds a new fleet, you destroy it."

During the next few days, as Di Lauria's fleet was readying to sail, the moment he woke, the admiral's first thoughts each day were planning the battle with the Angevin fleet. He'd lie awake in his cabin, eyes closed, imagining fleet movements and developing strategies.

In Malta, after their meeting with the count, Bastone and Mino returned to Gnejna Bay. Mino joined his scribe and first mate on shore, where the wheat was being distributed. A wizened farmer arrived at the beach with his donkey and cart, a common sight for the last several days. After filling his cart with wheat, he asked to see Bastone.

The man placed his right palm on his chest and bent slightly forward, addressing Bastone in Sicilian, "Signuri Ponziu." The farmer quietly stated the challenge words, "Animus tuus dominus."

"Antudu," answered Bastone.

Bastone marveled at his fortune. After he had gained at least partial cooperation with the count, his next task had been to find Bertinu, his contact in Malta. But it appeared Bertinu had found him instead. The man waved for Bastone to follow and began heading off the beach, the wheels of the loaded cart sinking in the sand, barely moving. The man was patient, speaking gently to encourage his donkey.

"Wait!" Bastone caught them, "I'll be right back." Bastone retrieved his crossbow and told Mino he would return in a few days with intelligence for King Peter.

Returning to the farmer with his cart, Bastone unstrapped his crossbow and hid it under the sheaves of wheat. They left the beach, heading inland toward the count's fief north of Mdina. Instead of using the customary goad stick, the Maltese farmer used gentle commands to lead his donkey. The donkey appeared to be moving at its own pace, the farmer merely accompanying her. The going was slow.

After creeping along the countryside, Bastone grew impatient with their progress. He asked, "Signuri, can we go faster?"

"She likes this pace."

"Yes, but can't you hurry her a little, erm, prompt the donkey?"

"She's doing her job. Would you like to pull the cart?"

"No! Aren't goad sticks used to make donkeys go faster?"

"Do you know much about animals, son?"

"No, I grew up in a city."

"You are a sailor. Do cats live on your ship, killing the rats?"

Bastone nodded.

"And does anyone use a goad stick on them?"

"No." Bastone remained silent after that.

Halfway to Mdina they turned east, toward the green Qliegna Valley, part of the count's fief. In an hour they reached the north slope, terraced and planted with vineyards. The fall rainy season had started in Malta, and the usual rivulet that traversed the valley had become a shallow river. While wading across, they made a stop for the donkey to drink and finally reached the south side of the valley where the gentler slope was covered with cotton fields.

A lone man came out of the copse of pine trees bordering the fields and waved. When they reached him, the man spoke in Arabic with the farmer. The men embraced, exchanging kisses on the cheeks. The stranger turned to Bastone. "Signuri Ponziu, I am Bertinu de Ponczu."

Bastone placed his palm on his chest, about to greet him as the elderly man had done, but Bertinu embraced him.

Bastone looked puzzled. "I thought, um, this gentleman was Bertinu."

"He is my father. I'll take you to Bormla Harbor." Bertinu pulled a rolled parchment from his tunic and handed it to Bastone, who opened it to find a map of the harbor.

"Grazzi! Bonu. I'll just have to mark the location of the enemy fleet and camp."

"*Pregu.* And my father will distribute the grain secretly to the peasants. You know of the count's tax?"

Bastone nodded.

"Ciau Patri!" Bertinu waved at his father as he departed.

Bastone asked, "I find it intriguing our surnames are alike."

"Where is your home?"

"Genoa, where my name is pronounced Ponzio."

"Hmm. Ponzio, Ponziu, Ponczu. Really, they are the same. Just a little different because of accents, no? My father's family came to Malta from Sicily before he was born. From Licata. He married a Maltese woman as did I."

In less than an hour, they left the small valley. The green vegetation fell away, replaced by sparse ground cover dotted with groves of salt cedar trees. Bertinu led Bastone up the ridge overlooking the harbor. Manfredo Lancia, the leader of the Maltese besieging the Angevins in

Castle Maris, had set pickets. After they passed a thicket of evergreen cedars, a voice from behind called out, "Bertinu, who's your friend?" Several of Manfredo's Sicilian fighters left the cover of the trees, smiling. They embraced Bertinu, who explained Bastone was a patriot sent by Peter for reconnaissance. Bertinu told Bastone he would be returning to check on him and said his farewells, wishing him good luck.

Enthused to be a speculatore once more, Bastone positioned himself in a copse of salt cedars on the north side of Xebarras Hill, overlooking the harbor.

The Angevins had moored their galleys across the harbor at the village of Birgu. He noted the Angevins had constructed their galleys with the traditional low bulwarks. The Aragonese and Sicilians had adopted higher fore-and-aft castles for their warships. As Bastone recorded the information and marked the number and location of the enemy ships on the map, he recalled Bertinu's surname. Had he found more distant cousins like he imagined he had in Sicily and Favignana? Intriguing, but the thought retreated as Bastone focused on his mission to verify the size of the Angevin fleet. He needed to send a map as soon as possible to Sicily.

He heard the pickets call a warning, and he looked up from sketching. Across the harbor, Angevin troops led by a troop of mounted knights were marching out of the landside gate of Castle Maris. In addition, a small galley was being rowed across the harbor's narrowest point, headed toward his position on Xebarras Hill. The two forces, along with the sortie from the castle, would trap Manfredo's fighters if they landed.

Bastone had twenty bolts in his quiver. Figuring the Angevins' distance and rowing pace, he could shoot three bolts per minute, putting much of the crew out of action. He began shooting when the boat was three hundred yards away, the bolts flying in silence, the clack of his bow tiller the only sound. From this distance, he could only see his initial shots vanish amidst the men aboard the boat. The

Angevin boat kept coming. Halfway across, Bastone saw his bolts impaling soldiers. Cries of pain echoed across the harbor. The Angevins reached the shore. Bastone kept his bolts flying, hitting several more of the enemy trying for cover in the undergrowth. A group of Angevins began moving up the hill toward him, another group hurrying along the peninsula to cut him off. Bastone suddenly realized Manfredo's pickets had not remained to oppose the landing, and his escape route was in danger. Almost out of bolts, he ran along the ridge, zigzagging to avoid the brush wood, branches, and limbs pulling on his clothes. Bastone covered over a hundred yards, encouraged that he no longer saw the enemy. But ahead, shouts burst from a thicket of gum trees.

CHAPTER X

The voices drew closer, the source concealed by a dense thicket of trees. Clenching his last bolt between his teeth, Bastone performed a routine ingrained from thousands of repetitions. Placing his foot in the stirrup at the end of the crossbow and pinning it to the ground, he crouched and looped the bowstring to a steel hook attached to his belt. He straightened his legs, bending the steel bow to lock the string in place. He inserted the bolt into a groove on the crossbow, dropping to one knee, taking aim. Only twenty yards from the thicket, when they emerged, he would not miss. This close, the bolt could penetrate a knight's heavy armor or go through two soldiers less protected.

As the evergreen branches parted, a man stepping out from the thicket glanced behind and yelled in Sicilian, "*Zittirisi*—shut up!" He looked in Bastone's direction, who had stood and lowered his bow. "I am Manfredo Lancia. Bastone, hurry, come, we are retreating."

Not waiting, he turned his back, reentering the thicket. Bastone followed the band of Maltese patriots hurrying along the ridge. They left the cover of the evergreen trees, the landscape dotted by scattered low-lying woody shrubs. The stranger talked as they trotted side by side. "My sentinels fled, but at least they gave me your location. Ha! You were worth rescuing. Your bolts slowed the attack across the harbor, so we now can make it to Mdina, ahead of the Angevin troops, but we must hurry. Their knights are on horseback."

The first few miles the small troop jogged across flat land, collecting more patriots retreating from the Angevins; then the road rose gradually, but steadily. They continued at a fast walk. "The Angevins, now reinforced by the men from their fleet, outnumber us," said Manfredo, catching his breath. "We can't stand and fight. A few miles up the road, we'll set an ambush."

The road passed through a stand of trees, where Bastone hid along with several crossbowmen. Manfredo sent the Muslim farmers who had joined the revolt ahead to Mdina a mile away. Bastone hoped the count would keep his promise and let the patriots enter the city.

The Angevin knights on horseback soon entered the forest, ahead of a column of infantry. Bastone shot his last bolt, impaling a knight, who fell off his horse. The other arbalesters hit several knights, sending the infantry for cover. Bastone fled with the ambushers to Mdina.

When they reached Mdina, the rest of their patriot fighters were gathered at the gate, prevented from entering the city. They shouted for the count, who stood atop the battlements, to let them in. Manfredo hollered over the din, drawing the count's attention. "I'm Manfredo Lancia, an agent of King Peter. The king has kicked Charles out of Sicily. He can't help you. Let these men in—your own vassals! The Angevins won't stop after slaughtering them. Mdina will be next!"

The count peered down at them through a crenellation in the wall but didn't respond.

The rumble of heavy cavalry sounded behind them. Bastone shouted in Genoese, attracting the count's attention, "Count Andreolo! We made an agreement. Mino, you, and I."

The count appeared to recognize Bastone. He let them into the city, then closed the gates. Within minutes, the Angevins arrived. From the top of the city wall, the count spoke with the Angevin leader. While the leader tried to convince the count to reaffirm his loyalty to Charles, a ripple of commotion passed through the Angevin troops.

A mob of peasants approached the Angevins' flank, armed with threshing flails, hay forks, axes, and other farm tools. Leading them was Bertinu, the tenant-in-chief, who had decided it was time to commit to the uprising. The Angevins retreated along the road, avoiding being caught between the peasants and Manfredo's soldiers in Mdina. Manfredo reorganized his men, uniting with the newly recruited farmers, and followed the Angevins, keeping them in sight the entire way to Castle Maris. After the Angevins withdrew into Castle Maris, Manfredo reestablished his siege lines.

Rushing to Gnejna Bay, Bastone found Mino's ship still anchored. Fishermen were ferrying bales of cotton to the *Lucia*. Mino was counting bales in a stack piled on the beach.

Bastone handed the rolled map to Mino. "This intelligence needs to be delivered to Peter as soon as possible!"

Bastone noticed Mino glancing at the stockpile of cotton bales, hoping he wouldn't delay casting off.

"Of course!" Mino headed toward the dinghy, stopping when Bastone didn't follow, repeating, "Let's go!"

"I still have work to do here." He handed Mino the map which showed the enemy positions and forces. "Have a safe journey, *mbare*," said Bastone. "When you get to Messina, tell Esmeray I am well."

The men embraced, Mino pounding Bastone on the back, "Ciau mbare!"

His concern for Esmeray surfacing, Bastone wondered if he was making the right decision to stay. But he remained on the beach, watched a sailor pushed off the dinghy, jump in to join Mino, and row toward the *Lucia*.

From reports by fishermen near Favignana, Admiral Di Lauria learned that the Angevin fleet he had engaged near Messina had sailed around the west coast of Sicily, then south out to sea. Di Lauria was certain that the enemy was heading to Malta. He departed Messina the next day with a fleet of twenty galleys, stopping at Syracuse as a port of call to rest the rowing crews. Mino, sailing from Malta, had planned once in Messina to immediately deliver the strategic information collected by Bastone, but discovered the admiral had anchored his fleet in the harbor at Syracuse. Among the flotilla, he found the flagship and delivered Bastone's map in person to the admiral.

"Merchant Nglisi," said Di Lauria in Genoese, "grazie mille for the map. And I thank you for delivering the wheat, an important part of our strategy." He held up his cup. "Now I must toast you and say goodnight. Cent'anni. We sail at dawn tomorrow and I must sleep on this new information."

Mino turned to leave, then paused. "There is a magnificent trading ship, the *Paradisio,* moored in the harbor. Is the ship with your fleet?"

"The *Paradisio* is sailing with us to deliver siege engines for the patriots in Malta."

Mino left with visions of owning a vessel like the *Paradisio*. It was over 100 feet long, with three masts, lateen sails, and luxurious cabins for high paying passengers. Each trading voyage would have triple the profits of his current ship.

The admiral studied Bastone's map. Bastone's notes confirmed the Angevin fleet from Marseilles was in Malta. His eyes widened upon learning the size and type of the enemy vessels, the number of fighting men, and the fact that the ships were not equipped with the tall fore-and-aft castles, as was his fleet. In the morning, after he woke, he remained in his bunk, his mind churning, envisioning new strategies for his battle against the Angevin fleet.

The *Lucia* docked in Messina, Mino heading at once for Castle Mategriffon, eager to inform Peter that he had delivered Bastone's strategic intelligence to Di Lauria. When he arrived, while Mino waited for his audience with Peter, he asked the steward to tell Esmeray he had news of her husband. He lingered outside on the walkway along the battlements, turning when he heard a woman's voice behind him. "Signuri Nglisi?"

A young woman approached, petite and fair-haired, wearing a triangular headscarf. Assuming her to be Esmeray, he bowed his head. "Signura Ponzio, Bastone sailed with me to Malta. He is . . ."

The fair-haired woman looked past Mino, "Oh, there's Esme!"

He turned to see a woman, her chestnut hair loose and glorious in the breeze. But now in the presence of a strange man, she was hurrying to tie her hair back with a woad scarf, the color matching her blue shoes. Mino was relieved the newcomer was Esmeray. He had been quite taken with the blonde-haired woman.

"Esmeray, I am Mino Nglisi."

She bit her lower lip and appeared to be holding her breath.

"Bastone is in good health."

Esmeray sighed, her shoulders relaxing.

"He sends his, er . . . love, still on his mission, signura."

Esmeray recovered, her voice steady and matter of fact. "I am not surprised. He is a *testa dura*. That hardhead will not quit until he is done."

"Come, Signuri Nglisi," said the fair-haired woman, "I am Giovanna di Lentini, Esmeray's mentor, and a lady of the queen. Let us wait in the hall and visit until they call you for your appointment with the king." A servant met them in the conference hall with a tray of ceramic cups.

They sipped diluted wine as Mino described Bastone's success in his mission as a *speculatore* and spoke of his own trading venture.

"Thank you for bringing the good news about Bastone," said Esmeray. "Did he say when he will return to Messina?"

"No, I am sorry, signura."

There was a lull in the conversation while they sipped wine. Mino feeling awkward arriving without Esmeray's husband was relieved when Giovanna changed the subject. "Signuri Nglisi, I have never seen boots as unique as yours."

He didn't know how to answer her question, but he was now glad he had changed the worn deck shoes for a new pair to meet the king.

"They convey sturdiness, thick leather," said Giovanna, "with three robust buckles. Not like those shoes the dandies wear with long pointed toes."

Mino glanced at Esmeray's shoes, which had pointed toes, and Giovanna noticed.

"No, not like hers. The pointed toes on the men's shoes are twice as long as the shoe itself. And they curl up." She snickered. "Esmeray's shoes are fashionable and in good taste."

A steward arrived, announcing the king would now see Mino. He excused himself, conveying his pleasure at meeting the women.

When he had moved outside of hearing distance, Esmeray laughed. "You were flirting, Giovanna!"

"I like him."

"Is it acceptable for a court lady to act in such a way?"

"This lady will, and with him."

Michael A. Ponzio

Children of the Middle Sea

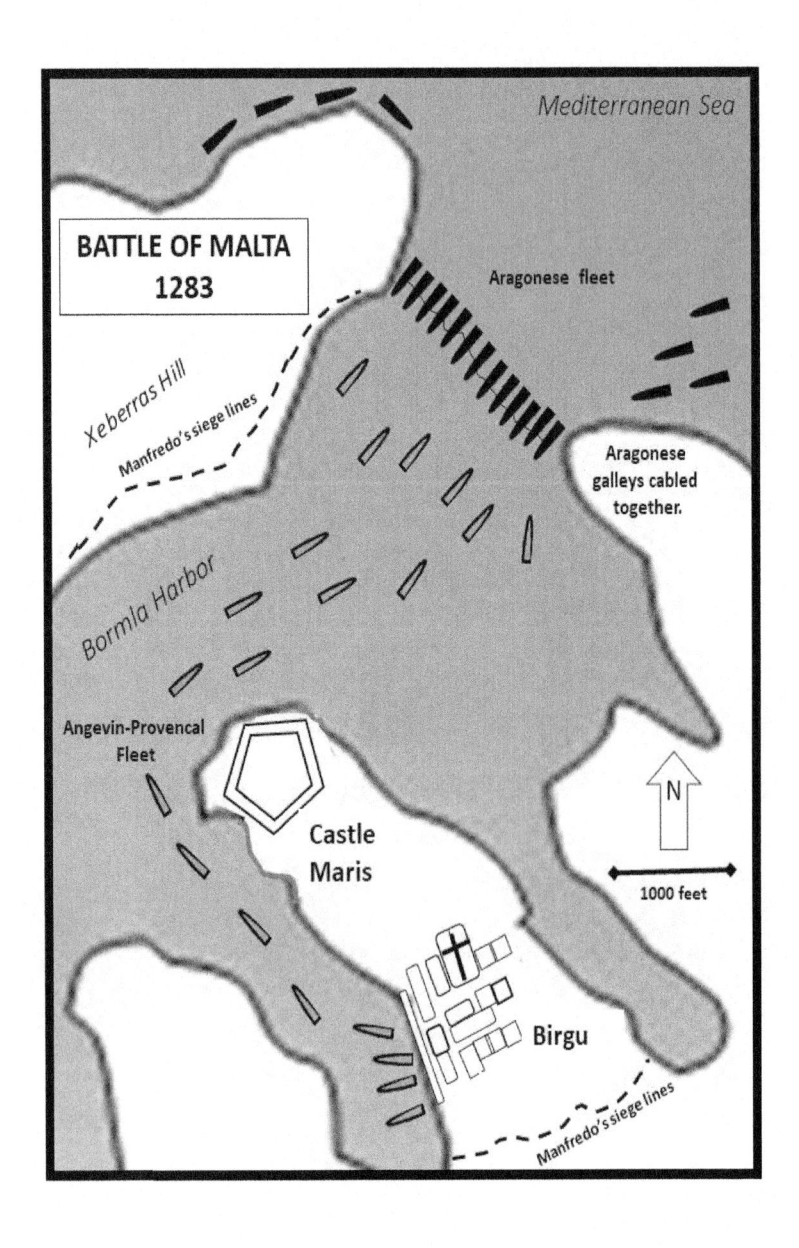

BATTLE OF MALTA 1283

Mediterranean Sea

Aragonese fleet

Xeberras Hill

Manfredo's siege lines

Aragonese galleys cabled together.

Bormla Harbor

Angevin-Provencal Fleet

Castle Maris

Birgu

Manfredo's siege lines

N

1000 feet

CHAPTER XI

After returning to Xeberras Hill, Bastone continued surveillance in the dim light before dawn. He hid in a copse of salt cedar trees overlooking the harbor. Counting the vessels again to verify the enemy's strength, he looked for any changes while he had been in Medina during the Angevin sortie from Castle Maris. Eighteen narrow, fast galleys remained, each with a minimum of 108 oarsmen and 50 marines. Also, several round-hulled cargo ships were still moored in the narrow cove, each capable of transporting hundreds of men at arms. Including the garrison in Castle Maris, Bastone estimated the Angevins had about 5,000 fighting men.

Bastone was reassured that the locations of the Angevin ships and their camp on the map he had sent to the Admiral had not changed. The camp remained between the village of Birgu and Castle Maris. Although the cove off Bormla Harbor protected their ships from the weather, Bastone noted their fleet was vulnerable to being trapped in the small waterway. He anticipated Di Lauria would use this intelligence to his advantage. Looking up from sketching, he spotted enemy scouts row a pair of dinghies into the main harbor.

Along the ridge from the direction of Mdina, Bastone saw a couple Maltese patriots approaching with Bertinu. He left the copse of small trees to greet them. As the men grew closer, each put his right hand on his chest, their way of showing peace and friendship. Bastone returned their gesture, recalling the exchange of kisses in their culture was for close relations. They sat in a circle facing each other under the mild sun and steady breeze.

Bertinu spoke in Sicilian. "Bastone, I have good news. Admiral Di Lauria's fleet has reached Malta. Anchored at Gozo, he is planning to sail tonight to trap the Angevin fleet in the harbor. He will attack the enemy tomorrow at dawn."

Bastone pointed at the Angevin dinghies that were now approaching the harbor mouth. "They'll detect Di Lauria's approach. I could go down to the shore and shoot the crew, but the lookouts from the castle would notice. They would merely send more scouts. And I can't see to shoot them during the night."

Bertinu placed his hand on the shoulder of one of his comrades. "There is another way. These patriots are lobster divers. They can stay underwater like fish."

He spoke to them in Arabic, one of them clenching a knife between his teeth, and moving his arms as if he were swimming underwater. Bertinu said, "Tonight they will eliminate the Angevin lookouts, and those in Castle Maris won't detect a thing."

Bertinu glanced at the fishermen, pointing to the sky.

They also pointed, saying, "*Insha'Allah*, God willing."

Bertinu departed, and Bastone bedded down in the hideaway with the divers. In the middle of the night, the Maltese fisherman stole down to the shore, performed their mission, and departed after their grisly yet successful endeavor.

Bastone slept fitfully, at one point dreaming he was in Favignana sailing on the *Aspasia* with Esmeray. As they had the spring before, they had joined the annual tuna hunt with the islanders. Although by tradition, the fishermen always sang a ritual chant when they hauled in the nets, Bastone found it odd they were instead sounding horns and beating drums. He woke to the sound of trumpets and drums from Di Lauria's fleet, calling the men to battle.

During the night, Di Lauria had directed his crews to moor their galleys, side by side, at the harbor entrance. The ships were then lashed together, blocking the enemy fleet from escaping the harbor. From his vantage point on the hill, Bastone also observed Di Lauria's brilliant positioning of his reserves, hidden behind the headlands at either side of the entrance to Bormla Harbor.

The Catalan-Aragonese banners of red and yellow flew above the fleet as the drums and bugles continued. Activity at the Angevin galleys, still moored in the cove, had just begun. Maltese fishermen, turned assassins, had eliminated the Angevin sentinels the night before. Bastone shook his head to clear the sleep, questioning why Di Lauria, with the advantage of surprise, hadn't attacked the moored enemy fleet. Would sounding the drums and trumpets instill the pride of the Angevins to come out and fight, especially the French Provencal knights, bombastic by reputation?

Bastone scanned the panorama, evaluating. The Angevins had moored their galleys in a narrow cove. With limited room to maneuver, Di Lauria could only attack using a small number of ships at a time. In addition, his ships would have to pass under the catapults of Castle Maris to reach the enemy fleet. Now Bastone understood why Di Lauria did not attack the Angevin fleet in the cove.

As he continued to watch, a lone dinghy from the Angevin fleet rowed out of the narrow cove, passing Castle Maris, moving toward Di Lauria's fleet. With the Angevin sentinels eliminated the night before by the divers, the occupants of the rowboat were scouting Di Lauria's fleet, likely counting the galleys.

Bastone picked up his crossbow and descended the hill heading to the shore of the harbor. There was not much cover, but he was determined to eliminate these scouts as well. The enemy rowboat halted to observe Di Lauria's galleys, outside of crossbow range. But the boat's occupants were easy targets for Bastone now that he was almost level with them. Bastone cocked his bow, setting a bolt in place. As he took aim, he glanced at Di Lauria's galleys secured together, the admiral's reserve ships hidden from his view now that he was at sea level. Bastone did not shoot, returning to his hiding place atop the ridge, allowing the enemy scouts to return to their fleet where they would report Di Lauria's fleet only had a dozen galleys. The Angevins would believe they outnumbered Di Lauria's fleet.

Soon, Angevin marines and sailors boarded several of their beached galleys, which were rowed to the exit of the cove where they awaited more ships to cast off. Knights from Castle Maris joined the fleet, their armor glinting in the light of the rising sun. A group of Angevin galleys was now approaching Di Lauria's vessels. When they were within a hundred yards, the battle began with an onslaught of arrows and bolts.

As crossbow bolts continued to fly between the fleets, the enemy galleys drew closer. Bastone had notified Di Lauria that the fore and stern castles of the Aragonese galleys were higher than those of the Angevin ships. But Bastone remembered the heavily armored Angevin knights who had boarded their galleys. The marines in Di Lauria's fleet were Almogavars, without armor. And the Catalan arbalesters wore only leather vests. Would the Angevins lob their missiles onto the decks of Di Lauria's galleys to counteract the height advantage?

The battle intensified as the Angevins brought more galleys to the front, raining arrows, javelins, and cross bolts on the Aragonese blockade. Slingers hurled rocks and clay pots of lime, intending to blind their adversaries. In contrast, the Catalans and Aragonese hunkered down behind the higher decks and bulwarks, except for a few crossbowmen who appeared, shot, and disappeared. Angevin galleys took turns moving close to the immobile Aragonese ships, exhausting their missiles. By noon, when the rate of projectiles slowed, Aragonese sailors removed the cables and ropes that had lashed the galleys together, spreading out to counterattack the Angevins in ship-to-ship battles. The entire Angevin fleet came forward, believing they still had the numerical advantage.

The Aragonese had withheld the bulk of their missiles, and now poured thousands of arrows and javelins into the Angevin galleys, decimating the enemy crews. Boarding the enemy ships, the agile Almogavars outmaneuvered the slower, armored Angevin knights, their ranks already reduced by the Catalan arbalesters. When Di Lauria ordered his reserve galleys to enter the harbor, the battle became a rout in favor of the Aragonese. The water of the harbor was stained red with the blood of the slain.

Night approached, halting the work of prisoners removing bodies among the flotsam to bury them on shore. Di Lauria had set up camps for his forces on nearby Marsamxett Harbor north of Xebarras Hill.

A Catalan officer found Bastone at his position overlooking the bloody waters, informing him Di Lauria wanted to see him. They descended to Marsamxett Harbor, where catapults and trebuchets were being ferried from a large vessel. The ship was the *Paradisio*, on which Bastone had served as an officer. He wondered if Captain Zaccaria was on board.

The Catalan officer left him in the Aragonese-Catalan camp at Di Lauria's tent, where a guard soon showed him in. Di Lauria and several men, including Zaccaria, sat on rough pine boxes around a wooden trunk being used as a table.

Zaccaria smiled and greeted Bastone, embracing him. "It has been a while!"

He introduced him to the admiral, a robust, muscular man in his forties with full beard. "The king's Admiral for Aragon and Sicily, Roger di Lauria." When he stood, he was half a head taller than Bastone.

Bastone bowed his head, "Admiral, congratulations on your victory today."

Di Lauria embraced Bastone. "Your intelligence was invaluable. Share wine with us."

An officer gave up his stool to Bastone and handed him a cup.

Di Lauria added, "We stopped another threat to invade Sicily. The Angevins lost almost 3,000 in battle. We captured ten galleys."

"Bravo, Admiral!" Bastone held up his cup.

The officers toasted. "Antudu!"

"I will call on the count in Mdina. He still has his gates closed. Bastone, you have negotiated with the count and know the situation in Malta. What advice do you have? I can't keep my fleet here for more than a few days. We don't have enough food to maintain a siege."

Bastone remembered the count valued above all, his title and the income from his lands. "He enjoys a lifestyle of wine, good food, and the wealth he gets from his fief. That is more important to him than political loyalty," said Bastone. "He also is Genoese and will drive a hard bargain. I believe he will move his allegiance to Peter if you guarantee he will keep his title and fief."

Di Lauria rose from the stool, his guests standing with him. He placed a hand on Bastone's shoulder. "Your negotiation skills will be needed. I will go to Mdina the day after tomorrow; please accompany me. Be here on the overmorrow at dawn."

Zaccaria departed with Bastone. "Come, be my guest in your old home. You can bunk on the *Paradisio*." They crossed the camp, heading for the shore. Zaccaria asked, "Where is your wife?"

"With child, waiting in Messina."

The captain slapped Bastone on the back and laughed. "Congratulations. A newborn child is the only thing that might slow her down."

At the waterfront, a pair of sailors with the *Paradisio's* harbor boat waited for Zaccaria. "Grazie, Captain. And when do you leave Malta? Will you give me passage to Messina on the way to Genoa?"

"Certainly," said Zaccaria. "While you are in Mdina with the count, I will load the *Paradisio* with cotton. Actually, Bastone, you may want to continue with me to Genoa. Your brother, Francesco, is alive and has returned home."

CHAPTER XII

Bastone rode next to Di Lauria, who had decided he would present a stronger image arriving at Mdina mounted. The admiral had chosen the largest steed among the horses offered him, likely a descendant of the pure-bred destriers that the Normans had brought to the island almost two centuries earlier. Manfredo Lancia rode just behind them, and contingents of Almogavar infantry escorted them. The horses progressed at a walking gait. "Bastone, I'm making a concession going to see the count. I destroyed Charles's fleet. You'd think he'd come to my camp. But I can't remain here long and must secure his cooperation, if not loyalty."

"Admiral, even the arrival of your fleet didn't appear to shake him. He's confident he can hold out behind his walls, especially now with the grain Peter sent."

"Yes, it didn't convince the count, but the wheat persuaded his peasants in the countryside to join the revolt. Now, with additional men and siege engines, Manfredo can seize Castle Maris."

"Admiral, would you consider letting the count keep his title and fiefs if he switches his allegiance to Peter?"

"Yes. But what stops him from closing his gates the day I sail?"

"Weaken him a bit, Admiral. Dismiss his Genoese mercenaries, his crossbowmen. Perhaps you could allow him to keep a squad of personal bodyguards."

"Hmm. Yes, and I will replace the count's garrison with Aragonese marines from the king's fleet."

The count welcomed Di Lauria at the city gate, exchanging embraces, and accompanying them to his castle. During the negotiations, the admiral gave the Genoese crossbowmen a choice to return to their home city or serve in his fleet. The count retained his fief. Di Lauria appointed Manfredo Lancia as governor of the island of Malta, overseeing the count.

The island was secure, but still short of food. Di Lauria set sail, along with ten captured enemy galleys and the *Paradisio*. A two-day stop on Gozo, the second largest island of the Maltese archipelago, resulted in the leaders there retaining autonomy after pledging loyalty to Peter and delivering a large cache of jewels to Di Lauria. The admiral took possession only of the enemy ships captured in battle for the king, distributing the plunder and valuables to his sailors and soldiers.

On board the *Paradisio* and bound for Messina, Captain Zaccaria invited Bastone to his cabin to share wine, updating him on events in Genoa. "After you and Esmeray fled Genoa, the Spinolas publicly accused you of killing Amilcare. A clan war went on for weeks. Their young men assaulted members of the Ponzio family on the streets, and your cousins retaliated. For months, members of the families only ventured out of their enclaves when accompanied by armed escorts."

Bastone turned hot with anger. "The lies! Amilcare was killed by his own cousins."

"But the Spinolas believed the lie," said Zaccaria. "One night, the Spinolas burned one of your Uncle Riccio's ships, but the fire destroyed vessels belonging to other merchants. The families who hold power, the Grimaldis, the Fieschii, and the Dorias, met with the warring families, coercing them to end the violence. The streets have been peaceful now for several months."

Bastone regretted leaving his family. He was determined to return to Genoa and see his brother. Would his family blame him for the violence?

Several days later, Bastone disembarked the *Paradisio* at Messina, Zaccaria sailing on to Genoa. For his service to the crown, the king invited Bastone and Esmeray to live at Castle Mategriffon. After a passionate reunion, they lay in bed, discussing their experiences while separated. Esmeray had not been happy, confined to the indoors at the castle, taking walks around the fortifications to relieve her discomfort. One day, a steward had accompanied her to the waterfront so she could check on her boat. Giovanna had gone with them, interested in seeing Esmeray's trohantiras. They found the *Aspasia* secure under the watch of the harbor master. It had been her only excursion outside the castle while Bastone was gone.

To avoid alarming her, Bastone kept silent about his close encounter with the Angevins. Instead, he talked about his friendship with Mino, of meeting Bertinu Ponczu, and of the voyage to Malta. Esmeray showed special interest in how Mino had piloted his ship to withstand the storm. Bastone also told her that the report of his brother's execution by Charles's men had been false. Francesco was alive in Genoa.

"Bastonino, he's alive!" said Esmeray. "How does this make you feel about, um . . . about everything?"

"Esme, when Zaccaria told me Francesco was alive, my first thoughts were selfish," said Bastone. "I was angry that I had wasted the last three years, risking my life on a vendetta against Charles, fighting with all my strength to stop his plans. But after the initial shock, I put aside my emotions, realizing it had all been worth it. I met you, *dolcezza mia*, my sweetheart, only because I was on a quest to avenge the murder of my brother."

Esmeray kissed Bastone, tears in her eyes. "But you must see your brother in Genoa . . . and go without me." She raised up on an elbow, peering at her husband. "I don't want to put our child at risk. If we ran into a winter storm, the rough seas would toss the *Aspasia* about like a cork."

Bastone frowned. "You're right, but we could sail instead on a large trading ship. I think my mother would accept you now, because my brother can marry into the Spinola family, and you will bring her a grandchild."

Esmeray's face reddened. "But I cannot accept your mother after she forced me into the nunnery. They cut my hair, put me in solitary confinement, and I barely escaped."

Bastone paused, saddened he'd need to leave Esmeray. "Fine, I will go to Genoa alone." He knew Esmeray was not a socialite, but she would be confined due to her pregnancy. "You will have Giovanna for company."

"Yes, we have become close friends. She has taken care of me like a sister. But I wish our child was already born, so we could return to our home in Favignana."

Bastone headed across Messina toward the south gate. After passing the synagogue, he continued along the narrow, cobbled street. Lining the way were shingles hung in front of the shops of Jewish professionals, such as doctors, lawyers, and accountants. Continuing through the merchants' quarter, he arrived at the church of San Filippo Neri. The first person he asked gave him directions to Mino's residence.

Mino welcomed Bastone, ushering him to the inner courtyard, where they relaxed in a garden under the pleasant October sun. Sharing wine, they traded stories of their experiences over the last few weeks.

"Bastone, your timing is perfect. I am sailing to Genoa in two days. Shipping cotton from Malta to Genoa has opened a new commercial route for me."

"What did you trade for the cotton?"

"Wheat, of course. Malta depends on Sicily for grain." Mino sipped his drink and said, "I have purchased a second two-masted ship to cover the routes to Collo, trading for honey. I'm unloading the wheat at Gnejna Bay again, but after Castle Maris falls, the port at Birgu will open."

Bastone raised his glass, as did Mino. They toasted: "Cent'anni!"

"Congratulations, Mino. Hmm, a second ship, very good! One of the huge round-hulled trading vessels?"

Mino knitted his eyebrows. "No, they are too easy for the pirates to catch! It is almost identical to the *Lucia*."

"What did you name her?" asked Bastone.

Mino smiled. "The *Giovanna*."

Several days later, the *Lucia* tacked with the mistral wind along the Italian coast, headed for Genoa. Two products widely used in Genoa, cotton from Malta and pine pitch from Linguaglossa, filled the hold. In Genoa, artisanal housewives working from their homes and small clothmaking guilds wove the cotton into durable fustian cloth. The Genoese shipbuilders waterproofed their ships with the pitch.

Waving from the main mast was the patriots' flag of Sicily, the Trinacria symbol on a field of red and yellow. Mino was confident if they saw any warships, they would be those of Di Lauria. The admiral had confined Charles's ships to their ports.

Averaging four knots, they reached Genoa on the sixth day out of Messina. After docking and unloading his cargo, Mino accompanied Bastone to meet his sister, Maria Grazia. Bastone and his sister were close, and when he returned home from the sea, he always went first to visit her. After introductions, they relaxed on sofas in her parlor as a servant brought cheese, bread, and wine.

Maria Grazia beamed. "I have missed you, brother! When you last visited, my husband was away. Once again, he is on a faraway trading venture, this time to the Black Sea. But tomorrow when they awake, my children will be thrilled to see their Uncle Bastonino."

She looked at Mino. "Please tell me about yourself."

Mino described how he and Bastone had met on their venture to Malta.

"Your Genoese is excellent, and you are very successful in trading. Perhaps you were destined to be a merchant?"

"I am Sicilian, signora, but yes, I pursue the life of trade."

Her smile faded. "Bastone, did you hear about the violence with the Spinolas?"

He nodded. "Captain Zaccaria told me." Bastone leaned forward. "Where is our brother?"

"Francesco is here. He was staying at our parents' house, but they became, um . . . impatient with him. Perhaps because Mother has been sick. His behavior has been erratic since he returned. He has been having trouble remembering. Perhaps he is suffering from his ordeal as a galley slave."

Bastone slapped his forehead as he said, "Teeth of Jesus! No! A galley slave?" He composed himself. "Will he still marry the Spinola woman—after all the fighting between the families?"

"When he arrived, he said Muslims had enslaved him on a war galley but couldn't recall how he had escaped. He did remember he was from Genoa, and he found a ship home. The leading families demanded the marriage go ahead as a stipulation to a truce to end the vendettas. The Ponzio and Spinola marriage would seal the agreement and bring about peace."

"Please, I must see Francesco."

Maria Grazia called for her domestic and left with her, returning soon with their brother. He didn't acknowledge anyone in the room. He was still gaunt from his months as a galley slave, but the resemblance to Bastone was clear.

Mino's eyes grew wide, his mouth fell open. "It's him! The man from Collo!"

"Collo?" asked Maria Grazia.

"Collo, in Africa. Doctor Procida and I were in Africa when King Peter rescued hundreds of galley slaves and subsequently treated them in Sicily. He—your brother—he was sick and came with us on the ship returning to Sicily. The doctor risked his life protecting him and treated him at a hospice in Trapani."

"Procida?" said Bastone. "You know him?"

Could Procida know Mino and his brother? Bastone tried to make sense of the new information.

Francesco, now seated, seemed to wake up from their chatter. He glanced around. "*Buon giorno.* Maria Grazia said my brother is here. Which one of you is Bastone?"

Bastone smiled, leaning toward Francesco. "Ciccio, it's me. How are you doing, my brother?"

Even with Bastone's use of his childhood name, Francesco didn't appear to recognize him.

"Do you know Maria Grazia is your sister?" said Bastone.

"Yes. At first I didn't recognize her, but she told me stories about when we were young, then I remembered her. She said I was rough on both of you."

Bastone didn't comment, although he recalled Francesco bullying them. Instead, he said, "Remember when three guys were ganging up on you near the Greek Tower? I wanted to fight them, too, but you protected me because I was too little, and made me leave, sending me home?"

Francesco focused his eyes on Bastone and said, "Yes, little brother."

Maria Grazia and Bastone exchanged stunned looks.

"Ho! That was fast!" said Maria Grazia. "It took me days to get Ciccio to recall the times he tore the heads off my dolls!"

Francesco sprang to his feet. "Yes, you are my brother and sister! I feel like my mind is clearing."

His siblings glanced at each other, smiling, but then Francesco put his hands on his temples. "Too much! Too many memories are coming at once!"

He collapsed into a chair, facing downward, holding his head. "I had to row, and row, and row. They slammed my head into the oar if I didn't row fast enough."

Bastone laid a hand on his brother's shoulder.

Maria Grazia handed him a cup, and Francesco drank. The wine seemed to calm him.

Mino stood. "Thank you, signora, for your hospitality." He nodded to Bastone. "Tomorrow, you will have time to take me to the *Factoria de Balestrai,* my friend? I am looking forward to seeing the new crossbow designs."

Bastone said, "Yes, I will meet you on your ship soon after the second hour."

The domestic showed Mino out.

Bastone watched his brother lean back on the sofa. Francesco was nowhere near ready to marry the Spinola woman. The next day, Bastone knew he must visit his parents. He was uneasy about the reunion.

CHAPTER XIII

In the morning, as soon as Bastone awoke, his first thoughts put him in a sullen mood, knowing he needed to see his parents. But his spirits lifted a little, remembering he also was to take Mino to the crossbow factory. After a quick breakfast with Francesco and Mino, the trio descended the steep lanes to the factory. Bastone hoped the stimulus of walking the streets of their youth might wake his brother's memories. After Mino purchased several laminated crossbows, Bastone and Francesco accompanied him to the wharf. Before Mino departed on the *Lucia,* Bastone entrusted him with a letter for Esmeray.

Bastone and Francesco climbed the slope to their parents' compound. On the way, they took a few shortcuts, wandering along the *vicoli*, the narrow alleys, where, as teenagers, they had fought common adversaries. Walking shoulder to shoulder down one of the narrow backstreets, Bastone reminisced.

"Ciccio, remember when we used to fight those *stronzi* in these *vicoli*? We still beat the rich turds, even though they had daggers against our sticks."

He glanced at his silent brother, wondering what would awaken his memories. Pausing where a fig tree had climbed a wall, Bastone broke off a dead branch and snapped it in two, throwing one length to his brother. Francesco did not try to catch it, the stick falling at his feet. Bastone weaved his stick through the air, beginning a mock attack trying to get Francesco to engage. When his brother didn't respond, Bastone recalled as youths, when one brother wasn't cooperative, the other would recite their secret saying. Reenacting, he placed his palms together as if praying, moving them up and down, "Be a brother!"

Francesco's eyes hinted of a familiarity with the phrase, but he didn't respond.

"Come on, Ciccio. Be a brother!"

Francesco surfaced from his torpidity, his eyes growing wide. He crouched, picking up the stick, and put up his guard. After several minutes of vigorous sparring, they were both wearing a few bruises and cuts. Francesco's awareness and the renewal of their relationship encouraged Bastone. When they arrived at their parents' compound, Maria Grazia received them at the door.

They entered a large courtyard, verdant with evergreens. A few late blooming flowers held their last petals in the otherwise fallow gardens. Scattered fruit trees stood dormant, waiting for the next spring. Surrounding the courtyard were the residences of the extended families of Bastone's parents and uncles. The large, two-story homes, roofed with terra cotta tiles, enclosed the quadrangle, creating a fortress-like enclave. But unlike the leading families of Genoa, the Ponzios had not erected a tower as a status symbol of their wealth. A gentle October sun provided just enough warmth in the enclosure to make it pleasant, although Bastone's mother had wrapped herself in a heavy cloak. She had always been sensitive to even a slight chill, but Bastone recalled Maria Grazia had said their mother was sick.

Bastone's father hugged each of his children close, patting them on the back, repeating, "Buona sera, buona sera." His mother greeted them with a quick embrace, bending forward at her waist, only touching shoulders. Before she sat, she coughed into a linen handkerchief, folding it before she pocketed it. Bastone noticed bloodstains on the cloth. They sat on stone benches around a table as a domestic served antipasti and glasses of a red tinted aperitivo.

Bastone, feeling awkward, began with small talk. "This aperitivo is rather sweet—but it's delicious. Where did you find it?"

"It's *rosolio maraschino*," said Bastone's father, "made in a convent in Dalmatia. Yes, the cherry is very sweet." He held up his glass, crafted with decorative ribs along the sides. "And this goblet is from Venice. The Genoese are getting better at blowing glass, but I will have to admit, those dastardly Venetians make the most elegant pieces."

Bastone suspected the talk annoyed his mother, as she soon ended the pleasantries. She coughed, then said, "Francesco, Maria Grazia said you are better. Do you? . . ." She coughed again. "Do you know your own parents?"

"Yes, Mother. I am feeling well. And your tunica is beautiful."

She dropped her goblet, glass shattering on the slate patio floor. A domestic promptly arrived and swept the shards away. Another brought a new goblet of apéritif. She swallowed a sip, then said, "Maria Grazia, how did you heal Ciccio?"

"Patience and love, Mother," said Maria Grazia.

Bastone, detecting that the comment likely offended his mother, tried to deflect his sister's innuendo, and said, "Familiarity. We reminisced about childhood times with him."

His father addressed Francesco, "Son, you look like yourself again, Bravo!" He glanced around. "I can't remember the last time our whole family was together. What joy!"

His wife loosened, permitting a weak smile.

"Mother," said Bastone, "ask Ciccio of, um, an amusing family occasion."

She appeared hopeful, looking at her oldest son and said, "Ciccio, remember, when you were a boy, pretending you'd been stabbed?"

Francesco's eyes lit up as he said, "I tucked a knife under my armpit, lay in front of the fireplace, and Maria Grazia poured red wine on me to look like blood."

"You made me go fetch Mother," said Bastone. "I screamed, 'Mother, come here, Ciccio is hurt!'"

"And she was fast. She got there before the domestic," said Maria Grazia.

Francesco added, "I'll never forget your expression, Mother. You were terrified that I was bleeding. Then suddenly you became quiet, seeing it was a jest. You were so angry you grabbed the poker next to the fireplace, instead of the broom."

"That's when you really got hurt, Ciccio," said Bastone. "Mother hit you in the head. Then there was real blood."

Francesco touched his scalp above his ear. "Yes, the scar is under my hair somewhere."

During their shared laughter, Bastone's mother pulled out her handkerchief. He saw her cough blood again. His mother was not merely sick. She had a serious malady. Recovering, she cleared her throat and asked, "How did you make the blood look so real?"

"We mixed a little honey in the wine," said Maria Grazia.

She had a wry smile as she peered at her daughter. "Hmm. We? Now I know you were involved, and not just an innocent onlooker."

The domestic announced *primi* was ready. They went inside and enjoyed *mandilli de seta al pesto*, thin silky sheets of pasta with pesto sauce, the first course of the dinner.

"Have you missed fresh pasta, my sons?" said their father.

Both Bastone and Francesco nodded with their mouths full.

He turned his attention to his wife. "And we must, um, reintroduce Francesco to his fiancé, seeing he's been away."

"Francesco should be married at the Cathedral of San Lorenzo," said their mother. "Of course, the Spinolas will agree. It's Genoa's most prestigious church."

With his parents' attention on Francesco, Bastone was relieved, avoiding a discussion of his flight from Genoa a year earlier. No one, not even Maria Grazia, asked about Esmeray. Francesco was on everyone's mind.

The second course was meat seasoned with *agliata* sauce, originating in Genoa, and one of Bastone's favorite condiments. Bastone ate, hardly paying attention to anything his family said, but he pondered how his brother's return would affect his family's view of Esmeray. He profoundly missed his wife, although he had been absent from Messina for less than a month, and was concerned how she was feeling. The meal continued with a green, leafy salad, followed by a dessert of fruit. The family resumed discussing Francesco's wedding but made no final decisions.

That evening, Bastone accompanied his father to the waterfront, stopping by the docks to see his uncle, Ponzio Riccio, who ran a shipping business. His uncle greeted him with his usual jovial bear hug. "Oh, what a joy! My favorite nephew has returned." He released Bastone from his clinch. "How is Esmeray?"

"She is with child, Uncle."

"Bellissimo!"

"And your family, Uncle Riccio?"

"Now that the street war is over, the family is well, except . . ." Tears welled and his voice quivered, as he divulged the tragic news that the Spinolas had killed one of his sons in a skirmish. Bastone's father put his arm around Riccio's shoulder as they shed tears together.

"I am so sorry, Uncle," said Bastone. He patted his uncle's shoulder. Why hadn't his parents warned him? They didn't discuss his mother's affliction, either. Plus, his father had not acknowledged Esmeray's pregnancy, although Bastone had just clearly told Riccio. Bastone felt as distant from his parents as he'd been when he was far across the sea.

Riccio recovered and said, "Grazie, Bastonino." Lowering his head in despair, his curly hair shrouding his anguish, he shook off the tears, and with chin up, renewed his characteristic zest. Slapping his kinsmen on the back, his arms around their shoulders, he guided them into his office.

Procuring a jug of wine, Riccio swigged. He passed it to Bastone's father, who wiped tears from his cheeks and also gulped from the jug, as if to gain strength. "Bastone, your mother is dying of the consumption."

In Messina, Esmeray continued her daily walks around the perimeter walls of the castle. She felt like a captive, although Giovanna and the other ladies-in-waiting were kind to her. As her pregnancy advanced, she had an overwhelming desire to be at home in Favignana, to clean and prepare the cottage for their child.

One evening, Esmeray had a nightmare. She was captain of a ship, and babies, all barely toddlers, made up the entire crew. They were all her children, and, in the dream, she knew she would never settle down to one home, but continually sail about the world. Esmeray woke, relieved it was only a dream, remembering Queen Constance had invited her to one of her ladies' gatherings. After breakfast, the queen asked Esmeray to talk about herself. Still rattled by the bad dream, she was at first inhibited and began slowly, but became more enthusiastic, describing her wide-ranging adventures. The women were fascinated. She told about her life as a girl in Anatolia in far off Asia, how she had grown up on a Greek island, and had even sailed to England with Bastone. By speaking, she reminded herself of her strengths, shed the worry from the dream and regained her confidence.

The next morning, Esmeray departed the castle for the city market, relieved to get away from the confines of the palace. She chaperoned the palace maids, who were attending the queen's master cook during an excursion to resupply the royal pantry. Although the mild October sun was pleasant, the dry scirocco winds from Africa carried fine sand, irritating Esmeray. A few times, she wrapped her blue headscarf around her face.

Leading their entourage was a squad of Aragonese soldiers, escorting them and clearing the way. Following were several donkey carts led by servants to transport the food to the castle. At the fish market, the chef examined piles of fresh fish, pointing to a few, which were loaded into the carts by the male servants. While the master cook was selecting cuts of pork, the maids chose vegetables and fruits. The cook's assistant paid the fishmongers and vegetable peddlers. As they passed the market stalls, Esmeray was aware they were moving away from the waterfront, where she had hoped to glimpse her boat, the *Aspasia*. Her longing for the sea and freedom of sailing pulled at her. But the clothier stalls reminded Esmeray she had promised to buy Giovanna a few bolts of cloth. Slipping from her group toward the colorful display of fabrics, she perused the red, blue, green, and yellow bolts. The sight of her beloved color, blue, reminded her of Bastone's brilliant cerulean eyes. A sadness pierced her joy in being free of the castle, wondering instead when he would return. After purchasing a few lengths of cloth, she returned to the group, the purchase of food staples now complete.

It rained as they returned toward the castle. Citizens along the streets were looking at the sky and shouting, "Blood rain—it's raining blood. A bad omen!" As they retreated inside, the residents held their hands up toward the sky, extending their index and little fingers upward, pinching the middle and ring fingers with the thumb: the sign of the horns to ward off evil.

With her face down, Esmeray walked in the drizzle. Then she looked up. The rain *was* red. She recalled the airborne sand, which was orange and reddish, stinging her eyes earlier in the day, and she was sure there was a connection. Her group increased their pace, finally reaching the castle. Once inside, she went to her room to change into dry clothes.

The strange rain had discolored her woad tunica with red spots. When she removed her outer garments, she gasped. There was also a red stain on her linen underwear. It wasn't the rain, it was blood from her womb. Was her child—their child—in danger? Esmeray's confidence was lost to fear and emotion. She wailed.

Esmeray was sobbing when Giovanna appeared. "Esme, what's wrong?"

Losing her composure and her usual good sense, Esmeray said, "It was raining blood! The Messinese said it was a bad omen, then this started." She pointed to the red stain, tears flowing.

"No, no!" said Giovanna. "That's superstition. It's the rain washing the red dust out of the sky! But do not worry." She found a blanket, wrapping it around Esmeray. "Lie down on the bed. I will find Dottore Procida."

Esmeray closed her eyes, recalling other times in her life she had been this terrified. Running from the Turkish raiders in the tunnels in Anatolia, her mother had helped her. Then, another time, when she was fleeing the assassins in Constantinople, Bastone had saved her. And the most terrifying instance—when she was captured by the Berber slave traders—again Bastone was there. She remembered, during those times, she had acted decisively, putting her fears away. Now, what could she do? Who, what, could she fight? She felt helpless, and she spoke to an empty room. "Where the hell is Bastone? Where is my husband?"

Giovanna returned with a midwife, who examined Esmeray. The midwife was reassuring. "*Zita*—sweetheart, hold your worries. I have seen this before. Bed rest will keep the baby safe."

Procida arrived and after the midwife described her examination, he disclosed a knowing nod. He placed a hand on Esmeray's forehead. "How long have you been with child?"

The company of the doctor and midwife calmed Esmeray. She glanced at Giovanna. "When I first came here, we thought it was about ten weeks."

Giovanna nodded. "Mm-hmm."

"Following that, Bastone spent two to three weeks in Malta. And he has been in Genoa for almost a month." She paused, looking into space, counting with her fingers. "So, I have been with child about twenty weeks."

"Do you have any cramps?" asked Procida.

Esmeray shook her head. "No."

"You must lay still until the bleeding stops." Procida looked at the midwife for confirmation. She nodded.

"I will be nearby if you need me, signura. Your baby will be fine." Procida took her hand and kissed it. He gestured toward the midwife. "Signura is very knowledgeable. She will guide you. You are in the best hands."

Esmeray looked from Giovanna to the midwife. "How long will I need to rest?"

"It could be days . . . or weeks."

Esmeray frowned.

The midwife noted her unease. "It will be worth all the frustration. I have given birth to four children. I am grateful for the Lord's blessing. After your first child is born, you will see life differently."

Procida, departing, bowed his head slightly. "There is no victory without sacrifice."

Esmeray was a fighter. The doctor knew how to encourage her.

CHAPTER XIV

The *Lucia* arrived at the Messina docks, where the port was bustling again, recovering from the revolt of the Sicilian Vespers. Mino had been notified before their arrival, had awakened and dressed. His thoughts organized the business for the day as he washed his face and brushed his hair and beard. Crossing the midship galley, he found Cardo eating breakfast. "Offload the fustian cloth and take it to the market stall." A sailor offered Mino a bowl of pasta, which he waved away. "Cardo, I'll go ahead of you and complete the contract to trade the cloth with the wine merchants by the time you deliver the cloth."

Mino turned to leave, the sailor handing the captain a cup of diluted wine. He quickly finished it. He was about to hurry to the castle as his feet hit the wharf, but paused when he heard, "Capitanu, *aspetta!*" The cabin boy raced along the gangway to the dock and handed Mino a belt, a sheath, and case dangling from it.

"Grazzi, sailor!"

He buckled it around his waist, patting the small leather case containing pen and rag paper for writing contracts. On the opposite side hung his dagger. He swiftly wrote a note, requesting an audience with the king, handing it to the cabin boy. He pointed up the hill. "Please deliver this to the castle steward." The boy sprinted away.

Arriving at the market, passing food vendors, his stomach muttering that he'd missed breakfast, Mino bought a few warm arancini, consuming the rice-filled balls as he headed toward the wine vendors. There, he made an exchange, trading his fabric for wine from Etna. He composed a short agreement for the vendor to give Cardo. On his way to Castle Mategriffon, he stopped at the cathedral, negotiated a price, and made a contract with the bishop's secretary to supply wax for the liturgical candles.

He proceeded to the castle, hoping Peter would give him an audience. As he trekked uphill, his thoughts were filled with plans. He reviewed his proposal to ship more wheat for the king to Malta. And while in Malta, he would obtain a beehive and develop an apiary to produce his own honey and wax in Sicily, saving shipping costs from Malta and Collo.

At the castle, Peter received him without delay. Mino reminded himself he was not haggling with another merchant—this was the king. He needed a different approach.

The king had a huge smile. "Signuri Nglisi, you'll be pleased that Castle Maris has surrendered to the Maltese, opening the port of Birgu to commerce."

"Excellent! I offer my services to continue shipments of wheat to the Maltese."

The king tightened his lips, paused. "The wheat I sent was free to the people. It swayed their allegiance to me, no? That is done."

"Your Highness, with Birgu open, the Maltese can export again and trade for the grain. We can send them wheat at a profit."

"We? Signuri, I have more important tasks."

"Sire, I will sell the wheat in Malta at reduced prices, proclaiming the lower cost is a gift from you to the Maltese. The people will remain loyal. As you say, you have more important issues here in Sicily."

The king folded his arms. "I'm not interested in being involved in that trade. And I have resumed the export taxes. How can you sell lower?"

"Charge me half the tax rate. People will appreciate your generosity. And you will still collect taxes. A small price to pay to retain *and* strengthen their allegiance."

"Signuri Nglisi, I accept your proposal."

Satisfied he had made a profitable agreement with the king, Mino sought Esmeray to tell her about Bastone's reunion with Francesco. The steward told him she wasn't available, but Giovanna would meet with him shortly. Mino was excited at the prospect of seeing Giovanna again. His news for Esmeray could wait. The servant seated him and brought him wine. Recalling her blonde hair and petite figure, but especially her intelligent eyes, he waited, savoring each sip of wine the steward had served him. When Giovanna arrived, she looked flushed. Mino came to his feet, removed his red watch cap revealing his dark, curly hair, and bowed, taking her hand. "Did you run here, Giovanna? Are you so eager to see me? I trudged up the hill solely to gaze upon your wondrous beauty!"

Giovanna looked down, blinking. Had she had found his jest mawkish? But she looked up, her blue eyes alive with a smile. She laughed, then said, "Yes! Learning of your arrival, I bolted out of class to see you!"

Enjoying the flirting, it was Mino's turn to laugh. "Class?"

"Teaching the court ladies from Aragon a Sicilian dance."

"A dance?" asked Mino.

"Yes, the *Tarantella*. I learned it from my mother. It's a Greek dance." She dabbed perspiration from her forehead with her headscarf. "The dancing warmed me."

Mino cleared his throat. "Um . . ."

She reddened further, but said, "That was . . . not an intended jest, but it was funny how it sounded. Really, I didn't want you to leave without seeing you."

His gaze settled on her. "Giovanna, will you marry me?"

She answered, as if expecting his proposal. "Of course!" She took a step, glancing over her shoulder. "Come, Esmeray should be ready by now. We can't keep her waiting to hear about Bastone."

On their way to Esmeray's room, Giovanna voiced her plans, describing how she must keep her position as a court lady, so they needed to find a house near the castle. She knew Mino must travel, but someday, she would like to sail with him on a voyage. Mino smiled to himself, envisioning them at sea on the stern castle of his new ship, named after her.

In Genoa, ascending the streets to the Ponzio enclave, Bastone's father apprised him of his mother's condition. Her behavior had deteriorated along with her health, even before Bastone's last visit, when she had so egregiously wronged Esmeray. She now spent most of her days in bed. His father apologized for his attack on Bastone's character during his last time in Genoa, explaining that his behavior was poisoned by worry for his wife. Bastone said, "I should have known something was wrong. It's likely too late for an understanding with Mother." Their gaze met, but he saw no answer in his father's eyes, and they continued uphill.

The next morning, Bastone visited the doctor who had been treating his mother.

"Signore Ponzio," said the doctor, "according to the *Doctrine of Signatures* of the ancient Roman physicians, Dioscorides and Galen, herbs that *look* like a part of the body will treat ailments of that same organ, limb, or part of the physique."

Bastone's eyebrows were furrowed tightly. "How can that be?"

"Signore, the Church endorses this philosophy."

Bastone hid his disdain. "Dottore, how have you been treating my mother?"

"First, I bled her, then I administered lungwort. As the *Doctrine* predicts, the spotted oval leaves of the lungwort mimic the diseased lungs."

"Have you seen it heal others?" asked Bastone.

"God has provided us with relief for every illness," said the physician.

Bastone looked up and sighed. "Physicians in Sicily must be licensed by the medical school of Salerno. What is your qualification, Doctor?"

The man was silent, appearing insulted. Bastone left, recalling what Procida had said. Garlic had cured a man with *mal aria*. Bastone would try anything. The *agliata* sauce prepared in the Ponzio kitchen contained garlic, so what was different from the ladies' food in Trapani? Bastone could not consult with the medical school in Salerno. That city was under Charles's control.

Bastone next paid a visit to the Hospitallers' villa knowing of their expertise in medicine. The Hospitallers in Genoa, however, were bankers, not healers, and they directed Bastone to the nearby Monastery of Santo Stefano. It rankled Bastone that he had to return to the location, a joint monastery and nunnery, where the abbess had held Esmeray captive. The barber-surgeon there directed him to the home of Simon Genova, a physician who traveled to monasteries across Europe, collecting information to write a medical lexicon.

Bastone found Simon's house. "It's fortunate you came today, signore," said Simon. "I am sailing in a few days to Constantinople. They have an extensive library and I hope to find medical knowledge of the ancient Greeks and Romans to add to my dictionary. You said Dottore Procida used garlic to ease *mal aria?* I have read a book by Dioscorides who stated garlic cleans the arteries, as well as helps the intestinal tract, and can treat animal bites, but I have never heard of it used to cure swamp fever. You said your mother's diet includes garlic. If you want to attempt a cure, I recommend a concentrated application, such as garlic oil. But one cannot just drink it. It is too caustic. I suggest soaking bread in the oil before your mother consumes it." He wrote instructions and handed the parchment to Bastone. "Please notify me of the results of the treatment."

Considering his father's comments, Bastone understood why his mother had been so ruthless. Though he forgave her, he could never forget, and would never trust her again. Arriving at his parents' home, he advised his mother to undertake the treatment that Doctor Simon had recommended. She agreed to start the concentrated garlic regimen.

Bastone sent a letter by Genoese trading ship to Messina, telling Esmeray he would return after Francesco's wedding, scheduled early because of his mother's health. The Spinola woman, who was previously betrothed to Francesco, had married someone else. Francesco, thirty-five, would instead marry the youngest Spinola daughter, seventeen, the age difference common in their culture.

At the wedding, Bastone searched the faces of the Spinola men, trying to find the relatives of Amilcare who had killed him, a death that had set off the feud between the Spinolas and Ponzios. He encountered tense stares from Amilcare's cousins, but he recalled it had been dark and he couldn't identify the murderers.

After the wedding, Bastone's Uncle Riccio offered him a job in his trading company based in Genoa, but Bastone reminded him Esmeray was with child and he could not accept at this time.

Over the next month, Bastone's mother followed the treatment, an oil made by boiling chopped garlic cloves in olive oil. The garlic didn't completely cure her, but the treatment stabilized her health.

After two months in Genoa, Bastone boarded the *San Giorgio*, headed for the island of Vulcano, thirty miles north of Messina. Bastone was familiar with the *San Giorgio*. Years earlier, the ship had sailed with the *Paradisio* when the Genoese had opened the sea routes to the North Sea, trading alum to be used by the cloth makers of Flanders and England. Now, the shipments to the north had become routine, the *San Giorgio* again taking on alum at Vulcano. Bastone continued to Messina, finding passage on one of the frequent crossings made from Vulcano.

Arriving in Messina, Bastone jumped off the boat onto the wharf, thanking the boatman, and hurried up the slope to Castle Mategriffon. Short of breath, he entered the castle to find Esmeray. She was walking along the battlements. They embraced, enjoying their reunion in silence for a few minutes. Bastone looked over his shoulder. Finding no one around, he kissed her lightly, resting a hand on Esmeray's abdomen. "Yes, I thought I felt the baby kicking. That's amazing! How long has this been happening?"

Esmeray placed her hands on his. "Just the last few days. Your arrival must have excited the baby."

That evening after dinner, they retreated to their suite. Esmeray had received his letter and knew of the affairs in Genoa. She was pleased that Bastone's relationship with his family had improved, but she still refused to return to the city. Bastone was relieved the bed rest had helped Esmeray. She could still stroll around the castle walls, and they visited the waterfront once to see the *Aspasia*. Doctor Procida had warned her against having intercourse because of her earlier condition. They found other ways to fulfill their passion.

As Esmeray's baby grew, Bastone sensed her melancholy increase with the loss of her freedom and increasing dependence on others. One evening, in their room, they lay together chatting. Suddenly, she sat up. "And you are not going anywhere until this baby is born!" Bastone agreed with her. Thrilled her spirit had resurfaced, the next day he found work as an accountant at a trading office at the port, where the owner, like many of the citizens living on the east coast of Sicily, spoke Greek as his first language, a proud descendant of colonists a thousand years earlier. Bastone being fluent in Greek helped him get the job.

By late June 1284, Esmeray's pregnancy was obvious, and her baby appeared to have dropped, foretelling an early birth. Giovanna sent for the midwives, a mother and daughter from the village of Il Ringo, about a mile north of the castle. The mother had impressed Giovanna with her qualifications and her references. Sixty years earlier, the King of Sicily, Frederick I, had required physicians and midwives to pass a test to obtain a license. The certification was no longer enforced, but the most reputable midwives continued the practice and obtained a license.

The midwife was licensed, as was her mother before her, and her daughter was now training under her. She had shown Giovanna the trappings of a prepared midwife, including a birthing stool, a sketch of a dragon, which was the symbol of Saint Margaret, the patron saint of pregnant women, and an eagle stone, a hollow geode for protection in childbirth.

Esmeray no longer accompanied Bastone to the harbor front, only straying short distances from her room. With her slight frame and enlarged abdomen, she spent many daytime hours in bed due to fatigue. The second week of July, she waddled outside, fortunate there was a breeze off the sea to temper the warm day. Looking down on the harbor, she imagined where Bastone worked. She felt a slight tug, followed by a damp warmth on her leg. She retreated to her room. Checking herself, she noticed a clear liquid on her legs. It was traced with blood.

Esmeray was not afraid, recalling the midwife had said this was normal: a sign she would soon go into labor. She called for help with a steady voice, "Maid! Maid, come at once!"

A young woman arrived, helping Esmeray remove her tunica and get into her bed. "Signura, are you comfortable?" Esmeray nodded. The maid hurried out of the room. Within minutes, Giovanna arrived, noting the red spots on Esmeray's linen undergarments.

"Everything looks the way it should, dear. And Esmeray, you are calm. Very good! I will be right back. I will send for the midwives from Il Ringo. And notify Bastone at the docks."

Esmeray forced a smile. "And Doctor Procida?"

"No. We don't have to inform Doctor Procida because everything is going as planned. Besides, it's the midwives who deliver babies."

The midwife arrived within the hour, her adolescent daughter carrying the birthing chair. Joining her hands together as if in prayer, she said, "Lady Giovanna, please." She tilted her head toward the door. Giovanna headed to leave and paused when the midwife added, "But wait outside. We may need your help."

Giovanna closed the door behind her. The midwife placed the eagle stone on Esmeray's belly. "Are you feeling urges to push the baby out?"

"I felt cramps in my belly a little while ago," said Esmeray. "Owww, another one!"

The midwife prayed, "O God, grant us through the intercession of Your holy virgin and martyr Margaret." She touched the eagle stone, "As this jewel, shone by the command of God in the first angel, little infant, come forth as a shining man abiding God."

"A shining *man*? What if my baby is a girl?"

The midwife paused, frowning, "Yes, I see . . . you are a, um, . . . a sensible woman. I will use the precise methods of Trotula di Ruggiero, who taught at the school at Salerno."

"Ohhh! It hurts so much!"

The midwife and her daughter helped Esmeray crouch onto the birthing chair, allowing her to sit upright to push. The midwife counted until the next contraction.

"Unu, dui, tres, . . ."

Esmeray groaned in pain again and the midwife said, "Breathe in. Now breathe out and push, young lady."

At each of Esmeray's contractions, the midwife repeated, "Push!" Almost overwhelmed by pain, Esmeray concentrated on the midwife's command and pushed, without realizing the passing time. She strained for nearly an hour, saying, "I'm so tired, I can't do it anymore."

They moved her to the bed.

"Women have been doing this since Eve," said the midwife. "You are strong. You can!"

"But it feels like I'm trying to push out my insides!"

"You must trust me. Bear down when I say so."

After over an hour of labor, she finally delivered a baby boy. The midwife cleared the mucus from the baby's nose and mouth, cut the umbilical cord, tying it with a wool thread. She placed the boy on Esmeray's heaving chest. She was covered in perspiration. Her breathing slowed. "Ohhh, what a relief. So painful. I never want to go through that again."

But the baby was not breathing. The midwife gave the baby small puffs of air.

"What's wrong?" cried Esmeray, holding her arms out to retrieve him.

Then the baby cried. The midwife examined the baby. "It is tiny. We should try to get him to suckle as soon as possible."

Esmeray had trouble getting the baby to nurse. The midwife dabbed a drop of honey on his tongue. "Signura Trotola said it will give him an appetite." The midwife swaddled the baby and gave him back to Esmeray. After several minutes, Esmeray got the baby to nurse.

Holding him transformed her. "Oh, it hurt so much, but he was worth it!" Esmeray recalled Procida's message—'There is no victory without sacrifice'. Only now did she understand how her mother and father had felt about her.

An hour passed, the midwife examining Esmeray every few minutes, and shaking her head. She murmured to herself, "Where is the afterbirth? She should have delivered it by now."

Esmeray wailed, "He's not breathing!"

The midwife blew in his nostrils and looked upward. "Saint Margaret, hear our prayers! Save this boy!" She rubbed the baby's legs and chest for long minutes but was unsuccessful in reviving him.

The midwife held Esmeray's hand and gently brushed strands of hair from her face. "Dear, I am so sorry." Her daughter handed her a small bowl of water. The midwife sprinkled drops on the baby's head. "In Saint Margaret's words, 'That this water may be for me a healing and an enlightening and a bath of baptism. Whoever hears my passion may from that time have his sins blotted out.'"

Esmeray held her hand over her baby's head. "Stop!"

"The rite is still sanctified, dear. The Pope has granted midwives permission to baptize the stillborn."

The midwife had misunderstood. Esmeray didn't care about the sanctity of the ritual and burst out sobbing.

Midwives did not allow men during the birthing and Bastone had been waiting outside the door with Giovanna for news of the birth. When he heard his wife's cries of anguish, he entered the room, Giovanna pulling on his sleeve, trying to stop him. Bastone shouted, "Esmeray!"

The midwife blocked his way. "During childbirth, women gain strength from women. Leave now! Your child didn't survive. Now let me save your wife. Your presence will only do harm."

Giovanna dragged him into the hallway. The midwife wiped Esmeray's forehead with a cool, wet cloth. Her daughter wrung her hands. "*Madre*, the lady's abdomen is still very swollen."

"It can take a month before a mother's belly shrinks."

"Yes . . . *Madre*." She chewed on her bottom lip.

"You still look worried. The added swelling is because the placenta has not arrived."

The midwife held Esmeray's hand. "Signura, I am going to deliver the placenta next. It will not be painful like birth, but perhaps a little uncomfortable."

The midwife pulled down the sheet. "Daughter, you have seen the placenta deliver after the baby, but I must coax this one out." She massaged Esmeray's abdomen with one hand, following the umbilical cord with her other hand, very cautiously trying to nudge the afterbirth. She glanced at her daughter. "I must be very careful not to pull too hard." She massaged Esmeray again and with patience after several minutes, her gentle touch delivered the placenta.

Giovanna sent a maid for fresh bedclothes. After the maids freshened Esmeray and changed the sheets, the midwife fetched Bastone and Giovanna. Bastone sat on a stool next to Esmeray and held her hand, not hearing the midwife give Giovanna instructions on the necessary bedrest for Esmeray. Giovanna thanked the midwives as they left, turned and smiled at Esmeray. "Gather your strength, sweet." She touched Bastone on his shoulder. "Signuri Ponzio, call for the maid if you need anything and send for Dottore Procida. He will be nearby."

Esmeray's eyes remained closed, but she forced a weak smile. "Hmm-mmm."

"I'm very sorry, Esme. I'll never leave you again."

He realized her exhaustion dulled her perception, shielding her from the emotional pain of losing the baby. It took extreme self-control not to show his own grief. Bastone lightly kissed Esmeray, then touched his cheek to her hand, resting his head on the bed. They dozed.

CHAPTER XV

Esmeray screamed in pain. Bastone saw blood had stained the clean bedding. Rushing to the door, he opened it and found the maid in the hall, her eyes wide. "Bring Dottore Procida right away!" He returned to his wife.

"What's happening!"

Bastone gently drew her hands to his chest to reassure her. "Esme, the doctor is coming."

"It hurts! Like when the bab . . ." She hung her head, sobbing. "No, it can't be real. I thought it was a dream. Did our baby die?"

Bastone forced his voice to be calm. "Esme, tell me what you remember."

"I had a beautiful boy, but he's gone."

He stroked her cheek. "Yes, my sweetness, but we still have each other."

"Owww! The pain is back again."

Procida hurried in, carrying his medical bag. "I sent a steward to retrieve the midwife. It will be an hour before her return."

The doctor turned to Bastone. "I am going to examine your wife."

"Of course, Dottore."

"Esme, I am pulling the sheet down."

Procida peered closer. "What? You gave birth two hours ago. But I see a head. There is another baby!"

Bastone and Esmeray locked eyes. He saw her fear change to determination.

Procida said, "Esmeray, press down."

The door burst open. The midwife rushed in with her daughter, crying out, "No! Only push when I say! Saint Margaret must have appealed to the Lord for you. I was still in the castle." The midwife took a garment from her bag. "Signura, we'll put this birth girdle on you. It's been blessed by Saint Sussana!" She flicked her hands at Bastone and the doctor. "Shoo! Shoo! No men allowed!"

Procida and Bastone exchanged glances, the doctor leading them out of the room, shaking his head.

"To the birthing chair." The midwife gestured to her daughter, who helped her move Esmeray from the bed to the chair, supporting Esmeray. Esmeray's head dipped forward from exhaustion. The midwife leaned in, face-to-face with her. She tipped Esmeray's chin up. "Look at me, now! What was the most terrifying event of your life?"

Esmeray sniffed, pausing in her sobs. "What?"

"You are not done!" said the midwife. "Can you recall a time when you were tired and scared, but didn't give up?"

Esmeray recalled battling a terrible storm at sea in her fishing boat. Instead of trying to defeat the sea, she had adapted to its rhythm, the crests, and the troughs of the storm waves, however violent.

The midwife said, "Esmeray, you have another child who wants to be born. Now push!"

Embracing that dark, terrifying night, when she had derived power from the sea, Esmeray found new strength.

Outside the birthing room, Bastone flinched, hearing Esmeray scream in labor. He went back to the door and grasped the handle, hesitating.

Procida grabbed his hand. "She is battling, and the women are with her. Don't go in."

His wife's sobs had transformed into powerful cries of effort, as if Esmeray had rallied.

Giovanna said, "Hear her! Esme *is* fighting!"

Bastone dropped his hand from the handle.

Procida put his arm around Bastone's shoulder. "Giovanna, I'll be in the Great Hall with Bastone. If the midwife needs me, tell me at once."

Guiding Bastone downstairs, Procida said, "The midwife has years of experience. I will help only if the midwife requests it."

Several minutes later, after arriving at the great hall, the two men sat drinking wine at the end of an enormous table. The vinous fragrance, the high ceilings, and the immensity of the hall calmed Bastone. Procida's voice echoed as he spoke, "Esmeray is in the most capable hands."

Bastone drank, then peered at the ceiling.

Procida looked up. "Like a cathedral, no? Inspiring? Bastone, do you draw strength from the Lord?"

"Even as a boy, I perceived my parents attended Mass only to be part of society, although they also taught us the Christian morals. Our family was large and protective. That is where I drew strength. I suppose I view religion as they did."

Bastone drank again, putting down his empty cup, gazing at Procida. Yet, my family has been in turmoil for the past few years. I met Esmeray. Now she is my strength."

"She is a fighter, son! It's good we left the birthing room. She might have made you the object of scorn, blaming you for putting her in that condition."

Procida's words brought on a reluctant smile from Bastone.

Loosened by the wine, Bastone's voice broke as he said, "The first baby was too small, dying minutes after birth . . ."

"I'm so sorry," said Procida. "But have hope, son. Now she is giving birth to a second child."

After they talked through a half jug of wine, the steward arrived to report the midwife was asking for them. At the birthing room, maids were departing with the birthing chair and the stained bedsheets. The midwife's daughter opened the door.

Esmeray rested in bed with fresh sheets, sitting up against pillows. Her eyelids heavy from exhaustion, Esmeray squeezed out a weak smile when she saw Bastone. In the crook of her arm she held a swaddled newborn, only the tiny face visible. The midwife and Giovanna sat nearby.

"Husband, meet your daughter, Aspasia," said Esmeray.

"A daughter! And is she? . . ."

"She is healthy, signuri," said the midwife.

Bastone sat on the bed and kissed his wife, then his daughter. "A beautiful name—Aspasia—your boat's na . . . er, your mother's name."

From the doorway, Procida said, "Bravo, Esmeray and Bastone!" The doctor glanced at the midwife. "Exceptional work, signura! Can we discuss a time for Esmeray's next health appraisal?"

The midwife stood to go with the doctor, pausing, "Signura Ponzio, among the other directions the doctor and I will list for you, the top priority is to remain in bed for a four-week lying-in period. If you need us, we will be downstairs."

The midwife paused a second time. "I am sorry for your baby boy. But your daughter is strong, and I am certain you will want a priest to baptize her. After I inform the Church, I will be back to escort your husband and daughter for her baptism." Receiving no response, she said, "Of course, you are tired and want to be alone with your beautiful new girl."

They departed, leaving the couple alone. The steward closed the door, giving them privacy. Bastone kissed Aspasia's forehead and stroked his wife's hair, hoping she would not become upset about the baptism. She did not comment, trying to get the baby to nurse. "She doesn't want to nurse. Look at that stare! *Testa dura*!"

He suggested, "Please try to sleep, *dolcezza mia*." Removing his shoes, he lay next to her. They slept.

A few hours later, Bastone woke, pleased to see Aspasia was feeding. "Bravu, Esme!"

After a knock, Procida came in. "The midwife sent a message that the priest will baptize Aspasia tomorrow morning. *Tutti va bene*—everyone is fine?" said the doctor.

"Yes, Dottore Procida, thank you," said Bastone.

After the doctor shut the door, Esmeray said, "I should have told him we will not baptize Aspasia."

Bastone had dreaded this conversation, although he knew it would come. "I was baptized, you were baptized."

"Our daughter can make her own decision . . . when she is older."

"Esme, I understand, but denying her baptism will cause people to reject us—reject her."

"My mother wasn't baptized," said Esmeray.

"Really? Oh, oh, yes, your mother was Turkish and . . . Muslim. But please have Aspasia baptized," said Bastone. "What if my family asks?"

Esmeray's eyes narrowed. "I don't care. I won't go to Genoa, anyway."

"Esme, remember when my mother said she would accept us getting married? You agreed to convert to the Catholic Church."

She winced, squeezing her eyes shut, then said, "Yes."

"And what did you tell me when you had agreed to become a Catholic?"

For a moment, Esmeray stared at the wall. "That it was nothing."

"So, this baptism would mean nothing to you. It would have no power."

"It's not the same."

"Esme, let me take Aspasia tomorrow. Neither of us will ever tell our daughter it happened, unless she asks."

Children of the Middle Sea

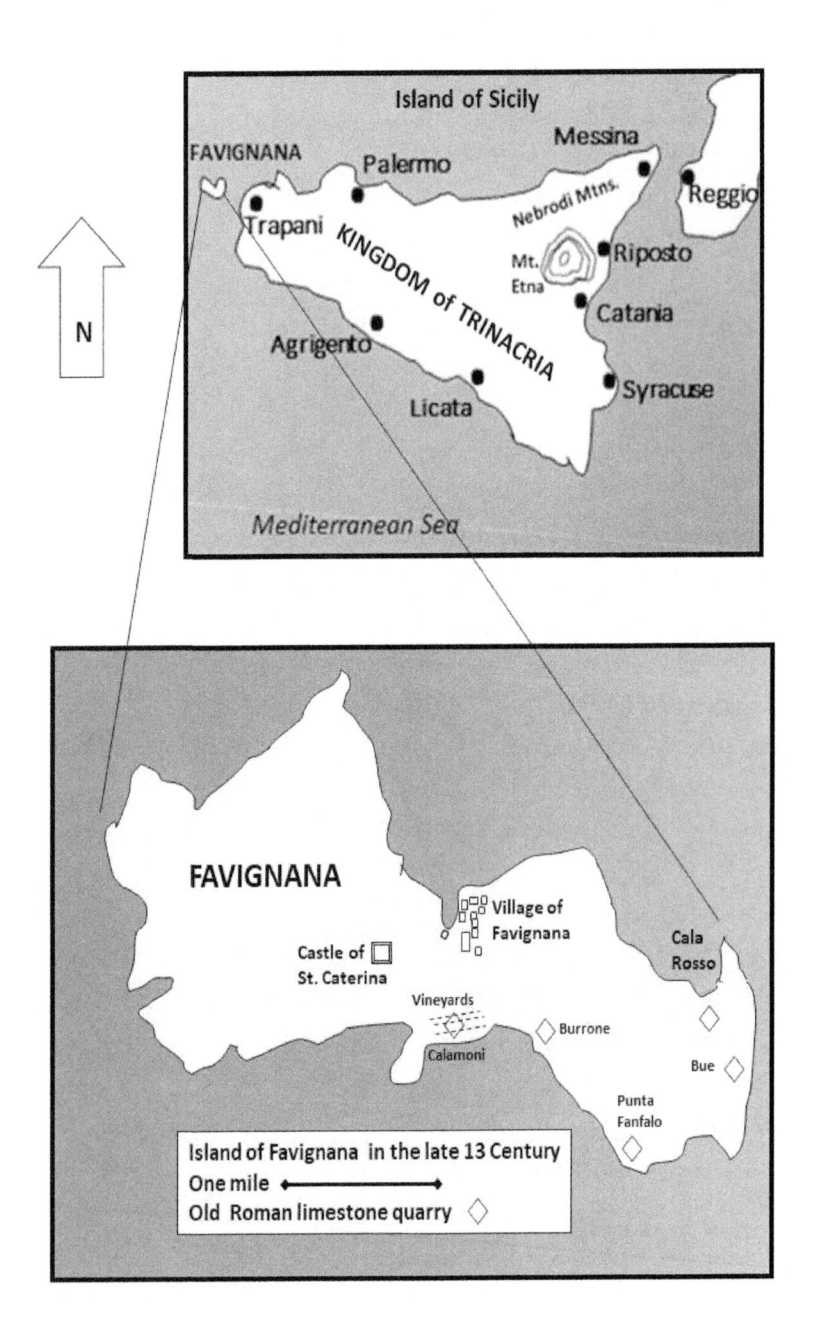

CHAPTER XVI

Esmeray, Bastone, and their daughter, Aspasia, woke at dawn, as they had almost every morning for the last five years. It was summer and another tranquil day as they sailed along the island of Favignana, collecting the catch from their fish traps. Esmeray sat beside Aspasia at the tiller, supervising her as the girl steered. Bastone shielded his eyes from the glare, looking for the next trap, recalling as they had cast off that morning a villager had told him news of the war. Admiral Di Lauria, leading the Sicilian navy, had defeated an Angevin fleet at the Bay of Naples. The Sicilians captured Charles's son, who had commanded the Angevins. Other than scattered reports, Bastone seldom thought about the war, hundreds of miles across the sea. Instead, Bastone and his family enjoyed a peaceful life in Favignana.

Bastone saw their gourds floating ahead, marking the location of one of their traps. "Capitanu Aspasia, trap ahead—furling sails!"

The boat coasted, Bastone dipping the oars to control their approach to the floats. Aspasia sprang up. "No! Sit down," said Esmeray. She took the tiller. "And?"

Aspasia said, "Per . . . perm . . ."

"Permission."

"Permission to . . . will you take the tiller, Mamma?"

Esmeray smiled at her daughter. "Granted."

The girl hurried to the bow and plopped on her father's lap, Bastone reacting with, "Oof!" He had just enough air to add a weak laugh. "Aspasia, you are getting big."

She grabbed the oars, grunting with each pull, and rowed with her father as Esmeray steered to the floats. Aspasia gripped the trap line, pulling hand over hand with Bastone's help. As the trap surfaced, she said, "This one is full!" Nearby swam a pod of dolphins. Aspasia let go of the rope, pointing, "Look, *Delfini, delfini!*"

Bastone transferred the fish to a canvas bucket as Aspasia leaned over the water toward the dolphins. "I wish I could swim with them!" Her father placed his hand on her shoulder, although she was already an excellent swimmer. It would not surprise him if she dove into the water.

"Aspasia!" Esmeray was standing at the tiller, her hair blowing in the wind as was Aspasia's. The girl was a smaller version of her mother but with darker tresses. Esmeray shouted, "Viva!" She then dove into the water. Aspasia followed. Both swam to the dolphins, the creatures lingering, showing interest in the visitors. Bastone laughed to himself. Daughter like mother.

After Aspasia and Esmeray swam for several minutes, Bastone called them back to the boat. "We need to finish the trap run and go to the market!"

They pulled themselves back into the boat. "Did you see, Papa? There were baby delfini, too!"

"Old sailors say that they've seen dolphins save people from drowning, even rescuing saints," said Bastone.

Aspasia grabbed a fish from their bucket and threw it to the dolphins. "Then they should get a prize!"

Finished with the traps, they returned to the harbor. A small Aragonese war galley on routine patrol was departing. Nearing the beach, Aspasia saw Petru waving to them. "Uncle Petru!" She dove into the turquoise water, swimming to shore. Esmeray stood at the tiller to get an unobstructed view of her daughter, making sure she steered away from her. *Delfinina*—her Little Dolphin—was sometimes too enthusiastic and reckless. Aspasia swam to shore and hugged Petru.

After her parents beached their craft below the village, Aspasia helped them haul their catch up the path which twisted through the rocky outcroppings surrounding the beach. They joined other fishers at the outdoor market, a couple of awnings to provide shade, trading fish among themselves according to their personal tastes.

The patrol boat had brought news of King Peter's death, which was on everyone's tongue in the village.

Today, the fishers were selling part of their catch to soldiers who had trekked down from Castle Saint Catarina. As the soldiers mingled with the villagers, Bastone asked the garrison officer, "*Amicu,* how did Peter die?"

He shrugged his shoulders, "Old age."

A soldier said, "Yes, old for a warrior. They said he was forty-six."

"He was a warrior, but also wrote lyrics for the troubadours in his court," said the officer.

Bastone recalled hearing a few of his songs in Messina. The songs Peter wrote were parodies—political propaganda against his adversaries. Bastone never liked Peter, but being a speculatore, he gave the late king credit for his guile. Bastone was more interested in the political changes. "And how will Peter's death affect Favignana—affect us?"

The officer touched his palms together, then spread them wide apart. "Peter split his lands among his sons. Alfonso, the oldest, got Aragon. James is the new king of Sicily, and his younger brother Frederick is prince regent. I don't think Favignana will be affected."

Another soldier arrived, slapping Bastone on the back, "*Ou, Bastuninu*—Hey Stickman, how will the wine be this year?"

"We're almost finished pruning. The buds will burst open soon."

"Ha, buds, vines, grapes. When will the new wine batch be ready?"

"Something wrong with last year's wine?" asked Bastone.

Pinching together his thumb and index finger, he made a pulling motion across his chest and said, "Your wine is *pirfettu*! But we're worried we might run out."

"You men drink wine like water!" said Esmeray.

"Who drinks water?" said the soldier, laughing with his comrades as they headed to buy wine at one of the few shops in the village.

Returning to their cottage, the family had breakfast together, then Bastone made his daily walk across the small island to join Vincenzu and his apprentice at the vineyards. As the men concentrated on their work, Vincenzu repeated instructions he had voiced a hundred times. "Remember to cut each vine above the second bud." Bastone didn't need reminding. Over the last five years, he had absorbed everything Vincenzu had taught him about cultivating grapes and producing wine. He enjoyed working with Vincenzu, who was pleased to have his assistance in caring for the vineyards.

As they continued to prune the vines under the gentle March sun, Vincenzu repeated the importance of the *Favonio*, the warm wind that constantly blew from the west. The inhabitants had named the island after the incessant wind. "Bastone, mbare—the Favonio brings seeds of the Neptune grass, which grows between the vines to provide nourishment." He glanced at the sky. "The seagulls glide over the island riding the same wind, dropping guano and fertilizing the soil. The wind blows insects away that could damage the grapes. And, the Favonio brings the sea itself, the salt air, to mingle with the soil and wine berries. The Favonio is a gift from the Roman god of the sea."

Bastone laughed. "It's good we don't have a priest on the island. He wouldn't want to hear that."

"Hmm? Oh, yes, yes." Vincenzu chuckled. "It's like putting one's faith in—in a saint—don't you think?"

"How do you mean?"

"People pray to saints for help. Are saints gods?"

"Something to think about, Vincenzu." Bastone found free thinking people like Vincenzu—like his own Esmeray—rare. And neither had been formally educated. He was quiet, pondering this when Vincenzu continued on a philosophical monologue, asking himself questions and not expecting answers. Bastone never tired of hearing the same stories again and again.

"Son, this dry, sunny climate is perfect for the grapes, but too much wind could desiccate the soil. So, the ancients planted the vines on the leeward side of the cliff, part of the old Roman quarry, to protect the grapes from too much wind. I continue the legacy of ancient winemakers, but my time is limited. You enjoy this work, no?"

"Very much."

"Do you remember who started the vineyards on Favignana?"

Bastone recounted the history once more, again recognizing Vincenzu was preparing him to take over the vineyard. He could not fulfill Vincenzu's wishes, because he would miss cherished time on the water with his family, especially being present as Aspasia grew.

Bastone began, "The ancient Phoenicians brought the *Zibibbo* grapes to Favignana to make the white, sweet wine—the fishermen's wine—thousands of years ago. Then the Greeks arrived, with red wine berries, which the Romans also grew. The Arabs halted winemaking, but the Normans revived the craft. Sicilians brought a red grape, *mascalese*, but the hardiest grape in the vineyard is the *malvasia*, from the dry plains of Greece."

Bastone respected and loved Vincenzu, and within several days found a worthy apprentice to train under Vincenzu. He recruited a young man from the village who didn't take to fishing.

After a day of hard work, Bastone, Vincenzu, and his young apprentice sat at the edge of the vineyard, a stone's throw from the sea lapping at the rocky shore, watching the sun approach the horizon. They shared a skin of white wine from the Zibibbo grapes. Vincenzu recited a peculiar adage: "The wine of Favignana has flavors of sea salt, crusty soil, and . . . yes, even tuna."

Bastone enjoyed Vincenzu's sayings, and though he found tuna tasty, he never imagined the flavor in the wines. The aged vintner continued, "I had a dream that the sea used to cover the island. Look, the soil is full of seashells and skeletons of creatures from the sea—giving the wine its special character—yes, a fisherman's wine."

Bastone trickled a swallow of wine into his mouth, experiencing the sweet and faint salty taste of the Zibibbo grapes, but he never understood what Vincenzu meant by the "flavor of crusty soil." He passed the skin to Vincenzu, who sipped. "I imagine a whiff of the sea." Then after he swallowed, he smacked his lips and said, "Just then, yes, for just a blink, then it was gone—a vision of shells and fishbones." Bastone was grateful he didn't mention the tuna taste.

Celebrating the completion of pruning for the season, they finished the wine. The men embraced. Bastone and the young man headed north to the village. When Bastone arrived at home, Esmeray and Aspasia had finished working in their small garden and were preparing the evening meal.

It was almost June. The flowers had dropped from the grapevines, and the wine berries emerged, still small and hard. The bluefin tuna had begun their annual migration past Favignana. During the previous weeks, the island's fishermen had prepared an immense floating trap by anchoring mile-long nets on the sea bottom to funnel schools of tuna. Nearly all the men of the island took part in the traditional hunt, the *mattanza*.

Esmeray and Bastone had both taken part in a mattanza before Aspasia was born, although Esmeray's involvement had been controversial. The traditional role of the women of Favignana was to support the communal hunt by gathering in the village to pray for their men.

Now in the village with Aspasia and the fishermen's wives, Esmeray imagined Bastone was several miles out to sea, joining in the backbreaking work of hauling the enormous fish into their boats. Esmeray joined the women in the plaza. Most were praying silently, but a few appealed aloud to Saint Peter for the safety of their husbands. Aspasia, now five, was more aware, and her mother told her to remain quiet and respect the women praying. Mother and daughter closed their eyes, silently wishing for Bastone's safe return.

After the men returned from the tuna hunt, Bastone arrived with their fishing boat laden with tuna. Esmeray and Aspasia joined him on board to help transport the catch to Trapani. Many of the fishers from Favignana took their families to visit the city to sell the tuna, also buying products not available on their island. Most would also attend Mass, although as it was not Sunday nor a festival day, the service would be Low Mass, an abridged ceremony.

After selling their tuna, Esmeray, Bastone, and Aspasia left the waterfront. The day was warm but comfortable. Arriving at a plaza in Trapani, they found a food vendor and had some *arancini*. Covered with breadcrumbs, the snack was the shape and color of a tiny orange. Aspasia took another bite. "Mmm, this one is filled with cheese!" Breadcrumbs spilled from her mouth.

Esmeray glanced at Bastone. Both were laughing. She said, "Yes, delicious!"

"Which is your favorite, Delfinina?" asked Bastone.

"Hmm. The rice, no the fish . . .?"

"It is called pork."

She finished an *arancinu*. "No, this one. I like the cheese."

Aspasia seemed interested in watching as several families from Favignana entered a church across the plaza.

Esmeray noticed. "Let's go find duci," she suggested. "Remember how much you liked the sweet *marzipane*?"

Aspasia pointed at the church. She was five years old, but had never been to Mass. "Our friends from the island are going there, look! Can we go, too?"

Bastone matched eyes with Esmeray, knowing what her answer would be. They had discussed going to Mass, Esmeray insisting she would not take her daughter until she was old enough to make her own decision about the Church.

Favignana had no priest nor church. Aspasia asked, "What is that place?"

"It's called the Church of Saint John the Baptist," said Bastone.

"People go there to pray," said Esmeray.

"Oh. Like when the fishermen's wives pray during the mattanza?" Esmeray didn't answer. "Yes," said Bastone.

"I want to see what's inside," said Aspasia.

At first, Bastone wondered if Esmeray would deny her daughter, but he also knew she wouldn't restrict Aspasia's inquisitive nature. Esmeray held Aspasia's hand and headed across the square. "Let's go."

They entered the church, stopping just inside the door, closing it behind them, their eyes taking a minute to transition from the bright daylight to the dark. There were scores of people standing on the opposite end of the chapel, as the priest, his back to them, recited in Latin. The interior was dark, except for faint light from a few windows and candles around the altar.

Bastone took his daughter's hand. "Do you want to join the others?"

She resisted, then tugged back, whispering, "No, no. I don't like it. It's dark." When they returned outside, Aspasia brightened.

At home, they had read *The Song of Roland* to her several times. Although the document was very expensive, it was important to them to give their daughter an education. She was fond of the story, intrigued by the names of faraway places. Bastone sketched a map of the Mediterranean from memory, having studied on his sea voyages, showing her the locations of the legend. When the Normans had ruled Sicily centuries earlier, there had been *jongleurs*, itinerant minstrels, who sang the epic poem in French at festivals. Disdaining the French language because of the brutal occupation by the Angevins, the native bards had translated the poems into Sicilian, and the jongleurs sang in the vernacular.

Aspasia displayed her excellent memory, saying, "The priest said words from the book we read."

"You mean the story about the knight, Rolando?" said Esmeray.

"Yes."

"What words did you recognize?" asked Esmeray.

"I think he said, God, father. . . but . . . Mother, can we go get sweets?"

Aspasia darted down a nearby alley toward a peddler hawking his wares in Sicilian, shouting, "Duci! Pasticcinu! Marzapane!"

Esmeray shouted, "Aspasia, stop!" The girl skidded to a halt. "Don't be heedless. Think before you act!"

Aspasia waited for Esmeray and Bastone to reach her. Her mother said, "But because you listened and stopped, we all get *duci*." They headed to the street vendor with his cart of sweets.

The Sicilians and Favignanesi were fortunate to have a peaceful holiday in Trapani. As Aspasia's family enjoyed sweets, the vendor told them good news. In distant Aragon, Di Lauria, leading the Sicilian fleet, had repulsed a French invasion. And Charles's plan to reinvade Sicily had been cancelled, because the despised king, whom Bastone had fought against for years, had died of a fever.

Children of the Middle Sea

CHAPTER XVII

As the sun was rising above the hills of Favignana, the fishers completed their daily run, heading to the village to trade. Esmeray and Aspasia had returned to their cottage. Bastone was about to leave for the vineyards when two ships entered the harbor. The lead ship was a small war galley, a coastal patrol boat of the Kingdom of Trinacria. Flying at the mast was a banner— half red and half yellow, at its center a trinacria—Medusa's head surrounded by three legs. Following the galley was a round-hulled *navi mercantile* with two masts, flying a white flag adorned with the red cross of Saint George, the flag of Genoa.

While the ships were dropping anchor, the commander of the castle garrison arrived, a knight from Trapani, having trooped down from Castle Saint Caterina with a squad of soldiers to meet the ships' delegation. He was the king's representative on the island, but was rarely involved with the village. Most of the inhabitants of Favignana belonged to the three families with the surnames of Campu, Torrente, or Ponziu, who together resolved matters.

The crews launched dinghies to shore. Fishermen waited on the beach for the visitors. Francesco was a passenger in one of the rowboats. Guilt consumed Bastone, his scalp becoming prickly with heat. He could not remember when he had last thought of his parents or siblings, not even his beloved sister, Maria Grazia. His brother might be bringing dreadful news about their family in Genoa.

Bastone waited at the top of the bluff as his brother wound through the sandy path among the black rocks. It had been five years since Francesco had been rescued from enslavement. He appeared to have recovered, his face and body robust again. A pair of his sailors, each with a wooden cask on his shoulder, preceded him up the path. As they passed Bastone, he overheard one say, "The king awarded a contract to the Genoese for a trading station on this island. But who would want to live here?"

Francesco reached Bastone. Both held unabashed smiles. The brothers embraced, drew apart, paused, then clasped a second time. "It's good to see you, Francesco."

"Yes, it's been too long, brother."

Bastone, recalling the sailor's remark moments before, placed his hand on Francesco's shoulder, guiding him toward the village market. "It looks as if you have business to discuss?"

Francesco updated his brother on the family. "Mother has improved, but eats so much garlic, she reeks of the odor!"

Bastone laughed.

"She thinks you cured her, Bastone."

"And Father?"

"He only visits the crossbow factory once a week, but he is fine, just slowing with age. And Maria Grazia is well. She sends her love."

"Did you already know I was on Favignana? You didn't look surprised to see me," said Bastone.

"Mino told me you were living here."

They soon arrived among a crowd of Favignanesi fishers.

Half an hour later, the visitors and the fishers faced each other across a table. The villagers had converted the stalls of the small fish market to an outdoor meeting space. Suspended between posts, old sailcloths shaded them, flapping above the men in the incessant west wind. It was warm, but the breeze and the canopy made a comfortable setting. The villagers had turned the event into a feast, grilling fish, the appealing scent of burning wood and smoked meat coming and going with the wind. They had sent for their wives to bring more food. Francesco shared the casks of wine he had brought. Francesco and the garrison commander sat on one side of the tables, Ponziu Petru, Campu Vincenzu, and the head of the Torrente family occupied the other side. Petru, Vincenzu, and the family leaders asked Bastone to join them in the negotiations. Scores of fishermen stood around the canopy, waiting to hear the news. Nearby, a few sailors and the garrison soldiers ate and drank.

Women placed grilled fish and hard bread on plates on the tables. Petru said, "Please, *mancia*—eat, then talk." He smiled and raised his cup. "Cent'anni!" Others followed. They ate with their hands, dipping their fingers in a bowl of sea water when finished, wiping them dry on their tunics.

After informal introductions, Francesco handed a one-page document to the garrison leader and said, "In this deed, the co-regent of Sicily, Frederick, grants the mineral rights of Favignana to the group of Genoese investors that I represent."

Nattering and rumblings of discontent came from the crowd. Francesco kept his gaze fixed on Bastone until the noise subsided. Then he scanned the faces in the crowd. "The mining will not affect your homes, the village, or interfere with fishing. We are reopening the old Roman quarries at *Cala Rosso* to mine the limestone."

A voice of anger emerged from the crowd. "Who will work the quarries?" Others sounded their irritation.

Torrente stood, confronting several men. "*Paesani*, please! If you want to sit at the table, I will trade places with you. Otherwise . . ."

The men quieted.

Torrente asked, "Yes, who will work there?"

"We will bring skilled *pirriaturi*," said Francesco. "These stonecutters will need apprentices. We will provide training for the Favignanesi. It would mean paying jobs for the island, paid in silver coin."

"That may be good," said Torrente. He surveyed the villagers. None of them shook their heads. With the cue, Torrente continued. "What about laborers?" he asked. "How will you move the stone blocks?"

Francesco hesitated, then said, "Workers from Africa."

"Slaves? Muslim slaves?"

Francesco nodded.

A woman cried, "Don't bring any *Saraceni* to Favignana!" She made the sign of the horns with her fingers. "*Diavuli*—Devils!"

Angry voices erupted from the crowd. One said, "Who will keep them at Cala Rosso?"

The garrison commander spoke above the noise, "My guards!"

Outbursts from the people halted as one of the commander's soldiers shuffled to the front of the crowd, his eyes heavy from drinking. The man slurred as he said, "Shir, dids zu call?"

A shout from the crowd, "Si, si, our brave soldiers will guard us!" The people roared with laughter.

They wiped their eyes and calmed, then poured wine all around. Vincenzu swished the wine in his cup, swallowing, whispering to Bastone, "This wine from Trapani is good, but it's not the fishermen's wine."

Bastone sensed his mentor was worried about the threat of imported wine, reducing the demand for their local vintage. He knew the Genoese could force their will on the island because the king had granted mining rights. Yet he knew he must negotiate to give compensation to the Favignanesi. Would the bargaining proceed smoothly with his brother, or would it be as difficult as when they had been young, when Francesco had criticized Bastone's every action, every comment?

Bastone placed one palm on the table, leaning slightly back on his stool, and turned his body at an angle, keeping eye contact with his brother. "Will you reopen other mines?"

Francesco nodded. "The other four, if needed. We own the mining rights."

Bastone clasped Vincenzu's shoulder, who sat next to him. "Signuri Campu's family has been growing grapes for generations in the ruins of the mine at Calamoni."

Francesco did not hesitate. "We will not reopen the mine at Calamoni. I guarantee we will not disturb his vineyards."

"Where do you plan to take the limestone?" Torrente asked.

"Mostly to Palermo."

Bastone said, "A shrewd Genoese never sails an empty ship. What cargo will your ships have when they return to Favignana?"

"We will bring Trapani wine to the island with each returning barge."

Bastone worried the imported wine would hurt Vincenzu's vineyards. "I propose trading an equal amount of Favignanesi wine for the wine from Trapani."

"What if the people of Palermo don't like this wine?" said Francesco.

"The same goes for the fishermen," said Bastone. "Today your wine is free, but will they pay for it? I will buy half of your wine, guaranteeing purchase, and trade for the other half."

Bastone and Francesco stood, hands reaching out to clasp, but Vincenzu barked, "*Aspetta!*"

They sat down. Vincenzu held up his hand, touching his thumb and middle finger together, frowning, as he said. "*Tantacchia.*"

Bastone had seen the gesture used only a few times. It meant 'too little', the Favignanesi wanted more concessions.

Vincenzu glanced at him, then at Francesco. "You should also bring the Favignanesi other goods—of their choice—on the returning ships."

Francesco nodded as several people responded with applause.

Bastone and Francesco shook hands. The people accepted, gauging by their cheerfulness and lack of protest. The Favignanesi would gain a few jobs as stone cutters, and they could sell the surplus from their catch to feed the workers at the mines.

Bastone was about to take Francesco to meet his family, when he realized Esmeray and Aspasia, hearing about the visitors, had returned to the village. Bastone was pleased to see Esmeray's genuine smile as she greeted Francesco. Aspasia laughed and squealed when his brother picked her up to kiss her cheeks. The family made the five-minute trek together to their home, its white limestone walls bright in the sunlight as they approached.

They sat outside the cottage under the arbor, ivy vines growing overhead, providing shade. Francesco discussed the family's welfare in Genoa, while Bastone informed his brother about their peaceful life on the island. Esmeray and Aspasia looked eager when Francesco suggested they come aboard his ship. A short hour later, arriving at the harbor, the family squeezed into a dinghy, a sailor rowing them toward a cargo ship. Aspasia saw the ship's name carved into the hull. "Mar, mari—what does it say?"

"Good try, Delfinina. The ship is named the *Maria Grazia*, after your aunt."

On board, Esmeray eagerly described the workings of the rigging and sails to Aspasia. Her daughter was tugging on the steering oars, marveling at how much larger they were than the tiller on their fishing boat. Francesco and Bastone leaned on the taffrail, peering out to sea. Francesco said, "Will you consider returning to Genoa?"

Bastone glanced at his brother, then returned to gaze across the water. "During my last visit, our parents seemed to accept me again, but neither asked about Esmeray."

"Uncle Riccio told them Esmeray was with child. Bastone, you are a lucky man." He glanced at Aspasia, inspecting the ship. "Aspasia is curious and vibrant! And Esmeray, beautiful, intelligent . . . plus her skills sailing."

Bastone squinted, tilting his head, wondering how Francesco knew of her past. Francesco noticed. "Uncle Riccio told me all about her, and you, on the *Paradisio*. I know you are proud of her."

Francesco added, "I have a boy, a year old, and a girl, three."

"Late congratulations! Bravo, Ciccio!" said Bastone.

"Cousins should be together," said Francesco. "And Maria Grazia's children. Don't you think Aspasia should meet them?"

"Esmeray will never return to Genoa," said Bastone. "The memories are too painful."

"I have a proposal—Esmeray and you could return—perhaps a compromise, not a full commitment," said Francesco.

Bastone turned to face his brother, raising his eyebrows, wondering what he meant. Behind Francesco, Esmeray and Aspasia playfully sparred with belaying pins as they laughed.

"I own a quarter of this navi," said Francesco. "Uncle Riccio owns the rest. We want you to be captain. It's a tough crew to manage. Zaccaria told me you commanded the respect of the often surly crew on the *Paradisio*. And your skill as an officer of the arbalesters is renowned throughout the Genoese fleet. Return with your family to Genoa. Esmeray and Aspasia would sail with you. Once settled, you'll spend most of your time at sea, sparing her from family gatherings. Think about it. Ask Esmeray. I'll wager she'll want you to accept."

CHAPTER XVIII

Francesco remained on the *Maria Grazia*, waiting for the captain of the Sicilian galley and a few prominent Favignanesi, including Torrente, to join him on his ship. He planned to entertain the islanders to explore other profit-making ventures. Bastone and his family returned to their cottage, where he wanted to talk with his wife in private. Esmeray ushered Aspasia to the garden to weed, telling her she would soon join her to help.

Aspasia's eyebrows knitted. "Alone? We always do it together."

Esmeray looked behind her daughter to see their white cat approaching. "Ciciri is here. She will keep you company while your papa and I talk."

The girl picked up the fluffy cat. Stroking its cheeks, Ciciri purred in response. Aspasia, now contented, headed toward the garden saying, "Ciciri, let's go to the garden and pull the weeds."

Esmeray and Bastone sat under the arbor, watching their daughter busy among the rows of vegetables, talking to her cat as she worked. Bastone asked, "Dolcezza mia, do you miss our days of sailing across the world?"

Esmeray scowled, but kept her voice hushed. "Please don't tell me you are going on a mission as a speculatore."

"No, no. Uncle Riccio and Francesco, who own the *Maria Grazia,* offered me captaincy of a vessel for their trading company."

Esmeray searched his eyes. "And?"

Why disturb their safe, idyllic life in Favignana? Now that Esmeray was a mother, he was certain she preferred keeping a stable home for Aspasia. She had talked of her frustration at not having a place to call home and was worried that Aspasia would meet the same fate. Hesitating to answer her, he fell into Esmeray's gaze, recalling what he loved most about her—her self-confidence, grit, and her passion for adventure. Bastone had already decided not to accept his brother's offer, but now wavered.

An unforgettable scene flashed in his mind, the day, years ago, when he had met Esmeray—a bolt shot from a crossbow had barely missed her as she stood on the deck of her fishing boat. Fearless and unwavering, she had ignored the close shot, looked up from the deck and *demanded* to board the *Paradisio*. Then he recalled her escape from the Berber slavers at sea, her bright red scarf and beautiful chestnut hair in the ocean wind proclaiming her freedom. A plan burst into his mind, knowing what he would say to her.

"I could accept the job as captain, and I would consult you on all the decisions," said Bastone.

She frowned. "What would I do on the ship, just be your wife?"

"No, you would be first mate and . . ."

Esmeray said, through clenched teeth, "That would be worse than captain. I would have to be a sergeant to a bunch of ogling sailors. At least on the *Paradisio*, I gained their respect after I showed I could do sailors' work."

Bastone recalled his brother mentioning the crew was hard to supervise.

"I want to be the captain, not first mate," said Esmeray, raising her voice.

Aspasia, weeding on hands and knees, sat back on her heels, looking up.

Bastone kissed Esmeray. "I'm sorry, Dolcezza, I thought . . . I'll do what you want."

Aspasia relaxed, continuing her chore. Ciciri was batting around the piles of weeds.

Esmeray said, "After Aspasia was born, I was relieved when we returned to Favignana, providing a safe home for her. But yes, traveling on the open sea again would be exciting. If it was next year or later, I might have said yes, for Aspasia's sake. But she is too young now. And I would only agree if I would be the captain."

Bastone told his brother his decision not to accept the offer to be captain.

"That's the problem with strong women, like Esmeray, she is a *testa dura*."

Bastone's eyes grew wide, not expecting such a strong reaction from Francesco. He was glad Esmeray and Aspasia had already said their farewells and departed.

"Mother said, ever since you married that . . ." Francesco ceased when he saw Bastone's face transform, his nostrils glaring, his jaw clenching, not trying to hide his displeasure.

"No, no. I'm sorry, Bastone. But, but . . . consider my offer. I'll be back periodically to check on the mines."

He embraced Bastone and departed for the dinghy to his ship. He halted and glanced behind. "Good luck, brother. If you change your mind in the next few days, I'll be nearby at the Cala Rosa mine."

After Charles's death, his son, Charles II, had inherited the kingdom, but he was still a hostage, imprisoned at Castle Mategriffon in Messina. The populace took to the streets surrounding the castle, demanding his execution. But Queen Constanza, still with much influence, slipped him out of Messina and incarcerated him a hundred miles down the coast in Cefalu.

With relative peace in the waters around Sicily, over the next several months Francesco reopened the mine at Cala Rosso, and the benefit from the mining activities on the island was encouraging. He hired several Favignanesi and trained them as stonecutters, enabling them to develop their skills and earn an income. The villagers profited, spending longer hours fishing, selling their surplus to the mine to feed the workers. Also, the fishers that had previously sailed to Trapani to hawk their fish now sold them to the nearby miners, supplying food for the Muslim slaves who did the backbreaking work. The slaves slept in the quarries under guard. Francesco insisted on long workdays, but instead of seeking vengeance for having been enslaved himself, he established rules that treated the slaves humanely, ensured they were well-fed, and even permitted them to cultivate their own hypogean rockeries—belowground gardens inside the discarded sections of the quarries.

Bastone heard in the village that his brother had returned to inspect the operations at Cala Rosso—Red Cove. The area was so named because the water in the cove had turned red with blood during an ancient sea battle. A thousand years earlier, the Romans had destroyed a Carthaginian fleet in their war for control of Sicily.

Bastone had sailed past the rocky cove many times, paying little attention, other than noting the cliffs had unusual configurations. Now, as he approached the shore, he could see that the tall unnatural shapes were manmade. Miners had excavated the limestone-shell tuff at the shore, working their way inland. The cliffs were of various shapes—rectangular, square, and others pyramidal.

Moored nearby on the shore where the land sloped more gradually, were two *schifazze*—flat-bottom scows fitted with sails to transport the limestone for the short crossing to Trapani. The miners cut the limestone into blocks, brought it down the slope in carts, and loaded it onto the scows. Each *cantuna*—block—was one foot by one foot by two feet, weighing about 200 pounds.

Bastone tied up to his brother's ship, the *Maria Grazia*, anchored in the cove. The shoreline was rocky, but the seabed of the cove was sand, giving the transparent water an intense shade of turquoise, especially brilliant on this sunny day. Although Bastone had become accustomed to the beauty of the aquamarine water, he still paused before he climbed the rope to the ship's deck, appreciating the contrast of the blue green sea under the white cliffs.

The brothers traded news of their families over wine, the conversation moving to politics. "I heard about the riots in Messina," said Francesco. "They wanted Charles beheaded. I don't blame them."

"But Constanza prevented his execution. He is a very valuable hostage."

"Where were King James and Prince Frederick?"

"James was in Palermo," said Bastone, "and Frederick was on his way to Messina. Constanza acted without them. Sicilians have great respect for her and appear to have accepted her decision."

Outside Francesco's cabin, they heard a crewmember shout, "Ahoy—*du'navi*—two ships abeam!"

Francesco furrowed his eyebrows. "They are not ours. Both scows are already here." He ducked through the door to outside, Bastone following him. The pair of ships was sailing westward a few hundred yards off the coast. Each flew a red and yellow banner with a trinacria. "Sicilians. I'll wager they are going to the village to trade," said Francesco, "but we own the trading rights here."

He glanced at Bastone. "You can disembark, or we'll tow your trohantiras and you can sail with us. We can't catch the ships before they reach the village, but I intend to find out what they are doing here." Francesco turned and shouted to his first mate, "Weigh anchor and get underway! We are sailing to the village."

An hour later the *Maria Grazia* approached the harbor. The Sicilian trading ships had already anchored and a dinghy was being rowed toward the shore. Francesco had mustered his arbalesters, who stood ready at the bow. As they glided into the harbor, suddenly Francesco snatched a crossbow from the nearest arbalester. With both hands, Francesco thrust the weapon into Bastone's midsection. He barked at a marine, "Give me a bolt!" Handing the arrow to his brother, Francesco said, "I know you can hit the passenger in that rowboat from here!" Bastone hadn't witnessed such rage in his brother since their teenage years. Francesco leaned with his elbows on the bow rail, waiting for Bastone to shoot, squinting at the distant target. "Eliminate their captain and they will leave without a fight. They're as good as pirates, anyway."

Bastone glanced at the arbalesters. They appeared uneasy, perhaps even shocked. It seemed to be the first time they had seen his brother's extreme mood swings, while Bastone had experienced his brother's unpredictable personality his entire life. It wasn't Francesco's enslavement that had brought about the behavior; he had returned to his innate temperament.

Francesco snapped his head toward Bastone. "What are you waiting for!" He handed the weapon and bolt to the closest arbalester, who placed his foot in the stirrup, pinning the bow to the deck. He straightened his legs, cocking the bowstring, placed the bolt in the groove, offering it to Bastone, who refused to accept it.

Francesco ordered the officer of the arbalesters, "Shoot the man in the dinghy!" Getting no cooperation, he aimed the weapon. The *Maria Grazia* had neared the closest trading ship. Carved on the bow was *GIOVANNA*. Now closer, Bastone recognized the passenger in the dinghy.

"No!" Bastone shoved the crossbow away from its intended target, but a sharp clack announced the release of the bolt. In a blink, it punched into the sea.

Bastone grasped the crossbow, his brother relinquishing it without a struggle. Handing it to an arbalester, he rested his hand on Francesco's shoulders, looking him in the eyes. "Ciccio, you almost shot Mino. He must have a good reason to be here."

Francesco calmed and went ashore with Bastone, where they shared wine with Mino in the shade of the village market, while his wife, Giovanna, visited Esmeray and Aspasia at their cottage. As the men socialized, Francesco learned that Mino, who was sailing to Collo, Africa, with a load of salt, had stopped at Favignana, so he and his wife could visit Bastone and Esmeray. Mino didn't want to depend on a trading convoy to sail to Africa, although piracy was widespread. Instead, he sent both his ships, with crews trained to fight, including experienced arbalesters.

Bastone continued to be reminded of his brother's changeable moods, as Francesco was now at ease with Mino, smiling, laughing, and telling stories. He and Mino traded information on their commercial ventures, each benefiting from the exchange. Mino finished his wine, holding the jug and flicking his chin up, the gesture asking if they wanted more. Both raised their cups. Mino poured, toasting, "Saluti!"

They drank, now savoring the wine in silence. Bastone broke the quiet. "Mino, how did you manage to convince Giovanna to accompany you?'

Mino chuckled, then said, "After Esmeray left Messina, Queen Constanza missed your wife's stories about her sailing adventures. Constanza encouraged Giovanna to take a voyage with me, so she could entertain the queen by reciting her own experiences."

Francesco said, "My wife wouldn't set foot on a ship, and I wouldn't want her there, anyway. There are crewmen on my ship who believe the old sailors' tale that women are bad luck on ships."

Mino set down his cup. He leaned toward Bastone and said, "Bastone, of course we have called on your island to see you. And Giovanna wanted to take a sea voyage before we had children. We will stay ashore in Messina for the birth of our first child. With good fortune, that will be next year. When the time comes, would you and Esmeray take over the *Giovanna*?"

Francesco's eyebrows furrowed, his jaw dropping when Bastone answered, "I accept your offer. Yes, I will captain the *Giovanna*. A fine vessel! I know Esmeray would support me. And as luck would have it, here comes Esmeray. Ask her. She'll agree!"

The women arrived in time to hear Mino say, "No, I fancied Esmeray would be the captain."

Francesco spit out wine. "What!"

Francesco poured himself more wine and gulped it. Mino explained why his plan would work. The crew had become familiar with Giovanna being on board, accepting her presence without problems. She did the scribe's duties, spending her time in the captain's suite or with her husband atop the stern castle. Mino had a loyal first mate, who was also the officer of the arbalesters. The first mate knew of Bastone's and Esmeray's heroics in the revolts, agreeing to relinquish the duty as officer of the arbalesters to Bastone. As Mino disclosed each detail of the plan, no one noticed Francesco's face reddening with anger.

Beaming, Esmeray glanced at Aspasia, appearing excited. "I will accept your offer as captain, Signuri Nglisi," Esmeray said. Bastone was certain his wife and daughter were envisioning grand adventures on the sea.

Mino and Giovanna both smiled. "So, I will finish this summer's trading voyages to Africa and back," said Mino. "That will give you two months to get ready to take over the ship."

While Esmeray and Bastone were engrossed in Mino's proposal, they were unaware that Francesco had been stewing in reticence. They were surprised when he loudly interjected, "Why didn't you accept my proposal last year?"

His outburst stunned them. Bastone did not answer, but Esmeray said, "It's not the same, Ciccio. Aspasia was too young. We told you that."

"If that's true, accept my proposal instead. Keep it in the family. *Il sangue non e acqua*—blood is thicker than water."

"There are other significant differences, brother," said Bastone.

Francesco stood, wavering from drink. He banged his cup on the table, causing Aspasia to whimper. Bastone stood. "Ciccio!"

"Don't Ciccio me! Mother told me you wouldn't marry into the Spinola clan after they received word of my execution. You didn't support the family then and now you are abandoning the family once again!"

He turned to go. Aspasia jumped up crying, and ran to him, Esmeray right behind her, fearing Francesco in his inebriety might harm her. But before she caught Aspasia, the girl reached her uncle. Aspasia hugged him. He calmed, patting her on the head. "I'm not mad at you, Dolcezza." He kneeled and kissed her cheek. Standing, he glared at Bastone, then stormed away with no words of farewell, heading toward the beach.

CHAPTER XIX

At dawn the next morning, Bastone, Esmeray, and Aspasia arrived at the harbor to begin the trap run for the day. As the crews of Mino's ships, the *Lucia* and *Giovanna*, were readying to cast off, Bastone rowed toward the *Giovanna* so his family could say farewell. They came alongside, shouting goodbyes as Giovanna and Mino leaned over the taffrail, waving. Aspasia and Giovanna threw kisses to each other.

Bastone continued out of the harbor, passing his brother's ship at anchor, where there were only a few sailors on deck. Aspasia peered at the vessel. "Are we going to say goodbye to Uncle Ciccio?"

Esmeray was at the tiller. "No, he is still asleep. He had too much to drink."

Bastone flashed a dissenting glance at his wife, but then agreed with a nod, thinking it would be a good lesson for their daughter. Esmeray said, "Sleeping off his grogginess, I'm sure."

It had been the first time Aspasia had seen someone drunk. "Mamma, Papa, you both drink wine."

"But not too much, Aspasia." Esmeray signaled for Bastone to raise the mainsail, then said, "*Delphinina*, you love to wake up every day, looking forward to the sea, yes?"

"*Certu*—of course!"

"If you drink too much, as your uncle did, you will sleep late, be sick, and miss a day of your exciting life."

Aspasia quieted, staring upward as if in thought. Esmeray hoped she was absorbing what she had said. "Mamma, can I work the tiller?"

They left the harbor, sailing west along the coast, approaching the location of the closest fish pots. Aspasia pointed to the floats made of gourds to mark the locations. Esmeray had painted them white, although the pigment had faded. Aspasia insisted on helping Bastone pull up the fish trap, woven in a conical shape from strips of cane. "This one is full of calamari!" he said, a fish she did not favor. "We should trade these squid."

The next trap had several eels and a rare *branzinu*. "I like the bass!" said Aspasia. "I'm getting hungry thinking about how good it will taste."

By midmorning, they had emptied their traps and sailed back to the village. Francesco's ship was still moored in the harbor. Gliding past the *Maria Grazia*, Aspasia stood, waving both arms. "*Ziu* Ciccio! Uncle, wake up!"

A crewmate came to the side rail. "He's waiting at your house!"

Bastone left a couple of eels with Petru, filleting the rest of the catch. He also was looking forward to grilling the fish. The white meat of the sea bass had a mild flavor, and he never tired of sweet eel fillets, chewy but not rubbery when grilled.

They approached their white limestone cottage, brilliant in the morning light. Francesco, awake but heavy-lidded, was slumped in a chair, waiting outside in the arbor's shade. Ciciri was napping on his lap. Aspasia ran ahead of her parents. "Uncle, Ciciri likes you!"

She kneaded the cat behind its ears. Smelling the scent of fish, Ciciri licked the girl's fingers, purring. Francesco patted his niece's head. "How are you, dolcezza mia?"

"Fine, Uncle Ciccio. Hey, your name and my cat's name are . . . the same? Ciciri and Ciccio!"

"Similar," Bastone said. "Aspasia, what is ciciri?"

"Chickpeas!" She laughed, rubbing the cat's nose. "Yes, I see a line on her nose. Just like a chickpea!"

Francesco laughed with her.

Esmeray had waited quietly, keeping a few steps back with Bastone. Francesco, who had focused on Aspasia, said, "Esmeray, please forgive my behavior last evening."

Bastone resisted looking directly at her, but detected a tentative nod.

Aspasia went to Bastone. "Can Ciciri have a piece of fish, please?"

He pinched meat from the bass, handing the flakes to his daughter. "Feed it to Ciciri by the garden." She ran, and the cat sprang to the ground, chasing the girl.

Bastone moved a chair near Francesco. Esmeray stood, folding her arms across her chest and pursing her lips. Francesco leaned toward them, placing his palms on the table. "Your daughter will not see me drunk again. And of course, you both should join any ship you choose. I also understand, Esmeray, that you don't want to go to Genoa. Yet, nothing is more precious than family. Think how excited Aspasia would be to see her cousins."

Both Bastone and Esmeray remained silent. Francesco had already tried this reasoning to persuade them. Bastone knew he had to let his wife answer, if at all. She was avoiding eye contact with Francesco, but he knew his wife. There was hope. At least she was not giving him her *Medusa* stare—a look that could turn a person to stone.

Francesco peered at his brother. "Mother is bedridden now."

He turned to Esmeray. "You could take Aspasia to visit Maria Grazia and her family and never have to see my mother."

Esmeray uncrossed her arms, sat at the table with them, looking Francesco in the eyes. She tilted her head, as if she wanted to hear more.

Francesco continued, "Genoa, the great city, awaits Aspasia's visit. She will gain many new experiences sailing across the sea. I'll return periodically to check the mines, so you'll have plenty of chances to come back to Favignana."

Francesco paused, waiting for her answer. Bastone sensed Esmeray was considering the proposal when she lifted her eyes toward the top of the arbor, pausing in thought. She turned to Bastone, her slow blink and almost imperceptible nod signaling she would go to Genoa.

GENOA

CHAPTER XX

The trading ship *Maria Grazia* sailed on course to the island of Corsica. On deck, Esmeray helped a sailor coil rope as they watched Aspasia tailing the ship's mouser. "Be careful, little girl, Zazu doesn't care for people." The cat moved away just before she could get within an arm's length, then stopped, glancing back, repeating the sequence each time she tried to reach him.

Aspasia crouched down, peering at the black cat. "He doesn't even want this scrap of fish."

The sailor finished his task. "I'll show you." He lay down on his side, sounding through his teeth, "Pspsps." The cat turned toward him, sitting on its haunches. Then the man blinked slowly. "Watch Zazu's eyes."

"He's doing it, too!"

"Now throw him the fish."

"He's eating it!" She sat on her heels to watch the cat. "His name is Zazu? What does it mean?" She didn't wait for him to answer. "My cat's name is Ciciri—it means chickpeas."

The sailor laughed. "Ciciri—you pronounce it as a Sicilian would—you would pass the test!"

"Test? Pronounce?" Aspasia stumbled over the word.

"Erm . . . it means Ciciri is a good name for your cat."

She smiled. "Hmm. What does Zazu mean?"

"Zazu means *moving*, in the Hebrew language."

"Like when he moves away from me?" She frowned. "Ebru?"

"The language spoken by the Jewish merchant in Messina who gave us Zazu."

"Mamma teaches me Greek and Papa teaches me Sicilian."

"You are a smart girl. How old are you?"

"*Cincu*"

"Five! Very good. You would say, *cinque,* in Genoese. Your cousins in Genoa will understand *cinque*."

Zazu had departed. "Each time you see Zazu, blink slowly, give him food, but don't touch him until he asks you."

Aspasia forehead crinkled. "Huh?"

The sailor nodded a thank you at Esmeray, departing as he said, "Aspasia, you will know when Zazu wants you to touch him."

Wearing her sailor's clothes of cut off pants, loose tunic, and floppy watch cap, Esmeray watched him cross the deck. "I liked the way you listened and learned from him, Delfinina." She laughed. "Although the lesson wasn't about sailors' duties."

Francesco had agreed to let Esmeray work with the sailors, informing the crew it would only be temporary. Within hours after Esmeray joined the crew, her skills as a sailor were obvious and the occasional grumbles that had been coming from the crew ceased. Esmeray wanted to show her daughter that women also could do hard work. She insisted her daughter watch the crew work, but from a safe distance, and not interfere.

The ship had been sailing on a port tack for three days, reaching the halfway point to Genoa, and anchoring at Porto Cardo on the northeast coast of Corsica. Departing the port, the *Maria Grazia* continued tacking using the nor'westerly mistral winds, sailing at five knots on course to Genoa. The sun was setting off the ship's port, the third day out of Corsica. Bastone, Esmeray, and Aspasia gazed in silence across the sea as the bow waves spread abeam of the hull. Trailing the ship was the stern wake, appearing an effervescent white in the rays of the setting sun. Zazu arrived after having finished his patrol below deck. He had befriended Aspasia during the passage, and now rubbed against the girl's legs, even tolerating her petting him a few times before he departed for the hold to hunt rats.

"We should arrive in Genoa soon," said Bastone.

"How do you know, Papa?"

Bastone began to describe the method of dead reckoning to his daughter. "Do you remember watching your mother uncoil rope from the stern and count the knots in the line?"

Aspasia nodded.

"The number of knots told her how fast we are sailing. She determines the distance to Genoa from the maps. And then she can figure . . ."

Aspasia nodded, pointing east, just above the horizon. "Look, the first star of the night!" He would have to explain it to his daughter another time.

Esmeray and Bastone exchanged glances. He was sure his wife was recalling the first time she had seen the welcoming light after they survived a violent storm at sea.

"Delfinina, it's the great lighthouse at Genoa. *La Lanterna*."

"Light . . . house. Lantern?"

"It's a tower, higher than the steeple of the church in Trapani. Monks keep a fire lighted at the top, so Genoese sailors can find their home. The first sighting of *La Lanterna* tells us we will arrive in Genoa in four hours."

"The light also warns sailors, so they won't shipwreck on the rocky shore at night or in a storm," said Esmeray.

Aspasia quieted, watching the light across the sea. Bastone hoped Esmeray's decision to come to Genoa, with Aspasia gaining many new experiences, pleased her. But what would happen when they arrived in Genoa? How will his mother react?

The harbor at Genoa was always teeming with trade ships, but as the *Maria Grazia* approached the entrance, Bastone noticed the waterfront and docks were more crowded than usual. War galleys filled the city's harbor, suggesting a significant portion of the navy had been summoned. As soon as they disembarked, they learned that Genoa was mobilizing the fleet for another battle with the powerful maritime republic of Pisa, confirming Bastone's premonition that war was on the horizon.

Esmeray and Bastone, holding Aspasia's hands, keeping her safely between them, worked their way through the crowd of sailors and marines gathered at the waterfront. Bastone was not surprised by his wife's sullen expression. They had left their quiet island and entered the havoc of a city on the verge of war.

They passed by a remarkable building, the Palace of the Sea, the waterfront customs house. Aspasia tugged on their hands to stop. Because of their abrupt halt, pedestrians jostled them. It was nothing out of the ordinary for the city, but Bastone saw his wife's gloomy mood turn to annoyance.

"Mamma, what is that beautiful building?"

"We can't stand here, Aspasia. We are in the way!"

Aspasia looked up at her father with brow furrowed.

"Mamma's just tired from the voyage, Delfinina." As they moved on, Bastone said, "It's where merchants trade. Like our little fish market in Favignana, but larger."

Aspasia seemed to return to herself. "*Assai granni!*"

"Delfinina, we are in Genoa. Here you would say, "*Molto grande!*" She smiled. "Si, Papa, molto grande!"

Aspasia had many more questions, Bastone answering them, hoping it would give Esmeray time to defuse her anger. Perhaps when they got to his sister's house she would calm herself.

They hiked the steep route through the city to the home of Maria Grazia, his sister. After an emotional reunion, they shared almond pastries and sweet white wine with her family. A domestic showed Bastone and Esmeray to their room, while Aspasia played outside with her cousins and aunt in the courtyard.

The servant left, closing the door. The instant the latch clicked, as if she had been containing her emotions, Esmeray gnashed her teeth and said, "Why did I agree to come here!" Esmeray balled her fists, eyes fixed on the ceiling, shrieking, "I have come to Genoa twice and both times there has been a war!" She continued to pace across the room, holding her temples, peering at the floor as she walked back and forth.

"It is fate," said Bastone. He had never seen her like this. Calming her at this moment would not include touching her. Esmeray pounded her fists on the table, scowling at the ceiling.

He kept his voice even. "We will endure this, just as we have survived worse times before. But fortune is on our side. Esme, Maria Grazia told me the Pisans just raided Corsica again. If we had arrived a day or two later, the Pisans might have captured or killed us."

Bastone paused, as if he was going to say more. She peered at him. He tarried, finding it difficult to tell her what he must do. Esmeray erupted. "What? No!"

"And I must fight along with my countrymen to defend Genoa."

His wife slumped down on the bed. "I am worried about Aspasia."

"I will not . . . we will not . . . our family will let nothing happen to her. The Genoese families may fight and bicker among themselves, but when there is an outside threat, we are unbeatable when united. The Pisans could never invade the city. All the fighting will be at sea."

Esmeray calmed, and went to Bastone, embracing him, her voice softening. "I am afraid for you, tesoro."

Their lips came together, mouths opening, sharing the warmth. He locked the bedroom door, pulling off his tunic, as he returned to Esmeray. She had already removed her tunica. He paused, exploring, enthralled. They embraced, deep in the other's arms, Esmeray shuddering with the contact. Bastone's body throbbed from the closeness, as Esmeray softly moaned. Their anxieties melted away, the fears of the upcoming battle forgotten.

CHAPTER XXI

Wearing leather gloves, Simon held an iron ladle in the flames as his assistant blew through a reed tube at the base of the fire. The lead ore in the spoon turned white at the edges as it melted. Today, he was melting lead ore using a charcoal fire in his courtyard. Simon, the most skilled physician of Genoa, prepared his own medicines.

He had received a letter from Rome offering the role as physician to the Pope, but he had delayed travel, staying to heal many sailors injured in the recent sea battle with Pisa. Now he was preparing one of the hundreds of formulas he had collected during his travels and research. It was a formula in his compendium, *Clavis Sanationis*, The Key to Healing, which he had written in three languages: Latin, Greek, and Arabic. The encyclopedia contained the recipes for medicines from ancient Greece, Rome, and the Muslim world.

After the lead melted, the assistant kept blowing, evaporating the liquid. The residue that remained was a bright orange-red powder—*red lead.* The fumes shifted with the wind, making them both cough. Simon waved the smoke away. He removed the ladle from the fire and set it on a stone pedestal, allowing the residue to cool.

Holding out his hands, the doctor said, "*Olio.*" The assistant poured olive oil on Simon's palms and he rubbed it to cover his fingers and hands. He tapped the powder from the ladle into a bowl, added shredded rose petals and honey, and kneaded the mixture, producing *oleum rosarum,* a paste that he used to treat head wounds.

He wiped his hands with a cloth, instructing his assistant, "Put the salve in a crock and gather linens for fresh bandages, while I clean my hands and dress for our appointment with Signore Ponzio." The doctor headed toward the house, pausing. "And also bring a vial of the *oleum mandragoratum*."

The pair were soon climbing the streets and stairways to the neighborhoods above the harbor of Genoa. Although fit and in his thirties, Simon felt weary, his legs heavy from little sleep. Every step was an effort. His days had been long, all his waking hours spent treating his wounded countrymen who had been injured in the sea battle. His thoughts turned to the thousands of unfortunate enemy Pisans held in the penal camp outside the city. He was a devoted and compassionate physician, also wanting to help them. The Hippocratic oath from the school of medicine in Salerno resonated in his mind: *I swear by the Lord, that I will come for the benefit of the sick.* But although many of the captured sailors needed his help, the Genoese authorities had forbidden it.

They reached the family enclave of Bastone's sister, Maria Grazia. The domestic guided them to the second floor, where they heard long, low moans of pain as they headed down the hallway. They entered a bedroom, Simon greeting Esmeray, who sat next to the bed, her face grim with worry. She had been at Bastone's side since his comrades had rescued him several days earlier. There were dark circles under her eyes, and her tunica was wrinkled and disheveled from sleeping in the chair next to his bed. The doctor felt Bastone's forehead. "He has no fever. I have fresh salve for your husband. Has he awakened at all?"

"Only to vomit," said Esmeray, shaking her head. Bastone continued to moan as he lay on the bed.

"Often? Like the first days after the battle?"

"No, only once today."

"That's a good sign, Signora." Her back became less rigid, and her face softened.

He removed the bandage wrapped around the top of Bastone's head. Bastone groaned louder, but his eyes remained closed. He had lost a patch of hair from the side of his head, revealing a lump with a deep red bruise on it. "The laceration is only superficial, but see the redness? It is inflamed, and the salve in the poultice will heal his injury, but it has to be changed frequently. His helmet had a dent the size of a walnut, likely from a heavy lead shot. The slinger must have been very close. The helmet may have saved his life . . . if he survives this inflammation."

His assistant handed the doctor a patch of linen saturated with the oleum rosatum salve. He wrapped it around Bastone's head, holding it in place by tying strips of cloth.

"Is the salve working?" asked Esmeray. "You have given him a fresh poultice several times, and he is no better. And he is in constant pain."

"It will take weeks to heal. And frequent changes of the poultice." He gestured to his assistant. "The *mandragoratum*, please."

He traced a finger across Bastone's forehead, rubbing in a dollop of mandrake paste. "We must use this salve with great care, in small applications."

"Many knights and sailors need my attention across the city. Signora Ponzio, replace his plaster often. Two changes daily, for ten days. You must follow this regimen for him to survive. I will leave the *oleum rosatum* salve with you."

Esmeray nodded.

Simon stepped back from the bed. "Signora, this *mandragoratum* will ease his pain. I will leave this vial, the mandrake, with you, if you promise not to let anyone other than you apply it, exactly as I did. One time per day. Never internally. It would kill him."

"Si, dottore," said Esmeray.

"If he wakes, he should drink plenty of water. He can eat a pottage of milk and wheat. Add honey and serve it hot. When he improves, if he gets dizzy while standing, he should return to bed. The doctor counted off days with his fingers, saying to himself, "This is the seventh day of the month." Then he addressed Esmeray, "I'll return on the *ides* in eight days."

Esmeray changed Bastone's dressing twice per day over the next several days. Awakening from his semi-conscious state, he opened his eyes. Esmeray noticed the pain seemed to worsen now that he was more aware. With each application of mandrake, his pain subsided, but after just a few hours he began moaning again and Esmeray had to stop him from fiddling with his bandage. When she asked him, he remembered nothing of the sea battle with the Pisans.

Bastone improved each day as Esmeray continued to change the poultices. She decided it was time for Aspasia to see her father. Esmeray took a bath and changed into a fresh tunica. To avoid alarming their daughter, she timed the visit just after the effects of the mandrake had dulled Bastone's pain.

Maria Grazia held Aspasia's hand as they entered the bedroom. Aspasia ran to her father and hugged his chest. "Papa!"

He patted her on the head. "My little dolphin. Have you been having fun with your cousins?"

"Yes, Papa."

Bastone's sister smiled, looking at Esmeray.

"And *Zio*. Have you seen your uncle?" said Bastone.

"Can I go see the big walls?"

Bastone and Esmeray shared bewildered glances. Maria Grazia said, "We have been going to Mass at San Lorenzo's. I would have thought the immense cathedral would impress Aspasia, and we visited the waterfront, strolled through the custom house, the beautiful Palace of the Sea. Aspasia was very interested in the variety of ships, but when she saw the gate towers high atop the surrounding hills, she insisted we visit the city walls. Francesco volunteered to take her."

Esmeray was about to decline Aspasia's request when Bastone said, "I'm recovering, Esme. And you need fresh air, no?"

After ascending the narrow, steep streets, they finished the climb up a long flight of stairs to the highest point above the city. Esmeray saw Aspasia was at ease, clasping Francesco's hand as they hiked. Esmeray had some reservations about her brother-in-law's ever-changing moods and kept a watchful eye on him. Francesco's personal guard from the Spinola clan escorted them.

Genoa was founded along the semicircular waterfront of the harbor. As the city grew, the citizens had built their residences stepwise up the slopes to the crests of the encompassing hills, giving the appearance of an amphitheater facing the sea. Along these ridges, over a century earlier, the Genoese had erected new walls, which protected the city from *Barbarossa*, the emperor of the Holy Roman empire, who had ravaged many other Italian city states.

They reached the *Porta Soprana*. The city gate was massive, flanked by two semi-circular barbicans. Appearing heedless of their arrival, a pair of Genoese soldiers manning the gate crouched nearby, playing dice, with helmets and weapons strewn on the ground. Their lack of vigilance was not surprising. There was little pedestrian traffic near the upper city walls. In addition, Genoa had just won an overwhelming victory over Pisa, their archrival, destroying or capturing most of the enemy's fleet. Genoa was no longer on alert.

Pausing in the portal under the towers, Francesco stopped to read aloud the inscription on a plaque. *"I am defended by soldiers and surrounded by amazing walls. If you come in peace, you may touch these doors. If you come looking for war, you will retreat sad and defeated.*"

"What does that mean, *Zio*?" asked Aspasia.

"It means these walls will protect us," said Francesco.

As Esmeray watched them, her thoughts returned to Bastone. She had given the pain medicine to him just before Aspasia arrived, so he was under the influence of the mandrake. Bastone had encouraged them to go on the excursion, but she shouldn't have agreed. Now suddenly, the heat of fear engulfed her. She should have kept Aspasia safe at the house.

The guards looked up from their game, collected their gear, and departed. A band of men, thugs by their menacing look, arrived, fanning out, blocking Francesco and Esmeray's passage through the gateway. Francesco held Aspasia's hand, not showing any sense of alarm. A thug tossed a pouch to Francesco. With one hand, he caught the tiny cloth sack, coins jingling. Francesco stepped back as if offering his niece to the men and gestured toward Esmeray.

Esmeray yanked Aspasia from Francesco, backing toward the wall, clutching her daughter with both arms, as the girl whimpered. Esmeray's eyes were ablaze, her body tensing, as she scanned for a way for them to escape. She snapped her secreted quill knife off her necklace, hiding the blade behind her wrist.

Drawing near, the gang surrounded them. Francesco pointed to Esmeray. "You stole my brother and ruined our family. Take them!" Aspasia sobbed. He tilted his head toward Aspasia, who screamed when the guard moved to grab her. Esmeray stepped in front of her daughter, shielding her, and swung her quill knife, slicing a deep cut in the guard's cheek, forcing him to retreat.

From behind, a thug choked Esmeray with his arm, but she forced her jawbone down, blocking his forearm from crushing her throat, then slashed his arm and jabbed the knife repeatedly into his groin. He groaned, staggering away, bleeding profusely, as the brigands formed a semicircle around Esmeray, her back to the wall.

Francesco stepped back, as did his guard, his cheek bleeding. The man stabbed in the groin was on the ground, holding his hands between his legs on his blood-soaked tunic. Esmeray brandished her tiny blade, backing against the wall, her other hand keeping Aspasia behind her. The girl was sobbing.

They closed in, a thug seizing Aspasia by the wrist. Francesco shouted, "No!" He broke the man's grip, freeing Aspasia. "I'm keeping the girl. Take the woman!" Francesco drew his dagger. Blades flashed, blood spattering as Francesco kept the attackers at bay. Esmeray grabbed Aspasia's hand and fled down the street to the nearby buildings, tugging her daughter along, glancing behind.

A thug broke away from the cluster around Francesco. Knowing she could not outrun him, Esmeray turned and faced the man, keeping Aspasia behind her. He slowed at the sight of her crouching form, knife ready, eyes wild. A mother, ready to protect her daughter at all costs. The hesitation was enough for Francesco to tackle him from behind, stabbing him as they struggled.

Francesco regained his feet. "Run!" He held his ground as the rest of the thugs approached. Esmeray picked up Aspasia and raced down the street toward the city's labyrinth of alleys and steep streets.

Francesco threw the pouch of coins at the attackers, the cloth sack breaking open as it hit the pavement, the metallic ringing drawing their attention. As the brigands scrambled to collect the coins, Francesco retreated to the top of a flight of stairs where the street narrowed.

But the money wasn't enough to satisfy the brigands. They drew close, looking past Francesco, greedily eyeing Esmeray and Aspasia. Esmeray, having difficulty making the descent down the flight of steps carrying her daughter, exhausted, put Aspasia down. The girl was frozen with shock. Esmeray frantically dragged Aspasia along the steps, glancing back at Francesco, confused why he had planned their abduction, then changed his mind. Esmeray was just thankful his love for Aspasia exceeded his hate for her.

The thugs attacked.

Children of the Middle Sea

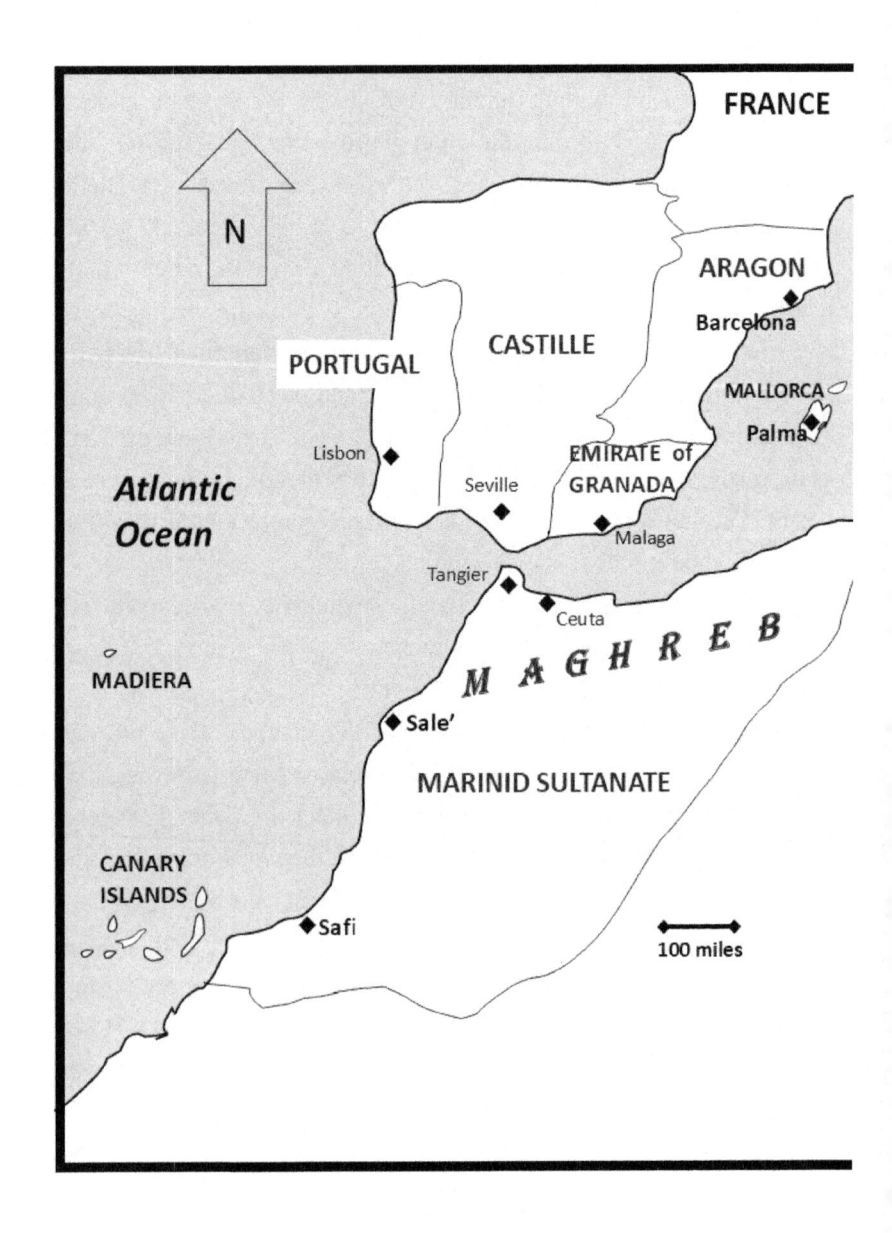

N

FRANCE

ARAGON
- Barcelona

PORTUGAL

CASTILLE

MALLORCA
- Palma

- Lisbon
- Seville

EMIRATE of GRANADA
- Malaga

Atlantic Ocean

- Tangier
- Ceuta

MAGHREB

MADIERA

- Sale'

MARINID SULTANATE

CANARY ISLANDS

- Safi

100 miles

Michael A. Ponzio

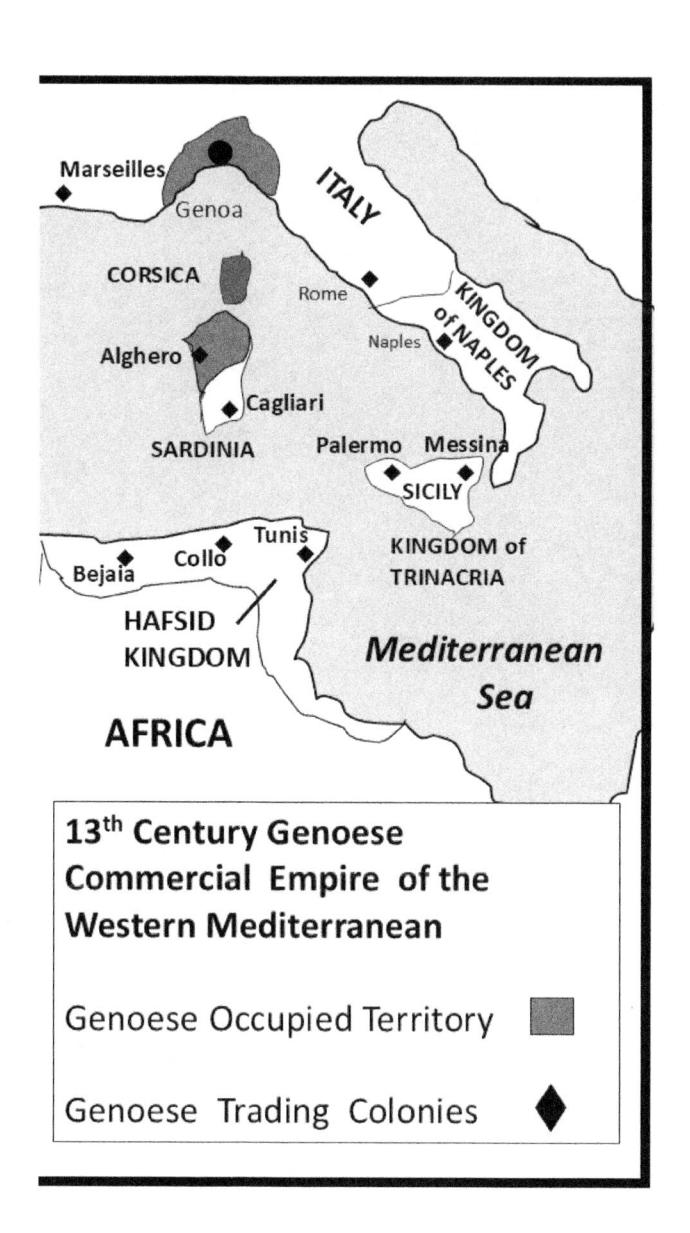

13th Century Genoese Commercial Empire of the Western Mediterranean

Genoese Occupied Territory ▬

Genoese Trading Colonies ◆

CHAPTER XXII

When Bastone had been wounded during the Battle of Meloria, the Genoese fleet had destroyed most of the Pisan navy. As a result, the Hafsids in Africa agreed to a new treaty granting Genoa additional trading rights. The Genoese presented a formal agreement in Tunis, which was certified by the Caliph of the Hafsid Kingdom and Admiral Zaccaria on behalf of the Republic of Genoa.

Mino didn't waste any time procuring a copy of the treaty in both Arabic and Latin. He loaded the holds of the *Giovanna* and her sister ship, the *Lucia,* captained by Mino's nephew, Cardo, with wine, lacquer, aloe, linen, and alum, and sailed for Africa.

Now, as the ships rounded the last cape before the open sea to Africa, Mino gazed from the stern castle. He pondered taking high risks with this new commercial venture amidst the political turmoil and dangers of war, not questioning, but solidifying his decision, exhilarated with the gamble. He was headed for Bejaia, a bustling port, ranked second only to Tunis, the capital of the Hafsid Kingdom. The city was an important trade center for the region known as the *Maghreb,* which stretched across North Africa.

After a two-day crossing, the sister ships reached Tunis, offloaded cargo, loaded more goods, and set sail for Bejaia in the evening. Below him on the deck was his wife Giovanna, conversing with the Genoese merchants and their families. These colonists had boarded the ship in

Tunis to emigrate to Bejaia. Mino planned to expand the Genoese *fondaco*, the merchants' quarter. For many years, Pisa had maintained close trading arrangements with the Emir of Bejaia and had developed a sizable fondaco. Mino's plans would challenge the Pisans' dominance of trade with the city.

He descended to the deck, catching his wife's eye as she socialized, and gestured with a tilt of his head for her to join him as he entered the captain's suite. Stepping over the raised threshold, the petite woman still had to duck to enter, joining him in the cabin. Mino embraced her, taking his time to place a slow, warm kiss on her yielding lips.

"Mmm, so, you cannot wait until tonight?" said Giovanna, holding him close, her fingers running through his dark hair.

Mino gave her an affectionate squeeze, a quick kiss, and held her at arm's length. He gently released her. "Let's review the Hafsid treaty again. The caliph in Tunis approved the treaty, but the emir who rules Bejaia must also agree. I want to know it well enough to answer the emir's questions."

Giovanna rolled her eyes but added a genuine smile. "Fine."

He retrieved the Latin copy of the Hafsid-Genoese treaty of 1287 and placed it on the table, pulling over a stool to study the details of the document. As he read over the conditions once more, Mino contemplated the agreement's impact. The establishment of a large fondaco in Bejaia had the potential to increase his trading opportunities and make him very wealthy.

Three days later, an hour after sunrise, Mino was finishing breakfast in his cabin with his wife, when they heard the watchman call out from the crow's nest, "Ahoy, Bejaia!" They went on deck for their first view of the town. The sheltered harbor was on the western end of the Gulf of Bejaia. Hemmed in by the Tell Atlas Mountains running parallel to the Mediterranean Sea, the town was a verdant oasis, receiving plentiful rainfall. Cedars, pines, and cork oak trees covered the upper slopes. Below, the Hafsids had planted the hills with orchards of olive and fig trees, as well as fields of rye and wheat. Beyond this maritime range was a plateau where goats and cattle fed on dry grasses. The Hafsid people exploited these resources for export from Bejaia. Beyond the plateau was a second range, the Saharan Atlas Mountains, a barrier from the vast desert.

After docking, Mino watched the crew use the mast booms as cranes to transfer the containers of goods to the wharf. As he surveyed the other ships at port, most flying the Hafsid flag, he thought of his friend Bastone. Waving in the breeze, the kingdom's banner displayed a crossbow on a red field.

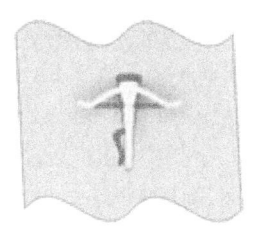

His wife, the ship's scribe, was tallying the shipment. As the sacks of alum were unloaded, she said, "I remember stopping at Vulcano to load the alum. And we brought Florentine and Genoese linen? Does anyone here use the alum for weaving or dyeing?"

"There are a few. Bejaia exports hides and wool that are made into clothing in Italy. But my plans include making cloth here at the trading colony, with Genoese tradespeople."

Giovanna finished counting the bales of linen and entered the numbers into the logbook with her quill. The sailors were hoisting barrels and smaller casks of wine to the dock. After several minutes, she asked, "And wine? It looks like the European merchants here drink quite a lot!"

Mino spoke under his breath, "Many Muslims here drink wine, although their religion bans the practice. And if caught drinking wine, a Muslim can receive forty lashes."

They transferred the goods to donkey carts. The Genoese colonists disembarked, the women covering their heads and wearing linen veils.

In Sicily, Giovanna always covered her hair while at the castle and in public, but she now added a veil to follow the local custom. She wore a lavender veil and head covering to brighten her woad blue tunica. Mino recalled her saying if she must conform to the Hafsid traditions, she would enjoy choosing an attractive head dress and veil. A year ago, Mino would have never thought of getting married, and definitely not of bringing a woman along on a trading voyage. But now as he glanced at Giovanna, as always, her appearance stirred and comforted him. But would her presence affect his sharp-edged trading abilities?

Leaving the waterfront, the ship's party led the donkey train through narrow streets, arriving at a roofed, open-air building. Mino and his crew set up their wares and he directed the Genoese colonists to continue to the fondaco. Giovanna watched the market activities with fascination. Hafsids and Europeans played chess on boards placed on crates. Groups of sailors rolled dice, betting, and cheering. Food stalls drew crowds of hungry merchants. The colorful spices and clothes contrasted with the mud walls and dusty pavement.

"Mino, it's thrilling to be in the souk's hubbub and activity!"

"Yes, it's exciting, but this market is not the Arab bazaar. It is called the *dugana*—the custom house—the only place we can trade, except, of course, at the fondaco. Foreigners may not trade at the souk, and the emir discourages us from even visiting."

"Well, we can't go to the souk, but perhaps the souk has come to us?"

Mino smiled, noting her enthusiasm appeared undeterred.

An interpreter arrived from the Genoese fondaco on Mino's behalf. The local merchants and buyers engaged him and began negotiating prices. Giovanna stayed out of the way, several steps behind Mino as he negotiated, but ready to tally any transactions. When the local officials arrived, requesting the taxes due for the import of goods, she confirmed the sum of money with her own calculations. Bejaia leaders welcomed European traders because they provided a significant income for the government through taxes and custom duties.

The trading went well, but near sunset they loaded what goods they had kept as well as those gained and headed to the fondaco. Giovanna walked beside her husband as he spoke to the interpreter.

"Your excellent Genoese has a slight Catalan accent." said Mino.

"You are quite perceptive, Captain. My family is from Andalusia. We came here because of the wars in Spain.

"Do you live at the fondaco?"

"No, in the city."

"You are Muslim?"

"I am Christian. My family came to Bejaia to flee the violence."

Mino's eyebrows raised. "Despite being Christian, is your family better off here than in Christian Spain?"

"The Catholics taking over Spain restricted our faith practices. They said we were doing it wrong. But here, we are *dhimmi,* protected people, because we have submitted to Muslim rule over us. They allow us to practice our religion, discreetly."

They approached the southwest city gate, *Bab el Kasbah*. Looming above them to their right was the Kasbah of Bejaia, the emir's palace and citadel, its stone walls tinted a faint orange in the sunlight. Upon entering the gate, the guide pointed at a group of buildings a few hundred feet away. "European merchants like you have the emir's protection as long as you follow the rules, stay in your compound, and leave only for trading at the *dugana,* or boarding your ship."

The Pisan fondaco occupied the greater part of the foreign merchant quarter, containing warehouses, outdoor ovens, a bathhouse, workshops, a church, and houses. Bordering the Pisan compound were the smaller Genoese, Sicilian, and Catalan fondacos.

They reached the Genoese fondaco, consisting of only one building, divided into living quarters for a single family and for storage. There was not enough space to accommodate the goods Mino had brought with him. A low wall made of dried clay surrounded the building, creating a small courtyard which included fig trees and an outdoor bread oven. The score of colonists from Tunis would have to camp outside the walls until they built new houses.

The next morning, Mino and his men went to the custom house market to buy fabric for the colonists' shelters. Not finding any pieces large enough for tents, he went to the wharf and bought sailcloth from an artisan. To Mino's misfortune, the harbor master stopped them as they were returning to the fondaco and took him before the emir. He had conducted business outside the customs house and fondaco. The emir fined Mino and warned him that another violation would endanger his permission to trade in Bejaia. Mino didn't plan on committing a second infraction or even returning to Bejaia. Esmeray and Bastone had agreed to take over command of the *Giovanna*. He had a surprise for them when he returned to Sicily, planning to persuade them to manage the expansion of the Genoese fondaco in Bejaia as well.

CHAPTER XXIII

Riding in the dinghy next to her mother, Aspasia cradled a wicker basket in her lap. Although the sea swells were modest, the prisoner in the basket carried on with sorrowful wails. As a sailor rowed, the rhythmic creaking from the oarlocks penetrated the cat's moans. "Mamma, Ciciri is scared of the water."

"She'll be better when we get on the ship, Delfinina."

They reached the *Giovanna* anchored in the harbor at Favignana. There was a dull thump as the dinghy bumped the ship's hull in the light chop. A sailor dropped a knotted rope from the ship's deck. The oarsman snatched the wavering line and tied it to the basket. As a crew member hoisted the cat to the deck, it protested with loud yowls.

A crewman lowered the rope again. Esmeray braced her feet against the hull, pulling herself up and climbed onto the deck. Next, Aspasia clung to the oarsman's back, her arms around his neck, and he ascended the hull. Halfway up, Esmeray said, "Sailor, halt. Aspasia, grab the line and climb the rest of the way."

"Mamma!"

Esmeray was confident Aspasia would be strong enough. She had been helping her parents pull the lines to haul in their fishing traps for over a year. Usually, her daughter was fearless and would have welcomed a new challenge, but Esmeray guessed the absence of her father had troubled Aspasia.

Esmeray stood above on the deck, hands on hips. "You said you wanted to be a sailor. Board the ship like one."

The girl pulled herself up and stood on the oarsman's shoulders. She grabbed the knots hand over hand, using her feet against the hull. When she reached the deck, Aspasia hurried over to the basket.

The first mate directed the crew to hoist the dinghy on board. Esmeray glanced beyond the stern to make sure they had already secured her fishing boat in tow, then addressed the first mate, "Get underway."

Aspasia's cat, Ciciri, stopped yowling, but stayed in the basket peering over the edge across the deck. After zigzagging around the scrambling feet of the crew, the resident mouser, a black and white cat, drew near, halting several feet from the basket, peering and sniffing. Instead of hissing at the newcomer, he exchanged slow blinks with Ciciri.

Three days later at sea, Esmeray stood atop the stern castle, speaking with the helmsman, who was piloting the ship toward Messina. Having turned over the command of the ship to Esmeray, Giovanna and Mino were sleeping late in their suite, as they had been doing the last few days, serious about starting a family and settling down when they arrived at Messina.

Esmeray wore baggy sailor pants, gathered at the knees, over stockings. She also wore a loose linen shirt and a maroon *bag hat*, which distinguished her from the crew who had either knitted watch caps or cotton head rags in woad blue.

The bag hat draped down the back of her neck, enclosing Esmeray's long hair. In cooler weather, she added a dull red waistcoat. At night, when virtually alone on the deck of the stern castle, she removed her bag hat, letting her hair fly in the wind. When she went ashore, she would change to a long tunica, add a waistcoat, plus leather shoes, and tuck her hair into her hat.

Esmeray watched Aspasia return from the bow where the girl had emptied the chamber pots at the head. Aspasia had been quiet since they had left Palermo, and she wondered if her daughter missed her father. Keeping her busy might help. "Aspasia, did you bucket sea water through the lattice at the head?"

The girl looked up, "Yea."

"What's that, sailor?" Esmeray had instructed the girl to address her as captain when around the crew.

"*Si, Capitanu*, yes!"

Aspasia ran up the steps to the top of the stern castle. Esmeray stood, arms folded. "And?"

"Permission at the stern castle, Captain."

Esmeray smiled. "Granted." She could see tears about to flow.

"I miss Papa."

Esmeray turned to the helmsman. "Stay the course. First mate has command while I am in my cabin."

"Si, Capitanu," said the helmsman.

Esmeray put her arm around her daughter's shoulder, leading her to the captain's suite below.

The crew had accepted Esmeray as captain primarily because the first mate had approved which was a critical hurdle. She didn't want to lose respect while being a mother in front of the crew. She was relieved that Aspasia had not sobbed on deck, but held her tears until they entered the captain's suite.

Aspasia and her mother had agreed to keep Ciciri in the cabin until the cat acclimated to her new surroundings. Weeping, Aspasia moved to the bed and petted Ciciri, who had awakened from dozing. Her mother sat next to her, knowing at this moment, the cat would help her more than her words could. Esmeray recalled horrors from her own childhood, but she had grown resilient, eventually healing with the love of her father. Now her daughter was coping with traumatic events. The thugs had assaulted them in Genoa. And then there was the funeral.

Esmeray remembered something her Sicilian midwife had recited. *Na bona matri vali centu maestri*—a good mother is worth a hundred teachers. Esmeray was determined to stay strong after the terrible events in Genoa and to help Aspasia recover her adventurous spirit.

Michael A. Ponzio

Three Capes of Sicily

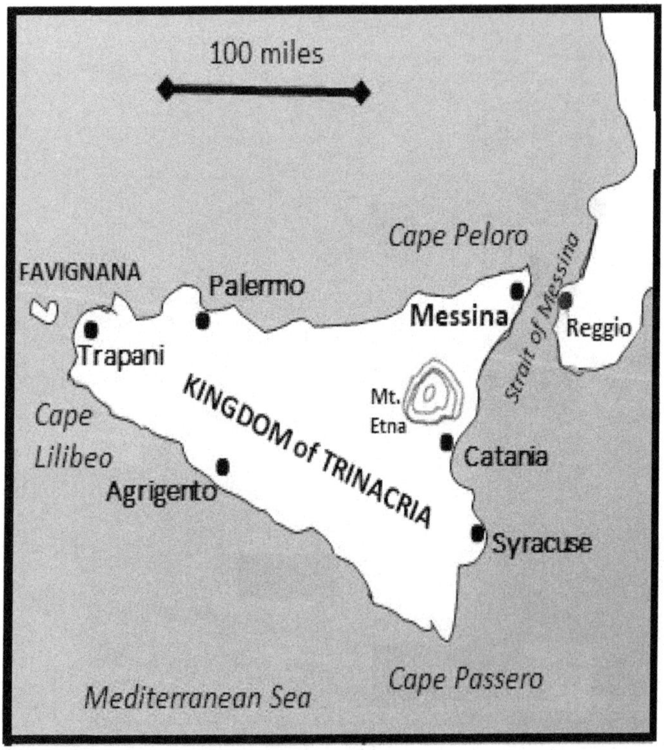
100 miles
Cape Peloro
FAVIGNANA
Palermo
Messina
Strait of Messina
Reggio
Trapani
KINGDOM of TRINACRIA
Mt.
Etna
Cape
Lilibeo
Catania
Agrigento
Syracuse
Mediterranean Sea
Cape Passero

CHAPTER XXIV

One week after leaving Favignana, the *Giovanna* sailed at night along the north coast of Sicily, guided by the mistral winds. The helmsman on shift, assisted by a handful of watches, navigated toward Messina. The *Lucia* followed, the helmsman sailing within sight of a pair of lanterns hanging at the taffrail of the *Giovanna*.

Yearning for Bastone, insomnia plagued Esmeray. Leaving her daughter asleep in the cabin, she climbed the stairs to the stern castle, nodded at the helmsman, and continued further aft to the taffrail. She removed her hat to free her hair in the wind. In tow was the *Aspasia*, the fishing boat which she had built with her father and named after her mother. Esmeray thought of Bastone again, recalling when they had traveled hundreds of sea miles on her cherished boat.

She surrendered herself to the salty smell and taste of the air, her long tresses billowing in the unceasing wind. These sensations had always distracted her from melancholy thoughts. Tonight, absent was the hubbub of the crew, allowing her to appreciate the music created by the elements. The wind whistled, and the ropes creaked among the rigging, accompanied by rhythmic splashes on the hull and the snap of flags rippling at the masts. This music consoled her for an hour of formless meditation. Her thoughts clearing, she was about to return to her cabin when the clouds veiling the full moon drifted apart. The brilliance of the moon reminded Esmeray of her wedding night.

Bastone had told her of the vow he'd made to himself during one of his sea voyages. One night on watch in the crow's nest, he'd become entranced by the music of sailing, heightened by the beauty of the full moon. But he had realized what was missing. It was someone to share his love of the sea. As he confessed that finding her had made it all perfect, she had shed tears—as she did now because of his absence. Finally, she grew weary, returning to her cabin to sleep.

In the morning, crewmembers served Esmeray and Aspasia breakfast at the midship galley. The sailors had boiled the dried pasta, which kept well in storage, in a mixture of half seawater and half fresh water. Today, they added chickpeas, which preserved well on the voyages. After they finished their pasta, mother and daughter stood atop the stern castle. The two ships approached the Cape of Peloro, the northeast point of Sicily, also called Punta del Faru. Using her hand to shade her eyes, examining the coast, Esmeray said to the helmsman at the steering board, "I see the tower." Aspasia leaned on the taffrail nearby, gazing at the landmark, a stone tower in ruins.

"Si, Capitanu. Yes, that's it," said the helmsman in Sicilian.

Esmeray recalled that years earlier when she had been a sailor on a large trading ship all the sailors had spoken Genoese. She had learned the crew's language, which was very different from her native Greek. Now, her crew spoke primarily in Messinese, a dialect of the Sicilian language, the native tongue of most of the forty-man crew. While she was pregnant living in Messina, she had learned the local dialect so now she could converse with the Sicilian sailors on the *Giovanna* who were from Palermo or Catania. And although Genoese and Sicilian had both descended from Latin, the handful of the crew from Genoa had struggled to understand Sicilian, which included Arabic, Greek, and Norman French words. But the Genoese had adapted. Mino had also found a handful of Christian sailors in Bejaia, immigrants from Andalusia, who had fled the Christian-Muslim wars. They spoke Pisan and Arabic because of the century-long presence of the Pisan fondaco in Bejaia.

A flash of anxiety passed through Esmeray as her thoughts returned to the Genoese sailors in the crew. Two were brothers from the Spinola clan. They must certainly remember their family had alleged that Bastone murdered their kinsman years ago. But the accusation was false; Bastone had seen the Spinola man's own cousins kill him. Esmeray had inherited the crew from Mino and couldn't get rid of the Spinolas without reason. The brothers were from a prominent family and both valuable arbalesters. And how would it affect the crew? She would keep close watch on the pair.

Esmeray was an expert in sailing dynamics but was still learning about navigating long distances. She thanked the helmsman, saying, "Grazzi, sailor, for your guidance. We'll round the cape here."

All hands were on deck. She cupped her hands, shouting to the crew, "Prepare to come about!" The sailors headed for their stations at the rigging and sails. Seeing the crew in position, Esmeray shouted, "Come about now! *Aviri li mura a sinistra*—tack to port!"

The first mate used his salty language to encourage the deckhands working the ship's ropes. The crew worked hard and fast, adjusting the sails and changing the ship's direction towards the southwest to sail parallel to the Sicilian coast.

Esmeray turned to the helmsman. "Your timing is excellent! You were right. The current in the strait has shifted toward the south. *Benissimu*—very good!"

"Si, Capitanu."

His dutiful manner and the crew's respect for her as captain, even without Bastone's support, should have buoyed her mood. Instead, again, she was reminded of her husband's absence.

Esmeray glanced over her shoulder. The *Lucia* was performing the same maneuver. As a sailor, she had come through this strait several times. She recalled the first passage while sailing on the *Paradisio*, a large *navi mercantili* with twice the capacity of the *Giovanna*. Upon intercepting one of the frequent whirlpools, the ship had twisted and turned in the vortex, timbers creaking with protest. Noticing that the phenomena had unsettled Esmeray, the sailors had tried to frighten her, saying that the whirlpool heralded sea monsters. She, however, had found the jest amusing and had enjoyed the thrilling ride across the whirlpool. The *Paradisio* had never been in danger of sinking.

Her daughter pointed to the landmark at the cape, the ruins of a stone tower. "Mamma, is that a lighthouse? Like in Genoa?"

When Esmeray hesitated to answer, the helmsman said, "*Signurina* Aspasia, you have been to Genoa? That is so far! You are a brave sailor like your mother?" He glanced at Esmeray, her smile telling him to continue. "Yes, long ago the tower was a *faru*, a lighthouse built by the Romans. Now the tower helps sailors from crashing on the sandbars."

Esmeray appreciated the helmsman's manner with Aspasia, remembering Bastone's fatherly mentorship. But she couldn't rid herself of the empty feelings that emerged with virtually every thought, every action, every turn since Bastone had gone. She missed her husband terribly.

However, remembering what she had recited to her daughter the night before now calmed her. They had sailed under the clear night sky, filled with the wonder of thousands of bright stars. It was a quote from Marcus Aurelius's *Treatise to Himself*, which Esmeray had been using to educate Aspasia. *"To watch the course of the stars as if you revolved with them. To keep constantly in mind how the elements alter into one another. Thoughts like this wash off the mud of life below."*

Sailing now, with the tides shifting in their favor, the ships made it from Cape Peloro to Messina in an hour. They entered the harbor by midmorning and the fishing fleet had already been out and returned with their catch, the fishers setting up the market along the wharf. The crew of *Giovanna* docked the ship and secured the lines. They began transferring the trade goods to shore—terra cotta amphorae of honey, wax, and bails of hides they had shipped from Bejaia in the Hafsid Kingdom of Africa. The *Lucia* anchored in the harbor, waiting for a space on the wharf.

A squeal from the stern castle pierced the commotion of the busy waterfront. "Papa!"

The gangplank sprung up and down, creaking under Bastone as he boarded the *Giovanna*. His daughter bounded down the stairs from the stern castle to the main deck. Despite wanting to follow, Esmeray held back in front of the crew.

She was complete once again. In the past, she claimed that her sole requirements in life were the sea, Bastone, and her boat. Now her world included Aspasia.

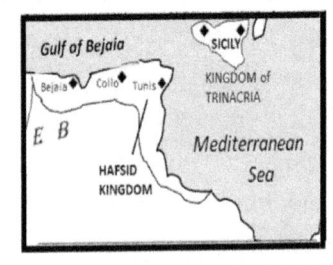

Children of the Middle Sea

Gulf of Bejaia

SICILY
KINGDOM of TRINACRIA
Bejaia • Collo • Tunis
HAFSID KINGDOM
Mediterranean Sea

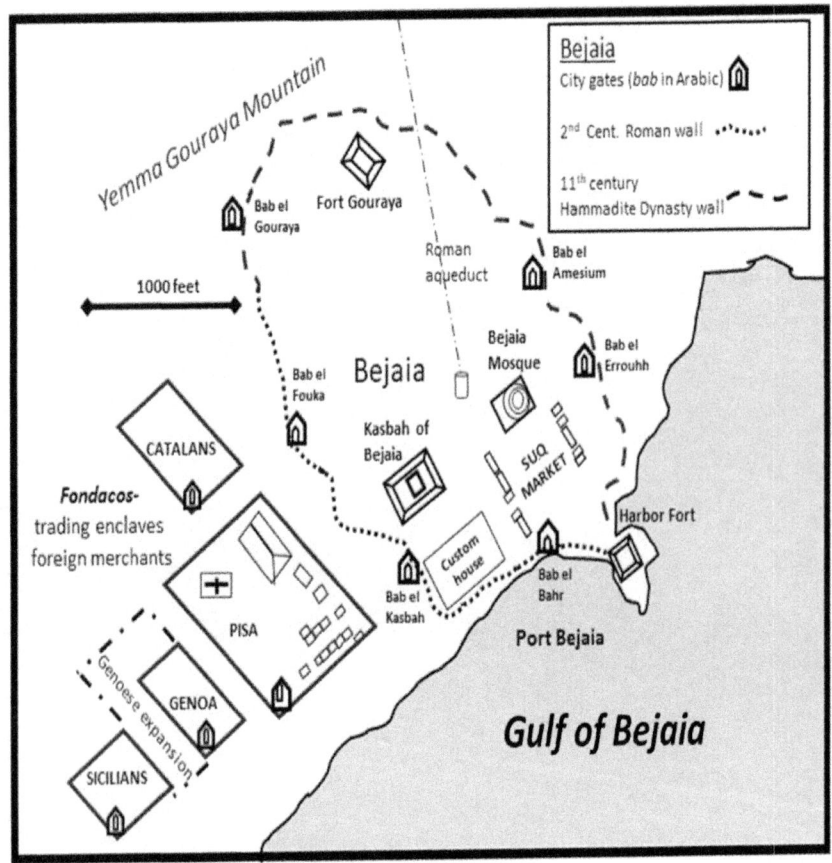

Bejaia
City gates (*bab* in Arabic)
2nd Cent. Roman wall
11th century Hammadite Dynasty wall

Yemma Gouraya Mountain

Bab el Gouraya
Fort Gouraya
Roman aqueduct
Bab el Amesium
1000 feet
Bab el Fouka
Bejaia
Bejaia Mosque
Bab el Errouhh
CATALANS
Kasbah of Bejaia
SUQ MARKET
Fondacos – trading enclaves foreign merchants
Harbor Fort
PISA
Custom house
Bab el Kasbah
Bab el Bahr
Port Bejaia
Genoese expansion
GENOA
SICILIANS

Gulf of Bejaia

204

CHAPTER XXV

The next day, the *Giovanna,* loaded with barrels of wine, departed Messina accompanied by the *Lucia,* its hold packed with finished cloth. The vessels sailed north through the straits, then northwest to Isola Vulcano, where the islanders mined alum. Esmeray, captain of the *Giovanna,* stood on the stern castle alone in thought, gazing across the seas, enthused to be at sea piloting the large vessel. Despite facing bias for being a woman, she triumphed through intelligence and hard work. She had to stay alert and fight for her place in the world. Before, there had only been Bastone supporting her, but now she was reassessing her world. There was also hope for her daughter's future if there were more men like Mino. He respected her and her abilities enough to hire her as captain and leader of the trading voyage.

When they arrived at Vulcano, waiting for them on the dock were 200 bags of crystalline alum, used to fix color when dyeing cloth. After the sailors unloaded a portion of the wine, they looped a rope over the mizzen mast boom, tied batches of the bags to the line and hoisted them over the main hatch, lowering them into the *Giovanna's* hold. Each bag, tightly woven of hemp, contained one *cantarium,* a measure equal to 117 pounds of alum.

After two days at sea sailing to Palermo, the ship no longer smelled. There, the crew stowed wooden casks filled with olive oil in the *Giovanna's* hold. Now packed with trading goods, the *Giovanna* and *Lucia* crossed the open sea to Bejaia.

Plying the seas toward the southwest, Esmeray enjoyed the salty wind atop the stern castle. She watched Bastone drill the arbalesters. Over time, they increased their shooting rate from two to three bolts per minute. He had issued them round shields, a light and maneuverable design he had seen used by the Catalan crossbowmen at the battle in Malta.

Many states in both cultures sanctioned corsairs to raid and plunder foreign lands and ships. Muslim and Christian pirates were always a threat on the open sea, but Esmeray was confident they could fight off an attack.

As Esmeray watched the men train, she saw her daughter returning from one of her chores as cabin boy, emptying chamber pots and washing down the head with buckets of seawater. She called, "Aspasia. After you finish, grab two of the belaying pins and come up here."

Esmeray entertained Aspasia with a game of tossing belaying pins. The club shaped batons, inserted at the ship railing to secure rigging, were also used by the sailors as weapons. After gaining her attention with the game of catch, Esmeray taught her daughter how to use the clubs to defend herself.

The next day, Bastone issued the arbalesters a second crossbow. Sailors were paired with each arbalester and practiced cocking and loading the spare bow between simulated volleys.

During the days at sea, Aspasia also studied the crew in action, learning how they worked together to sail the large ship. Her mother warned her to avoid distracting the crew, saving her questions for later, and to never be alone with any of the crew.

The third day out of Palermo, Esmeray noted she had not seen Aspasia in a while. Not finding her in their cabin, Esmeray was perturbed she didn't see Aspasia on deck. None of the crew members had seen her. She remembered a few times her daughter had gone below, looking for the cats. When she got to midship, she heard the strum of Aspasia's *oud*, a stringed instrument popular in North Africa. The music came from the hold. One of the Spinola brothers was sitting on the hatch, the sliding door cracked open. He was pulling fibers from remnants of rope, a customary duty for sailors. The fibers were spun to make yarn for mending sails.

Esmeray halted in front of the man. He looked up, continuing to pull apart the rope.

"Sailor, get up!"

He leisurely stood and moved aside, spitting on the deck.

Her eyes narrowed.

He responded in a monotone voice, "Scusi, Capitano."

Esmeray refrained from thrashing him for his insolence, controlling herself, knowing sailors must be disciplined in front of the crew. She slid the hatch door open, glaring at him as she descended the ladder into the hold. He leered at her, prompting her to climb back onto the deck, halting inches from him, her face tilted up to his. His odorous breath was overpowering. She glanced around. The first mate and crewmembers on deck were not looking her way. Careful not to attract attention, Esmeray placed her left hand gently on his shoulder as if to give him friendly advice, then smashed her knee into the man's groin. He let out a subdued groan, his eyes watering, as he hunched over, but recovered, biting his lip.

"Don't ever look at me that way again," she said, teeth clenched. He could not reply.

Esmeray descended into the hold. "Mamma!" Several paces along the keel were Aspasia, holding her oud, a cat next to her, and the other Spinola brother.

"Sailor!" shouted Esmeray. "What in God's bones are you doing down here?"

The cat fled. The man held up rope remnants. "Getting more ropes, Capitano." The Spinolas stubbornly spoke in Genoese, instead of Sicilian.

"Aspasia . . . ?" Esmeray assumed the worst. Reacting right now would not correct the problem to keep her daughter safe. She simply said, "Sailor, get back on deck. Aspasia, come to the cabin."

Esmeray called Bastone to their suite, asking Aspasia what had happened below deck. Aspasia denied being touched by the sailor. He had only asked about the cat. Esmeray and Bastone traded wary glances, their eyes narrowing in agreement. They reminded her not to be alone with any of the sailors.

Esmeray matched Bastone's grim look. Had the Spinola brothers planned on harming Aspasia? If it was an innocent coincidence, and they punished the brothers now without evidence, the crew wouldn't like it and the siblings would seek revenge. Esmeray informed the first mate about the incident, and he stated the Spinolas have had to be disciplined before. She instructed him to keep an eye on the brothers and told him that the Spinolas be assigned different shifts and never be scheduled for a night watch.

Later that evening, as Aspasia slept in the captain's suite, Esmeray and Bastone leaned on the ship's rail, alone at the stern. The ship's wake trailed the *Giovanna,* the froth of the spreading waves gleaming in the light of the gibbous moon. Bastone put his arm around Esmeray's shoulder. "Is this your dream, Esme?"

She kissed him lightly. "It is beyond my dreams, Bastonino." Her elbow on the rail, she turned toward him. "Our little Delfinina is safe. You are here. We are at sea."

The wind whistled through the rigging, masts creaked, and waves splashed against the hull. They gazed at each other, the rolling of the deck and the music of a ship at sea, comforting.

"And we have more challenges than we expected now that Mino tricked us! *Que forbu*—what a character!" Glancing behind, she thought the helmsman might have heard her outburst, and softened her voice. "We had agreed only to take over the *Giovanna*, but he added enlarging the fondaco, knowing it was vital to make the trading expeditions to Bejaia successful."

She embraced him, whispering in his ear so the helmsman would not hear. "When you stayed in Genoa to grieve with your family for your brother and father, I was confident in my command as captain, knowing you would return to us."

Bastone laughed. "Esme, you are a skilled captain, and the officers, as well as the crew, respect you." Her stare was penetrating. "Um . . . like the way you are now. You can stand up for yourself."

Her face softened into a smile. "Yes, Bastonino, but our greatest strengths come about when we act as partners."

A memory of their time in Genoa pierced her happiness. The attack's horror surfaced again, heat rising within her. Francesco's sacrifice had enabled Esmeray and Aspasia to escape, but then Bastone's father had died, heartbroken when he'd learned of Francesco's death.

Bastone's words brought her back. "Esme, I will hire a builder to supervise the construction of the fondaco so I can be at sea with you."

Esmeray placed her hand on his. "And we can share the pleasure of watching Aspasia grow and experience life."

The next morning when they docked at Tunis, Esmeray and Aspasia remained on board the *Giovanna*. Bastone supervised delivery of the olive oil to the customs house. To meet the *halal* standards of the Quran, the Muslim customers poured the oil into their own containers. Bastone returned the empty terra cotta jugs to the hold.

Leaving Tunis, they sailed along the North African coast for three days, reaching the Gulf of Bejaia early in the morning. The cloudless shoreline of the gulf curved in front of them, and the Atlas Mountains, which had been off their portside, now loomed ahead of the *Giovanna's* bow. Aspasia, with her parents at the stern castle, studied the town of Bejaia glowing in the morning sun. With the port nearing, Esmeray had already changed from her trousers into a long tunica in her favorite color, blue from the woad plant. She wore her maroon hat and would add a veil before going ashore.

As the ship approached the harbor, Aspasia pointed. "Will we live there? The houses climb the hill, like in Genoa. And the mountains are green, not like the brown hills in Favignana."

Esmeray left the first mate in charge of the *Giovanna* once the crew had unloaded the goods onto donkey carts. Bastone dispatched a messenger to the Genoese fondaco for an interpreter to meet him at the customs house. He and his family, along with a pair of arbalesters, entered the town through the waterfront gate, *Bab el Bahr*. Directly ahead, bordered by the mosque and lined with shops, was the city market—the souk. The recent arrival of a caravan heightened the usual bustle of activity. The Berbers, dressed in their flowing robes to protect them from the Saharan sun, led a camel train. Many of the camels were saddled with evenly cut slabs of salt, creating a balanced load.

European traders were prohibited from doing business in the souk. Instead, Bastone turned towards the custom house with a train of donkey carts following him. They soon reached an open-air roofed structure, providing shade from the July sun. Bastone set up his wares and Esmeray and Aspasia sat waiting, sipping from a waterskin. The breeze off the sea was warm but soothing. The translator arrived from the Genoese fondaco, introducing the emir's officials to Bastone, and he paid the import taxes. Then he began negotiating with local merchants to trade goods.

Within several minutes, the Pisan merchants glared darkly at Bastone and his men, openly displaying their contempt at the Genoese and Sicilians' presence. A few Pisans went out of their way, intentionally bumping and elbowing Bastone as he moved around looking for customers. The body contact was not the incidental jostling and bumping typical in Genoa and other cities. Bastone did not react, knowing the local authorities would likely blame the confrontation on him as a newcomer.

The Hafsid authorities did not prohibit foreigners from visiting their market at the souk, but they discouraged them. But Hafsids freely roamed through the *dugana*, the customs house market, selling their wares. A smiling vendor hawked grilled chicken on a stick. Esmeray waved him over to distract Aspasia before she could notice the harsh behavior of the Pisans. She pulled out a silver penny and offered it. The vendor appeared displeased, speaking in an irritated tone in Arabic. "This should be enough," said Esmeray.

The interpreter, nearby, noticed, and he handed a coin to the vendor, who smiled and moved on. The interpreter said, "Scusi, Signora Ponzio, forgive me for not helping you sooner."

"What was wrong?" asked Esmeray.

"Your penny. It is Messinese. Most vendors will take any silver money. But he must have been a very devout Muslim. He wouldn't take the money because Muslims do not allow images on their coins, especially of people."

Aspasia finished eating. "Can I see?"

Esmeray showed her a couple of Messinese silver coins, each about the size of a thumbnail. One had the eagle of Messina stamped on it. "This one has a bird," said Aspasia as she held it up. "There's a man in a hat on this one."

"That's King James of Sicily," said her mother, "wearing his crown."

Aspasia looked at the interpreter expectantly, who pulled out a Hafsid silver coin and handed it to the girl. She examined both sides. "What are the scrabbly lines?"

"They are letters," said the man.

"I am learning letters, but . . ." She looked confused.

Esmeray said, "They are the letters the people use here in Bejaia."

"Oh."

The interpreter offered the girl the coin. "You can have this one."

"That's kind, Signore," said Esmeray, "but please, here." She traded the Messinese coin for the Hafsid money. "A fair exchange?"

He nodded, smiling, "Si, Signora. One Hafsid dinar for one Messinese denaro."

A smile of satisfaction spread across Esmeray's face that her daughter's first encounter in Bejaia had been friendly. Moreover, she was relieved that Aspasia had not seen the aggressive behavior of the Pisan merchants or, even worse, violence.

Bastone and his family headed to the Genoese fondaco. They passed under the archway of the Bab el Kasbah, the southwest city gate, and paused just outside the walls, waiting for Aspasia, who had stopped a few steps back to examine a stone plaque at the gate.

A hundred paces outside the city walls was the sprawling Pisan fondaco, the size of a small village. A tower rose above the ten-foot stone walls, but there was no cross or bell at the top. The Hafsids allowed the Christians to worship as they wanted inside the fondacos, but they prohibited the display of crosses or the ringing of church bells.

Esmeray queried Bastone, "When we passed the souk, I saw that the caravan had brought salt. So Mino figures he can compete with the local trade?"

Bastone chuckled, "Mino. What a merchant he is! During his visit to Bejaia, he learned the details of the salt trade. The tribe of nomadic herders, Berbers, live on the plateau beyond the hills. They travel south across the great desert and trade for salt at the Taghaza mine, hundreds of miles away. It is surprising the Berbers bring *any* salt to Bejaia if the tale Mino told me is true. There is a kingdom south of the salt mines called Mali, where the merchants trade gold—pound for pound—for salt. Most of the desert-mined salt goes south, with little reaching Bejaia. Mino will seize the opportunity."

"Mamma, look! I know these letters." Aspasia was holding up the coin the interpreter had given her, comparing the Arabic script to the Latin engraving on the plaque. "This sign has our letters, not the ones on this coin." Aspasia read out loud, "Ga . . . Gaius . . . Mamma, read it . . . please."

Esmeray translated the inscription on the plaque, *"Town counselor of Saldae, Gaius Cornelius Peregrinus, dedicates this gate to Imperator Gaius Aurelius Valerius Diocletianus."*

Aspasia appeared puzzled.

Bastone said, "The Romans built the wall and dedicated it to their um . . . their king."

Aspasia raised her eyebrows. "The Romans built it. Like the old lighthouse we saw?"

Esmeray gently placed her hand on the girl's shoulder. "Excellent memory, Delfinina."

They passed the Pisan walled enclave, arriving at the gate to the Genoese fondaco, which faced the sea. A few hundred paces more along the shore, merchants from Sicily occupied another fondaco. Between the two enclaves were tents where the Genoese colonists were living until they built permanent houses. Bastone entered the gate to the fondaco with his family, as the donkey train loaded with the goods he had bartered followed.

They came to the largest house in the fondaco, its lime-plastered walls brilliant in the sun. The gabled roof was covered in terra cotta tiles. A man and a woman exited the house which was the fondaco's residence, office, and warehouse. As they approached them, the man gestured for the donkey handlers to take their carts to the newly built warehouse to unload. The colonists had recently completed a few smaller cottages nearby, inside the walls, with flat roofs in the local style.

The man and woman hurried toward them, both smiling and extending their arms wide. Esmeray was sure they were the couple that managed the fondaco. Closer now, Esmeray could see they were elders, although they appeared quite energetic. The woman hugged Esmeray as the man embraced Bastone, slapping him on the back, welcoming them in Genoese, "Benvenuto! Benvenuto!"

Esmeray glanced at her husband. The warm greeting also pleased him.

The woman hugged Aspasia again, then pinched the little girl's cheek, "*Chi beddicu*—what a cutie!"

Aspasia giggled, then said, "Mamma, they know Sicilian, too."

"Signuri and Signura Ponzio, and . . . ," the man paused, looking at Aspasia expectantly.

She responded to his hint. "My name is Aspasia."

"And Signurina Aspasia," he said as he gestured toward the house. "This is your new home."

"But this is *your* home, Signuri Scorzuto," said Esmeray.

"Please call me by my given name—Baldu." He glanced sideways at his wife. "My wife, Richelda. But we have a new house." He pointed to the nearest whitewashed cottage.

"The small house suits us perfectly. Signuri Ponzio, as the fondaco's new leader, you must reside in the main house.

CHAPTER XXVI

Bastone woke the next morning, reflecting on Baldu's statement: "You're the leader of the fondaco." He had a responsibility to Mino, but also to numerous investors who were depending on him. Mino had adopted the Genoese method, which was to gain multiple investors to raise money for the expeditions. The capital came from a wide range of society. Not only did wealthy merchants and nobles invest in the trading ventures, but middle-class citizens such as craftsmen, artisans, and even working-class people bought shares.

Bastone rolled out of bed, hearing Esmeray and Aspasia talking in the next room, remembering he needed to review the investor contracts. While examining the list, he noticed that Anneta Lingosa, a tavern owner, had found a witness to sign her contract instead of a notary. He knew that domestic servants, and laborers, and the poor did this to avoid the cost of a notary when they invested their meager funds. Mino honored such documents.

He finished ciphering, irritated because the Roman numerals were difficult to multiply and divide and required long multiplication tables and an abacus. He had seen the Arab traders using different numbers. The Catholic church was suspicious of the Muslims' system, especially the numeral zero, and had banned its use. The Pope had assumed the zero represented nothing and was thus demonic, because

God had made everything. But Bastone knew that many Italian merchants continued to use it secretly.

He joined Esmeray and Aspasia in the next room, noticing their conversation becoming heated.

"I want Ciciri and Tangier here with me, Mamma!"

"Aspasia, the cats have a duty on board the *Giovanna*. Also, we will be sailing soon, and you will see them aboard."

Bastone entered the room. "What's going on?"

Mother and daughter glanced at Bastone, both with blank looks, then faced each other again and continued arguing.

"Then bring Ciciri here and leave Tangier on the ship," said Aspasia.

Esmeray folded her arms over her chest. "The cats don't want to be separated."

There was a knock on the door. Bastone saw through the window that it was Richelda, the elderly woman they'd met the previous evening. "Enter!"

She opened the door, carrying a wooden tray covered by a linen cloth. The delicious scent of freshly baked bread filled the house. A diminutive black cat with a star-shaped white patch on its chest was close behind her.

Aspasia crossed the room and crouched near the feline. "*Chi beddu gatta*—what a beautiful cat!"

"Si, si. And she *is* beddu, but she is Genoese, so her name is Bella."

"Is she your cat?" asked Aspasia.

"One does not own a cat," said Richelda. "A cat chooses you." Bella purred and closed her eyes as Aspasia stroked her back. "Aspasia, this is Bella's house. She's thrilled you are here."

Richelda removed the cloth, the aroma of the round loaf filling the room. She handed the bread to Esmeray, who placed it on the table. "Please stay and eat with us," said Esmeray. She set four unpainted terra cotta cups on the table, the fired clay a burnt orange color. She added a small measure of red wine, then filled them with water.

They sat around the kitchen table, pulling off chunks of bread and eating the warm, crusty treat.

Bastone thought nothing could improve its taste, not even olive oil. Aspasia dropped pieces on the floor for Bella. Pausing between bites, Richelda looked at Esmeray and said, "I will take you outside and show you the oven."

"Um . . . thank you, Richelda, but I'll be at sea most of the time."

The matron tilted her head toward Bastone and said, "Then I will show your husband the oven."

Esmeray's eyes grew wide. Bastone missed the jest because he wasn't listening. The silence that followed caught his attention and he looked up. His blank face made Aspasia and the women break into laughter.

Finishing breakfast and thanking Richelda, Esmeray returned to the port, escorted by one of Bastone's arbalesters. She supervised the loading of the *Giovanna* and readied the vessel to set sail within a few days. Bastone updated the accounts, taking Aspasia with him to survey the expansion of the trading compound. Outside the gate of the fondaco, the workers were shirtless, sweating from exertion under the warm sun. They had pounded four posts into the ground and attached wooden planks, creating an enclosure four feet high, eight feet long, and two feet wide.

Several men got on top of the form, straddling it. Donkey carts had arrived, filled with baskets containing a mixture of gravel, sand, silt, and clay. Christian and Muslim, European and African laborers worked together, slinging baskets to the men on top of the form, who added the earth to the enclosure. After the crew poured a layer of earth about two feet deep, they pounded it with heavy poles, compacting the soil. They added another shallow layer and continued ramming the earth, stratum by stratum, until the workers had filled the form. The workers had compacted the soil in the enclosure into a hardened block. They removed the wooden form and reassembled it at the end of the completed section, repeating the process. Building a four-foot wall, section by section, between the Genoese and Sicilian fondacos took the entire day. The next morning, they constructed a wooden form on top of the completed sections and increased the wall's height to eight feet.

The following day, Bastone went to examine the progress of the wall, only to find a section had collapsed. There was a dispute among the laborers, as they blamed each other for shoddy work. The foreman, examining the pile of rubble, asserted that the damage was intentional. He pointed out gouges and indentations in the wall, signs that vandals had used the workers' mauls and compacting tools. Recalling the Pisans' aggressive behavior at the market, Bastone was sure they had destroyed the wall.

When the foreman convinced the workers that they were the victims of sabotage, the men picked up their tools and together repaired the wall. The scene reminded Bastone that men of various backgrounds, like the crew of the Giovanna, could cooperate. A spark of optimism rippled through him as he recalled decades earlier, before Charles had invaded, the Christian, Muslim, and Jewish inhabitants of Sicily had coexisted under King Frederick II. This policy had vanished under Charles. Now that the Sicilians had expelled the tyrant Charles, Bastone wondered if the island might return to a multi-religious society. These idealistic thoughts evaporated as the problem with the Pisans' resistance to his arrival occupied his mind. Bastone directed the workers to remove their tools at night. He also arranged for an increase in the night watch.

By day's end, workers had completed repairs on the wall. After the crew had departed and Bastone examined it, Esmeray and Aspasia arrived to walk back to their house for dinner. The light of dusk bathed the terrain as the sun fell behind the mountains. In the evening light, Aspasia noticed along the entire length of the wall were waves of varying tones of earth colors, created by the horizontal layers of compacted earth.

"Papa, it looks like someone painted stripes on the wall, Beddu!"

CHAPTER XXVII

Over the next year, Esmeray, Bastone, and Aspasia followed a routine, sailing between Sicily and Bejaia, trading Marsala salt for hides and wax, finished cloth from Messina for honey, and Sicilian wine for red coral. They had left their fishing boat, the *Aspasia*, in Bejaia, having taken it out of the water for re-caulking and wood repairs. Bastone had hired a Hafsid boatman to restore the vessel. As payment for the work, the boatman could use the *Aspasia* for one year to harvest coral from the shallow sea near Bejaia. Bastone, once a spy posing as a merchant, now embodied the Genoese saying: To be Genoese meant being a merchant.

Once again, the *Giovanna* departed Messina after delivering pelts and hides for the women of the city to use in making clothes for export. They reloaded the ship with linen and silk cloth and finished clothing. Stopping in Palermo, Bastone traded the goods for wine. The *Giovanna* sailed around the northwest cape of Sicily, Cape Lilibeo, arriving in Marsala, where the *Lucia* was waiting.

At Marsala, Esmeray stood atop the stern castle as the crew loaded bags of dried sea salt into the holds of ships. Sitting nearby on the steps leading to the deck, Aspasia practiced chords on her *oud*. The *Giovanna's* second mate, Ayman, an Arab from Bejaia, had taught her how to play. She was a fast learner, now thrumming soothing, open tones. Across the salt pans of Marsala, the slow turning of windmill blades was mesmerizing, as they pumped the aquamarine seawater into a lagoon, where the water took on a pink tinge as it evaporated. There, another windmill moved the concentrated brine to the drying lagoon. Laborers dredged the sea salt, piling it on the bank of the lagoon to dry. Other workers shoveled dried salt into hemp bags for shipment.

A flash of worry hit Esmeray. As she watched the workers, she envisioned their daily routine, especially at the end of the workday, going home to their families. Were they content and happy? A pang of guilt arose. Esmeray's thoughts backtracked into a mental duel that had recurred several times since the day they left Favignana. Was her love of the sea risking Aspasia's life? Her family? Should she have stayed in Favignana? Life there had been routine and secure. She enjoyed the freedom of sailing on her fishing boat, free from societal expectations. It did not bother her that she didn't feel the closeness in the small commune. She realized she was only happy at sea. But would Aspasia be enthused with the same kind of life?

So far, they had been lucky, avoiding pirate attacks during the trade voyages. As a deterrence, Mino sent at least two ships on trading runs and also coordinated with other shipowners to form convoys to sail together for safety. He provided arms and training for his sailors in case of an attack. Recalling Bastone's skill and leadership, Esmeray's fears eased, and her thoughts returned to preparing for the voyage to North Africa.

After loading the salt, which also provided ballast for the ships, they cast off toward the southwest. Recognizing the approaching sunset, Esmeray and the helmsman agreed to sail at night. The sky was red in the west, which Esmeray knew predicted favorable weather. She was aware that the helmsman knew the stars to follow to Cape Zebib. A familiar sensation engulfed her as she began another voyage, her heart stirring with the thrills of the sea.

Leaving Sicily for open water, Esmeray insisted on testing the ships to see how fast they could make the crossing to North Africa.

She had discussed the notion with her helmsman, first mate, and captain of the *Lucia*, who had all agreed. They would keep lanterns at bow and stern and stay together. The pair of ships departed Marsala tacking windward using the scirocco winds, the *Lucia* following the *Giovanna*.

Esmeray, satisfied with the running, left the first mate to oversee the ship and joined Bastone and Aspasia in their cabin. Bastone sat at a small table reviewing the cargo inventory. Aspasia was on her bunk with the cats, petting Ciciri and Tangier.

As Esmeray entered, she said, "Delfinina, the cats will need to go out soon. They do their best hunting at night."

"Mamma, why is he called Tangier?"

Bastone answered without looking up from his document. "Because Mino made a goal to extend his trading voyages to Tangier. It's farther along the coast than Bejaia."

"We want to go to Tangier," said Aspasia, speaking for the cats and herself.

A sense of satisfaction washed over Esmeray as her daughter displayed a lack of worry about the upcoming move. Her daughter was eager for new experiences and to see unknown places.

"Maybe we will go there on one of our trading voyages," said Esmeray.

Bastone, although focused on the inventory, still found time to comment, "Our treaty with the Hafsids only allows us to trade at the ports of Tunis, Bejaia, and Ceuta."

Esmeray unrolled a map, showing Aspasia the location of Ceuta and Tangier, west of Bejaia. "Aspasia, perhaps if we go to Ceuta, we can visit Tangier," said Esmeray.

Bastone glanced at his wife, subtly shook his head, and returned to studying his figures. Abruptly, he raised his voice, "How did the Romans build the roads and aqueducts using this cumbersome number system!"

Both mother and daughter looked at him, eyes wide at his outburst. Esmeray appeared irritated and Aspasia looked puzzled. He said, "I'm sorry, my sweet ones."

He opened a letter of instructions Mino had given him on their recent stop in Messina. Esmeray held a finger up to her lips for Aspasia because she didn't want to irritate Bastone. It was quiet in the cabin for several minutes as he read the letter.

Bastone abruptly cursed in Sicilian. "*Bedda Matri*—Good Mother! It can't be that simple." He penned a few numbers on scrap parchment, doing a few calculations. To himself he said, "It works!"

Esmeray, who had only heard Bastone swear in his native Genoese, laughed to herself. "Bastonino, what is it?"

"Mino said we must adopt the . . . um, Hindi-Arabic numerical system, or we will fall behind the other merchants. When we reach Bejaia, I am to seek the director of the Pisan fondaco, Inghio Bonnaci. His great uncle introduced the Arabic number system to Italy."

"That's going to be a challenge, tesoro mio," said Esmeray. "Pisans are still bitter over the sea battle with Genoa, and their merchants at the Bejaia fondaco do not appreciate our expansion. Too much competition."

"We'll figure something out," said Bastone. "We've had tougher challenges."

It was morning, and the crews had been busy, the ships sailing in tandem, close-hauled, beating windward all night. In twelve hours the ships had sailed 100 miles across the sea that separated Marsala and Cape Zebib. Turning west at the cape, they continued along the coast about a mile off the mainland, passing the small port of Bizerte, the northernmost town in Africa. The southwest winds changed to easterlies, a frequent occurrence in summer. With the boost, they ran downwind along the coast after the change. The ships sailed nonstop for the next two days, with the crew sleeping on the deck when off duty.

On the third morning out of Cape Zebib, Aspasia was on the stern castle, eavesdropping on her mother's conversation with the helmsman. The sun was rising behind them. On their port side, a pair of single masted dhows, the type used to trade along the coast, sailed out of the mouth of Collo harbor.

"Delfinina, we have sailed past this town before. Do you recognize it?" asked Esmeray.

"Yes, I remember it. It's the one with the mountain that sticks out in the sea. It's Collo." The girl pointed. "Mamma look . . ." Esmeray cleared her throat. "I mean, Capitanu, look at those ships," Aspasia said. "The sails have two points, and . . . not three points like ours."

"Good eyes, Delfinina. Yes, our sails have three sides and three points, but the dhows' sails are, um, flat at the bow's end."

The helmsman said, "Our sails with three points are called *lateen* sails, capisci?" Not expecting an answer, he gestured toward the Arab ships, "The Africans fit their dhows with *settee* sails."

"Lateen sails have three points. Settee sails have two points and something else . . ." said Aspasia to herself.

Dhows turned, sailing east, disappearing in the sun's glare. The *Giovanna* and *Lucia* continued west, nearing the tip of the Collo peninsula. Ahead was another cape a mile distant, the northernmost summit of the Tell Mountains running into the sea.

The watch yelled, "The dhows have come about!"

Esmeray asked, "Are they following us?"

Esmeray shouted across the ship's deck to the first mate, "Reef the mizen sail, *un pocu*—just a little."

The *Lucia*, a few ship lengths behind, caught up to sail fifty paces beside them, heeding gestures from Esmeray, reefed and slowed to match speeds. After several more minutes, Esmeray said, "They *are* following us. The dhows had been gaining on us, but now have also slowed."

She saw Bastone had also heard the watch, his commanding voice rising above the background sounds as he organized the arbalesters and their weapons. Esmeray shouted at the wind, "We can't outrun them, but if they get close, with Bastone and Cardo leading them, our arbalesters will let them know *nun stamu schirzannu*—we aren't joking around!"

As Bastone joined Esmeray, eyeing the pair of dhows behind them, she said, "Even though we are heavily loaded, they are not gaining on us and continue at the same distance."

Esmeray had a dubious look. "If they were planning to attack, why didn't they intercept us before we crossed Collo's harbor?" Esmeray waved at the first mate. "Reef just a little more and signal the *Lucia* to keep pace." She pinched the air with thumb and forefinger. The *Giovanna* slowed. "Hmm, see, the dhows have also furled their sails a tad, slowing to match our speed again. Are we really under threat?" asked Esmeray.

"The dhows behind us are acting peculiarly," said Bastone.

Esmeray yelled toward the midship for the second mate, "Ayman, to the helm!"

The second mate, an Arab sailor from Bejaia, hurried to the stern castle. "Yes, Capitanu."

"What do you know about the dhows?" asked Esmeray.

"They may be trouble," Ayman said. "They're not fishing and they have no banners. The Hafsid caliph requires all traders to fly either the Hafsid flag or the banner of their city."

As the *Giovanna* and *Lucia* let out their sails again to increase speed, a third dhow, hidden by the Collo peninsula, sailed into view on a line to cross their path. "Now I know they are after us! We can't outrun them," said Esmeray, directing the helmsman to steer away from the third dhow to gain time.

Bastone had already ordered his squad of arbalesters to midship with their shields, extra crossbows, and sailors as reloaders. Esmeray noticed they were getting ready to ascend the stairs to the stern castle, and kneeled to face Aspasia, holding her shoulders. "Delfinina, remember when we ran from the wicked men in Genoa?"

Her daughter nodded.

"Go hide in the hold. *Capisci?*"

"Yes, Mamma."

"You are brave, Delfinina."

"Like you, Mamma."

Although pleased Aspasia imitated her, Esmeray berated herself, doubting her decision to take on the captaincy, exposing her daughter to this imminent danger. Before Aspasia's birth, Esmeray never let herself get distracted during a crisis. But now, thinking of the risk she was causing Aspasia, her resolve faltered. Bastone's eyes flashed alarmingly, making her feel like she was descending into a deep well. Then, as had become a mark of their relationship during monumental challenges, they fixed their eyes on one another, stiffening their determination.

Aspasia ran down the stern castle steps before Bastone's arbalesters hurried up the stairway. They gathered at the aft of the ship's stern castle. The side bulkhead was only a foot high, topped by the taffrail, a waist high open railing, offering no protection against bolts and arrows. The arbalesters leaned their shields against the taffrail, crouching behind, ready to shoot at the pursuing dhows. Sailors squatted behind them with more loaded crossbows.

Aspasia reached the main hatch, descending into the hold full of sacks of salt. She walked along the top of the rows of sacks until she came to bales of finished cloth stored in hemp bags. Knowing it was the cats' favorite place to hide and nap, she wriggled into one bag, peeking over the edge.

Above, on deck, Esmeray asked, "Bastone, can you hit the ships tailing us?"

"Not with a straight shot. I could loft the bolts, but it would be a lucky hit. I think they are staying out of crossbow range . . . on purpose," said Bastone.

The *Giovanna* and *Lucia* continued sailing parallel to each other, as the pursuing dhows remained distant. The third dhow was getting closer to the *Giovanna*. Bastone sent several of his arbalesters to the bow and said, "Don't shoot until I order it!"

The ships approached another headland, the Cape of Kbiba, when a war galley, with all oars rowing, glided from behind the cape. "*Denti di Gesu*—teeth of Jesus," said Bastone. "Four ships. No way out. And a Pisan galley joining the Arabs, not afraid to show their colors. All pirates!"

Esmeray's heart was hammering, but she again matched steely eyes with her husband. He quickly devised a plan, but it would take all her skills as captain to succeed. To trust in each other was their best chance.

CHAPTER XXVIII

The *Giovanna* turned abruptly, causing the hull to creak and groan, but the bags of salt lining the keel held fast, counterweighting the tendency for the ship to heel. The sudden change frightened Aspasia. Tangier appeared, followed by Ciciri. Flicking their tails with agitation, Aspasia sensed they were confused why she was so deep in the hold. They jumped on top of the adjacent sack. By stroking their backs and scratching their ears, Aspasia calmed both the cats and herself.

Esmeray sensed the easterlies slowing and the renewal of the scirocco blowing from the southwest. She ordered the helmsman to turn the ship north, heading straight towards the Pisan galley. With the scirocco blowing, the *Lucia* and *Giovanna* sailed side by side, their sails full of wind. The boost increased the distance between the Sicilian ships and the dhows, but only briefly. The pursuers changed course as well.

Bastone shouted to his arbalesters, "*A portu!*" Without delay, they lined the port side of the stern castle with their round shields propped against the railing. Nearing crossbow range, Esmeray, with a shield strapped to her back, conferred with the helmsman one last time on their strategy. She projected her voice toward midship. "Hold the trim!" After the crew tightened the lines, the first mate signaled for them to seek cover. Esmeray joined the arbalesters behind the row of shields along the port side. With shields on their backs, Bastone and the helmsman gripped the steerboards.

The *Giovanna* continued to run downwind on a course to ram the Pisan galley. Esmeray's stomach churned, having second thoughts regarding this aggressive plan. She wanted to flee instead, but trusted Bastone's recommendation: when surrounded with no escape, one must attack the strongest threat first. Still one hundred yards away, the silent flight of crossbolts launched from the deck of the pirate galley soon made itself heard by a cacophony of thuds and clatterings as the missiles pierced shields, bounced off masts, and skipped across the deck.

The single dhow that had emerged from behind the cape was still on an intercept course and Bastone's arbalesters loosed their bolts at it. They traded their crossbows to the attending sailors for a second crossbow strung and loaded, which they shot for a second volley. Now fifty yards from the pirate galley, Bastone's arbalesters on the stern castle, over a man's height above the deck of the pirate galley, shot into the ranks of the Pisan ship, decimating the crew. The enemy crossbowmen were still reloading. Seconds later, Esmeray shouted, "Now!"

As the *Giovanna* loomed over the galley, the helmsman and Bastone struggled to maneuver the steering boards, turning broadside to the other vessel. A sequence of loud cracks ensued as they broke off the oars along the port side of the galley. Following the glancing impact, the *Giovanna* slowed but then disengaged and proceeded past the enemy ship with the *Lucia* sailing on the steerboard side.

Approaching from behind, the two dhows were closing in, launching a barrage of arrows onto the decks of the *Giovanna* and *Lucia*. The Sicilian arbalesters on both ships retaliated with a deadly barrage of bolts. They overwhelmed the enemy with steady flights of arrows.

Although the crossbows had taken a heavy toll on the enemy crews, the dhows kept coming. The pirate galley came to a standstill in the water, as many of its oars were broken, forcing the crew to raise the vessel's sails. Three dhows were converging on the *Giovanna and Lucia*.

The dhows had reefed their sails, slowing to wait for the galley to get under sail and join them. Esmeray believed joining forces with the *Lucia* might be their only chance. Bastone shot her a knowing glance. Their eyes met, both understanding their shared thoughts. He released his grip on the steerboard and waved and shouted at the *Lucia*, getting the captain's attention, and then bumped his fists together several times. His nephew, Cardo, the *Lucia's* skipper, quickly acknowledged.

Esmeray shouted to the first mate, "Reef the sails!" She ordered the helmsman to steer closer to the *Lucia*. When they slowed enough, sailors from the *Giovanna* hurled coils of lightweight throw lines to the *Lucia's* crew, who hauled across heavier ropes attached to the cords, using the lines to tie the ships together broadside.

The galley and dhows were now all under sail, the four enemy vessels converging on the Sicilian ships. The crews of the *Giovanna* and *Lucia* prepared to repel them as Bastone's crossbowmen loosed bolts at the enemy. The crossbowers on the pirate galley dueled the Sicilian arbalesters, drawing their fire, enabling the dhows to reach the *Giovanna*. One dhow slammed into the *Lucia* as pirates jumped aboard. The other two dhows discharged corsairs onto the *Giovanna's* midship deck. The battle erupted into hand-to-hand combat. Sailors stabbed and cut with daggers. Both sides wielded belaying pins as bludgeons or threw them, the missiles cartwheeling through the air. Arabs slashed with their curved scimitars, the bright steel flashing among the combatants.

Esmeray, on the stern castle above the fierce combat on deck, panicked, seeing Arab pirates near the ship's main hatch. Driven by emotion, she rushed down the steps to secure the door.

Well trained, better equipped, and with their advantage atop the stern castle, Bastone's arbalesters had eliminated the enemy galley's crossbowmen. He turned his attention to the lower deck, but he could not shoot among the fighters without hitting his own crew. In the turmoil, Bastone had lost track of Esmeray. Glancing about, he caught a glimpse of her hurrying to the deck.

He was about to follow her, and despite the clamor, Bastone detected the telltale creak of a crossbow being drawn. Bastone turned to see the Spinola brothers, one kneeling, aiming a crossbow at Esmeray. He lunged, pushing the crossbow aside, as the clack of the trigger sounded.

Was she hit? But the Spinolas were attacking him and Bastone couldn't look. One brother raised his crossbow to bludgeon Bastone as the other discarded his bow, drawing his dagger. Bastone leaned away from the overhead strike, parrying the bow with his left arm. He encircled the attacker's bow, locking up the weapon and the man's hands as he kneed him in the groin. The other Spinola lunged. Bastone intercepted his dagger with his bow and string, entangling the blade, drew his own dagger, and in two swift arcs slashed both the Spinola brother's carotid arteries.

Blood spattered on him as they fell to the deck. Bastone shouted for his men to follow him. He descended to the main deck and fought through to reach Esmeray. The Spinola bolt had deflected off the steps and had pierced the shield on Esmeray's back. She lay face down near the hatch door.

Bastone reached Esmeray, her face down on the hatch, an arrow lodged in her back. He dropped to his hands and knees, tears blurring his vision, unaware the surrounding battle had ended.

CHAPTER XXIX

"Esme!" Bastone saw blood on her tunic. "Esme! Esme!" She was breathing, but not moving or responding. He was careful not to move the arrow, to minimize the loss of blood. Still kneeling, Bastone grabbed a sailor by the wrist, "Bring the surgeon!"

Bleeding from a neck gash, the man collapsed after taking a step. Bastone glanced around the deck, covered with bodies and slick with blood. Screams from both the wounded and those struggling to help obscured Bastone's plea as he stood and yelled for the barber-surgeon. There was no response, but his outburst restored Bastone to his senses. He would save his wife himself.

An image from years earlier flashed into Bastone's mind. A crossbolt had impaled his comrade, Luciano, during the revolt in Sicily. Bastone had watched a trained barber-surgeon remove the bolt from Luciano's leg. He tried to recall the steps. Put pressure on the wound. Don't pull the arrow out until you control the bleeding. Does the bolt have a barbed end? Bastone's mind spun. He cleared his mind by shaking his head. He ordered himself, "Slow down, stop! One step at a time!"

Bastone continued to speak to himself. "Stop the bleeding." Without moving the shield on Esmeray's back, Bastone lay on his stomach, peering between her back and the shield. The bolt had punctured the shield below her right shoulder, but only a small crimson stain was visible. "How?" The bolt had barely penetrated the shield. It should have gone deeper. "Thank God. The shot must have ricocheted." He let out a long sigh.

Bastone used his dagger to cut a piece of his tunic for a bandage. He was about to remove the shield when his wife raised her head and groaned. "Esme, don't move!"

"Hmm?" she pushed herself up with her hands.

"Don't move, you'll . . ."

The shield fell away, the arrow with it, as she sat back on her heels, rubbing her forehead. Bastone, expecting a gush of blood, pressed the cloth on the wound. "Can you stand?"

She nodded, still holding her head. As he helped her to their cabin, keeping pressure on her wound, the barber-surgeon arrived. Forcing his words between breaths, the surgeon said, "Bastone, are you able to take care of your wife?"

"She had an arrow in her back. I am going to check. I may need your help."

"Send for me if necessary. They have started a fire to cauterize the men's wounds." He rushed to midship, where sailors had built a fire on the galley slate.

In the cabin, Bastone guided Esmeray, helping her sit. "I'm afraid to remove the cloth."

She was groggy. "Hmm?"

Bastone eased the cloth from the wound. "Esme, it's only bleeding a little. I'm going to pull off your tunic, so I can clean it, va beni?"

"Huh-huh."

The puncture was not deep. "A miracle! Dolcezza! The crossbolt barely pierced the shield."

Esmeray squirmed, as he poured wine over the wound. "Oww—that stings! And, oh, my head!"

He dried her back, noticing a lump on her forehead when he bandaged her wound. "You must have hit your head on the hatch when you fell."

He gave Esmeray sips of diluted wine, reviving her.

She cried out, "Where's Aspasia?"

Esmeray tried to stand but was unsteady, Bastone catching her. He helped her put on her tunic and led her to the bunk. "Esme, lay still, I'll go get her."

Bastone rushed across the deck, weaving among the injured sailors, screaming while their mates sealed their wounds with red-hot daggers. He slipped on the bloody deck, barely keeping his feet, and evaded crewmen throwing dead pirates overboard. The dhows were fleeing as the lifeless galley floated nearby, a drifting graveyard.

Bastone reached the hatch at midship and found Ayman waiting. "Sir, I didn't let anyone below." They climbed into the hold, calling for Aspasia, feeling their way in the dim light along the bags of salt. "Aspasia! Where are you? Aspasia!"

Ayman moved pass the bags of salt, reaching the bulk sacks packed with cloth, hollering, "Aspasia, Aspasia!"

From the dark, "Meooow!" Ayman jumped back. The male cat, Tangier, blocked Ayman's path. "*Gattu*, you scared me! Where is Aspasia?"

The cat cried out with drawn-out yowls, then appearing to sharpen his claws, scratched the side of a large hemp bag. Ayman noticed a bulge in the sack. "Aspasia, it's me, Ayman. Come out."

Aspasia peeked out of the top of the large bag, emerging with a belaying pin in her hand. "Ayman, I thought you were a pirate!" Bastone reached them. "Papa!"

When they returned above, sailors were splashing buckets of seawater, rinsing off the gory deck. Esmeray was holding a book, standing over a row of bodies. Crewmen had crossed the deceased sailors' hands over their chests.

Aspasia ran across the deck and cried, "Mamma!"

Esmeray kneeled, the bandage tightening, pain shooting from the puncture in her back. The surgeon told her she would need stitches.

She hugged her daughter, squeezed her eyes closed, not trying to hide her tears.

"Mamma." She glanced at the bodies. "I am sad."

She kneeled down and embraced her daughter. "It's natural to be sad. I'm glad you told me. We're all sad, Delfinina."

Esmeray stood, wiping her face. Aspasia held her mother's hand. The first mate announced the captain would recite a eulogy for the deceased. The crew took off their watch caps and listened.

Esmeray opened the book and read to the men in Latin: "If there are gods and they are just, then they will not care how devout you have been, but they'll welcome you based on the virtues you have lived by. If there are gods but unjust, then you should not want to worship them. If there are no gods, then you will be gone, but you will have lived a noble life that will live on the memories of your loved ones."

They didn't comprehend her reading, but they knew the words were in the priest's language—the language of the Church. The sailors likely recognized a few words, such as *Deus*. They answered, "Amen."

One by one, the crew gave up the dead to the sea. After they released the last of the deceased overboard, the pain Esmeray had been suppressing returned. She was about to go find the surgeon when Ayman drew near. "Capitanu."

She concealed a wince and gathered her energy. "Ayman, thank you for finding Aspasia."

"My honor, Capitanu." After a pause, he asked, "Capitanu, I read our holy book, the Quran. I have heard that the Christian Bible is also a book of wisdom. May I ask you to interpret the words you recited?"

She translated the verse into Sicilian. The man's thick eyebrows knitted together so harshly, he appeared to be in pain. Esmeray thought she had offended him, now wishing she had not translated the quote. Anxiously, she waited as he turned his head to stare into space for a few moments. Then he relaxed. "At first, I thought the verse rang with blasphemy. But then I realized, yes, the deceased may have had different beliefs—there were words for everyone. What prophet did you quote?"

Esmeray answered with a wry smile, "Marcus Aurelius."

CHAPTER XXX

After the pirate attack, the *Lucia* and *Giovanna* sailed west for several days and were now an hour away from Bejaia. With the ships was the galley they had captured from the pirates, under sail by a skeleton crew of sailors from the *Giovanna*. At the stern castle Bastone pursed his lips with a look of concern. "Do you think it's safe for Aspasia to spend so much time in the hold by herself?"

Esmeray said, "We both have been going below to talk, so she knows she's not the only one feeling sad. But she is consoling herself by playing her oud, don't you think? And the cats must sense her feelings. Every time I go below, one is there napping beside her or comforting her."

Esmeray reached behind her shoulder and rubbed. "Hmmm . . . it itches."

"Careful, that's too hard," Bastone said. "You'll break the stitches." Bastone kneaded her back, taking care not to touch her injury. "I am so relieved the shot didn't penetrate. There were hundreds of bolts flying in every direction during the fight. The one that hit you must have bounced off the deck—or was a misfire."

Esmeray glanced at the helmsman, who hadn't appeared to notice Bastone massaging her. "Bastonino, please, you shouldn't touch me in front of the crew."

Bastone withdrew his hand and pounded his fist on his chest in mock salute. *"Si, Capitanu!"*

Esmeray laughed. "And yes, I am very lucky." She was relieved Bastone hadn't praised God for her fortune. Feeling a wave of elation and warmth pass through her, their family safe after the bloody attack, a lone tear rolled down her right cheek. She laughed inwardly, recalling her mother had told her that if the first tear came from your right eye, it was a sign of happiness.

Bastone held his arms wide, looking left and to the right, measuring *their world.* "Dolcezza, we are alive—alive to see this magnificent day! We've traveled the world, surviving hazards together. Aspasia is safe, and you're a captain at sea! Don't you think God has blessed us?"

Esmeray tilted her head back, puffing her cheeks, blowing in exasperation. "Let's discuss this in the cabin."

In their suite, Esmeray removed her tunic and lay on the bed on her stomach. "Now you can scratch my back."

Bastone massaged her, avoiding her wound. "Dolcezza mia, I'm sorry that I mentioned God. It is a habit of speech. I'm not sure if He does anything to help or harm people."

Eyes closed and between moans, Esmeray answered, "Va beni, Bastonino."

"The men appreciated your eulogy. You were gracious. And being in Latin, I'm sure they thought it was from the Liturgy, giving respect for the dead."

Esmeray's eyes remained closed as she smiled.

I see that look. "They didn't know you were being irreverent."

Esmeray propped herself on her elbows. "I wasn't irreverent."

Bastone raised his voice, "Saying there was no God?"

She spoke calmly. "It was a quote by Marcus Aurelius. He didn't deny the existence of God, but offered comfort according to one's beliefs."

"Hmm." His voice grew louder again. "But what if one of them had known Latin? He would have told the others . . . ?"

Esmeray rolled over on the bunk to her knees and sat on her heels. Seeing how Bastone was peering at her, she folded her arms to cover her breasts. Raising her eyebrows, she peered at Bastone. "Later, my husband."

His gaze returned to her face. "Va bene. None of them would know Latin. I need to read this passage myself." He gave her a quick kiss of reconciliation. "Have you been reading Marcus Aurelius's book to Aspasia?"

She nodded.

"What are Aurelius's thoughts on fate?"

She tilted her head back, staring upward. "Let me see if I can remember. Yes, he advised a person should not complain when they have bad luck. Rather, one should declare, *'It's good luck to bear the unfortunate, neither crushed by the present nor fearful of the future.'*"

Esmeray returned to lie on her stomach, arms at her sides, turning her head to the side with an impish smile. "You can continue your massage, Bastonino."

Bastone leaned over and kissed Esmeray. The door opened. Aspasia entered, hopping over the raised threshold. "We're almost home!"

Their arrival at the Bejaia, accompanied by a warship, drew a lot of attention from the people on the waterfront. The crews of the *Lucia* and *Giovanna* docked and began unloading the ships. Bastone posted watches on the galley, moored in the harbor. He left for the *Bab el Kasbah*, the emir's palace, to explain the war galley and report the attack by the corsairs.

At midship, Esmeray supervised and tallied the goods brought ashore, explaining the counting method to Aspasia. The ship's cats scampered across the deck to the port side, one heading toward the bow, the other toward the stern, diverting the girl's attention. She ran after Ciciri, finding the cat at the end of the mooring rope, which secured the bow to the wharf. The cat was resting on its belly, forepaws curled underneath his chest, staring down the length of the mooring rope. "Ciciri, what are you doing?"

"He's waiting for a rat," said a sailor. "That's how they get on the ship—along the ropes."

Aspasia bolted toward the stern, running under a bundle of salt bags the sailors were hoisting to the wharf. Esmeray looked up from her logbook. "Aspasia!"

Her daughter ignored her mother and ran on, the swinging bags just missing her. Aspasia hurried to the stern, where Tangier lingered at the aft mooring rope, like the other cat, ready to pounce on any ambitious rodent.

At the palace, the scribe received Bastone, informing him that the emir already knew of the battle. The emir found it disturbing that the merchants of the fondacos, whom he considered his subjects, were fighting among themselves. The scribe instructed Bastone to return to the palace on the following day along with the director of the Pisan fondaco, Inghio Bonnaci, to discuss the incident at length.

Bastone pondered the scribe's words as he walked back to the Genoese fondaco. News traveled fast. The emir had already learned of the sea battle, although according to the scribe, he thought it was just Pisans fighting Genoese and Sicilians. The emir didn't know, or wouldn't acknowledge, that rogue Pisans had become pirates. Bastone needed to convince the emir that he was only defending himself. The Pisans from the local fondaco might have encouraged the pirates, or, even worse, the emir could be in collusion with the Pisans.

As Bastone prepared the next morning to visit the emir of Bejaia, Abu Zakariya, he dressed his best to show respect. He wore a clean linen tunic, belted. A finely crafted dagger, a common accessory for distinguished men, rested at the belt. He dressed in leggings and a surcoat of green linen cloth, which he wore only on formal occasions.

Although it was not his usual garb, he unexpectedly felt comfortable in the clean, seldom worn clothes. Could he assume the role of a gentleman merchant? Comfortably directing the trading voyages from Bejaia? He laughed out loud. No! That would never be him, especially with Esmeray as his wife.

Ayman accompanied him as an interpreter. It was only a five-minute walk to the emir's palace, across a small plaza from the customs house. On the way, Bastone reflected that the surnames of the emir and the Genoese merchant, Admiral Zaccaria, were pronounced alike, though spelled differently. He mentioned the happenstance to Ayman, who said, "Yes, Zakariya is a holy name. According to the Quran, Zakariya was a Jewish priest, the guardian of Maryam, the Virgin Mary of the Christians."

Bastone noted the coincidence. He would find the right time to use the similarity in names in the upcoming meeting with the emir. They passed through the southwest gate into the city where the palace was on a rise to their left. The guards expected them, allowing entry. The director of the Pisan fondaco, Inghio Bonacci, waited in the atrium. He stood to greet them, flashing a genuine smile. His aquiline nose was narrow, and he had a gentle, intelligent face. He also was well dressed with leggings, a surcoat, and a maroon bag hat like Esmeray's.

Bastone made sure he began their conversation with respect and embraced him as was customary for gentlemen of the Italian maritime republics. He continued, "Signore Bonacci, I have heard that your great uncle was a genius in mathematics. I have been studying his methods."

"Thank you, Signore Ponzio. My uncle had no children, so I continue his work and encourage its use."

Inghio glanced at Ayman. Bastone gestured as he said, "Oh, scusi, Second Officer Ayman, my interpreter." Ayman placed his right hand on his chest and nodded. Inghio returned the greeting. Bastone added, "You have heard the rumor that the sea fight was between our fondacos?"

Inghio hesitated, then nodded. Bastone did not perceive any deceit in his manner, then said, "Before we see the emir, whatever the issue he brings up, I propose an agreement. We put the rivalry of our home cities behind us and work together."

Inghio paused, taking in the offer, then said, "Agreed." The men shook hands.

An attendant escorted them to a large hall where the emir received visitors. The banner of Bejaia, with an image of a crossbow, hung on the wall. Flanked by standing guards, a scribe at a writing table, and another attendant, Zakariya sat, his back straight, head erect, and forearms and hands on the chair's armrests. Before the meeting, Ayman had told Bastone that in the Quran, Muhammad made it clear that Muslims should bow to no person. Ayman recommended he imitate Inghio. As the visitors approached, and after a subtle nod by the emir, Inghio halted twenty steps away, placed his palm on his chest and tipped his head toward the emir. Bastone and Ayman did the same.

Bastone noted the emir's turban. The cloth was deep blue, its weave more intricate than the white turbans he saw at the souk. Bastone was certain the rich blue color had been made from *indigofera*, an expensive dye imported from India, rather than from woad, grown across Europe. Zakariya wore a cotton *boubou*, a loose gown, a lighter blue, the color representing the sky and divinity in the Quran.

After the emir nodded to Bastone, he spoke, the standing attendant translating. "Your Highness, thank you for receiving us. Four days ago, near Collo, three dhows, along with a galley, assaulted our ships. We repelled the attack and captured the galley."

The emir raised his eyebrows, saying a few words, his interpreter translating. "His Highness asked, how could two merchant ships defeat four ships of determined fighters?" Aymen nodded, showing the translation was correct.

Bastone intended to find common ground. "I was fortunate to serve as officer of the arbalesters under Benedetto Zaccaria on the *Paradisio*."

After the emir's translator repeated Bastone's words in Arabic, the emir's face brightened as he said, "Zaccaria! The Genoese, Admiral Zaccaria? Months ago, the admiral commanded a Castilian fleet made up of his own galleys and defeated the Marinids at the straits to the Ocean Sea. Without intending to, he aided me, weakening the Marinids, my rivals to the west."

The emir tilted his head, and paused in thought, then continued, "The admiral and I share a holy name from the scriptures. And we are both warriors. I have battled for years to become the ruler of Bejaia, liberating the city from the caliph in Tunis."

He peered at Inghio, then settled his gaze on Bastone. "Zaccaria won a magnificent victory at the Battle of Meloria. His Genoese crossbowmen were a major factor. Were you there?"

"Yes, Your excellency. I was an officer of the arbalesters, Your Highness," answered Bastone.

The emir glanced at the Bejaia flag with the crossbow, his man translating. "Bastone, the emir has instructed that you compare methods with his master arbalester."

"Of course, Your Highness," said Bastone. "It will be an honor."

The scribe whispered to the emir. He appeared irritated, then regained his poise, stiffening his back, and spoke to Inghio. "I will not stand for the attacks on trading vessels."

"But Your Highness," Inghio held out his palms to his side. "We didn't . . ." The Pisan silenced himself, appearing uncomfortable.

Bastone quickly said, "Your Highness, I am certain the Pisan fondaco had nothing to do with the assault on my ships. I searched the enemy galley. The pirates were renegades with no state association, and there was no sign they had ties with the Pisan fondaco here in Bejaia."

Neither the emir nor Inghio commented. The great hall absorbed the lies in silence. Bastone also had lied. He believed the emir had lied and Inghio concealed something. But Bastone's declaration freed the parties from complication, and they returned to business, trusting but not trusting each other.

CHAPTER XXXI

Bastone thanked Ayman, who departed for the waterfront. Bastone and Inghio left the palace, headed toward the fondacos outside the city walls. "Thank you for your support with the emir," said Inghio.

Bastone believed that Inghio and the emir had conspired to sabotage Mino's investment. But he collaborated, knowing Inghio continued playing his own role of deceit. It reminded Bastone of the thrills of deception during his days as a speculatore. He had thrived on challenges, but now he longed for freedom.

Several years earlier, during the uprising of the Sicilian Vespers, Bastone had negotiated, deceived, and cajoled pirates, spies, kings, and emperors across the Mediterranean. He trusted very few people and was ready to manipulate others. When he had met Esmeray, he almost lost her because of the deceitfulness ingrained in his behavior. But his love for her tempered him.

Bastone gently placed a hand on Inghio's shoulder. As both men halted, Bastone faced him, relaxed his eyes, giving the man a warm, friendly smile. "Signore Bonacci . . . Inghio, *paesanu*, as we agreed earlier, although our home cities fiercely compete, here we can cooperate, no?"

"Yes, that's the spirit!" said Inghio. "What can I do for you?"

"Teach me how to use your uncle's ciphering. Tell me about the zero."

After a brief walk, they arrived at the Pisan fondaco. Within the walls, a plaza was bordered by colonnades, with a church at its head, and market stalls within. Cobblestones paved the plaza and the alleys between the fondaco's buildings, but splashes of vegetation created a pleasant contrast to the lime plastered church and arcades. Thriving among the buildings, along the walls and across the plaza, were many date palms providing shade, bunches of sweet fruit hanging near the top of the trees. Trellised fig trees grew on the columns of the shop arcades and the sides of cottages. Native grasses, thistles, and peonies, with pink or magenta flowers, grew on the fringes of the plaza. The church's bell tower had neither a bell nor a cross, as stipulated by the local decrees.

Inghio welcomed Bastone into his whitewashed house. As they headed for his office, he politely asked a servant to bring wine. Inghio gestured for Bastone to sit, pulling a chair next to him at a round table with four ornately carved chairs, the furniture made of walnut. Shelves lined the walls, full of books and scrolls. The window shutters were open, letting in dry, fresh air and filling the room with light. There was a large folio made of bound parchment on the table. There were no decorations on the cover, only the title *Liber Abaci*.

Inghio placed his hand on the oversized book. "This is my great uncle's masterpiece, *The Book of Calculations*." Opening the book, he said, "The first section introduces the Hindi-Arabic numbers. My uncle learned the system during his travels with his father, trading with Arab merchants."

"What is Hindi?" asked Bastone.

"It is the major language of India."

"Yes, India, from where we import black pepper?"

Inghio nodded. "And are you familiar with the numerals?"

"My partner in Messina sent me a brief description."

Inghio showed Bastone how to use zero and how to convert between the Roman and the Arabic number systems. They took a break, enjoying wine, dates, cheese, and bread. Bastone, involved in studying the math and now relaxed, reconsidered Inghio. Perhaps his demeanor was authentic.

Returning to the book, as Inghio turned the page to the next section of the document, Bastone pointed. "A number is on top and another on the bottom of a line."

"Those are called fractions, which I will explain later. Being a merchant, you will be more interested in the next section. It gives examples of how to calculate interest and profit, *without* using an abacus."

"Bellissimo! Please, continue."

Because the pirate raid had depleted their crews, Bastone and Esmeray were forced to delay their next trading voyage to Marsala. Besides the loss of life, several of the injured were still recovering. Esmeray's wound had healed without infection. During the interval, Bastone tried to recruit more crewmen. Over the next few weeks, Ayman persuaded several of his cousins to join, and Bastone found a few sailors in the Sicilian fondaco. Bastone planned to ask the emir for help to find more sailors. He sent Ayman to request an appointment with the emir.

Before Ayman returned, Inghio visited, inviting Bastone and his family to attend Mass at the Pisan church the following morning. Although he knew it would be a challenge to convince Esmeray to go, Bastone agreed to attend. Bastone knew that after Mass, the men lingered in the plaza discussing trade prospects. If Inghio introduced him to other merchants, he could learn more about the workings of their fondaco. After explaining his motive, Esmeray agreed to join him. Their attendance at Mass went without incident, and Aspasia appeared indifferent. Bastone thought his daughter was unusually quiet about the affair, wondering if his wife had prompted her to not ask her usual many questions.

That afternoon, Bastone practiced multiplication with the Arabic numbers as Inghio had taught him. He compared the results with his usual method with an abacus and Roman numerals. The new method gave faster results. He also penned a letter to Mino on a sheet of rag paper, describing the pirate attack and the delay in the return of his ships.

Looking out of his office window, he saw a group of Genoese residents gathered near the fondaco gate talking to an unfamiliar man, who by appearance was a European sailor. One pointed in his direction, and the stranger headed toward Bastone's house. He was intercepted by Baldu, the elderly supervisor of the Genoese compound. Bastone called through the window, "It's fine, Baldu. Bring him in!"

Inside, the three men shared greetings and wine, conversing in Genoese. The stranger introduced himself as Tedisio Doria. "I left Genoa—I have forgotten how many years ago—with Ugo and Guido Vivaldi on a voyage to reach India by sea."

Bastone slapped his forehead and said, "Mother Mary! That was 1277! Years ago! Two galleys captained by the Vivaldi brothers. You were with those ships? Your ships sailed with our trading convoy on our voyage to England. After we passed through the Pillars of Hercules, your ships turned south, yes? Did you reach India?"

Tedisio finished his wine and put down his cup. "It does feel like a lifetime ago. How long has it been? Ten years? More? But, no—I didn't go as far as India."

Bastone poured more wine for them. "What happened? And how did you get here? No one in Genoa knows the fate of the Vivaldis."

"A few weeks after we sailed south from Valencia—yes, it was 1277, about ten years ago—we reached Safi, a very remote trading colony, on the west coast of Africa. We then continued south, visiting an island in the Canary archipelago. I was with the party that landed to explore. Our Berber guide referred to the people of the Canaries as Guanches. They were initially friendly, but a fight arose when bartering for food. I became separated from the group. The landing party retreated to the ships and sailed on. Likely, they assumed the Majos had captured or killed me. Thus, I don't know what happened to the Vivaldis. The local tribe, who call themselves Majos, must have thought I wasn't a threat and let me join them, marrying into their group. The most primitive Majos live in caves near the sea, but inland, a king leads, and they have built a few stone houses. And I never saw the Vivaldis again."

Baldu asked, "How did you get to Bejaia?"

Tedisio sipped, raised his cup, and toasted, "Salute! I have missed good wine. It is expensive to trade for in Safi." Baldu poured him another cup. "Grazie! How did I get here? A few years ago, the sister of the Vivaldi brothers set out from Genoa on a ship captained by her husband, Lancelotto Malocello, searching for her brothers. They arrived at Tyterogaka, the island where I was left behind, and built a score of stone houses, with plans to use the hamlet as a base to further explore and find Lancelotto's brothers-in-law. After returning to the island from one of the few expeditions south along the African coast, finding no clues of the Vivaldis, the crew and officers settled there, a few marrying local women. Lancelotto built a fort and now governs the colony. The Genoese and the Majos tolerate each other. The climate is mild but very dry and the fish are plentiful. Lancelotto sent me back with a handful of men to recruit more colonists. We bought a dhow in Safi, sailed along the coast, arriving here, and will continue to Genoa soon."

The men savored the wine, Bastone and Baldu taking in the fantastic story. "I'm sailing to Genoa tomorrow. Are you interested in joining me when I return to the Canary Islands?" said Tedisio.

"It sounds intriguing," said Bastone, "but that is a major decision. I am deeply invested here with family and business. I cannot give you an answer now." He retrieved the letter he had written to Mino. "Will you deliver this letter to Mino Nglisi in Messina?"

Tedisio raised an eyebrow. "Hmm. We'll follow the Sicilian coast and might call on Messina."

Bastone was not surprised, recalling, *Genoese therefore* . . . and added, "Nglisi might be interested in investing in your return voyage to the Canaries."

"Yes, I'll deliver the letter."

Bastone removed the letter from the leather packet and penned a few more sentences. "I am introducing you to Mino and recommending the proposal in my letter." He returned the letter to the case and gave it to Tedisio. "He lives in the merchant quarter. Just ask for him by name."

Tedisio appeared enthused. "I might recruit more colonists there. And, on my way back, I will call on Bejaia to see if you are interested in joining us."

They shook hands. After the explorer departed, Bastone recounted the story of the Vivaldi brothers to Esmeray. He could tell, as her eyes grew wide, that the tales piqued her interest in adventure and faraway places. Aspasia appeared eager as well. Bastone knew Esmeray was a dreamer, sensing her aspirations were in the clouds. Perhaps Esmeray would always seek another adventure. Will she ever be content to settle in one place? And was it important to him?

Hearing rumors that the emir was planning to lead an expedition to Collo to restore his influence there, Bastone and Inghio planned a way to exploit the venture. Several days later, Bastone and Inghio again stood before Emir Zakariya at the Bejaia Kasbah, this time as business partners.

Bastone addressed the emir, "Your Highness, I will sail to Sicily, calling on Tunis on the way, to inform the caliph that Collo is harboring pirates. Don't you agree he should know?"

The emir cleared his throat. Although twenty steps from the emir, Bastone could see him clench his jaw, forcing his words through his teeth, controlling his anger. "I have declared Bejaia a free city under *my* rule. You don't need to bother the caliph. I'll go to Collo and take care of the issue. The city is under my authority." Bastone glanced at Ayman to make sure the translation by the emir's scribe was correct. Ayman nodded.

The emir's jaw muscles relaxed as he calmed. "But, Signore Ponzio, I do have a favor to ask you. My arbalesters want to share crossbow skills with you." He cleared his throat once more. "They need to be well prepared for our venture at Collo. And I will consider using the galley that you captured to serve as my flagship for the undertaking."

Bastone kept a stoic face—hiding satisfaction that the emir had taken their bait with a strategy Inghio and Bastone had planned together.

The emir focused on Inghio. "Signore Bonacci, it is a Pisan galley, no? There are men in your fondaco with experience in navigating the vessel?"

"Yes, Your Highness."

"How many oarsmen are needed?"

"It is a small galley, Your Highness. Forty."

"I don't have that many slaves available for rowing," the emir said.

"Your Highness, are you aware the Genoese and Pisans pay their oarsmen?"

"Yes . . . at what rate?"

"One or two Genoese lira per day."

The emir scratched his chin, looking at the scribe, who nodded. The emir considered. "Hmm."

"And, unlike slaves that you must feed and shelter, you only pay oarsmen the days they are at sea. I could enlist a score of Pisans to row—half of the crew."

"Yes, that will work," said the emir. "So, what are your terms to lease the galley?"

Despite the risk of losing the valuable ship, Bastone decided to take the emir's venture without Mino's approval. "The galley is for your use with two conditions."

The emir raised his eyebrows.

"Your first sailing to Collo is at no cost," said Bastone. "But the oarsmen's wages are your responsibility. For future voyages, the lease for the vessel is one thousand lira per day, or the equivalent in goods."

The emir nodded and said, "Agreed. What is your second condition?"

Bastone wanted to protect the asset. "I propose that my two ships, with a score of skilled arbalesters, escort you to Collo."

"Also agreed," said the emir, smiling.

CHAPTER XXXII

After the emir announced he would pay oarsmen to row the captured galley, men volunteered from the European fondacos and Bejaia. A week later, on a day with clear skies and calm seas, the emir departed Bejaia for Collo aboard the galley as his flagship. A flotilla of dhows escorted the galley.

Finished consulting with the helmsman on the Giovanna, Esmeray readied to cast off. She descended to the deck, casting a distaining glance at the emir's ships. She joined Bastone in the cabin. "I still don't think it's wise to sail with the emir to Collo. Why did you agree to escort him without talking with me first?"

"I'm sorry, dolcezza mia. I just wanted to safeguard the galley."

"I know you, Bastone. You now regret committing the galley without getting Mino's approval."

"And I know Mino. He doesn't mind taking risks for profits."

"We are not a warship. We're risking another fight with the same pirates we barely survived! Think of Aspasia's safety. What if it's a trap? We are going to trust the emir?"

"As I promised, we will not enter the harbor. I told the emir we would escort his ships as a show of strength, but not join in battle."

Two days later, as the emir's fleet approached Collo harbor, two large dhows, neither flying banners, exited the harbor toward the east. The emir landed without opposition, confirming the pirates had fled on the departing dhows. Relieved there was not a fight, Esmeray ordered the *Giovanna* and *Lucia* to sail north, avoiding the pirate dhows and crossing the sea to Marsala, Sicily, where the *Lucia* docked and traded its cargo for a load of salt.

The *Giovanna* continued along the coast where Sicilian galleys kept the sea free of pirates. After unloading goods at Palermo and completing the trade voyage in Messina, they visited Mino and Giovanna. As they relaxed on padded sofas, Aspasia played across the room with the Nglisi's daughter, a toddler learning how to speak, with a nanny supervising.

The Genoese explorer, Tedisio Doria, had kept his word in delivering Bastone's letter a few weeks earlier, so Mino and Giovanna knew of their battle with the pirates. But as Bastone and Esmeray told them the details of the attack, Giovanna squirmed and wrung her hands. Mino pursed his lips and squinted. Bastone described how Esmeray was shot, tears welling up in Giovanna's eyes. She bit her lip, standing and hugging Esmeray. "You are brave! Are you all right?"

"Yes, yes. I am fine. The bolt hit me in the back and went in just a little." She held up her thumb and index finger, a tiny space between them. "*Sulu un pocu!*" Smiling, she glanced at Bastone. "*Tesoro mio* promptly bandaged me!"

Mino stood and slapped Bastone on the back. "*Un pocu? Un pocu?* What warriors! Very brave! You are quite a couple."

Suddenly, Giovanna's eyes grew wide and her mouth dropped open. "Where was Aspasia during the fighting?"

"We hid her safely deep in the hold."

Giovanna let out a long sigh. "She was not hurt? She didn't see the bloodshed?"

Esmeray shook her head.

They paused, comfortable in silence, savoring the wine.

Mino put his arm around Giovanna's shoulders. "We are joyful. Your family is safe!"

"And we are fortunate to have such caring friends!" Bastone toasted. "Saluti! And Mino we captured a Pisan galley in the battle. You have a third ship!"

Mino, showing a huge grin, toasted again, then furrowed his brow. "Where is it? How did you find a crew to bring it to Messina? I want to see it right away!"

"It's still in Bejaia. I leased it to the emir."

Mino sighed, as if all his joy had been deflated, then just as fast, his eyes grew wide. "But who cares about the ship. We are ecstatic you are here!" He assumed a devilish look. "But tell me. What is the ship's name?"

Bastone and Esmeray exchanged empty glances.

Mino held up his cup toward his daughter. "Then I christen her, *Rosa*!" They toasted. "Saluti *Rosa*!"

A few days later, the crew of the *Giovanna*, loaded with trade goods for Tunis and Bejaia, was preparing to cast off when a ship arriving from Genoa docked nearby. Two men in brown monks' habits disembarked. One was young, the other older, with hair, beard, and mustache white with age. Aspasia watched from the top of the stern castle as the two men went along the dock, querying those on one ship after another, the crewmen shaking their heads in refusal. The crew of the *Giovanna* was busy readying to leave port. Aspasia was playing delicate arpeggios on her oud as the elder man called from the wharf, "Young lady, you play the strings with considerable precision!"

"Grazzi!" said Aspasia.

"Is your ship sailing to Tunis?"

"Yes."

"Such a smart little girl. May I speak to your captain, young sailor?"

Aspasia ran down the flight to the captain's suite, returning with Esmeray.

"Signore, I mean, signora, er . . ." The older man hesitated.

"Capitanu will do," said Esmeray.

"With respect, Capitanu, you are the first female captain I have met."

Her expression remained stoic. "You asked for the captain, signuri."

"Yes, yes. I seek passage to Tunis."

"Our only guest suite is being used."

Bastone joined Esmeray, took one look at the visitor, and said, "Dottore Lullio!"

"Do I know you, son?"

"I visited the monastery at Miramar to consult your wonderful maps. They were a great help on our voyage to the North Sea."

"I'm sorry, I don't remember you, but yes . . . I remember the visit by Admiral Zaccaria, no?"

Esmeray said, "The doctor wants to go to Tunis."

"We are going to Tunis," said Bastone. "Come aboard. We're ready to depart, but where's your baggage?"

"We don't have a cabin for him," said Esmeray.

Lullio placed his palms together as if in prayer. "My fellow traveler and I are missionaries, doing the work of Jesus, living a simple life as he did. We will sleep on the deck. And we travel just as we are."

Bastone glanced at Esmeray, who shrugged and returned to the stern castle.

The *Giovanna* departed Messina and sailed to Marsala, joining the *Lucia*, which had been loaded with salt. Together, the ships crossed the sea to Tunis. On the trip from Sicily to Africa, Lullio joined

Esmeray and Bastone at midship with Aspasia, enjoying pasta with them. Esmeray had finished her food and stood to leave, pausing to wait for her daughter. Aspasia was done eating but she remained seated, Bastone sensing she was interested in listening to Lullio. Esmeray knelt down next to her daughter. "Aspasia, you have chores." Bastone was certain Esmeray didn't want Aspasia to hear what the Christian mystic said. Aspasia wisely avoided talking back to her mother. As they departed, Esmeray said, "I'll be at the helm."

As Lullio watched them leave, he looked heavenward, his lips moving in silence. He turned to Bastone. "Thank you for taking us to Africa," said Lullio. "I have a letter from Pope Nicholas to the caliph, appealing to him to consider accepting the teachings of Jesus, who the Muslims consider a prophet."

Bastone looked incredulous. "The Pope writes to the caliph?"

"Yes. They have been corresponding for a few years. I am more than a mere messenger for the Pope. I have studied the works of Mohammedan writers and with that knowledge, I have developed a system of rational and scientific arguments to convert Jews and Muslims to Christianity."

"Scientific? What do you mean, scientific?" asked Bastone.

"It is the art of using knowledge and facts. I have written a book in which I show how to use mathematics and shapes to solve philosophical problems. The caliph is a very educated man and reads Latin. I am sure he will be open to discussion."

Bastone shrugged. "Dottore, I understood little of what you said, but I wish you the best of luck in Tunis. But be careful trying to convert Muslims."

"Thank you for your concern, Bastone," said Lullio, "but God will protect me."

The next day, when they reached Tunis, Lullio and his companion disembarked. Bastone offloaded goods, trading for local products to take to their next port of call, Bejaia.

Several days after departing Tunis, the two ships arrived in Bejaia. It was late September and, with the onset of inclement weather, crossings to Sicily would be less frequent. Having more time in Bejaia, Aspasia studied Latin, improved her writing, and Bastone taught her the Hindi-Arabic numerical system. In her free time, she played with the children of the Genoese and Sicilian families inside the walled enclaves of the fondacos. She was not allowed to leave the compounds without her parents.

Esmeray met Sautara, a girl from the adjacent Sicilian fondaco. They delighted in romping through the fondaco, hiding, dashing between houses, fleeing from imaginary phantoms. Sometimes, the girls secretly left the fondaco and played with children at the Pisan compound. Another time they went to the seaside, Aspasia showing Sautara her family's fishing boat beached near the port, being leased by a local Hafsid to harvest coral. Emboldened that their forays had gone undiscovered, Aspasia and Sautara slipped out of the fondaco one day and played hide and seek with Hafsid girls near the souk. The boys were in their own groups, wrestling, sparring with sticks, or racing.

Over months' time, Aspasia frequently snuck out, making friends with the Hafsid girls, while Esmeray had become annoyed by the neighbors pressuring her to attend church. Richelda, the elder supervisor's wife, made a habit of knocking on their door every Sunday morning, insisting that they attend Mass with her at the Pisan church. Esmeray agreed to go with Bastone, after he convinced her he needed to attend to strengthen political and commercial ties.

On most Sundays, about one hundred people attended Mass at the small church. Most of the congregation were Pisans, with a score of Genoese and Sicilians at Inghio's invitation. Everyone stood during Mass, the priest facing the altar reading from a missal, a book containing all the scriptures and chants needed for the Mass. There was no chorus, but the priest and his young apprentice sang the choral sections.

The Christian mystic, Ramundo Lullio, who had crossed the sea as a guest on the *Giovanna*, had arrived from Tunis a few days earlier. The caliph had issued him a letter with permission to evangelize, but only at the customs house market. He had preached at the market several times over the last few days without incident. Inghio invited Lullio to attend the Mass at the Pisan church and, recognizing that Lullio was a zealot, he had secured a promise not to interfere with the priest's homily.

Bastone recalled years earlier at Aspasia's birth, Esmeray had said she didn't care whether Aspasia was baptized. Afraid she might change her mind, he had taken his daughter to a priest for christening. Thus, Aspasia could receive the Eucharist. The family knelt for communion, Esmeray joining, to not cause an issue.

As a child, Bastone remembered that as soon as children could chew, they received communion with the adults. But the Church had changed, now restricting communion to those older than seven. The priest included Aspasia as she held out her hand, accepting a piece of bread, and sipped from the chalice.

As they walked home, Aspasia asked, "Do people understand the Latin words the priest says at Mass?"

Bastone glanced at Esmeray as if to pass the question to her. She answered, "No, most people know only a few Latin words. I can read most Latin texts, but I did not understand every word he said. You are learning Latin, Delfinina. Did you understand it?"

"Hmm. When the priest handed me a piece of bread, he said, 'This is my body' and when I sipped from the chalice he said, 'This is my blood,'" said Aspasia.

"And?" asked Esmeray.

"It sounded funny—no, not funny. I mean—it sounded weird," said her daughter.

They walked on in silence, Bastone repressing the urge to explain the symbolism.

Aspasia said, "It was even stranger when the priest said, '*Resurrexit a mortuis*'—he got up, er, he got up, again, from the dead? What's that mean?"

Bastone said, "He rose from the dead."

"I know that can't happen," said Aspasia. "I saw the dead men on the ship. None of them came back alive."

CHAPTER XXXIII

The scirocco remained steady for several days, a sign the weather had improved. Esmeray and Bastone were at the harbor front, readying a shipment to Sicily as Richelda stayed with Aspasia at their house knitting, while the girl read the exhortations of Marcus Aurelius. The elderly woman fell asleep in the chair. Aspasia snuck out of the fondaco once again with her friend Sautara. In Bejaia, as they played hide and seek with their Muslim friends, they saw a troop of the emir's soldiers rush toward the souk. Esmeray and Sautara followed to investigate.

At the souk, Aspasia recognized the missionary Lullio, who was preaching in Arabic and declaring that Christ was God. A crowd of men raised their fists and jeered at him.

Aspasia covered her mouth with her hand. "Sautara, why are they so mad at him?"

Her friend tugged on her arm. "We should go!"

Aspasia was frozen to the spot. "He's not a bad man!"

A few angry men pushed and struck Lullio's disciple. The girls stepped backwards, then turned and broke into a dash along the street. Aspasia looked over her shoulder as they ran and saw the soldiers pull Lullio from the crowd and drag him away.

Aspasia and Sautara hurried across the souk, weaving among the market stalls and shoppers, running toward the city gate. Esmeray and Bastone approached from the waterfront. Esmeray shouted, "Aspasia!"

Aspasia glanced toward the crowd of pedestrians funneling through the gate but kept going. "Aspasia! Stop!" This time she halted.

"What are you doing in the city!" Esmeray looked at Sautara. "And I know your parents don't want you to leave the fondaco." Tears ran down Sautara's cheeks as she kept her eyes downcast.

"Home. Right now," said Esmeray. Clutching her daughter's arm, she started toward the city gate to the fondacos, Sautara following behind them.

"But Mamma, that missionary who was on our ship . . . the man we left in Tunis. He's in Bejaia."

"We know, we saw him at Mass last week," said Esmeray.

Bastone said, "He had a document that he claimed gave him permission from the caliph to evangelize and to preach at the customs house."

"But he was speaking at the souk. And people were angry! Soldiers came and took him away!"

Esmeray, her grip still firm on Aspasia's arm, halted. "You were at the souk!" A group of women nearby noticed her outburst. Esmeray took a deep breath and sighed. Her voice softened. "I'm just glad they did not hurt you, Delfinina." Her eyes met with Bastone's. "If that man wants to make trouble, that's *his* problem."

Aspasia looked at her father, who answered, "Lullio broke the caliph's decree."

As the family continued to the fondaco, Esmeray said, "I am surprised the caliph approved of Lullio even preaching at the customs house, where the market is filled with Muslims every day."

Bastone glanced at Esmeray. "The caliph in Tunis gave consent to preach, but the emir doesn't recognize the caliph's sovereignty over Bejaia."

Several days later, the captain of a ship arriving from Messina brought a letter from Mino and delivered it to Bastone at the fondaco. The captain had his son with him.

Bastone invited them into the house. As they sat at the table, enjoying figs and diluted wine, Bastone asked the captain about his voyage and the sea conditions. Esmeray and Aspasia arrived and joined them. The boy's eyes sparkled when he saw Aspasia.

After Bastone introduced Esmeray, the captain placed a hand on his son's shoulder. "My son is the cabin boy for our ship."

Esmeray smiled, leaning on her elbows toward the boy. "Are you learning how to sail? Do you want to be captain someday?"

"Si, um . . ." His eyes darted to his father and back. "Si, Signura."

Esmeray glanced at her daughter. "Aspasia is a . . . my cabin . . . boy." She laughed. "Or cabin girl?" Aspasia sat up straighter, issuing a genuine smile at the boy. The boy's mouth hung open.

The captain's head tilted, an eyebrow raised. "Signura, you are a captain?"

Bastone answered, "She is captain of the nave *Giovanna.*"

"Very good!" said the captain. "And Aspasia, do you want to be captain of your own ship?"

"Si Capitanu! And I can pilot a trohantiras."

The parents laughed, but the youths shared frowns.

Figs and bread were passed around the table. "What is happening in Sicily?" asked Bastone.

The captain tore off a piece of bread, pausing. "King Alfonso died. James is now the king and governs Aragon. His younger brother, Frederick, is regent of Sicily. His mother, Constanza, and the Sicilian parliament support Frederick. And Sicily was still safe when we left Messina, but there have been sea battles near Calabria and Aragon. When we return, I'm not sure what we'll find." He bit off a mouthful of bread. "Mmm."

Esmeray said, "Captain, please stay a little longer. She nodded in the direction of the outdoor oven. "I have pasta baking. There is plenty for everyone."

Bastone thought the invitation was uncharacteristic for Esmeray. She didn't care for visitors. But then he recognized that his wife wanted to give Aspasia and the boy time together. They had shown interest in each other.

As they ate, the adults talked while Aspasia and the captain's son carried on their own conversation After their guests left, Esmeray asked Aspasia, "You got along fine with the young man."

Aspasia nodded. "Maybe because we are both cabin boys."

Bastone opened the correspondence from Messina. "I wonder if Mino will tell us to cast off for Sicily." He handed the letter to Aspasia. "Delfinina, read it to us."

She sat at the table, scanning the document. "Papa, this isn't Latin!"

"Mino writes in Sicilian. It is unusual, but now more common, dolcezza mia. You will recognize many of the words . . . and many will just have different endings. Try."

At first, she stumbled over words, but with his help, improved. Aspasia read over the polite greetings and news of Mino's family, then read about the war.

"Charles II of Naples, the son of the late King Charles, launched a new fleet to reconquer Sicily. Di Lauria, however, commanding the Sicilian navy for Aragon, defeated the Angevins, keeping Sicily free. There is word Charles is preparing another fleet, making the safety of the trading routes uncertain. Rekindling of the war will delay your trading voyages to Sicily.

Aspasia's frown matched her parents'.

The next Sunday, Richelda once again shepherded Aspasia and her parents to the church. After attending Mass, the family went to the harbor to meet the man leasing their boat. On the way they saw the missionary. Bastone greeted him, "Dottore Lullio, we missed you at Mass." He sensed his wife was impatient to go.

Lullio bowed his head. "Good morning, Ponzio *famiglia*."

Esmeray did not return his greeting.

Aspasia, however, was not shy. "Did the soldiers hurt you at the souk?"

"Aspasia!" said Esmeray.

"No, no. It's alright," said Lullio. "You know of my . . . er, arrest?"

"I . . ." Aspasia looked at her mother. "I was there in the souk. I saw you."

"No, little one. They did not hurt me. The Lord protects me. The emir . . ." he glanced at Esmeray and Bastone. "The emir isn't bad. He just said I couldn't speak at the souk." He looked at Bastone. "The Pisans didn't let me attend Mass. They said my presence will threaten their fondaco." He motioned for his apprentice to follow. "The Lord will guide us." The missionaries departed, Lullio saying goodbye.

Aspasia and her parents passed through the sea gate, reaching their fishing boat beached south of the harbor on a sandy strip. Izem, the fisherman leasing the boat, stood waiting to cast off to gather red coral, also called *precious* coral, because for thousands of years royalty had valued the rare commodity for jewelry and ornamentation.

"*As-salamu alaykum*—Hello!" said Izem. "Let's harvest the blood coral."

Izem and Aspasia boarded the fishing boat, its bow grounded. Esmeray and Bastone pushed off, jumping on, familiar with the vessel having sailed it for years. Izem took the tiller as Bastone rowed the boat across the harbor. Esmeray had removed her veil, but kept her headscarf, waiting at the mast to hoist the mainsail first. Aspasia asked Izem, "Why did you call it blood coral? Because it's red?"

"Yes, and do you want to know how the coral got that name?"

She nodded.

"Ages ago, a vicious monster named Medusa had hair made of snakes. Her eyes were so terrifying that anyone who looked at them turned into stone. A hero named Perseus used his shield as a mirror to avoid looking directly at her and cut off her head. The drops of blood fell into the sea and made the beautiful red coral we now harvest."

It did not surprise Bastone when Aspasia laughed. She enjoyed hearing magic tales, because to her they were funny, not believing them.

They sailed along the shore. After a half hour, Izem shouted, "This is the best place to find coral." He pointed at several other boats nearby and a ship a few hundred yards offshore. "They are searching for coral. That boat is from the Pisan fondaco. That one over there is Catalan, and there's one from the Sicilian fondaco, and the other . . . I am not sure. Maybe it belongs to that ship offshore."

Bastone squinted. The ship's flag had a yellow fleur-de-lis. The image of the lily was large, covering most of the dark blue field, so even from this distance he could tell it was the flag of Provence, loyal to Charles II and thus an enemy of Sicily. "I think they are from Marseilles. And far from home," said Bastone.

At the stern, Izem hefted a rig made from two timbers, each six feet long, joined in the shape of a large x, and held together with heavy iron bands. Small nets hung from the timbers. A rope connected the rig to the stern. He lowered the device into the water, the iron weights sinking the rig. They sailed down wind, dragging the rig along the sea bottom. After a short time, Izem pulled the rig up to the side of the boat, collecting pieces of red coral snagged by the nets.

"Here is our treasure," he said.

Izem then pointed to a boat fifty yards away, where a man surfaced and handed his partner on the boat an array of unbroken coral branches, the shape of a Jewish menorah. Izem cried, "That is perfection! The diver is Cola . . . Cola Pesce, from Catania—he swims like a fish to the bottom and retrieves the red coral branches, unbroken.

Those are the most valuable. Few men can hold their breath as long, or dive as deep as *Pesce*—The Fish."

Aspasia had stopped her forays into Bejaia. Her Muslim girlfriends, now ten years old, were no longer allowed on the street without a male family member accompanying them. Aspasia spent most of her time with Sautara or either studying or sailing with her parents. They had begun trading along the North African coast to raise money to pay their crew, as they waited for news from Mino when to resume voyages to Sicily.

Izem had made enough money harvesting coral and planned to build his own boat. Aspasia, recalling her mother had built their fishing boat with her own father, was interested in the undertaking. Izem harvested coral in the mornings, and in the afternoons, the Ponzio family, still waiting for news of their next trade voyage, helped him build a dhow. They worked on a secluded beach near the harbor, and Esmeray was relieved to be free of scrutiny from the public.

Years earlier, Esmeray and her father had built their fishing boat by nailing cedar planks to a frame, edge to edge, to form the hull. For waterproofing, they hammered hemp ropes soaked with resin into the joints between the planks. She was surprised to learn the Hafsids did not use iron nails to make the dhow hulls, but instead sewed the planks together.

After purchasing cedar timbers from trees harvested in the nearby Atlas Mountains, Izem spent the first few weeks shaping them into planks to match edge to edge to form the hull. He then disassembled the hull, wrapping each plank with a long mat woven from fibers of palm stalks. After matching the planks back together, using a hand drill, he bored holes through the planks. Esmeray and Aspasia threaded twine made from palm fronds through the holes. Bastone and

Izem pulled the twine through, anchored their feet against the hull, pulled, and tightened the line by twisting it with a stick then tying it. As they stitched the planks together, they compressed the mats of palm fiber, forming a watertight seal. To preserve the joints, Izem soaked them with pomace olive oil—cheap, low-quality oil from the final press. As the last step, Izem would coat the hull with a mixture of lime and fat as an antifouling treatment, preventing barnacles and wood worms from damaging the planks.

Day by day, they continued the meticulous construction. One Friday, Aspasia helped Izem, feeding him the palm twine through holes in the planks as he tightened and knotted the cords. She said, "Our priest said Christians shouldn't work on Sundays. Today, Friday, is the Muslim holy day and you are working."

Working next to Aspasia, passing twine through the hull to Bastone, Esmeray's voice was firm. "Aspasia!"

Izem paused in his task, stood, and peered over the rim of the hull, smiling. "Signura, it is fine. May I explain to her?"

"Yes, go ahead."

"Aspasia," said Izem, "on Fridays, Islam's holy day, men are required to attend prayers at the mosque, but afterwards we can work. On days other than Friday, we can pray at any location. But we always pray to *qibla*—the direction to Mecca. Muslims forbid women from attending prayers in the mosque, so they pray at home." Izem dropped out of sight behind the hull and continued to work. "I am pleased you are curious about our people, little one."

Finishing the day, Bastone and family bid Izem a good evening. Esmeray adjusted her head scarf and replaced her veil as they crossed the beach and headed toward the city gate.

"Mamma, I don't want to wear a veil."

"You won't have to worry about that for a few years."

"Soon, we'll be sailing again, and you'll be free out at sea, Delfinina," said Bastone.

"Mamma, you probably wish they didn't let women go to the church, like the Muslims."

The following Sunday morning, Esmeray argued with Bastone about attending Mass. "I'm not interested. You can go."

Bastone's voice was sharp. "Do you know how Aspasia's life will be affected if she rejects the Church? When she grows up, people will shun her. And the Church is vindictive. She would be safer being a Muslim or Jew! The Catholic Church despises heretics more than followers of other religions!"

Esmeray's tone of voice matched his. "Yet I have done well!" She then quieted. "I am smart enough not to reveal my beliefs to the wrong people."

Bastone lowered his voice and cradled his wife by her shoulders, saying, "Yes, you are my Dolcezza." He turned to regard their daughter, her eyes wide. "Aspasia is bright, but she is still a child. Her behavior could reflect on the family."

Richelda's knock on the door signaled her arrival to usher them to Mass, as she did every Sunday. The three exchanged looks, their eyebrows raised. Aspasia said, "Papa, I'll go, and Mamma can . . . rest."

Esmeray studied her daughter. "No, you . . ."

Aspasia looked at Esmeray. "It's alright, Mamma." She turned, directing her voice toward the door. "Come in, Signura Richelda!"

The next few weeks, Bastone and Aspasia went to Mass without Esmeray. She had convinced Richelda that she was feeling sick, but she sensed that the older woman was becoming suspicious.

CHAPTER XXXIV

Bastone and Esmeray were restless to hear from Mino. Their short trade runs along the North African coast had generated little money, leaving insufficient funds to pay the crews of the *Giovanna* and *Lucia*. Also, Hafsid merchants complained to the emir that Bastone was interfering in local trade. Esmeray had kept the crew busy repairing the rigging and sails, while Ayman and the Hafsid sailors had found work in Bejaia.

Esmeray consulted Izem about cleaning the *Lucia's* hull. He took them to the Wadi Soummam, a river a mile south of the city that flowed into the Gulf of Bejaia. There was a low bluff along the riverbank used by local shipowners to careen large dhows, exposing the hulls for cleaning. The *Lucia's* captain, Cardo, approved of the location and was familiar with the method. He used dinghies to pull the ship upstream to the shallows alongside the bluff. The crew tied ropes to the masts and pulled, tilting the ship to expose one side of the hull. Sailors scraped barnacles off the hull, working from the deck of Esmeray's fishing boat, tied off and floating alongside. Leaving Cardo to supervise the work, Esmeray departed in a dinghy, a sailor rowing her to the harbor and escorting her to the fondaco.

Shortly after Esmeray arrived at her house, Richelda called on her, accompanied by a pair of Genoese women who routinely attended Mass at the Pisan church. Aspasia was in the next room with Bastone, studying. Esmeray welcomed the women, who were familiar to her, and asked them to take a seat around the kitchen table. Esmeray poured a splash of red wine into each of their cups, then added water. Richelda said, "Please, a little more water. It has been very warm and dry. And dear, our visit isn't only social."

"Please enjoy," Esmeray said, waiting for Richelda to speak as the women sipped the wine. Richelda glanced at the other visitors. "The ladies have a complaint about Aspasia's behavior at Mass."

Esmeray's eyes widened. She had expected them to ridicule her for not attending Mass. Only Bastone and Aspasia had been going. She bristled at the criticism of her daughter, but softened her gaze to appear receptive, waiting for their comment.

A woman next to Richelda said, "Last Sunday during Mass, Aspasia snickered while the priest was reciting the liturgy."

Esmeray almost laughed, but she sensed in Richelda's darting eyes she should take the woman seriously. She asked, "Did she interrupt Mass?"

"No, but I saw and heard her."

"Did my husband notice?"

A second woman spoke, "We know she's a hellion, leaving the fondaco and running on the streets with the Hafsid children."

Esmeray answered, "She doesn't do that any longer." But seeing their stony faces, she realized no words would defend her daughter and she was ready to ask them to leave.

The woman added, "If you attended Mass, perhaps your daughter would behave."

Esmeray stood abruptly. She had not intended it, but her heel caught the spindle of the chair, flinging it backwards against the wall with a loud crash. She stood motionless, hands on the table, eyes straight ahead, as Richelda gestured for the women to leave, saying, "I'm sorry, Esme!"

Richelda steered the women out the door. One of them said, "God knows what that girl was doing with those Muslim boys!"

Esmeray remained unmoved, controlling her anger, staring at the far wall. Bastone and Aspasia had heard the commotion, hurrying from the next room. "What was that noise?" said Bastone.

Aspasia pointed to the chair. "Mamma?"

Richelda returned later, apologizing. She said the women had mentioned Esmeray's absence at Mass, and they wanted to encourage her to come to church, but they hadn't appeared hostile. Richelda had come with them hoping to temper comments and make sure they behaved in a Christian manner.

Two weeks later, a convoy of Genoese, Pisan, and Sicilian trading vessels arrived at the port of Bejaia. The sailors reported that the threat of war had decreased. A Genoese captain from the convoy delivered a letter from Mino.

Bastone, Esmeray, and Aspasia sat around the kitchen table, enjoying figs, bread, cheese, and diluted wine. Bella, the house cat, napped on Aspasia's lap. Bastone read Mino's letter to them. "Conditions have improved across the sea." He glanced at his wife. "Captain Esmeray, you are to load the *Giovanna* and the *Lucia* with trade goods and sail to Sicily."

Bastone paused. Cheered by the news, they grinned at each other, then Bastone continued reading. "While King James was occupied with a French invasion and defending Sicily from the Angevins, Castille has taken territory from Aragon in Spain. James, weary of war, has commanded a halt to offensive action against the Angevins in Naples." He glanced at Aspasia, raising his eyebrows. "Any questions, Delfinina?"

"Papa. I'm ten. Yes, I understand. James is the king of Aragon. You told me about the Angevins. They are our enemies because they were cruel to Sicilians before we threw them out." Her parents laughed.

"*Multu beni*, Aspasia." Bastone continued, his brow furrowing with worry. "No!" He looked up from the letter. "James is proposing to give Sicily back to Angevins to make peace." He drank, then poured straight wine in his cup.

Aspasia tensed, shrinking back, nestling with the cat. She petted Bella, whispering, "Bonu gatta, bonu gatta."

Esmeray said, "It is the Pope who is causing these evils. He didn't help the Sicilians when they asked for his protection. Those poor people! After all their sacrifices expelling Charles."

Aspasia hugged Bella closer, trying to ignore her parents' outburst.

Bastone continued reading, his tone more hopeful. "Queen Constanza and the members of the Sicilian parliament strongly oppose a return to Angevin rule, and the people support them. Sicily can remain free if Frederick resists James."

Aspasia looked up. "Papa, will you have to fight again?"

With a lull in the war, over the next few weeks Bastone purchased goods to take to Sicily while Esmeray readied the *Giovanna* to sail. Cardo hired local workers to help his sailors finish scraping barnacles from the *Lucia*, after which they coated the hull with a mixture of fat and lime.

Bastone and Aspasia had not been attending Mass after the visit by the local women criticizing Aspasia's behavior. While Esmeray and Bastone prepared the ships at the harbor, Richelda stayed with Aspasia at their house. Esmeray and Bastone returned home one evening after a long day of preparing ships.

Bastone entered the house, hugging Aspasia and kissing her on the forehead. "We'll be ready to cast off in a few days, Delfinina!"

Esmeray stepped outside where she and Richelda talked. Within moments Esmeray returned, her mouth set in a hard line, nostrils flaring, eyes of lightning—her face like a storm.

Bastone's eyes widened. "What's wrong, Esme?"

Aspasia went to Esmeray, grasping both her hands. "Mamma!"

"Richelda just told me the women have spread gossip, accusing me of acting like a man and being a witch! They say I have cast a spell on both of you to reject God!"

"No!" Bastone embraced her, pulling Aspasia close to huddle with them. He said, "*They* are the evil ones!"

Esmeray calmed. She knelt in front of her daughter, gently placing her hands on the girl's shoulders to face her. "I am sorry, Delfinina. I should not have yelled."

Aspasia chewed on her lower lip, holding back tears.

"Their words don't matter. We are strong! We don't need them, right? Delfinina?"

Aspasia nodded and didn't cry.

"All we need is our family—each other—our boat, and the sea."

Aspasia smiled and nodded again. "And the cats."

That evening, after Aspasia went to sleep, Esmeray and Bastone talked further about what Richelda had said. "Bastone, other accusations were made by women, but I didn't want to mention them in front of Aspasia. They said I had failed at raising Aspasia. Her intelligence and adult-like knowledge led to the belief that she is a changeling, a devilish incarnation. I've had enough. We must leave Bejaia."

"I'm sorry, Esme."

She sat on the edge of the bed, staring ahead, with her arms crossed. Bastone joined her, placing his arm around her shoulders. "Mino won't like that. What about our contract with him? You would probably lose your command of the *Giovanna*. Are you willing to do that?"

"Yes."

Bastone kissed her on the cheek, refraining from intimate consoling, sensing she was inaccessible at the moment. "Va beni, Dolcezza mia."

The timing would be right. They had already prepared a shipment to Sicily, and the truce gave them the confidence they could sail to Messina and end their contract with Mino.

Bastone invited Cardo to his house and informed him he was leaving Bejaia. Cardo sipped wine and smiled. "Did Mino decide he couldn't stay cooped up in Messina? When does he arrive?"

"No. He's not coming."

Cardo lost his smile. "Did he break his contract with you?"

"No, I'm breaking the contract."

Cardo's bushy eyebrows knitted together, and he banged his cup on the table, spilling wine. "You are abandoning my uncle. After all he's done for you?"

Bastone did not answer, let Cardo finish his drink, calming him, then said, "I will recommend you become director of the fondaco."

Cardo turned his command of the *Lucia* over to his first mate and took charge of the fondaco. He wrote a letter to his uncle Mino giving it to Bastone to deliver to Messina.

The *Giovanna* and *Lucia*, loaded with hides, honey, and wax, joined a few of the ships that had arrived weeks earlier and together crossed to Sicily. In tow behind the *Giovanna* was the *Aspasia*, their prized trohantiras, the family's fishing boat.

Reaching Palermo, the honey was unloaded, and they continued to Messina to deliver hides and wax. Bastone did not look forward to their meeting with Mino, to tell him they were ending their agreement to run the fondaco in Bejaia. Esmeray was moody, Bastone sensing it was very difficult for her to give up her captaincy after her dream had finally come true. The *Giovanna* and *Lucia's* profitability relied on the fondaco in Bejaia. Bastone wished for an alternative where Esmeray could remain captain. If not, Esmeray insisted they return to Favignana.

In Messina, at their villa overlooking the harbor, Mino and Giovanna welcomed the family. Giovanna introduced her second child, a year old boy. Her daughter was now three and was excited to have Aspasia as a playmate. Giovanna summoned the nanny, who took the children outside to the garden.

A servant brought cheese, bread, and olives, along with a pitcher of red wine and a vessel of water, placing them on a low refectory table carved from dark walnut. The couples sat on wooden chairs that matched the table. Giovanna poured a dash of wine, then added water to their cups. They talked about their children and the intermittent danger of war affecting the shipping company. Before Mino delved into business, Bastone handed Mino the letter from Cardo, who laid it on the table. Bastone said, "Perhaps you should read it now."

Mino's head tilted down, but his eyes peered at Bastone in disapproval. "You know its contents?"

"Um . . . no . . . I am only guessing," said Bastone, "but I will explain."

Mino sat back with a mischievous smile.

"We must withdraw from our tenure at the Bejaia fondaco." Bastone paused, glancing at Mino, then Giovanna. Curiously, he didn't detect a disapproving response, even with his skills as a former spy.

Mino opened the letter, scanning it. "Yes, I see. Cardo has assumed the directorship of the fondaco. That's good news."

Bastone and Esmeray glanced at each other, their eyes widening with surprise.

Mino stroked his chin, pausing. "Hmmm, but a Sicilian leading the Genoese fondaco?"

"The Genoese and the Sicilian compounds in Bejaia share a common wall, allowing free passage between the fondacos," said Bastone. "They cooperate and support each other, and the Genoese at the fondaco have known Cardo for years."

"You think it'll work?" Mino questioned.

"Do you remember when I told you about the resin production at Linguaglossa? That is a successful Genoese-Sicilian venture."

Mino said again, "Are you sure it will work?" He then laughed, "*Scherzu*—I'm jesting!" Mino drank, adding, "*Tuttu a beddu*—all's fine! Please share your reason for leaving Bejaia. I know you have been landside for longer than usual, but this war can't last forever, and you'll be at sea more often." He glanced at Esmeray with his last words.

Bastone held his wife's hand as he said, "We want Aspasia to live in a community where . . . um . . . I don't know how to say it . . ."

"It's fine, Bastone," said Esmeray. "Let me tell them."

"Esme, they have accepted our resignation, you don't have to . . ."

But his wife continued, recounting how a group of women at the fondaco had criticized her for acting like a man, spreading rumors she was a witch keeping Bastone and Esmeray away from Mass. Esmeray didn't mention she did not attend church.

Giovanna waved her hand beside her head. "Are they crazy? It's good you left, Esme."

A series of relaxing chords from Aspasia's oud reached their ears from the garden.

Giovanna's eyes grew wide. "And they knew she played a lute? Esme, you can't go back to Bejaia *or* live in Messina. Lately, there has been much talk of the *streghi et favulli*—witches and fairies." She held up her right hand, joining the tips of the middle and ring fingers to her thumb, while extending the index and little fingers. The sign of the horns to ward off evil.

"You believe them!" said Esmeray.

"No. No!" cried Giovanna. "I just made the sign out of . . . out of habit." Giovanna poured more wine for herself and the others, diluting it with water. "The sound of Aspasia's lute reminded me of the fairies. Good fairies bring food gifts, while evil fairies—witches—strum lutes to mesmerize and harm people. The folklore, I admit, *is* fascinating, although morbid."

"Giovanna!" said Mino. "I apologize. My wife has read a poem that describes the horrors of going through Purgatory and Hell. The ghastly punishments that sinners undergo captivated her."

They peered at Giovanna as if expecting a denial. She didn't have to comment; her subtle smile was endorsing. After a pause, she said, "The poet Dante Alighieri wrote the tales while living in Genoa, exiled from his native Florence. He had not published it yet, but I got a copy of the draft. Instead of writing the poem in Latin, he penned it in Tuscan."

Bastone and Esmeray's eyes widened.

Mino said, "I have read it. Before Dante's poem, I had only seen literature written in Latin or Sicilian. It was challenging to read."

"And Queen Constanza is a character in the poem," said Giovanna.

Esmeray didn't believe in Hell or Purgatory, but she still cared how Constanza was portrayed in what she considered a tale of superstitions. "What, no!" said Esmeray. "Who would write a story with Constanza in Hell? She was kind to me. And the Sicilian people love her."

"She was in Purgatory, having her soul purged to earn her heavenly reward."

"That's better," said Esmeray. "She deserves more."

Giovanna reached across the table and touched Esmeray's hand. "*Scusi*, Esme, for mentioning the Sicilian witches. I was just warning you to be careful. Perhaps your crew heard the women's gossip in Bejaia about you and Aspasia? Would any sailors spread those lies?"

Bastone and Esmeray exchanged glances. They drank in silence.

Map

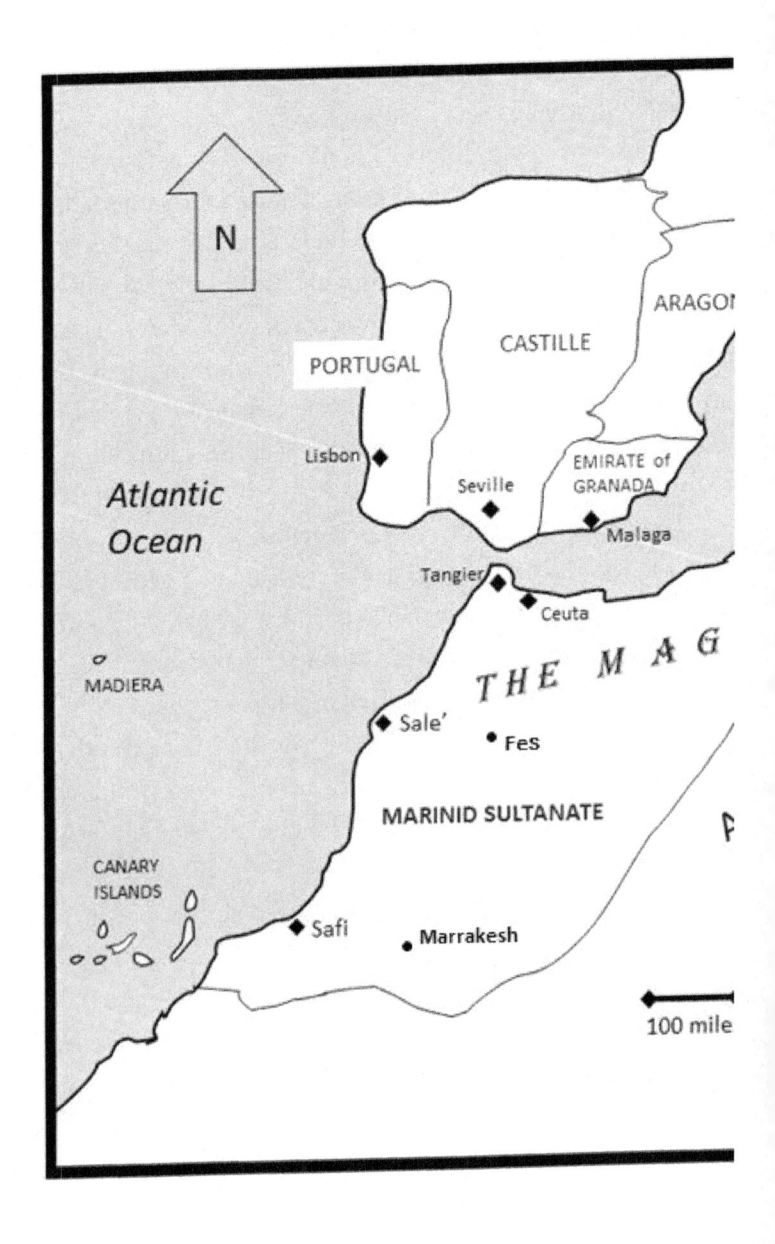

Atlantic Ocean

PORTUGAL — Lisbon
CASTILLE — Seville
ARAGON
EMIRATE of GRANADA — Malaga
Tangier
Ceuta

THE MAG...

MADIERA

Sale'
Fes

MARINID SULTANATE

CANARY ISLANDS

Safi
Marrakesh

100 mile

Michael A. Ponzio

13th Century Genoese Commercial Empire of the Western Mediterranean

Genoese Occupied Territory

Genoese Trading Colonies

CHAPTER XXXV

"But you must hear my plan!" Mino leaned forward as he described his scheme. "Remember Tedisio Doria, the Genoese explorer, who called on you at Bejaia? He stopped in Messina, delivered your letter, and continued to Genoa to recruit colonists to settle the Canary Islands. A few weeks ago, he visited me a second time on his return to the islands. A Genoese ship carrying settlers and adventurers for the colony sailed with his dhow. I made a contract with him to ship goods, including wine, to the Canaries. You are the man . . ." Mino paused, glancing at Esmeray then back to Bastone, clearing his throat, "you are the *partners* who can undertake this enterprise."

Esmeray let out a sigh of disbelief. "Are you serious? The round trip to Safi is a month of sailing and the Canaries are beyond Safi."

Mino crossed the large room and retrieved a scrolled parchment from a desktop. He unrolled a map, securing the ends with jugs to keep it flat, showing them the western Mediterranean. Pointing at the southern coast of Spain, he said, "We will ship wine from the Genoese fondaco located in Malaga."

Bastone asked, "Can you sell enough wine to make the venture profitable?"

"Yes. The Genoese merchants at the fondacos along the African coast will buy wine for themselves and to sell to the local people."

"Wine from Malaga?" Esmeray asked. "The port is in the Emirate of Granada." They produce wine? Even with the Muslim prohibition against alcohol?"

Mino smiled. "We now sell wine to the Hafsids in Tunis and Bejaia. As you saw in Bejaia, a significant number of Muslims secretly drink wine. The emir's predecessors, the former rulers of Granada, did not destroy all the Roman vineyards, but kept a few of them to produce raisins. My contacts at the fondaco in Malaga say the emir, however, devotes a third of his vineyards to produce wine for his royal household."

Giovanna stood and refilled their cups as Mino continued, "Bastone, your experience as a speculatore, your shrewd methods of negotiation, and the way you persuade people without threatening them, will be valuable in starting this venture. And Esmeray, I already knew you were a skilled captain, but Cardo's description of how you took command against the pirate attack has confirmed my confidence in you. Bastone, I recommend you convince the emir to convert more of his raisin crops into wine making. Draft a contract with the emir, as my representative, to export the wine to the African coast and the Canary Islands."

Mino sat back and sipped, as did the others.

Bastone said, "What's the source of their wine now? Perhaps from Castille?"

"Yes, but their prices are high. We can underbid them, but only if you ship the wine from Malaga. You will need to change your home port to be nearer the trade runs."

Bastone glanced at Esmeray. Her expression was stoic. Bastone sensed they needed to talk in private. He said, "We will think about your proposal."

Bastone and Esmeray slept well that night in their guest room, comfortable with a thick mattress and soft pillows. Aspasia had her own room, enjoying the company of the house cat sleeping with her. It was July, but the sea breezes and dry air made a restful night. Bastone dreamed that he and Esmeray were crossing the sea in their fishing boat, pounded by the winds and waves of a storm. Real to his dreaming consciousness, he was reliving the time they had crossed from Sardinia to Genoa during a tempest. The fears of capsizing and drowning which had engulfed him were absent. Instead, they were enjoying love making as the trohantiras peaked with the crests and slid down into troughs between the waves.

He woke from his dream. Esmeray was straddling him, her body glistening with perspiration in the light of the full moon. Exhausted, he muttered, "Esme?" Basking with fulfillment, she said, "I know you were dreaming of me, Bastonino!"

They lay together in silence, arms wrapped around one another. "Should we accept Mino's offer?" whispered Esmeray.

"Because you question the decision, we need more time to decide, Dolcezza," said Bastone.

They quieted in thought, falling into a slumber.

It seemed like just several minutes later, the steward knocked on the door, waking them. Pulling the bed covers over them, Bastone said, "Yes?"

The steward opened the door and placed a steaming pitcher on the dresser next to the washing bowl. "Hot water, signore. Master Nglisi expects you at breakfast in an hour."

The families ate together, enjoying fresh bread, figs, and juice from the blood red oranges. Finishing, Aspasia and the nanny took the infants to the garden.

"*Mbare,* we have not yet decided on whether to go to Malaga."

"Please, tell me your concerns," said Mino.

Esmeray leaned forward, "I am thrilled to continue as captain of the *Giovanna,* but . . ."

Mino turned his head to listen as she hesitated.

"I told you of the women's hateful behavior in Bejaia. Similar problems could arise at the Malaga fondaco."

Silence filled the room as everyone appeared lost in their own thoughts.

Esmeray broke the silence. "But I can't run away forever."

Esmeray surprised Bastone that she had shared her inner feelings with the group. "Esme, you *don't* flee confrontations!"

Mino added, "That's right, Esmeray—you, the brave captain who burned the Angevin fleet!"

Esmeray bowed her head in humility. "But now there is Aspasia."

Bastone said, "Dolcezza, do you recall what Marcus Aurelius wrote: 'People try to get away to the mountains . . .'" He paused, hoping she would continue.

Looking up, she said, "Yes, 'People try to escape to the mountains or countryside, but true escape lies within. Nowhere you can go is more peaceful—than your own soul.'"

Giovanna teared up, and she softly clapped along with Mino. He said, "There's good news about the fondaco in Malaga. It is small, the walled area enclosing a garden, a large villa, where two merchants live, and a warehouse. Another fondaco, managed by Catalans, is nearby, but the city has no Christian churches."

Esmeray appeared more receptive. Before she could reply, the steward cleared the table and brought a tray with cups, pouring water and wine for the two couples. The orange hue of the terra cotta tumbler contrasted with the dark walnut wood of the table. Mino raised his drink in their direction with a silent toast.

The steward announced Duke Gualtieri had arrived. Mino gestured to the steward and tilted his head towards the hall entrance. He then glanced at Giovanna and whispered, "Did you know your father was coming?"

She shook her head, her eyebrows raised.

The steward opened the doors of the double entryway, the duke entering with two men. Gualtieri had a broad smile as he approached Mino and his guests, who stood to greet the duke.

"Father!" Giovanna embraced him and he kissed her cheeks. Mino traded backslaps with his father-in-law, releasing him to Bastone, who greeted him with an embrace. Gualtieri took Esmeray's hands in his, as she offered her right cheek first, then left.

The steward departed, while the duke's guards positioned themselves on each side of the doors. Mino gestured with his hand toward the table. Gualtieri beamed at Bastone and Esmeray. "It is superb to see you both. I'm relieved to know that you're in good health..." He glanced toward the garden at Aspasia. "God has blessed you with a pretty daughter, no? *Beddu*!"

He drank, then said, "But I am afraid my visit is not social."

The cheer from their greetings ebbed. Bastone noticed that Giovanna squirmed, and her eyes darted toward Mino, who refused to look her way. Was Mino merely acting surprised that the duke had arrived? Had he invited the duke here to trap Bastone? It made little sense. Why had Mino offered them to command a trading venture in Malaga?

Bastone caught Mino's eye. He sensed his friend had not known the duke was coming. Without looking at Esmeray, Bastone knew she suspected the worst. Gualtieri wanted to recruit him for a hazardous mission. The war that had begun with the Sicilian Vespers' revolt a decade ago seemed never-ending.

Gualtieri inhaled deeply and sighed. "The Pope, King James, and Charles have made a treaty. James sold Sicily to the Angevins..."

Bastone spilled his drink. "No!"

Gualtieri paused as the others groaned in discontent. "The Pope has ordered the Angevins to occupy our island once again. But the Sicilian parliament, the people, and Queen Constanza have rejected the treaty and crowned Frederick as our king—King of Trinacria. He has pledged to defend Sicily against his brother, James of Aragon, who is allied with the Angevins."

Giovanna poured more wine for Bastone and the others, but did not add water. They drank with the grim shadow of war over them, but Gualtieri held his cup out, appearing to raise morale. "Saluti cent'anni! Take heart and thank God for Frederick!" They joined in the toast.

He put his cup down and leaned forward. "We have a monumental challenge ahead of us. The treaty requires Aragon to contribute forces to conquer Sicily, so it will be Sicilians against both Aragon and the Angevins."

Bastone said, "The Sicilian fleet has kept the Angevins at bay for a decade. With the Almogavars and Admiral Di Lauria . . ."

"Not anymore," interrupted Gualtieri. "Di Lauria remains loyal to Aragon."

The declaration stunned Bastone. Di Lauria had never lost a battle. Leading the joint Aragonese and Sicilian fleets, he had defeated one Angevin fleet after another.

Gualtieri had another shattering announcement. "Doctor Procida has also abandoned us."

Bastone blurted, "*Sciatiri e Matri*—Savior and Mother!"

"Bastone, you worked with him for many years. He trusts you," said Gualtieri. "He has sent speculatori to organize the Aragonese nobles in Sicily still loyal to James, as well as sway others to the Aragonese side. You may be the only speculatore who has the experience and skills to spy for him as well as spy on him. Come to my palazzo to discuss this proposal."

Esmeray resisted commenting, but she did not hide her frown of disapproval. Gualtieri had noticed. The Duke glanced toward the garden, then returned his attention to Esmeray and Bastone. "Circumstances have changed since your dangerous work during the revolt a decade ago. You have a daughter now." The duke focused on Esmeray. "I recall you were Bastone's confidante during the revolt, and you are welcome to the meeting as well. Both of you, please consider coming to discuss how you can help the cause."

That afternoon, Esmeray accompanied Bastone to Gualtieri's palazzo near the waterfront, Aspasia remaining at Mino's. They sat at a table studying a map of Sicily, daylight streaming through the unshuttered windows and illuminating the parchment. The unpleasant odor of fish and seaweed reached them from the nearby harbor, but soon the breeze replaced it with the fresh and salty scent of the open sea.

The duke marked a few places on the map using bronze coins. "The nobles in these towns have withdrawn into their hilltop castles. Frederick's men have them under watch. These others . . ." He marked locations on the map with silver coins. "These nobles are under suspicion for their refusal to contribute sailors to Frederick's fleet, despite not openly dissenting."

Bastone scanned the map. A bronze coin marked the city of Trapani. "Abate is among the barons opposing Frederick?"

"Not exactly. I believe he is watching the conflict, trying to stay neutral to see who takes the advantage. But he is withholding eight war galleys from Frederick."

Abate's lack of open support troubled Bastone. The baron was one of the most influential leaders who had aided Procida during the revolt.

Esmeray appeared to be counting the locations marked as disloyal to Frederick. "I see there are almost a score of nobles whose loyalty is in question, which makes them a significant threat. Is there any pattern or similarity among these towns?"

Gualtieri nodded, "Hmm." He stroked his beard. "Palermo, Messina, Cefalu, Catania—they are all loyal to Frederick. But of course! The treasonous towns are ports that are dominated by Catalan merchants, loyal to the Aragonese crown. And as for the undecided nobles, I am certain Procida will send agents to sway their loyalty to James."

A steward brought water and wine, each measuring their own blend of water and wine of the mascalese grapes from Etna. They paused from studying the map, savoring the drinks.

"Why has Procida betrayed Sicily?" asked Bastone. "The people revered him as a hero when he organized the revolt."

"After he invited King Peter to remove the Angevins from Sicily," said Gualtieri, "he was appointed as his chancellor. Although Procida is from Naples, he adopted Aragon as his homeland, where Peter awarded him fiefs."

Bastone had believed he and Procida had more in common. Both had lost family to Charles's cruelty. During the revolt against the Angevins, he and Procida had collaborated with the three most powerful nobles in Sicily: Abate, Caltagirone, and Alaimo. But Procida didn't love the people and land he had freed. He had only used Sicily as a pawn in his game to balance power.

Bastone loved the people of Sicily. He recalled how the people of Linguaglossa and those of Favignana, never having met him, had welcomed him like he was family. And during his years in Sicily, Bastone had been inspired by the people's bravery expelling the Angevins. The Sicilians had been merciless in their revenge against the oppressors but had also risked their own lives defending the French Angevins who had treated them fairly during the occupation, helping them escape Sicily.

Bastone wondered if he could revive a coalition of nobles like Procida had organized during the Vespers' revolt. But one was gone. Bastone had turned in Caltagirone for treason. King Peter had him beheaded several years earlier. Abate's position was unclear. He asked Gualtieri, " Duke, what is Lord Alaimo's status? He must still be a patriot. The hero who broke the siege of Messina."

The duke rubbed the back of his neck as he let out a long sigh. "You both have been away. James arrested Alaimo on false claims of sedition over a year ago. Alaimo was a true patriot of Sicily. James promised him a trial, but Alaimo disappeared without a trace. There was talk James had him drowned at sea. Bastone, we need you working for Procida again, but this time as a *contra* speculatore—a counter spy."

"How would I get Procida to add me to his spy network? He is in Aragon, no?" said Bastone. "To deceive Procida will be difficult. But just to arrange a meeting with him will be the most challenging task." Bastone paused with a wry laugh, then said, "It would be suspicious for me to sail across the Mediterranean and knock on Procida's door, proclaiming I am loyal to Aragon and eager to work for him again." Despite his sarcasm, his look became serious, stroking his chin with eyes turned upward.

Gualtieri touched his fingertips together, smiling. "I see your creative mind is stirring. I am certain you can find a way."

CHAPTER XXXVI

At Castle Mategriffon, overlooking the harbor in Messina, Frederick met with his new admiral, Conrad Doria, a Genoese he had employed after Ruggiero Di Lauria had defected to James and Aragon. Together, they crafted plans to defend against an invasion, dictating notes to a scribe as they talked. Years earlier, Doria and his brother had led the Genoese fleet to several victories over the Pisans, carrying on their family tradition in providing leaders for the Genoese Republic. Doria's exceptional skills as an admiral gave the Sicilians the best chance to match Di Lauria at sea.

During their meeting, a messenger arrived from Riposto, winded from rushing up the hill to the castle. The steward led him into the room. The messenger, catching his breath, forgot any formality and blurted, "The Angevins have taken Catania!"

Frederick commanded, "Speak man. Give me details."

"They have ten ships."

"What type of ships?"

"Um . . . yes . . . two large navi and the rest were galleys."

The scribe recorded the messenger's report as the king waved over his steward, who stood at the table in readiness. Frederick scanned the scribe's note, then handed it to the steward. "Notify the nobles at once."

Frederick peered at Doria. "Your opinion?"

"The Angevins have a much larger fleet, and we can't spare ships to relieve Catania," said Doria. "I recommend we patrol the straits day and night. If the enemy doesn't send more ships to Catania, it's a feint."

Frederick paused and said, "I agree. I will send a few knights to Taormina and Linguaglossa to organize fighters. They can block a move toward Messina by land. Unfortunately, we can't help Catania without dividing our fleet."

Doria returned to the map, "Which is what the Angevins want."

They dispatched messengers to warn the nobles in Messina that Catania had fallen to the Angevins. Gualtieri received the alert while still meeting with Esmeray and Bastone, reading the message aloud to them. He peered at the couple in silence. With the news, Bastone sensed the duke expected they would accept the assignment to contact Procida.

Bastone was certain Esmeray would be straightforward with Gualtieri. She didn't surprise him when she said, "We should leave now." Her refusal was definite.

Gualtieri appeared calm, but Bastone sensed the duke's disappointment when his eyes blinked thricefold. "You are an extraordinary couple," said Gualtieri. "If you change your mind, the Sicilian people will be grateful."

Walking back to Mino's villa, Esmeray said, "I want to be far away from the war when it starts. And I will not return to Bejaia."

"Esme, we are fortunate Mino wants us to continue trading for him. I'm sure you'll still be captain of the *Giovanna*."

When they returned to the Nglisi's villa, they accepted his proposal to ship wine from Malaga to the Canary Islands. Mino was eager to send his ships away to stay out of the conflict. He provided them with a copy of an old Roman map drawn by Plinius the Elder that he had obtained from the Genoese cartography school.

Within days the *Giovanna* and *Lucia* departed, their holds full of barrels of wine. The ships anchored in Favignana, waiting for a Genoese convoy sailing to the western Mediterranean.

Early the following morning, Esmeray stayed on the ship, checking the vessel for the voyage across the open sea, while Bastone went ashore, taking Aspasia with him. He went to the vineyards where he had worked, finding his mentor, Vincenzu. Older and slower, but still working and mentoring an apprentice, he welcomed Bastone, embracing him and pounding his back with joy.

While the men talked, Aspasia searched for Vincenzu's cats in the vineyard. Bastone asked Vincenzu's opinion on growing wine on the Canary Islands.

"How is the soil? How much does it rain?" asked Vincenzu.

"I heard that the islands have a dry, mild climate due to the sea breezes."

"If the islands are dry, with sea soils like Favignana, the *malvasia* grape will thrive." After Vincenzu pruned handfuls of the grapevines, placing them in a terra cotta jug of freshwater, Bastone sat with the aged vintner and his apprentice, savoring the mascalese wine.

"If I succeed in growing a vineyard," Bastone said, "in a few years, I'll bring you a jug of the wine to taste."

At Favignana's harbor, the sea was calm within the protecting bluffs, the water so crystal clear it gave the illusion the *Giovanna* was suspended in the air. A sailor called out, "Sails approaching from the northeast!"

Esmeray ran up the stairs to the top of the stern castle, hoping it was the Genoese trading convoy they were expecting. But instead of flags with the red cross of Genoa flying from the masts, she saw the yellow and red striped banners of Aragon, the invasion fleet the Sicilians were dreading. Esmeray hollered, "All hands on deck!" She shouted to the first mate, "Prepare to get underway!" Where was Bastone? Why was he taking so long ashore?

Within the hour, Bastone and Aspasia had not returned and thirty Aragonese war galleys along with a handful of cargo ships had anchored, blocking Esmeray's exit of the harbor. King James dispatched two dinghies from the fleet's flagship, one to the *Giovanna* and the other to the *Lucia*.

When the rowboat arrived at the *Giovanna*, an Aragonese officer demanded to come aboard. Esmeray signaled for the first mate to bring the uninvited visitor and his escort to the stern castle. The officer asked, "Where is the captain?"

"*Signuri*," said Esmeray, "I am the captain—Captain Ponzio."

"Uh . . . *signura*, er . . . Captain—I am appropriating this vessel for the Crown, King James of Aragon. You are the captain?" He addressed his escort. "I must report this to the king. Do not let anyone board this vessel until I return."

The officer returned with a contingent of Aragonese marines, who inspected the ship and determined it was secure. Esmeray met King James on the main deck as he boarded. Rather than curtsy, she bowed to him as a man would. James didn't appear insulted, tilting his head as he focused on Esmeray. She ignored his stare as he examined her from head to toe. James addressed the officer with him, "Just as you said—a lady captain."

Esmeray appeared unfazed. "Your Majesty, welcome aboard the *Giovanna.*"

James flicked his head towards the stern castle. "We'll speak alone." He gestured to the officer and men to remain as he ascended the stairs to the upper deck. Esmeray followed. They moved to a place on the stern castle where the crew couldn't hear them. He spoke to her in Sicilian. "I am curious, how in the world has a woman—a beautiful woman at that—become captain of a ship?"

She described how she sailed a fishing boat as a girl, followed by the years of rigorous work as a sailor on a large trading vessel. She spoke of the many trading voyages she'd led as captain and detailed the survival of brutal pirate attacks. As Esmeray told her story, she recalled how Bastone had taught her how to read people. She was quick to observe how the king's attitude transformed as she spoke. At first, James listened with his arms folded across his chest, displaying a crooked smile, and an eyebrow raised in sarcasm, then he unfolded his arms, leaned closer, nodding with growing interest.

When she finished, he raised his brows, his smile genuine. "Even though you are a woman, you certainly deserve to be a captain. What a story! So, now you are headed for Malaga?" He paused. "I am inclined to let you go. I respect strong women with guile. Like my sisters. They both refused proposals of marriage until they were betrothed to kings. And my mother, Constanza—she ruled Sicily when my father was away at war. But you . . . you are . . ." He cleared his throat. "Capitanu—you are making history."

Despite the danger, she had to speak her mind. "Your Majesty, it's your time to be remembered in history as a great benefactor to Sicily. When you governed the island with your brother Frederick, you treated the people well, earning the deep respect of the Sicilians." She paused, steadying her breathing to ensure her voice didn't become shaky. "But now, you are here to help the Angevins reconquer Sicily. I am concerned for the innocent children and families who will suffer when you help the Angevins return. They will certainly seek revenge."

James seemed unmoved.

Esmeray held her arms out to her sides, quoting in James's native language, "*La familia es todo*—Family is everything."

He shrugged. "Hmm. Yes, a proud Aragonese expression."

"Your Majesty, please don't make war on your brother. You will never forgive yourself if you lose him. I lost my brother to war and grieve his death every day." Esmeray noticed his expression soften, remembering Bastone's tutoring in persuasion: "Plant a seed, watch it grow, and nurture." She continued, "Think of your mother. What will the Angevins do to her without Frederick to protect her?" She detected the king's subtle flinch.

James glanced toward the stairs as if checking that someone might hear. "Yes, I love both my mother and brother, but I am committed to returning Sicily to the Angevins." He shook his head as if he'd spoken too much, and his body stiffened. "You are attempting to distract me." He frowned . . .

Footsteps sounded on the stairs. His officer appeared, and James nodded. "Your Majesty, Chancellor Procida is aboard and wishes to speak with you."

"Show him here."

The officer hurried down the steps, returning with Procida and Bastone. Both bowed to the king as the officer departed.

"Who is this?" asked James.

"Ponzio Bastone," said Procida.

James's forehead knitted with uncertainty.

Procida placed his hand on Bastone's shoulder. "He is the speculatore we were discussing. Bastone, along with his, um"—he glanced at Esmeray—"his wife, the captain, played a major role in the revolt of the Vespers. His skills as a speculatore are extraordinary, Your Majesty. I can send him to Trapani today and he will convince Abate to send you his warships."

The king's eyes widened, glancing from Bastone to Esmeray. "A fortunate coincidence Bastone is here. God's favor may be present." He chuckled, "But Bastone cannot do the impossible. The ships must be here before the morning. We sail tomorrow." James descended the stairs to the main deck to disembark.

Esmeray raised her hands and burst out, "Bastone, where's Aspasia?"

"She's safe in our cabin," said Bastone.

His wife's shoulders relaxed as she blew out a sigh of relief.

"We were waiting in the dinghy at the port side and not allowed to board until Doctor Procida arrived."

"Signora," said Procida, "when I heard the captain was a woman—and named Ponzio—I was certain it had to be you."

Esmeray remained stoic, expecting dire consequences with Procida's arrival. Yet, the doctor had treated her with the utmost respect years earlier, praising her abilities as a sailor and speculatore. She leaned forward, turning her head to her left, then right, accepting light kisses of greeting from him.

She expected Procida wanted Bastone for an undercover mission. They couldn't escape through the Aragonese fleet. How could her husband refuse? Esmeray sensed the doctor trying to lighten the mood as he said, "I talked to your daughter briefly. She displayed great maturity for her age. You must be very proud of her. Your accomplishments give her an example to follow."

Esmeray forced a smile, nodding. She suspected Procida was cajoling her.

"Bastone, I have a mission for you in Trapani." Procida added, "Esmeray, you and Aspasia will be safe here on your ship while Bastone is away."

Procida's manner and familiarity did not fool Esmeray. She and her daughter were hostages. Procida was coercing Bastone to undertake the mission and to turn against Frederick. She felt sick. Seeking vengeance for the slaughter of their troops during the Vespers, even more violence and brutal vendettas would mark the Angevins' second occupation.

The doctor continued, "Abate is harboring eight galleys. You must convince him to send the ships to join our fleet tomorrow as we sail to Sicily. Abate was your mbare during the revolt. He will listen to you."

Esmeray's hope sank that they would avoid this war. They had fled Messina to avoid the conflict, only to fall into working for the enemy—the enemy of an independent Sicily. Bastone would have no choice but to comply.

Children of the Middle Sea

CHAPTER XXXVII

Petru and Bastone sailed to Trapani on a fishing boat packed with tuna. Reaching the harbor, they sold the fish at the wharf, which the fishmongers hawked at the nearby market. Because Baron Abate alternately resided at three castles in Trapani, Bastone and Petru mingled with the citizens among the stalls at the market to find the whereabouts of the baron. Bastone learned Abate was at the Castle di Terra, a mile inland from the harbor. Petru waited at the waterfront as Bastone called on the baron.

In his receiving hall, Abate responded to Bastone's arrival. "Of course, I remember you," said Abate after a warm embrace. "You delivered the message to me in Palermo, beginning the revolt. We used the code word *Antudu*—Courage is your Lord. And I heard of your heroics later. Not just you, but your wife—um . . . Esmeray—the brave couple that burned the Angevin flect in Messina!" He led Bastone to join him at a table. The steward brought wine.

Bastone raised his cup. "And to you, Baron. You have fought bravely for Aragon under Di Lauria at . . . let's see . . . despite a two-to-one disadvantage, you triumphed in Naples and the battle off the coast of Catalonia—a resounding victory against the French."

They drank together. "Glorious memories, Bastone." Abate's smile faded. His tone became serious. "And who sent you?"

"Procida."

"Hmm. Just like old times, Bastone. I assume you want me to let James use my city as a foothold to conquer Sicily. But even if I allied with James, he'd take so many provisions from Trapani, it would impoverish the citizens. So, what is your alternative?"

Bastone said, "It's about your galleys."

The men spent an hour going over the details of the plan.

Bastone wasn't certain that Abate would release the galleys. Concerned about the short notice, he wondered if the baron would follow through according to the plan. Returning to Favignana by late afternoon, Bastone reported to the king's flagship. Procida met him on deck, and Bastone told him of the success with Abate.

"*Bonu, bonu,* I had great confidence in you." Procida lowered his voice. "I discovered the *Giovanna* belongs to Mino Nglisi of Messina. I traveled with him to North Africa years ago. He helped me save many sick men on the return to Sicily. I mistook one of them for you."

Bastone flinched. Procida had confused Bastone's brother for him. Francesco had told Bastone about a doctor in Trapani. So, it was Procida who had saved his brother. Bastone thought he masked his emotions, but Procida noticed.

"Bastone?"

He refrained from telling Procida about his brother's death. "That was my brother. I am in debt to you . . ."

"No, there's no debt. I'm simply a doctor." Procida paused, his eyes darting around.

Why was the doctor's response so impersonal, avoiding eye contact? Did Procida suspect their loyalty was to Frederick because Esmeray and Bastone commanded a Sicilian ship?

Bastone's unease retreated when Procida said, "I have asked the king to let you keep the *Giovanna* as compensation for gaining

Abate's ships. The king agreed because you are Genoese, and because of his respect for Esmeray. But he must stay unaware that the ship belongs to Mino, a Sicilian, or he will seize it. As of now, he will confiscate only the *Lucia* and her crew. Tomorrow morning, you and Esmeray can continue your journey to Malaga."

"Grazzi mille, Dottore!"

Procida led Bastone to the king's suite. The guard, recognizing the chancellor, knocked, opening the door. As they entered, they saw James at a table studying maps with his squadron commanders, who were standing.

"Your Highness, you wanted to hear from Bastone as soon as he returned," said Procida.

The king dipped his head, and Bastone bowed. "Your Majesty. Baron Abate has agreed to release his ships. The galleys will leave Trapani before sunrise and await your fleet at the Cape of San Vito."

The king looked at the map. "Yes, perfect!" Amid the captain's murmurs, James stood with a broad smile and slapped Bastone on the shoulder. "Excellent!" He glanced at Procida. "Chancellor, you were right. He succeeded. I didn't think it was possible."

Procida whispered in the king's ear, who nodded. "Bastone, I wish you smooth sailing to Malaga with Captain Esmeray. . . er, with Captain Ponzio." He glanced around at his officers. "She is the lady captain I was telling you about." The king's hand was still resting on Bastone's shoulder. "When he is on her ship this man is obligated to follow his wife's orders!"

Caught up in the mirth, Bastone involuntarily laughed with them, but wasn't amused.

James gestured that the meeting was over. Bastone bowed, and as he left the cabin, he overheard the king. "Send an officer to assess the crew of the ship we are confiscating. Don't interfere with the *Giovanna*, the other ship—the one that has a fishing boat tied to its stern."

Procida followed Bastone, clasping his shoulder as he was about to descend to Petru's boat. "*In boca al lupo,* Bastone—good luck."

"*Crepi,*" said Bastone as he rappelled down the rope. "And thank you . . . Doctor Procida."

Bastone said farewell to Petru as he boarded the *Giovanna*. After he told Esmeray they were free to leave with their ship, she insisted they talk in private in their cabin. He closed the door, and she hugged him, adding a long kiss. She drew back, still clasping his shoulders, beaming. Esmeray locked the door and pulled off her tunic. "Hurry, before Aspasia finishes her chores."

The sun was near the horizon. Aspasia spooned more pasta and chickpeas into her mouth, pausing as she said, "Mmm, mmm. This macaroni is good with olive oil." Still chewing, she mumbled, "Will they have olive oil in Malaga?"

"They will have plenty of oil, Delfinina," said Esmeray. She glanced at Bastone as they sat together on a coil of ropes. "Your papa made sure we had enough pasta. He can't live without it." As the sun went down, the breeze shifted, enveloping them briefly in the smoke from the cookfire.

Finishing their meal, Aspasia collected their wooden bowls and spoons, taking them to the port side to wash with seawater. Esmeray said, "I'm not so sure I trust James. We should leave—now." She stood, peering toward their sister ship anchored a hundred paces away. "The Aragonese are sending boats to the *Lucia.*"

"I heard James mention he was impounding the ship," said Bastone. "I wish we could do something about that. But, the king ordered his marines to leave the Giovanna alone. *Va beni?*"

She pursed her lips, continuing to stare at the *Lucia*. "It seems fine, at the moment. But when the moon is overhead, I'm going to wake the rest of the crew and cast off."

Esmeray ordered the crew to go to sleep early. Along with her daughter and Bastone, they also retired an hour after sunset, as the full moon was climbing above the horizon. In the next hour, there was a light knock at the cabin door. Bastone recognized the second mate's whispered voice. "Bastone, come out right away."

As Esmeray dressed, Bastone went to the main deck with Ayman. In the light of the full moon, he recognized two sailors from the *Lucia*, a few paces behind Ayman, water dripping from their clothes. Esmeray joined them. A few of the crewmen asleep on deck stirred in the warm July night but resumed dozing.

Ayman looked back at the men. "Tell the captain what you heard."

By his accent, the sailor was a Hafsid. He nodded at Bastone, "Signuri," and addressed Esmeray, "Capitanu. The Aragonese officer learned our ships are Sicilian and is going to report it to his commander. We slipped overboard as he departed on a dinghy."

Bastone locked eyes with Esmeray. Procida got the king's approval to release their ship because he thought they were Genoese. She had been right. They should have sailed earlier.

Esmeray whispered, "Ayman, alert the first mate, and both of you wake the crew. Be very quiet. Tell them we are going to steal out of the harbor. No talking among the crew. They must remain out of sight on the deck, ready to hoist sails when the command is given."

She directed her attention towards the two sailors from the *Lucia*. "You are now part of this crew." They followed Ayman for duty.

She nodded at Bastone, "Start warping the ship out of the harbor." He collected a few sailors and hurried to the stern. They moved their fishing boat, the *Aspasia,* from the stern of the *Giovanna* to the bow, secured a spring line, and began rowing the fishing boat, towing the larger ship out of the harbor.

Nearby, the Aragonese officer returning to the flagship from the *Lucia*, saw the *Giovanna* leaving. He shouted for the sailor rowing his dinghy to hurry. They reached the flagship where the king and most of the crew were asleep. Against the night watch's advice, he knocked on the captain's door. The captain rubbed the sleep from his eyes. "Why didn't you wake the first mate?"

The first mate and the night watch arrived out of breath. The officer said, "Give me permission to occupy the second cargo ship. Both ships are Sicilian, not Genoese. They are warping the *Giovanna* out of the harbor, but I can stop them with your help."

"James already issued a command not to confiscate that ship," said the captain. "Go back and do your duty. I'm returning to my berth." The captain was closing the door.

"Wait! They must have a reason for leaving in the middle of the night. Perhaps they are spies for Frederick? Perhaps they will give him the location of our fleet? Captain, at least halt their departure until we have interrogated them."

Addressing the first mate, the captain seemed to have awakened further. "Take my harbor boat and several arbalesters. Follow this officer's orders."

Bastone was thankful that fortune was on their side. The *Giovanna's* bow had been pointing west so they didn't have to turn the ship around. But they would need to pass among five or six Aragonese galleys to exit the harbor. It was slow going, the rowing difficult towing the cargo ship. The galley crews slept on the beach. Except for night watches, the galleys were unmanned.

As they passed the first galley, the night watch became excited and hurried away, returning with a second sailor, pointing, but they didn't intervene. Bastone and the sailors towed the *Giovanna* past the next few ships under the observation of the galleys' night watches without incident, confirming that the king had told his captains not to interfere with the *Giovanna*. The wind had been subdued in the harbor, but now they approached the sea. Bastone and three sailors, squeezed together on one bench, battled the rising westerly wind, two men per oar.

Ahead were the last two ships. They would have to pass between them to reach the open sea. Bastone was suddenly aware the launch from the flagship was pursuing them, when the Aragonese officer shouted, "Halt! Stop! Arbalesters, ready!"

Facing the pursuing boat as he rowed with all his strength, Bastone had his eye on a crossbowman stringing his bow at the front of the launch a few hundred feet away. He knew at this distance, in the light of the full moon, an arbalester would not miss. He shouted, "Row faster!"

While Bastone frantically rowed, peculiar thoughts flashed through his mind. Dying by crossbow would be merciful. No time for fear—just a clack of the trigger—and the silent flight of a crossbow bolt.

Although life-threatening, the thrill of danger shot through him, reviving sensations he had during his missions as a speculatore. Mad at himself for allowing the thought, he rowed harder than ever. He was no longer alone—he had to survive for Esmeray, for Aspasia.

Bastone screamed, "Pull, pull!" He shouted to the sailor at the *Aspasia's* tiller. "Turn hard to steerboard. Now!"

The tow boat veered right, slowly turning the *Giovanna* with it. Bastone heard Esmeray shout, "Make ready to hoist sails!" The sailors hurried to their stations. The tow boat had turned the *Giovanna.* There was the unmistakable thud of a crossbolt hitting the *Giovanna's* hull. Esmeray shouted to raise the lateen sails. Now leaving the harbor, the sails caught wind, the *Giovanna* gaining momentum. The vessel awakened for its run to the sea, as vibrations ran through the ship, causing masts and spars to creak.

The surge forward heartened Bastone. "Go, go!" Only two galleys left to pass. As the *Giovanna* sailed between the last two galleys, the wind faltered, blocked by the ships' hulls. Bastone heard the sails flap, losing the wind.

There were more thuds on the *Giovanna's* hull as the Aragonese drew closer. Bastone heard a scream behind him. He glanced back to see his helmsman down, impaled by a bolt. Bastone took his place. The *Giovanna* coasted without the wind. Bastone untied the towline. One of his oarsmen reached to grab the line for the jib sail. Bastone yelled, "Get down! Not yet." The sailor dropped to the rowing seat, unscathed when a bolt grazed the top of his head, taking his watch cap with it into the sea.

Both vessels continued drifting ahead, clearing the last two galleys, and the wind, no longer blocked by the last Aragonese galleys, again surged from the west. In anticipation, Esmeray had set sail to tack, the sails catching the wind. Bastone raised the *Aspasia's* sails, following as both vessels escaped out to sea.

Michael A. Ponzio

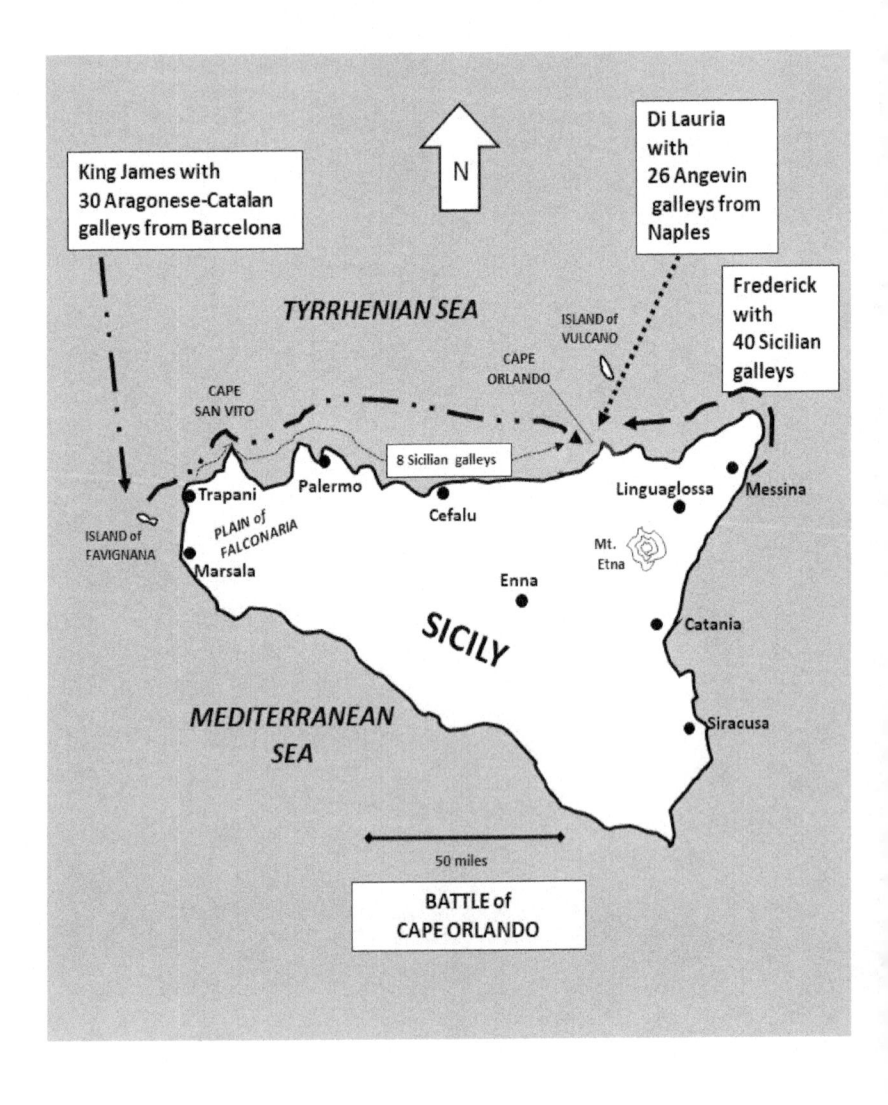

BATTLE of CAPE ORLANDO

CHAPTER XXXVIII

The following morning, James's fleet departed Favignana at sunrise, sailing east toward Cape Orlando to rendezvous with Admiral Di Lauria, who commanded a squadron of Angevin galleys. At Trapani, Abate's eight galleys sailed out of the harbor, heading toward Cape San Vito to wait for James's fleet.

Twenty miles north of Sicily on the island of Vulcano, the crews of Di Lauria's galleys spent the night ashore, the sulfur odor from the island's fumaroles permeating everywhere. While the Angevin sailors slept, a speculatore loyal to the Sicilians crossed from Vulcano to Messina on a fishing boat, notifying Frederick of the Angevin fleet.

In the morning, the Angevins boarded their ships. Twenty galleys cast off toward Sicily. Di Lauria kept six galleys at Vulcano as reserves, while at Messina, Frederick launched his fleet of forty galleys to intercept Di Lauria.

At the other end of Sicily, James, on the forecastle of his flagship, heard the watch in the crow's nest shout, "Sicilian galleys ahead at Cape San Vito!" The king shielded his eyes from the sun with his hand, squinting. The eight galleys ahead were stationary, their sails furled, their oars stored. Displaying a confident smirk, James whispered to himself, *"Trabajo excelente, Bastone*—excellent work! You have delivered the galleys from Baron Abate."

James ordered several galleys to row ahead of the fleet and make contact, but the stationary ships hoisted their sails and moved ahead.

The fleet followed under sail, bypassing Palermo where the populace was fervently against James, and avoided Cefalu, a fortified town that would also oppose his landing. They beached the galleys for the night on a remote pebble seashore past Cefalu, the cargo ships anchoring offshore. The eight galleys from Trapani had pulled ahead and their location was unknown. James was furious they had disappeared, but he had a timetable to meet. The cargo ships that accompanied his fleet had limited food and they would need to land soon and forage for supplies.

In the morning, Admiral Di Lauria with twenty Angevin galleys arrived at Cape Orlando, having evaded Frederick's fleet. The galleys were beached on the long sandy shore. James's fleet reached the cape as Frederick's ships appeared on the eastern horizon. Frederick, outnumbered, hesitated to engage, until the eight Sicilian galleys that had eluded James arrived, not to help James as he had expected, but to reinforce Frederick's fleet instead.

Frederick, at the advice of his admiral, Conrad Doria, and with the wind in their favor, chained the ships together into a huge fighting platform. Pushed by the wind, they attacked. James also chained his ships together and connected them with gangways to Di Lauria's beached ships.

The battle began with both sides releasing thousands of cross bolts, followed by the ships clashing, the adversaries boarding the other's ships, and hand-to-hand fighting. For hours, the combatants fought in the July heat. Many of the armored knights fell from heat exhaustion, including Frederick on his flagship. The fight went on until the galleys Di Lauria had kept in reserve at Vulcano arrived and attacked the rear of the Sicilian fleet. Outnumbered and now surrounded, Frederick's men detached his flagship, and he retreated from the battle. More Sicilian ships followed, taking flight, and both sides broke their formations. The fight turned into ship-to-ship battles, going in favor of the superior number of galleys in the Aragonese-Angevin fleet. The Angevins captured half of the Sicilian fleet, slaughtering the crews of the seized galleys, even those who surrendered. James stood on the forecastle of his flagship, disgusted with the massacre by the Angevins. He ordered his flagmen to signal his commanders to break off fighting.

Several Angevin galleys were on an intercept course for Frederick's ship. James observed the maneuver, now regretting he had agreed to help the Angevins invade Sicily. His own father had fought to expel the Angevins a decade earlier, and now he was fighting against his own brother. He had seen the Angevins massacre the Sicilian sailors on the captured galleys. What would happen when they caught Frederick's ship? What was it that the female captain had said? "*La familia es todo*—family is everything." Memories of his childhood with his brother Frederick flashed in his mind. James remembered how they had allied against their older brother when he had bullied them. More recently, they had been at peace governing Sicily together. What had he done?

James shouted for the first mate, running to the helm when he didn't get an immediate response. Reaching the stern castle, he found the first mate and helmsman. James pointed to the Sicilian flagship. "Get to Frederick's ship before the Angevins!"

The helmsman changed the ship's course as the first mate hurried down the stairs shouting to the crew, "Make full sail!"

James's fleet, under sail, raced the Angevin galleys, solely under oars, to Frederick's flagship. Aided by the westerlies, James was gaining on the galleys, but not fast enough to cut them off. He yelled, "Arbalesters to port side!" He was willing to switch sides and attack the Angevins to save his brother.

The crossbowmen hesitated, looking to their officer to confirm the engagement. He flicked his head portside. A score of arbalesters drew their crossbows. The officer shouted, "Keep your bows pointed down, don't aim yet—don't show your weapons."

Di Lauria's galleys and James's flagship were on a collision course, the Angevin sailors waving to the Aragonese, yelling and pointing. James stared at his helmsman. "Stay on course. Block the galleys!"

The officer of the arbalesters looked at James, waiting for the order to shoot. Abruptly, the westerlies gusted, boosting James's flagship ahead of the Angevin galleys. James passed behind Frederick's Sicilian flagship, crippled with torn sails, but it was still moving eastward. He scanned the stern castle but did not see his brother. A score of galleys in James's fleet followed his flagship, a long line of vessels, one by one, cutting off the Angevin galleys long enough for Frederick to escape.

Hours later, after James had collected his fleet and was sailing home to Aragon, he stood on the stern castle of his flagship staring across the sea. Bastone had promised him Abate's eight galleys, but instead had deceived him, sending the galleys to aid his enemy. James ground his teeth and squeezed the taffrail until his knuckles turned white. Although in the end they had not changed the result of the battle, James wanted revenge. Where was Ponzio Bastone?

Michael A. Ponzio

Children of the Middle Sea

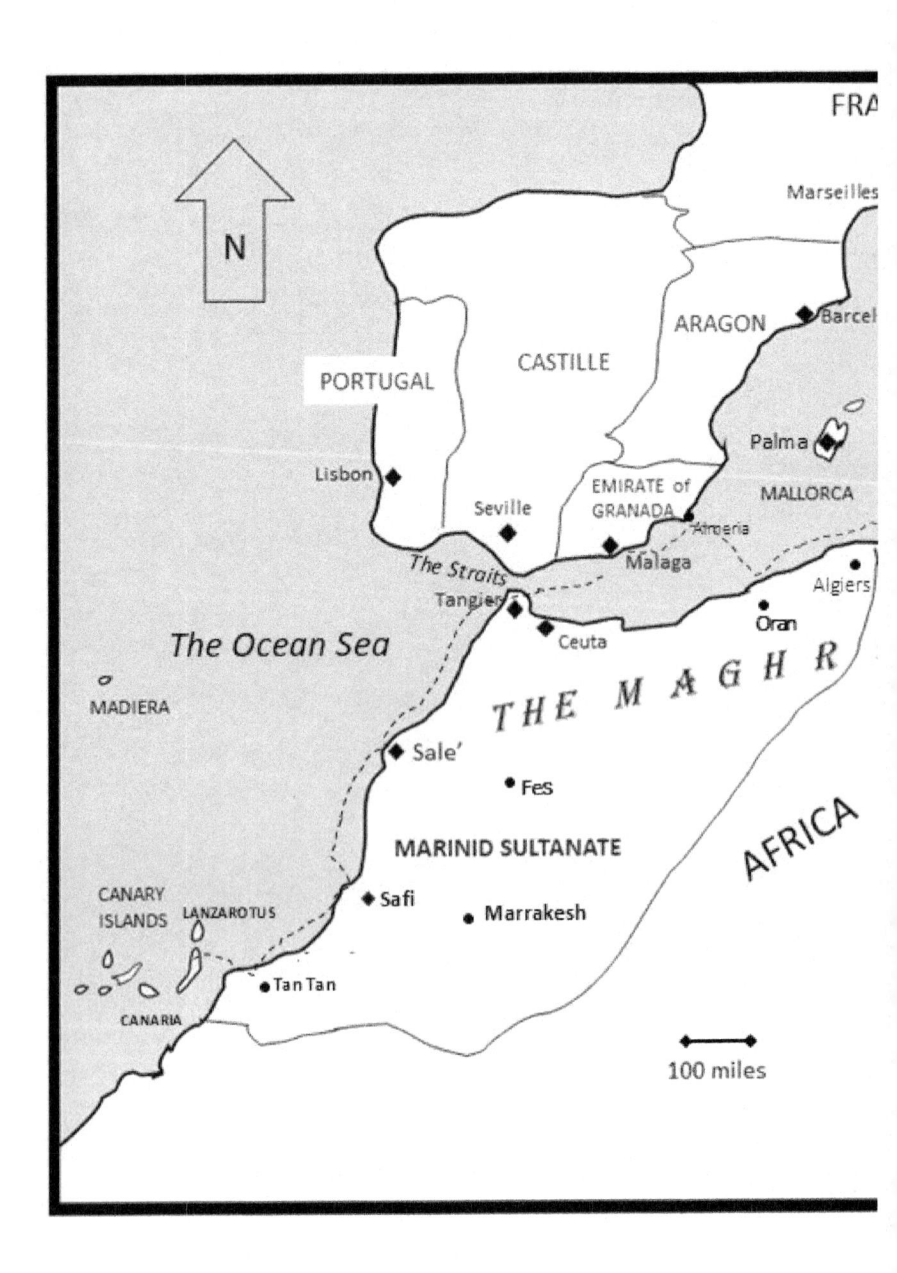

FRA
Marseilles
ARAGON
Barcel
CASTILLE
PORTUGAL
Palma
Lisbon
EMIRATE of GRANADA
MALLORCA
Seville
Almeria
The Straits
Malaga
Tangier
Algiers
Ceuta
Oran
The Ocean Sea
THE MAGHR
MADIERA
Sale'
Fes
AFRICA
MARINID SULTANATE
CANARY ISLANDS
LANZAROTUS
Safi
Marrakesh
TanTan
CANARIA

100 miles

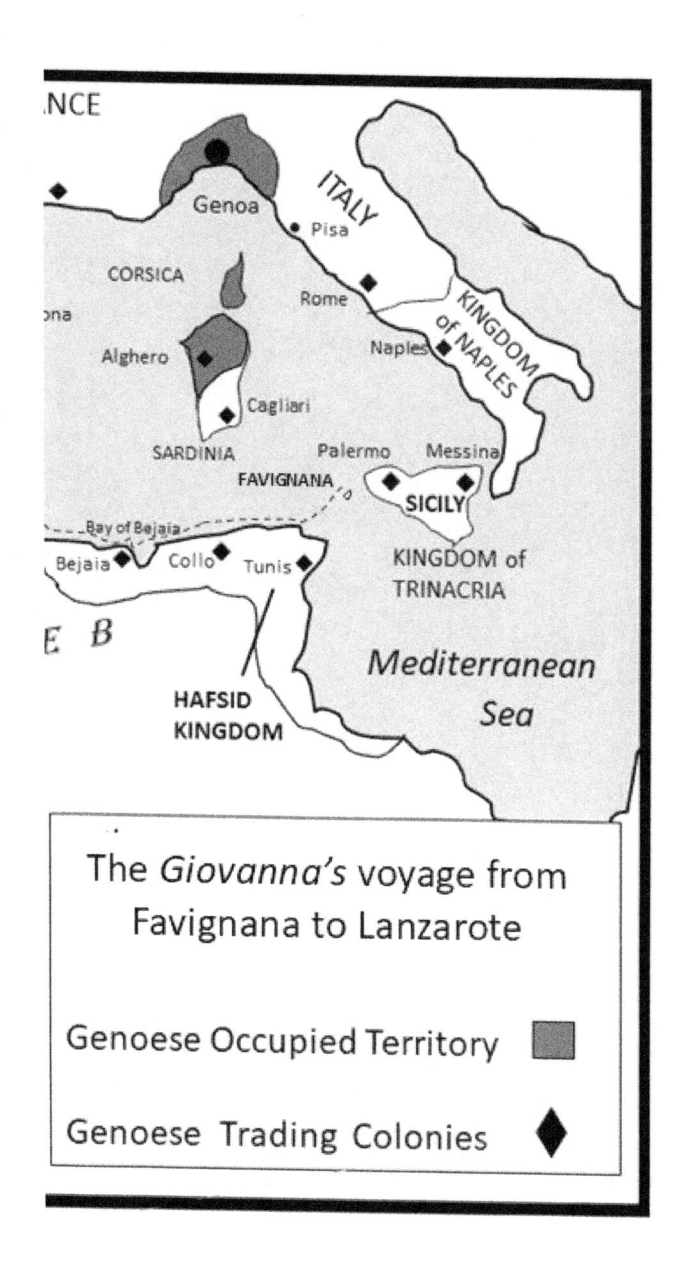

The *Giovanna's* voyage from Favignana to Lanzarote

Genoese Occupied Territory ■

Genoese Trading Colonies ♦

Children of the Middle Sea

CHAPTER XXXIX

Esmeray and Bastone agreed it would be safer to sail along the North African coast to reach Malaga. The alternate northern route, requiring a stopover at Mallorca, was controlled by King James. They were certain by now the king had discovered how Bastone had deceived him by diverting the galleys to Frederick. They preferred risking encounters with pirates over being captured by the Aragonese, with the potential execution of Bastone for treason.

Esmeray navigated the *Giovanna* across the sea to the North African coast, towing their fishing boat, reaching Bejaia in three days. They accepted Cardo's invitation to stay at the Genoese fondaco, selling wine to pay the crew's wages. During their layover, they sent a letter to Mino via a ship bound for Sicily to inform him of the confiscation of the *Lucia* and the *Giovanna's* escape to Malaga. A number of sailors quit when Esmeray told the crew of the plans to relocate to Malaga. Fortunately, several young men from the fondacos joined, replacing them. The crew was now composed of roughly equal numbers of Sicilian, Genoese, and Hafsid sailors.

Esmeray extended their stopover several more days, mingling at the customs house, seeking captains of ships arriving from the west. Esmeray learned that conditions along their planned route to the west had no unusual activity, other than scattered pirate raids in the straits to the Ocean Sea. Bastone was eager to learn about the fate of James's invasion of Sicily, but no ships had arrived from there with news.

Second mate Ayman searched for information at the souk. Ayman found two Arab captains who he knew personally and trusted, who were also preparing to sail their trading dhows west to the port of Oran within a few days. The Hafsid captains accepted Bastone's proposal to sail together.

While they were leaving the customs house for the fondaco, there was suddenly an uproar. Sailors who had just disembarked at the port arrived shouting about the war in Sicily. A crowd gathered around them as they spoke excitedly, accentuating their narrative with exaggerated hand gestures. "Antudu!" the crowd cheered, repeatedly shouting the rallying cry of the patriots during the Sicilian Vespers.

Bastone and Esmeray held Aspasia's hands and neared the edge of the crowd. A man yelled, "Frederick has defeated the Angevins. Sicily is free!" He raised a wine skin and sprayed a stream of the liquid in his mouth, then did the same to his fellow sailors. Bastone glanced beyond the celebratory crowd. When a squad of the emir's soldiers approached, he pulled Aspasia and Esmeray away, leaving quickly for the fondaco. Behind him, he heard a man shouting in Genoese with an Arabic accent, "Drink your wine back at your fondaco or we'll confiscate it!"

Walking to the Genoese trading compound, Bastone said, "The sailor at the customs house said Frederick won a battle. Could it have been against James's fleet?"

"The man was speaking Sicilian," said Esmeray. "Perhaps we can find him at the Sicilian fondaco later and ask him."

"If he's not drunk," said Aspasia.

"Good observation, Delfinina. His behavior was not mature. But sometimes it's fine to celebrate a little extra for a special event, as long as you respect other people."

When they returned to the Genoese compound, they heard music and cheerful shouting, unmistakable sounds of merriment, coming from the neighboring Sicilian fondaco. Esmeray and Aspasia remained at Cardo's house. Bastone and Cardo went to inquire about the situation in Sicily. The fondaco's small plaza was full of revelers. People were hugging and toasting. Others were dancing to a spirited melody created by a flutist blowing a *friscalettu*. Accompanying the flute was a musician thumbing a *marranzanu*, the jaw harp twanging in rhythm with jangles of a tambourine played by a young woman.

Bastone greeted a couple of sailors sitting at a table with a few locals, including the director of the Sicilian fondaco. The director pulled up extra stools and invited Bastone and Cardo to join the group, pouring wine for them. The others joined Bastone when he raised his glass, *"Saluti per cent'anni!"* He glanced around at the merrymakers, then peered at the Sicilian sailors. "So what happened in Sicily?"

The man smiled. "It will be a pleasure to repeat the story of our victory! The Angevin devils returned to Sicily on Di Lauria's and James's fleets. Frederick, outnumbered, bravely challenged the enemy at Cape Orlando. Of course, no one has ever beaten Di Lauria, and he was up to his tricks again, defeating Frederick's fleet."

Bastone uttered, *"Chi*—what!"

"The Angevins captured many Sicilian galleys, massacring the crews even after they had surrendered!"

Cardo exhaled. "Mother and Savior!" The others, hearing the tale before, merely shook their heads in disgust.

The spokesman sat back, continuing, "When the battle turned against Frederick, he escaped. Word is that James allowed his brother to get away."

Recalling that Esmeray had appealed to James not to fight his brother, Bastone had been alarmed—she had taken a dangerous risk talking to James that way. But Bastone wondered if she had influenced him to let Frederick go.

The Sicilian sailor continued, "James sailed back to Aragon, leaving the Angevins to land in Sicily alone. They besieged Trapani, but Frederick arrived with an army of patriots and Almogavars and challenged the Angevins to a battle on the Plain of Falconaria. The Angevin army had a thousand mounted knights! Frederick's foot soldiers withstood the charge of the knights as the Almogavars flanked them, dismounting the armored cavalry and killing most of them."

Bastone nodded, "As at Malta, where I saw the Almogavars outmaneuver the slower knights."

Cardo said, "This time they helped us, but they are mercenaries. We can't trust them."

"I agree," said the Sicilian sailor. "And at Falconaria, Almogavars fought on both sides of the battle. Frederick must have felt that distrust, too, because he convinced them there were richer prizes in the East, arranging for them to go to Constantinople and fight for the Roman emperor."

He swigged his drink, continuing, "Frederick marched into Trapani, victorious, avenging the loss at Cape Orlando. But unlike the enemy, Frederick spared the Angevins he captured."

Bastone reflected on the sea battle at Cape Orlando. Abate's galleys had not been enough to give Frederick the victory, but if Esmeray had helped change James's mind, the impact was enormous. Had Frederick been captured, he would not have defeated the Angevins at Falconaria. With James and the Aragonese withdrawing, the Angevins had a smaller force to invade Sicily.

Bastone was euphoric. He raised his cup, "Antudu!" The men at the table, still enthusiastic after scores of toasts, joined him.

The Sicilian sailor set down his cup. "And Frederick achieved one more victory! After the battle at Falconaria, Charles's other son, Robert, who had occupied Catania, advanced out of the city. Frederick defeated his forces and freed the city, chasing the Angevins out of Sicily again!"

Returning to the Genoese fondaco in the dark, the wine lowering his inhibitions, Bastone allowed tears of relief to fill his eyes. The vicissitudes of war in the decades fighting for Sicily's freedom flooded his mind. Would Sicily's freedom last this time? And Genoa. He missed his home, his country, his sister. Would he ever see her again? But Esmeray would not return to Sicily and would never go near Genoa.

Bastone and Cardo arrived at the house, swaying a little as they entered. Aspasia noticed, smiling, "Papa, the festivity must have been *a special event!*"

The *Giovanna* cast off from Bejaia with the pair of dhows. Sailing toward Algiers, they had left the territory of the Hafsid Kingdom and were now off the coast of the Marinid sultanate. Aspasia had finished her chores and studies, and she was at the bow with her father, watching a pod of dolphins swimming and jumping in front of the ship. "The dolphins are having so much fun they are squeaking. And look at that one!" A dolphin spiraled through the wake as it swam ahead at the point of the bow.

"I think you are right. They are playing. Perhaps they like the boost from the ship's wake."

Bastone nodded to a sailor who stopped to watch with them. "The dolphins are very smart, Aspasia," said the sailor. "I think they have a language."

"Ha ha. What are they telling us? Are they guiding us to port?" she asked. "Maybe they are good lu…"

The sailor shouted, "No! don't say it!"

Aspasia peered at him, scrunching her eyebrows. Bastone was silent, letting the sailor explain.

"Scusi, Signurina . . ." he glanced at Bastone, who nodded.

"Sailors are very superstitious. Old sailors believe it's risky to utter those words at sea. I'll share the words we shouldn't say on the ship once we're back on land." He showed a gap-toothed smile.

"Thank you, Signuri," said Aspasia. "I need to know such things to become a sailor."

He doffed his watchcap and nodded as he departed. Aspasia exchanged a knowing glance with her father. She was entertained, but he knew she was not superstitious.

At the port of Oran, Bastone bartered several barrels of wine for bulk sacks of wheat to trade in Almeria. The profits would ensure the trading voyage was lucrative. They would still have plenty of wine to trade further in their journey. There was a great deal of trade between Granada and Oran. Since the dhows that had sailed with them to Oran returned to Bejaia, Ayman and a handful of the Arabic crew from Bejaia found a group of dhows readying to make the day-long crossing to Almeria. With Ayman's influence, the captains agreed to let the *Giovanna* sail with their dhows. Castilian galleys had been patrolling the nearby seas to prevent pirate attacks. But at times, the Castilians had stopped the Oran trading dhows, falsely accusing the crews of being corsairs, confiscating goods and even sailors, so the Marinids welcomed the company of the *Giovanna*.

The *Giovanna's* call at Almeria, in the Emirate of Granada, was brief. Esmeray had dark memories of the port. It was where she had been kidnapped years earlier, and she was glad to sail on to Malaga. There, Grenadian dhows occupied the docks, so she anchored the *Giovanna* in the harbor, using the *Aspasia* to ferry them to the wharfs. They headed to the Genoese fondaco, with Ayman and several of the *Giovanna's* Arab sailors as escorts. Esmeray wore a veil. As they made their way through the souk to the fondaco, Esmeray and Bastone discussed their stay in Malaga. "Before we set sail to the Canaries in the Ocean Sea," Bastone said, "we must visit the waterfront and consult with the local captains."

Esmeray itched to sail as soon as possible. She felt cramped in the city and knew she would be even more confined at the fondaco. "I know where to sail," she answered. "I've studied the map of Plinius given to us by Mino. We sail south along the African coast for five days, then sail west one day to reach the islands. There are seven islands. The third one west is Canaria and I believe that's where Lancelotto's colony is located. We can ask at the Genoese fondacos along the way to be certain. And perhaps local fishermen can help? We can't leave the crew anchored here in the harbor for long, and we should move on."

They left the openness of the souk, entering a narrow street. Bastone gestured for two sailors to lead the way. Ayman and another sailor followed his family. "You are merely guessing which island Lancelotto is on. But you are right about leaving. And I want to plant my vine cuttings in the Canaries—they won't last forever in the jugs. It's agreed then. We will cast off soon, but I must at least contact the emir about the plan to ship his wine. He can think about it during our travel to the islands and back."

They arrived at the fondaco, a walled area enclosing a pleasant garden, warehouse, and villa where two merchants lived. A letter had been delivered from Mino for them to expect Bastone and his family. At Esmeray's suggestion, they gave the men a cask of Sicilian wine, which they were delighted to receive, and gladly obliged when Bastone requested they arrange a meeting with the emir to discuss Mino's proposal. Knowing of the emir's proclivity for wine, they sent a cask along with the message requesting an audience.

The subsequent meeting was a complete success. Returning to the fondaco with Ayman and the Genoese merchants, Bastone was sanguine and full of smiles as he described the encounter to Esmeray and Aspasia. The merchant fetched wine for the celebration.

He unrolled a parchment, placed it on the table, unsheathing his dagger to hold one end flat, keeping the opposite end from rolling back with his left hand.

Aspasia's eyes grew wide as her gaze passed from one end of the parchment to the other. "What a beautiful map! I love maps!"

"Where did you find this?" asked Esmeray.

"The emir was rather enthusiastic, knowing the map would ensure the success of our agreement. Mapmakers drew this at the monastery we visited in Mallorca. It's only borrowed for a day. I will copy the parts useful for us and return it tomorrow."

Aspasia pointed to an island on the map. "Papa, this is Mallorca?"

He nodded.

She glanced back and forth between her parents. "Let's sail to Mallorca."

Bastone's tone quieted, "Delfinina, perhaps someday. When it is safer."

"Look, there's a name written in Latin below the map. *Angelinus de Dalorto*," said Aspasia.

"Angelino Dalorto. He is the cartographer, Delfinina."

"Cartographer . . . hmm."

"A person who draws maps," said Bastone. "He lives in Mallorca. The emir said the Mallorcans have visited the Canary Islands." He pointed with his right hand. "These islands."

"And this type of map is called a portolan," said Esmeray; "it shows directions and distances between ports." Aspasia lowered her face close to the map, "Look, Mamma! That island is called *Insula de Lanzarotus Marocelus*. Our old Roman map had a different name for this island."

Now with more detailed directions to the Genoese colony of Marcello Lancelotto, Esmeray pinched her thumb and forefinger together, drawing her hand across her chest. "Pirfettu!"

After departing Malaga, they entered the straits to the Ocean Sea. Over a decade earlier, Esmeray had sailed her fishing boat on the same route. She used her experience to guide the helmsman of the *Giovanna* to navigate the difficult winds and currents.

The *Giovanna* turned south, sailing for a week off the coast of Africa, stopping at the small Genoese fondacos in the ports of Safi and Sali. As they sailed south, the weather became hotter and dryer. At the tiny fishing village of Tan Tan, they sailed due west.

A day later found them off the southern tip of an island. Aspasia watched the shoreline pass by with Bastone. "Papa, it's the island named after the Genoese explorer Lancelotto."

"Bonu, Delfinina. Yes, the Genoese named the island Lancelotto, but the native people call the island *Tyterogaka.*"

On the voyage from Malaga, Bastone recalled Aspasia had spent hours studying their maps. She then drew the African coast and Canaries by heart on scraps of parchment.

Bastone placed his hand on her shoulder. "Aspasia, you have an amazing memory! Do you remember what the native people are called?"

She nodded. "You told me—Guanches—no, Majos."

The *Giovanna* continued northward, reaching a series of coves, which strung along the coast. They caught first sight of the island's inhabitants, who were tending cultivated fields of wheat under the hot sun. Hardly glancing at the passing ship, several men and women continued working in the fields, wearing straw brimmed hats, loose shirts, and pants cut off below the knees. Their exposed arms and legs appeared well bronzed from the sun.

"Are the farmers Majos or Genoese?"

"I don't know, Delfinina."

She looked at her arm. The olive skin was the same tone as her mother's. Then she held her arm out next to her father's.

"Whoever the farmers are, they look like us."

"Aspasia. You are only ten, and you . . ."

"I'm almost eleven, Papa."

Bastone smiled, continuing, "You have been across the sea many times and seen many cultures and different kinds of people in your short life. Delfinina, think of the sea, the Mediterranean Sea, as a mixing pot . . ."

"A pot of macaroni?"

Bastone laughed. "Yes—of different types of macaroni, but as it's stirred, they all become cooked together."

"I understand, Papa. And you had to be cooked a little more than Mamma and I."

Bastone's eyebrows knitted. "What?" Then Bastone realized he might have underestimated his daughter's intelligence. Was she jesting?

Aspasia didn't answer her father's question but continued, "Remember when you went to Genoa for a long time? When you came back, your skin was lighter, but back in Sicily, you darkened once more."

"You amaze me again, Delphinina!"

Their ship reached the largest cove, which was a harbor formed by a sandy crescent beach a half mile long. The bright sun blazed over the shallow harbor, the strong sea breezes making the heat bearable. A Genoese ship, a few fishing boats, and a dhow were anchored in the cove. On shore, men came out of stone cottages to stand in the shade of palm trees. Behind the cottages were gardens and wheat fields. Beyond the cultivation, greenish-yellow sweet tabaibas, stunted trees, the tallest chest high, were scattered across the plain and climbed the volcano's slopes. Ravines were dominated by large succulents, some ten feet tall, capped by grey-white flowers. The vegetation's color contrasted with the tan desert landscape.

"So, this is Lancelotto's island!" exclaimed Aspasia.

"Is this all they have built? A few huts?" said Esmeray.

Bastone held a finger to his lips, pointing with his other hand. "Shh. Listen. Did you hear whistling? It sounded like it was coming from that mountain with a flat top—a volcano, I'm sure."

Esmeray peered at the volcano. "It might be the wind, Bastonino."

They remained silent, listening.

Esmeray scanned the cloudless blue sky. "Wait, I did hear—perhaps a bird whistle—yes, it did come from the direction of the mountain. Maybe a hawk?"

"No, Mamma, more like little birds chirping—or a flute. And I see bright flashes of light on the hill."

"Something metal reflecting sunlight?" said Esmeray.

"Shhh." Aspasia held her finger to her lips. They heard a pattern of songbird calls again for several minutes. The sounds halted.

On shore, a man climbed to the top of one of the stone cottages, and faced the volcano, a few miles distant. He whistled a rhythmic pattern of short high-pitched notes, resembling a lively bird song, which carried across the sunny, dry land toward the mountain. After several choruses, he paused.

Another series of repetitive notes were returned from the volcano, to which he responded.

Pulling with both hands on the taffrail, Aspasia bounced up and down on the balls of her feet. "They are whistling messages to each other! Let's go ashore!"

Bastone exchanged glances with his wife. Esmeray's eyes were soft and crinkled at the corners. Her slow blink reminded him of a contented cat, all the signs that his wife was at ease and content with their daughter's well-being. He sensed that, not just this moment, but finally, Esmeray had rid herself of the guilt she felt not providing Aspasia with a permanent home. Aspasia's home, their home, was wherever they were together.

Follow the story of Aspasia's family
in the third volume of the
Lover of the Sea series:
The Fortunate Islands
(Work in Progress)

Author's Comment

Thank you for purchasing this book. I know you could have picked any number of books to read, but you picked this book and for that I am extremely grateful.

I hope that it added interest, knowledge, and entertainment to your everyday life. If so, it would be appreciated if you could share this book with your friends and family and post comments on Facebook and X, formerly Twitter.

If you enjoyed this book and found some benefit in reading this, I'd like to hear from you and hope that you could take some time to post a review on Amazon. Your feedback and support will help this author to improve.

I want you, the reader, to know that your review is very important and if you'd like to *leave a review on Amazon, search the book on Amazon Books by its title or my name.*

Michael A. Ponzio Author Page
Michael A. Ponzio | Ancestry Novels (michael-a-ponzio-author.com)

Michael A Ponzio Author Facebook:
https://www.facebook.com/AncestryNovels/?ref=bookmarks

Author's Ancestry Novels website:
History & Historical Fiction: Pontius, Ponzio, Pons, and Ponce
https://mikemarianoponzio.wixsite.com/pontius-ponzio-pons

ABOUT THE AUTHOR

Since childhood, Mike Ponzio has read about history, trading books with his father, Joseph E. Ponzio. Mike's love of history, family, and his travels have inspired him to write *Ancestry Novels*. The stories chronicle the lives of historical characters which the author imagines may have been his family's ancient ancestors.

Mike met his wife, Anne Davis, in 1975 at a University of Florida karate class. Both continue to practice and teach Cuong Nhu Martial Arts. With John Burns, they wrote six instructional books on martial arts weapons. Mike retired in 2015, after working as an environmental engineer for thirty-seven years. Anne and Mike have raised four sons, who are also engineering graduates, following in the footsteps of their Davis and Ponzio grandfathers.

Ancestry Novels by Michael A. Ponzio

The Ancient Rome Series:
Pontius Aquila: Eagle of the Republic
Pontius Pilatus: Dark Passage to Heaven
Saint Pontianus: Bishop of Rome

The Warriors and Monks Series:
Ramon Pons: Count of Toulouse
1066 Sons of Pons: In the Wake of the Conqueror
Warriors and Monks: Pons, Abbot of Cluny

The Lover of the Sea Series:
Lantern Across the Sea: The Genoese Arbalester
Children of the Middle Sea
The Fortunate Islands (in progress)

Nonfiction Historical:
Brigadier General Daniel Davis & the War of 1812: The Destiny of the Two Swords
Memories of the Neracker Brothers: Sweet Cider & the Cider Mill